South San Francisco Public Library
3 9048 09175118 4

D0820008

CODE OF SILENCE

CODE OF SILENCE

Tim Shoemaker

ZONDERVAN.com/
AUTHORTRACKER
follow your favorite authors

ZONDERVAN

Code of Silence

This title is also available as a Zondervan ebook.
Visit www.zondervan.com/ebooks.

Requests for information should be addressed to:

Zondervan, *Grand Rapids, Michigan 49530*

ISBN: 9780310726531

Cover design: Cindy Davis
Interior design: Ben Fetterley and Greg Johnson, Textbook Perfect

Printed in the United States of America

12 13 14 15 16 /DCI/ 22 21 20 19 18 17 16 15 14 13 12 11 10 9 8 7 6 5 4 3 2 1

Dedicated to my sons and daughters-in-law

Andy & Laura, Mark & Sarah, and Luke
... and to the generation to come.

Special thanks to ...

Nancy Rue ... who mentored and encouraged
Kathleen Kerr ... who championed the manuscript
Kim Childress ... who helped make it stronger
Marlene Bagnull ... who invested in me from the very beginning
Terry Burns ... who believed this story needed to be published
Cheryl Shoemaker ... who loved and supported me

"Whoever of you loves life and desires to see many good days,
keep your tongue from evil and your lips from telling lies."

Psalm 34:12–13

CHAPTER 1

Cooper's leering opponent inched closer, fists raised and ready to strike.

"He's moving in for the kill, Coop," Gordy said.

Cooper didn't budge. *C'mon, you big moron.* He tapped the joystick. *One more step.*

The muscled fighter advanced. Swinging the control stick, Cooper drummed the punch and kick buttons on the arcade video game.

"Yes!" Gordy thumped Cooper on the back. "Nice move!"

Staggering backwards, the hulking villain wobbled and teetered.

With a whir of the forward control knob, Cooper smacked the buttons in a memorized sequence. "Say bye-bye, big guy." The stunned champion dropped face-down.

"How do you *do* that?" Gordy said, clamping both hands on Cooper's shoulders and giving him a little shake. "You've got all these secret moves and combinations."

Wiping slick hands on his cargo shorts, Cooper turned to face his cousin and smiled.

"I wish I could do that!" Gordy jumped and casually slapped the "Order Here" sign hanging from the ceiling.

Cooper glanced up at the swinging sign. *And I wish I could do that.* Dozens of finger smudges bordered the bottom edge—but none of them belonged to Cooper. Not that he hadn't tried when he thought nobody was looking.

Gordy brushed past him and tapped the joystick. "Just once I'd like to drop that thug."

Cooper looked up at him and smiled. "Drop a quarter in the slot, and I'll teach you."

Hiroko Yakimoto stood from the table next to them and closed her English book. "It looks like we won't get back to studying anymore tonight. Time for me to go." She slid her books into her backpack and wiped the table with a napkin. "I don't see why you two love playing that stupid old game every time we come here."

"Stupid?" Cooper stepped over to the table and picked up his monster shake. "The game is a classic."

"Classic waste of time." She smiled slightly and raised one eyebrow. "You're both thirteen years old, right?"

Cooper clutched at his chest. "Ow, owwww, Hiro, that really hurt."

"It's nothing but pointless violence."

Cooper acted like he couldn't believe what he was hearing. "Pointless?" Lifting the plastic lid off the quart-sized cup, Cooper stirred the chocolate shake. "If you'd ever make the effort to check this out, you'd see this game is all about the forces of good fighting the forces of evil in mortal combat." He pulled the straw out, slid it across his tongue, and stuck it back in the cup. "If you think about it, the Bible is full of this kind of stuff."

Hiro tossed her dark braid over one shoulder. "Oh, I get it now. Gee, maybe they should buy a few of these games for church."

Gordy snickered and grabbed a handful of fries.

Frank Mustacci shuffled around the corner from the ordering counter. Something about the owner of Frank 'n Stein's Diner always made Cooper smile. If Frank grew a white beard to match the hair rimming his balding head, he could get a job as a Santa in any mall. "Don't let these boys give you a hard time, Hiro. And tell your mom she can have her old job back any time she wants. I miss her around here."

Hiro smiled and nodded. Sometimes Cooper thought Frank treated Hiro like she was his own granddaughter.

"I ever show you this?" Frank held out a worn 4" x 6" photo with half a dozen tack holes at the top.

A glance confirmed exactly what Cooper expected. The picture taken nearly two years ago at Frank 'n Stein's Halloween party. And yes, he had shown it before.

Frank stood front and center wearing his white apron over a cheap Santa suit. Hiro's mom stood to his right, dressed in a traditional Japanese kimono. Hiro stood in front of Frank, swimming in her dad's leather Chicago Police jacket . . . her rich black hair woven into a single braid. Her smile lit up the entire picture—even though it had been the roughest year of her life.

Gordy stood to Frank's left. His white-blonde hair got washed out by the flash and was way shorter than he wore it now. Cooper stood next to him, hands tucked in his jeans. Both of them too cool for costumes. Except for Cooper's darker hair, they could have passed for brothers. Same lean build. Same height. Dead even. Eye-to-eye.

But that was before Gordy's growth spurt. Cooper was still waiting for his, which is why Cooper wouldn't mind so much if that picture accidentally fell into the fryer someday.

Frank tried to get a group photo at the last Halloween party. Thankfully Cooper avoided getting in the picture by being the designated photographer. He didn't want to look like Gordy's *little* brother.

"I love that picture, Frank," Hiro said.

"Me too." He slid the picture in his pocket. "You kids stay and finish your game." He held up a ring of keys and shook it like sleigh bells. "I just gotta lock the front door while I clean up."

"Coop." Hiro stepped into Cooper's line of sight. "I think we should leave."

Her playful teasing look had disappeared. Something else seeped into its place. Cooper stared, trying to figure her out. Sometimes her mood could swing faster than a punch from the fighter on the video game.

"Frank needs us out of here," she said. She nodded her head toward the door. Her eyes pleaded.

Frank wiped a greasy handprint off the front door glass. "Nonsense. You won't be in my way. I like a little company. You know that. And I have to put up Halloween decorations anyway." Frank turned the key in the lock and dropped the keys in his pocket. "Mind if I hit some of the lights?" He doused the lights to the eating area without waiting for an answer. "Otherwise somebody's liable to pull up to the drive-thru." He flipped over the CLOSED sign next to the door and nodded toward the windows. "The neon gives plenty of light."

BURGERS, FRIES, HOTDOGS, ITALIAN SAUSAGE & BEEF, and MONSTER SHAKES. Every window featured a different illuminated sign. Together they splashed enough colored light around the room to see clearly.

Frank opened a trash receptacle, pulled out the plastic liner, and twisted its neck as if it were a chicken headed for the broiler. "I'll be cleaning up in the kitchen. Call me when you're ready to go." He grinned at Gordy. "Or if you need more fries." Trash bag in tow, Frank squeezed through a narrow pass-thru in the front counter and lowered the hinged counter top back in place before he disappeared into the kitchen.

Hiro stepped closer. "Can I borrow your cell? Mine's dead."

He didn't have to check his pocket. He knew exactly where he'd left it. "Sorry. It's at home."

Gordy slapped a quarter on the table and slid several fries into his mouth. "I'm ready to learn those secret moves."

Drawing a cool mouthful of the chocolate shake through the straw, Cooper glanced at Hiro.

"Let's go." Hiro looked at Cooper and mouthed the words. "Please." Her eyes added the exclamation point.

Cooper set the cup on the table. "Why the big rush?"

Hiro folded her arms across her chest. "You wouldn't understand."

Gordy laughed and half choked on the fries. Doubling over, he coughed hard to clear his throat.

Hiro glared at him. Her mouth formed into a tiny line so tight her lips nearly disappeared.

Still wheezing a bit, Gordy dipped a fry into the ketchup and used it like a brush, painting a face on a napkin.

Cooper studied Hiro's face in the candied light of the neon signs. "Try me."

Hiro pulled a white sweatshirt over her head. "I got a bad feeling. Like we should go."

"Ahhh," Gordy winked at Cooper. "One of those 'women's intermission' things."

"*Intuition*, Gordy," Cooper said. "Women's *intuition*." He felt the hairs prickle on his arms. She'd had feelings like this before. He didn't understand it, but he wasn't about to underestimate it either.

Hiro slung her backpack over one shoulder. She strode to the front door, rattled it, and turned toward the ordering counter. "Frank?"

Gordy straightened up and cleared his throat. "What are you doing?"

"Leaving." Hiro didn't even turn to look his way. "You two can save the world from the forces of evil."

"It seems to me," Gordy flipped his napkin upside-down and carefully peeled back the paper, leaving a twin ketchup face imprint on the surface of the tabletop, "someone is acting like a little kid here."

Hiro glanced at the smiling ketchup face and nodded. "Exactly."

Gordy shrugged, mounted the stool in front of the arcade game, and dropped the quarter in the slot.

"Forget it, Gordy," Cooper said. "I'm not letting her bike home alone in the dark."

"What about my quarter?"

Cooper hustled toward Hiro. "Stay and play if you want. I'll teach you the moves next time."

Hiro glanced up at him, but didn't say a word. Standing directly below a poster-sized picture of Frank 'n' Stein's two owners, Frank Mustacci and Joseph Stein, she rubbed her hands up and down her arms.

"Hey, Frank. We're all done," Cooper called, peering into the fully lit kitchen. A wheeled metal bucket with a mop propped in it stood to one side of the preparation table, the floor all around it glossy with water. The stainless steel flat-top grill, fryer, and steam table gleamed in the overhead lights. From where he stood, Cooper could see through the kitchen to the back stairs leading to the second floor.

Hiro stepped in front of him and played with her braid the way she often did when she was thinking or worried about something. In this case it was probably both.

"Maybe he's up in his office."

Cooper tried to read her face. "How bad of a feeling are we talking here? Like *bad* bad, or just kind of bad?"

"*Bad* bad."

Spooky. He rubbed the goosebumps down on his forearms. For a moment Cooper looked over her head into the lifeless kitchen, listening for any noise from the floor above them.

"Frank," he called. "We're ready to go." Nothing. Like the dead air between stations on the radio dial. No noise, no static. A disconnected silence.

"Where is he?" Hiro's voice dropped to a whisper. Pacing along the counter that separated them from the kitchen, she stopped in front of the eight foot mascot—the legendary Frankenstein monster. Holding a Chicago-style hot dog in one hand and a monster shake in the other, the green-skinned beast sported a goofy grin.

Leaning to one side to get a better view, Cooper scanned the entire length of the kitchen. The back door stood open a crack. A clear plastic bag jammed with garbage sat just inside it with its top tied into a knot. "He must be taking stuff out to the dumpster." Cooper jerked his thumb towards the rear exit. "I'll grab my backpack. We'll slip through the kitchen and—"

WHAM! The back door flew open and Frank Mustacci stumbled through like he'd been pushed. He toppled over the bag of garbage and landed on his hands and knees.

"Stay down!" someone shouted.

Two uniformed men burst in from the shadows. One wore a clown mask—the other a slick-haired latex Elvis face. The clown pointed a can of spray paint at the security camera by the back door and blackened the lens.

Instinctively Cooper dropped out of sight behind the counter, pulling Hiro down with him. Adrenalin surged through his body. He glanced over at Gordy who was still sitting wide-eyed in front of the arcade game, like he was bolted in place. He was just out of the line of vision from the kitchen.

"What do I do?" Gordy mouthed the words.

Cooper didn't dare speak, but he shouted with his eyes. *Move!* Hiro motioned frantically for Gordy to hide. Gordy's eyes, wild with panic, darted around the room looking for some way of escape. Without a sound he slid off the stool and crawled under the nearest table.

Cooper licked dry lips and leaned in close to Hiro. Crouching, Cooper pressed his back against the only barrier between him and the kitchen. Had the men seen them? Cooper's heart punched out a warning in his chest.

The door slammed shut.

"Don't try anything stupid, old man. Do exactly what we say, and you won't get hurt." The man's voice sounded deep and strong. Like a DJ.

Frank groaned. "What do you want?"

Cooper could hear fear in Frank's voice.

"What do you *think?*" Mr. DJ said. "Empty the register."

A loud thump and another groan.

Cooper flinched, imagining poor Frank doubled over in pain. He heard a faint whimper escape Hiro's lips.

"Okay, okay," Frank gasped. "I'll cooperate. Put the gun away."

A gun—and they'd be coming his way. Cooper looked for a way to escape. The windows? They were big enough, but he'd need something solid to break through them. All the chairs and tables were securely attached to the black and white tiled floor—except the metal stool by the arcade game.

"All right, hotdog man," the other man said, clearly getting closer. His voice sounded permanently hoarse, like he'd been lead vocal for a heavy metal band for too many years. "You heard what the boss said. Keep moving, or I'll boot you again."

Cooper plastered himself against the counter. *We're trapped—and there's no way out!*

CHAPTER 2

Cooper heard shuffling feet on the other side of the counter. "That's it, old man. Nice and easy."

DJ voice was obviously the one in charge, and he sounded way too close.

Gordy pulled his lanky frame into a ball and stopped moving. Barely a second later, the register drawer clanged open.

The hair on Cooper's arms tingled again. He could almost *feel* the men on the other side of the counter. For a moment his mind looped frantically. *Dear God. Dear God. Dear God—please!*

"We'll take it to go," the man ordered.

"Wha—?"

"Put the cash in a bag, old man!"

Cooper looked out the window towards Kirchoff Road, hoping a car would pull in the lot and scare the robbers away. He focused on the headlights of an approaching pickup, willing it to turn in. *C'mon. Slow down.* Maybe a couple of burly construction workers would come by—hungry enough to stop and tap on the window. Regular customers knew Frank would open the door. Cooper watched for their turn signal to blink on and silently pleaded. *Help us. Please.* The truck passed without slowing. If only Cooper had remembered his phone.

No other vehicles were in sight. Cooper scanned the roads, then shifted his attention to the darkening sky, and then, with dawning horror, Cooper noticed their reflections. The front window reflected the scene inside the diner with mirror-like clarity. He could see everything. Cooper shuddered. Three men stood on the other side of the counter. Frank, easily a head shorter than either of the other two, emptied his own register and stuffed the bills into a paper take-out bag. Frank lifted the tray out of the register and fished a couple of bills from underneath. Cooper could see Frank's hands shaking as he set the tray on the counter and handed the bag of money to another man in a clown mask.

Cooper fought to control his breathing—keep it shallow. Afraid of making some kind of sound if he shifted his weight, he tried to ignore the cramping in his left calf. He stayed as still as the Frank 'n Stein's mascot grinning stupidly at him from the corner. *God, make this be over.*

Hiro touched Cooper's arm and nodded her head toward the window. In the deepening shadows at the base of the counter he could see himself and Hiro huddled like they were caught in the crossfire of a commando raid. If the crooks looked closely enough, they could see him and Hiro. Then it really would be over. A trickle of sweat broke free from his maze of blonde curls and crept down his forehead.

"Now. The combination to your safe," the DJ voice growled from behind the Elvis mask.

"*Safe?*" Frank's voice cracked.

Elvis backhanded him across the face. Staggering backwards, Frank cried out and groped the top of the counter for support. The register tray slid and clattered over the edge, showering coins onto Hiro and Cooper like a silver waterfall.

Hiro squeezed her eyes shut like she expected the coins to betray their fragile hiding spot.

"We know about the safe, old man, and how you don't trust banks."

Coins rolled across the checkered tile floor. Some circled, others spun, but within a few moments every coin lay still—exposed and powerless. Cooper knew the feeling.

"The combination." Elvis pressed in close.

"Nobody outside this store knew about the safe." Frank sounded confused. "Nobody."

"COMBINATION."

"Seventy-four." Frank's voice shook. "Ninety-three." Cooper heard him suck in his breath and stop. "It's *him*, isn't it?"

"Careful, old man. Give me the last number."

"It has to be," Frank said, as if it suddenly all made sense. "I gave him a chance."

"And this is *your* last chance." The man raised a pistol in a gloved hand. "The number." He pressed the muzzle against Frank's forehead.

Cooper heard a metallic click. *Give it to them, Frank. Give it to them.*

Frank hesitated, his reflection in the front window ghostly in his white t-shirt and apron.

Coop forced a dry swallow and silently begged Frank to cooperate. *Give him the combination. Please. Play it safe.*

"Okay." Frank nodded. "J-just put the gun down. P-please."

Elvis jabbed Frank in the forehead once with the gun. "That's better." He lowered the handgun and tucked it in his waistband. Holding empty hands up in front of Frank, Elvis leaned in close. "The number."

Suddenly Frank lunged—pushing the Elvis into the clown. The robbers stumbled backwards into the soda machine, and Frank reached for something under the counter.

Elvis regained his balance and swung at Frank's face. With a loud smack, Frank's head jerked to one side and his glasses skittered across the counter and tumbled to the floor.

Frank raised his hand over his head. A glint of steel flashed off the blade of a knife. Elvis caught his wrist in mid-air. The man with the clown mask slammed himself into Frank, pinning him against the counter. Frank grunted and gasped. The knife dropped from his hand. Elvis picked it up and jabbed the point under Frank's jaw. Squealing, Frank lifted his chin high.

"Last number."

Blood dripped down the front of Frank's t-shirt. Every ounce of strength drained out of Cooper at the same time.

"Eighteen."

Elvis lowered the knife and tossed it onto the counter. "Smart, hotdog man."

"Maybe a little too smart." The raspy-voiced clown spoke up. "He knows."

Stomach swirling with dread, Cooper watched. If only he could do something. Help Frank somehow.

Frank grabbed for the knife. Elvis blocked his reach with one smooth move and hammered him in the head with his fist. Frank's head snapped backwards. The clown, moving quickly, twisted Frank's arm behind his back.

Cooper tried to look away, but couldn't. Hiro buried her face in her sweatshirt. He prayed she wouldn't cry out.

With Frank unable to move, Elvis squared off and slugged him repeatedly in the gut. Cooper felt the force of it right through the counter and flinched with each blow, with each grunt from Frank. A raging growl came from under the Elvis mask that grew louder with each frenzied hit. With an inhuman roar, Elvis hauled back and delivered a crushing blow to Frank's temple. Immediately the owner buckled, and the clown let him drop. Frank's head whacked the open drawer of the register on the way down, and he crumpled to the floor with a dull thud that vibrated through the counter.

"Crazy old fool!" Elvis panted and massaged his knuckles with his other hand. "Did he think we'd just trust him not to talk?"

The clown bent down out of sight. "Looks like his neck is broken."

"Then he's double-dead." Elvis raised a lethal fist to his mouth and kissed it. "Sent him to the great hotdog stand in the sky."

The clown snickered, and Hiro's whole body started shaking. Cooper held her tight.

"I'll get rid of the other stuff," the clown said. "If someone looks in the window and sees the coins and money tray on the floor, the game's over."

Cooper held his breath — and clenched his fists.

CHAPTER 3

Forget it." Elvis grabbed the moneybag. "Mr. Lucky can do that job—and yank the surveillance tape. Let's get the safe."

The two men hustled out of sight.

The tapes! They'd be on them! Cooper could see one camera mounted on the ceiling in the dining area. It was recording all three of them. He heard the back door creak open.

"Are they gone?" Hiro whispered. Her face was drained of any color except the wash from the red-orange neon lights.

"Not for long," Cooper said. "We have to hide."

Chalky-faced, Gordy poked his blonde head out from under the table. "The bathroom?" He mouthed the words and pointed to the far end of the eating area.

Anyplace would be better than where they were now. Cooper nodded. "Let's go."

Hiro clung tighter.

"C'mon." Cooper jostled her. "We gotta hurry."

Releasing her grip, she crawled ahead of Cooper toward Gordy.

The back door slammed. Cooper and Hiro dropped flat on their stomachs. The hinged top overhead shielded them from immediate view, but Cooper still felt exposed. He inched backwards.

Frank lay belly up, partially blocking the other side of the skinny opening leading into the kitchen. Thankfully, only his motionless torso was visible. Endless stains marked his white apron—the most recent made in his own blood. Dizziness swept through Cooper's head.

The burglars returned with a third man. Elvis thumped up the stairs, the other two headed through the kitchen toward Frank. Cooper caught a glimpse of their legs. One wore commando boots and gray-blue pants with a dark stripe running up his leg along the outside seam. Cop pants—it had to be the Clown. The other, Mr. Lucky, wore blue jeans and pointy cowboy boots with alligator skin stitched at the toes. He stepped close enough for Cooper to see the loopy stitching on his boots. He paused next to Frank and nudged him with one sharp toe.

"Take a rag and wipe down this counter real good," Mr. Clown said, sounding as calm and detached as if he were ordering at the drive-thru window. "Then come up and pull the surveillance stuff. I'll hit the safe." The sicko turned on his heel and left.

Except for the ceiling creaking overhead, the room was eerily quiet. Cooper closed his mouth as if somehow that might muffle the noise of his heart drumming.

Mr. Lucky moved quickly. Straining to hear, Cooper froze and held his breath. He steeled himself to pounce on Lucky if he stepped on their side of the counter.

Cooper couldn't rip his mind free from the surveillance tape. He ran through his options. If they hid in the bathroom, the robbers might leave without ever noticing them. But what if there were monitors in the office? If one of the men caught a glimpse of them sneaking to the bathroom they'd be trapped. That left only one choice, but it was a long shot.

A muffled whoop sounded from upstairs. Apparently the combination worked.

"Bring a couple of bags up here." It sounded like Elvis. "There must be good money in hotdogs."

Mr. Lucky jogged through the kitchen toward the stairs. Cooper stole a quick glance at him from behind, but the man wore a sweatshirt with the hood up.

Hiro pulled out her phone and stabbed at the power button. She shook her head at Cooper. Dead. Like they all were going to be if they didn't do something. Cooper could kick himself for leaving his cell at home. He would never, *ever* go anywhere without it again.

"C'mon," Gordy whispered. His color looked better, and he'd shaken off the temporary paralysis. He motioned for Cooper to hurry. "Now's our chance."

Cooper shook his head. "The bathroom is no good." He pointed at the camera. "They'll see us in the monitors."

"We can't stay here." Gordy's words spilled out fast. "We'll end up like Frank."

Cooper looked over his shoulder toward the front door. "We've got to get out of here."

Gordy crawled closer. "How? The door is locked."

Cooper looked over the still form of Frank and through the kitchen. "Back door."

"Impossible." Gordy pressed in close. "The stairway to the office is right there. They'll hear the door opening and see one of us for sure."

Cooper knew it was way beyond risky. But to do nothing? Suicide.

"What about the front door keys?" Gordy whispered. "Check Frank's pockets."

The thought made Cooper's stomach crawl up his throat. Hiro stiffened beside him.

"One of us has to try," Gordy whispered. "And fast."

Cooper knew he had to do it. He crawled behind the counter, into the kitchen's entrance, and he reached for the closest pocket. Trembling, he slid his fingers inside. Part of him expected Frank to grab his hand and demand an explanation. He touched Frank's leg and recoiled slightly, but he pressed on until he reached the bottom of the pocket. Nothing—except the 4" x 6" photo. Pulling his hand out quickly, he looked at Gordy and shook his head.

"The other side!" Gordy hissed. Hurry!"

Cooper reached over Frank's belly and stretched for the pocket. Too far. Taking a deep breath and clenching his teeth, he climbed over, trying not to put weight on the man—as if it would matter. He buried his hand in Frank's pocket. Coins. Papers. *No keys.*

Hiro and Gordy watched. Cooper saw their anxious faces, softly lit by the neon light.

"No choice," Cooper shook his head. "The back door. All of us."

"I don't think I can do it." Hiro hugged herself and rocked. Tears flowed down her cheeks and clung to her chin. "They'll catch us."

It was a long shot at best. Even if they could sneak through the kitchen without a sound, the back door would definitely make enough noise for the men to hear upstairs. What if he made it out alive, but Gordy or Hiro got caught? Cooper couldn't live with that. He glanced at the back door—then stared. The keys hung from the lock.

Cooper whirled around to face his friends. "The keys are in the door." He motioned frantically. "I'll—I'll grab them and we'll all go out the front, OK?"

Both nodded, but their faces mirrored the doom Cooper felt.

"Wait for me at the front door." Cooper stood on rubbery legs. "And pray." He was an easy target out in the open. He wanted to run. Hide. But he had to do this. God, help him, he had to get those keys. "Grab the stool from the video game. If I get caught, bust your way out and get help."

Fighting his survival instincts, he took a step. Then another. Past the steel tables. He could smell the Italian beef even through the closed bins. The scent of onion rings hung in the air.

The flat-topped grill still radiated a last bit of warmth as he passed. Pausing at the fryer, he glanced at the dual vats of oil and listened. The voices overhead sounded confident, celebrating. Cooper wanted to scream or cry. Frank lay dead in his own diner, and the robbers were upstairs pawing through everything he'd worked for and saved.

Footsteps pounded down the stairs. Cooper grabbed a knife from the counter and dropped out of sight behind a walk-in freezer. He pressed himself against the wall and firmly gripped the wooden handle. His hands were slick, and his arms felt like cement had replaced the blood in his veins.

The footsteps raced back up the stairs again, two at a time.

Over halfway there. *Faster, Cooper.* Half crouching, he moved past boxes of napkins, straws, and cups.

The stairway leading up to the office lurked to his right. The keys … dead ahead. One key was fully inserted in the lock, four similar keys dangled from a plain silver ring below it.

"All right, pack it up." Clearly Elvis. "You got the security camera stuff?"

"It's all on an external hard drive," a muffled voice said. "Already down by the door."

Switching the knife to his left hand, Cooper gently pulled the key out of the lock. The quartet of keys below jangled a bit. For an instant, he froze. His pulse pounded high alert warnings in his ears. The keys settled, and he tucked them in his hand. A small auxiliary hard drive not much bigger than a cell phone sat on the floor just inside the door, wires poking out the backend. Something inside him told him to take it.

"All right, boys. Let's grab it and we're outta here."

Fueled by high octane fear, Cooper scooped up the hard drive and ran on tip-toe for the front door. Gordy and Hiro stood beside it, frantically motioning him to hurry.

Crawling over Frank again wasn't an option. Instead, Cooper vaulted over the counter. He caught a glimpse of something on the floor, but couldn't avoid it now. His right foot landed on the edge of the change tray, shooting it across the coin-littered floor like a loose skateboard. It ricocheted off the metal stool and clattered against the front wall.

Scrambling to his feet, Cooper dropped the knife and tightened his grip on the hard drive.

"The keys!" Gordy hissed.

Cooper stormed the door and stabbed at the lock with the key. It wouldn't go in.

Hand shaking, Cooper tried another key. Wrong again.

Footsteps thundered down the stairs.

"Please, God, *please!*" Hiro's prayer rose from just behind him.

The third key slid home. Gordy threw his body against the glass, pushing even while Cooper twisted the key in the lock.

The door burst open and the three tumbled out. Gordy and Hiro scrambled for their bikes. Cooper spun around, reached inside, and pulled the key from the lock. He needed to buy them more time.

"Stop that kid!" A voice roared from the kitchen.

Shouldering the door closed, he jammed the key in the outside lock and barely managed a full turn before the man on the other side slammed into the door.

"You're dead!" The clown growled, his mask pressed against the glass. "I promise we'll find you!"

Too stunned to move, Cooper caught a glimpse of the crook's eyes through the openings in the mask. Dark, bottomless, and cold. Like twin cigarette burns in a faded blanket. Shaking, Cooper jammed Frank's keys in his pocket and stepped back, stumbling over the curb and tumbling to the pavement.

The man tapped on the glass with the muzzle of the gun. "Drop the hard drive!"

Cooper was going to heave. Still clutching the hard drive, Cooper rose on unsteady legs and looked toward the street.

Hiro flew across Kirchoff Road on her bike, pedaling like mad. Gordy rode right behind her—gaining.

The window crashed behind him. Shards of glass strafed Cooper's back. Another crash. Sprinting for his bike, he jammed the hard drive into the pocket of his cargo shorts. He yanked his mountain bike off the ground and mounted it on the run. A third crash. Cooper glanced back to see the metal stool tumble into the parking lot and the man barrel toward him—ripping off his clown mask as he ran. He stood on the pedals, straining to build speed—fearing at any second he'd feel a hand pulling him off the bike or a bullet ripping through his back. Not slowing to check traffic, Cooper bolted out of Frank 'n Stein's lot.

His friends had a huge lead on him. Slicing through the Dunkin' Donuts entrance on the other side of Kirchoff, Gordy sped the wrong way through the drive-thru lane with Hiro only a half-length behind.

Cooper figured Gordy would stay on the pavement past the post office before ducking into the park. He pumped hard to catch up. Out of the corner of his eye he saw a startled face at the pick-up window as he passed. A car wheeled around the rear corner of the donut shop, headlights boring right into Cooper's eyes. Swerving, he slammed into the curb—and vaulted over the handlebars.

CHAPTER 4

Dark blurs and flashes of lights raced past his eyes as his feet swung over his head. Cooper slapped to the ground directly on his back and skidded to a skin-burning stop. The sky continued moving. He couldn't breathe. Rocking side to side, Cooper gasped for air.

The driver jumped from the car and ran toward him, his face twisted in concern. "Are you all right?"

Rolling onto his stomach, Cooper propped himself up on his hands and knees. With a gasp, he sucked in fresh air. His stomach lurched and a light-headedness swept over him. Cooper gagged once — and his stomach squeezed out his monster shake.

"Are you hurt bad?" The driver's voice again.

The fog in Cooper's head started to clear. He raised his head and looked across the street. A shadowed SUV with one headlight out rounded the back corner of Frank 'n Stein's. The high beams blinked on, pinpointing his escape like a pair of prison tower searchlights. A silhouetted form appeared from the same direction — running directly towards him. The clown just wouldn't quit. Cooper struggled to get up.

The driver stepped up and held him in place. "Hold on there, son. I don't think you should be moving."

Cooper had to get out of there. Now. "Let me go — I'm okay."

The driver looked worried, but backed off.

Too late.

"Police," the runner said, pushing past the driver. The Clown. His mask was gone, but his hoarse voice was unmistakable.

"Give me some room." Pressing one hand on Cooper's neck, the man kept Cooper sprawled on the ground and from getting any kind of look at his face. He felt the man's hand dart into the back pocket of his cargo shorts.

"What, no ID? Where do you live, kid?"

Cooper tried to stand, but the man leaned into him, keeping him in place.

Several people hurried out of the donut shop and formed a half-circle around him.

The man patted Cooper's front pockets, then drove his hand deep in one of them. "I want that hard drive."

Partially laying on his right side, the hard drive pressed into his leg just above the knee.

The man pulled out Cooper's house key. "Jackpot."

Cooper grabbed for it, but the man pulled back.

"I called 9–1–1!" a voice shouted from the pick-up window. "The police and ambulance are on the way."

For an instant Cooper felt hope.

The robber leaned in close. "I'll let you go—for now," he whispered. "You get me that hard drive. The bell tower. Sunday night. No cops. Got it?"

Cooper nodded.

"Say it." The man's lips brushed against Cooper's ear with every whisper.

"Bell tower. Sunday." Cooper tried to get on his feet.

"Good boy," the clown cop said. He patted Cooper's back gently, putting on a show for the bystanders. "And not a word to anyone," he hissed. The man squeezed Cooper's neck with an iron hand. "Or I'll find you if I have to try this key in every house in town. But you rode your bike, so I bet you don't live far."

The man leaned in close and snickered. "I gotcha, boy."

Cooper tried to pull free, but the man gripped Cooper's neck even harder. "And I'll kill everyone in the house. Your Mom. Your Dad. Brothers. Sisters." The man thrust his fist in front of Cooper's eyes and opened it for an instant—just quick enough for him to glimpse his house key. "I'll kill them all—and I'll save you for last. Understand?"

Cooper nodded.

"Now get outta here before the circus starts." The man released his grip and stood.

"He's alright," the man announced. "Just shaken up a bit."

Cooper turned to look down the road—half expecting to see flashing lights. He struggled to his feet.

Head down, the man backed through the crowd and disappeared.

Cooper staggered toward his bike, feeling a measure of strength pulsing through him again.

"Really," the driver put one hand on Cooper's shoulder, "wait for the paramedics to check you out."

"Send them across the street," Cooper said, picking up his bike and swinging a leg over the seat. "The owner of Frank 'n Stein's . . . there was a fight . . . I think he's dead." Pushing off, he leaned into the pedals like his life depended on it. As far as he was concerned it did.

Cooper didn't look back. Didn't dare. The wind shrieked in his ears, an unearthly voice that said he was doomed. The robber got a good look at his face—and had his house key.

He spotted Hiro and Gordy waiting in the shadows between a couple of parked mail trucks. They took flight again as soon as Cooper got close. Together they raced down the bike trail along the creek through Kimball Park.

Minutes later they ditched their bikes behind the shed in Cooper's backyard. With a six-foot cedar fence securing the backyard like a stockade, they were safe from detection. Still, Cooper stood at the corner of the shed and listened. Sirens wailed in the distance, but other than that, quiet. No rumble of a car passing slowly. Not even a dog barking. If the men had tried to tail them, they weren't following anymore.

"What happened back there?" Tears streaked Hiro's face.

"He took my key. Says he'll find me."

Hiro sucked in her breath.

"He wants the hard drive. Sunday night."

"Three days from now." Gordy plowed both hands through his hair and held his head. "Why didn't you just give it to him?"

"Then he'd have all of us. Right now I don't think he knows you two exist. By the time he got to the door, you were gone."

"And it was dark." Gordy said it like he desperately wanted to believe it.

Hiro swiped at her tears. "I had that *feeling.* Like I got the day my dad ..." She shook her head. "But that car—it looked like it hit you. Are you okay?"

He rolled his shoulders. "Yeah," the palms of his hands still stung, but the fall hadn't broken the skin. "I think so." He looked down at his cargo shorts. No tears or rips. In fact, nobody would even notice he'd taken a dive—from the front, anyway. His back burned but his t-shirt wasn't sticking. Hopefully that meant he wasn't bleeding.

"What about Frank?" Hiro hesitated. "Do you think he's ..."

Cooper's mind went back to the scene. Searching Frank's pockets for the keys. He was dead alright. And the men who did it intended to get rid of the eyewitness.

Hiro must have seen the answer in his eyes. "We have to call the paramedics. Just in case."

"Done. I told someone at Dunkin' Donuts Frank needed help. They called 9–1–1."

"I thought we were toast." Gordy paced in a tight pattern, jamming his hands deep in his pockets. "That was close. Too close." He hustled over to the fence and tried to peer through the slats.

"We're safe — for now," Cooper said. "We just need to stay that way."

"Thank God," Hiro said. "We need to call the police."

"No." Cooper struggled to harness his thoughts. His brain still felt like it was somersaulting the handlebars. "We can't tell anybody — especially the police."

"What!?"

"Two of those guys wore cop clothes. What if they're cops?"

"No way," Hiro whispered.

"It's possible." Cooper raked a hand through his hair. "Look, your dad was a cop, and your brother is a cop, and someday you'll probably be a cop, so don't take this personally. But maybe they dressed like cops because they *are* cops. Not everybody is as honest as your family. Chicago and corruption kind of go together — and Rolling Meadows is part of Chicagoland."

Hiro grabbed for the necklace around her neck and closed her fist around it.

Gordy turned from looking through the fence. "And one had a gun. Right? What does that tell you?"

"He's a dangerous criminal."

Gordy stepped closer to Hiro. "Or maybe he's a cop. You gotta admit it's possible."

Hiro stared at the ground. "Possible. Not probable."

Seeing the opening, Cooper pushed ahead. "As long as we stay quiet about this, the creeps won't know who *we* are — no matter if they're cops or not. We'll stay safe."

"What?" Hiro said. "I can't tell Ken? Are you trying to tell me I can't trust my own brother?"

"Look, Ken is still a rookie," Cooper said. "He's a good cop, but a rookie."

"Meaning?"

"He'll have to report everything. Our names and addresses." Cooper lowered his voice. "What if the wrong cop hears about it? What's to stop him from finding us and making sure we *stay* quiet?"

Hiro groaned. "We'll be letting those monsters get away with murder."

"We'll be staying alive," Cooper said. "Besides, what kind of a help can any of us really be? They wore masks. All I saw were his eyes. I couldn't identify him in a lineup."

"What about Frank?" Hiro whispered his name. "He's been like a grandpa to me."

"To all of us," Cooper whispered. Frank took the time to sit down and talk with them. Not just about the weather, but about life. With no kids of his own, he'd sort of adopted the three of them in his own way. Even helped with homework when he could.

"Nothing we do is going to bring him back—and you know it." Cooper stared at his hands, wishing he'd stood up and used them to help Frank when he needed it instead of hiding behind the counter. Not that he would have been much of help. "I just want to make sure none of us joins him."

More sirens echoed through the night. Hopefully that would keep the robbers off the street and in a hole somewhere.

Cooper listened for a moment. "Look," he said. "That guy with the clown mask has my key. He said he'd find me. Said he'd *kill* my mom and dad … and anyone else in the house."

Hiro came closer. "We need help. Protection."

Cooper shook his head. "We need to keep our mouths closed."

Hiro looked him in the eyes, like she was searching for the answer. "This is too big. Too dangerous."

Cooper glanced at the back of his house and nodded. "Exactly. So don't ask me to trust the police. Not when a couple of them might want to kill my family."

"What about the hard drive?" Gordy's eyes were wide.

"We'll figure that out later," Cooper said. "But right now we have to be together on this."

Gordy peered over his shoulder, as if to make sure somebody wasn't scaling the fence. When he turned back, shadows covered most of his face. He cleared his throat. "So we don't tell a soul. Right?"

"Exactly. Not even our parents. It's our secret." Cooper looked directly at Hiro. "We have to lay low."

"Lay low? Now *you* sound like a criminal." Hiro lowered her head. "This seems all wrong. They have to be stopped—whoever they are."

"We *are* stopping them," Cooper said. "We're stopping them from finding us and adding three more murders to the neighborhood." *No, not three more. What about Mom and Dad and Mattie? If that hard drive got out, they'd be dead too. We're talking six murders besides Frank.* Cooper rubbed the back of his neck with his open palm. And getting in the house wouldn't be a problem. The image of the man holding his house key played back in his mind and caused Cooper's stomach to flip just as violently as he'd done on his bike.

Hiro looked up at Cooper. "I had this weird feeling—just before it happened." Her shoulders shook as she sobbed. "I'm sorry. I'm just so scared."

Cooper put one hand on her shoulder and the other on Gordy's. "This is about our survival. I say we make a three-way promise not to tell a soul about this."

"Like a pact?" Gordy's eyes darted from Hiro to Cooper.

"Right. A code we all agree to live by. A Code of Silence."

Hiro stared, zombie-like. "If a fish could learn to keep its mouth shut he'd never get caught." She blinked. "My dad used to say that. People go to jail because they can't keep quiet."

"Exactly," Cooper said. "And they get themselves killed that way, too. We all have to stick together on this. All in—or it won't work."

Laying a hand on each of his friends' shoulders, Gordy nodded. "I'm in."

Cooper nodded. "Hiro?"

Hesitating for an instant, Hiro slowly put a hand on each of their shoulders. She looked at Gordy, then faced Cooper, her cheeks wet and glistening in the moonlight. "In," she whispered.

CHAPTER 5

Cooper took a deep breath and let it escape. "We keep quiet and this will all blow past." Striding over to the double-door entrance of the shed, he spun the dial on the combination lock. A moment later he rolled his bike inside next to his old one.

Gordy joined him inside. "What about the hard drive?"

"We bury it for now." Cooper worked his way to the back of the shed and dumped a plastic garbage barrel filled with basketballs, footballs, bats, and street hockey sticks. "Nobody will ever find it." Placing the hard drive at the bottom of the dark green container, he heaped the balls and gear back on top of it. Backing his way out of the shed, he stacked a sled, a couple of snow shovels, and the lawnmower in front of the barrel.

"Cooper?" his mother called. "Is that you?"

"Yeah." Cooper's heart jumped. He stepped past Gordy into the yard. "Right here." His mother stood in the open doorway of the house, hugging herself in the cool October air.

"Are Hiro and Gordy with you?"

"Yeah. We were just putting my bike away."

Gordy poked his head out of the doorway wearing a smile like a cheap mask. It did little to hide the guilty-as-sin look in his eyes. Thankfully, the shadows worked in his favor.

"Gordon," she said. "Your mom has called here twice looking for you. I told her I thought you were heading to Frank's for a little studying and after-dinner snack."

Gordy's smile went plastic, and his eyes widened. "Well, ah, we—"

"We changed our minds," Cooper burst in. "We just biked to the park for a while, then came back here."

The lie came out fast and smooth as though Cooper had rehearsed it a dozen times. Hiro stepped into view from the other side of the shed with her bike. Skin pale and eyes wide, she looked haunted.

"Hi Hiro," Cooper's mom smiled. "Are you keeping those boys out of trouble?"

"Definitely trying."

"Good girl," Mom said. "Keep them on their toes."

Cooper exchanged glances with Gordy. They'd *all* need to be on their toes ... or they'd end up flat on their backs like Frank.

"I'd better get home." Gordy gripped the handlebars and pushed his bike toward the cedar fence. He turned and waved to Cooper's mom. "See you, Aunt Dana." Without a word, Hiro followed.

Cooper hustled up beside them. "Let's take the bus tomorrow." He wasn't so sure riding bikes to school would be a good idea. "We can meet at the stop early."

Hiro nodded, but looked like she was in a different world.

Cooper put a hand on Gordy's shoulder. "Make sure Hiro gets home okay. I'd do it myself, but ..." He tipped his head toward his mom.

"I don't need a bodyguard," Hiro said, walking faster to keep up.

"We could *all* use one right now," Gordy said, hesitating as he neared the fence. "It's safer if we stick together." He took a deep breath and slid the bolt to unlock the gate. Looking both ways, Gordy rolled his bike out of the backyard.

Hiro waved a weak goodbye to Cooper and his mom, then disappeared into the darkness.

His mother closed the door partially and huddled behind it like she was waiting for him. Cooper's chocolate lab nuzzled past her and wriggled out of the house. Bounding to greet him, the dog zeroed in on him like a heat-seeking missile.

"Hey, Fudge." Cooper dropped down on one knee and braced himself. She collided into him, all wiggles and wagging tail. Cupping her head in his hands, he scratched behind her ears and under her collar. Fudge whimpered and whined happily.

When he stood and started toward the house, Fudge trotted beside him and sniffed at the hem of his shorts as if to find out where he'd been and who he'd been with. Whatever scent she picked up, it glued her to his left leg. Like some kind of tired wind-up toy, her tail slowed and finally stopped swinging altogether. Fudge prodded and poked at the pocket of his cargo shorts, but her nose never left contact with it, even as he stepped into the kitchen.

"Did you brush by a cat or something?" Mom frowned. "Look at her, she's trembling."

The hair around Fudge's neck grew stiff and started rising. Cooper put one hand between her head and his pants, gently trying to push her away. She pushed harder as if drawn by an invisible magnet.

"She's so intense, you'd think she smelled a chocolate bar in your pocket," Mom said.

Cooper shook his leg to break Fudge free. Not chocolate. Blood. Maybe his shorts absorbed microscopic particles of Frank's blood when he climbed over him. Now Fudge picked up on it. The scent of death. "C'mon Fudge." He picked up her chin and leaned close to her face. "No." Ears plastered back against the sides of her head, Fudge looked at him with deep caramel eyes. Sad, *knowing* eyes. Thankfully she couldn't talk. She'd have to live by the Code of Silence too.

"Warm me up, Cooper." Mom reached out for a hug. He was barely taller than her, which wasn't saying much. Cooper held her tight, wishing he'd never gone out that night. Never went to Frank 'n Stein's. Never—

"Cooper." His mother held him by the shoulders at arm's length. "You're shaking too. What's wrong?"

"Nothing," he said, avoiding her eyes. "I guess it got a little chillier outside than I thought it would. I should have worn my jeans."

"And your sweatshirt." She rubbed his back. "October is nearly over."

Cooper winced at the stinging flashes of pain. "I think I'll hit the shower." He needed to be alone. Think. Wash the blood off.

"I tried your cell." She pointed to his cell on the counter.

"I forgot. Sorry." She had no *idea* how sorry. He unplugged it from the charger and pocketed it.

"And then I started hearing sirens just before I checked outside." She gave him one last squeeze and let him go. "Sirens tell the world something bad has happened."

Worse than bad. The last twenty minutes had been like something out of a horror movie. More sirens wailed now. Cooper closed the door. "I'm home now, so it looks like you worried for nothing." He slid the deadbolt in place.

She smiled. "I'm just glad you're safe."

Safe. He intended to stay that way.

"Uh, Mom, I lost my house key."

"Is it up in your room?"

"Nope, I took it with me. Had it in my pocket." He pulled his pocket inside out. "Gone."

Mom smiled. "It's not the first one you've lost. I'll get a copy made."

"Yeah, but somebody could use it to get in our house."

If his mom was concerned, she didn't show it. "You didn't have a ring on it—no ID on it at all, right?"

Cooper shook his head. "Just the key. But I was wondering if we should get the locks changed—just in case."

His mom straightened a hand towel hanging from the oven door handle. "We'll be fine. I don't think whoever finds it will try every lock in town."

That's exactly what he intends to do. "But just to be *safe* ..."

Mom laughed. "Since when did you start worrying so much? That's *my* department. I'll see what Dad thinks."

Swing and a miss. And to push it any more would draw more attention to it than he needed.

She pointed to a tray of chocolate chip cookies cooling on the counter. "I need someone to test this batch."

He was in no mood for cookies. He wanted to turn out all the lights and be sure the deadbolts were in place on the front door. Hide. Take a shower and scrub every trace of blood, every scent of Frank's death off him. A wave of weakness rolled over him and settled there. His mind shifted to an image of Frank's body on the floor of his diner.

"Think I'll take a shower first."

She handed him a cookie anyway and leaned against the counter by the sink. "I talked to your dad on the phone while you were out. The photo shoot went well. He should be home by noon tomorrow ... and he's bringing a surprise with him."

Cooper chewed a bit of cookie he didn't remember putting in his mouth. Wake up and find out this whole thing had been a bad dream ... *that's* the kind of surprise he wanted.

She smoothed her shoulder length hair. "Something Dad has wanted for a long time."

Cooper's little sister ran into the kitchen. "Tell me too," Mattie said. At six years old, she acted like the entire family revolved around her—or should.

"I'll tell both of you after Cooper gets cleaned up."

Mom started giving Mattie a little hint, but Cooper couldn't focus on it. Right now every thought in his head revolved around Frank 'n Stein's. He only zoned-out for a minute, but apparently he missed something important. Somehow Mattie got the idea Dad was bringing home a pony. She pranced and galloped around the kitchen, pawing at the air.

Mom kissed Cooper's forehead. "He can't wait to show you, so do me a favor. Hurry home after school tomorrow. No snack stops at the mini-mart or Frank 'n Stein's."

Frank 'n Stein's. Cooper's heart lurched.

His mother started to leave the kitchen with Mattie. "You won't forget to come right home, will you?" she teased, calling over her shoulder. "I can pin a reminder note on your backpack if you think it will help."

His *backpack.*

Panic clenched his stomach and twisted it. Dizziness surged through his head. Cooper grabbed the edge of the table to steady himself. His mother wouldn't be pinning any note to his backpack. Not tonight. He'd left it under the table at Frank 'n Stein's. The backpack pinned *him*—to the scene of the crime.

CHAPTER 6

Gordy mounted his bike and followed Hiro down the drive, scanning up and down the street for a car with one headlight. He'd feel a lot safer when he got home.

"I don't need an escort," Hiro said over one shoulder.

And I don't want to be one. But he followed anyway and kept an eye out for suspicious cars, staying a couple lengths behind Hiro.

She didn't slow as she approached her house, but picked up the pace instead.

"Hiro," Gordy called after her. "What are you *doing*?"

She lowered her head to be more aerodynamic and seemed to pump harder, widening the distance between them. She zipped down School Drive, across Campbell Street and picked up the bike path through Kimball Hill Park.

She was heading right back to Frank 'n Stein's. *I don't think so.* Gordy stood on the pedals and closed the gap within seconds and pulled up alongside.

"You crazy?"

"Frank was good to my family. And you know it."

Yeah, yeah. After her dad died Frank gave her mom a job as a bookkeeper. Helped her get her degree and a higher-paying job. He ought to know the story. Their moms and Aunt Dana had been close since college. "It's too dangerous to go back there."

"Then go home." Her mouth formed a tight line. She kept pedaling along the asphalt bike path.

Oh, nice. And how heroic would that look? "Exactly what are you planning to do? He's dead."

She flashed an angry glare. "Stop saying that. Just stop it."

He coasted for a second and let her get a lead on him. He glanced down at the creek to his right. Black and rushing away from Frank 'n Stein's — which is exactly what they should be doing. When Coop heard about this he wouldn't believe it. Then again, Hiro did have her own mind on things. There would be no turning her back now.

Hiro biked over the creek on the pedestrian bridge and picked up the trail bordering the creek on the west side to Kirchoff Road.

Good. It was the longer way, but definitely safer than racing through parking lots and crossing the four-lane. At least she was using her head a *little.*

Flashing lights lit up the sky around Frank 'n Stein's. Hiro took the bike trail under the Kirchoff Road bridge that looped around and ramped back up to the street level on the other side. She crossed the creek and coasted to a stop at the diner parking lot. Gordy stopped beside her and put a leg down to take in the scene. Police cars. Paramedics. A growing crowd gathered outside a yellow police line.

All the glass had been knocked out of the front door of Frank 'n Stein's now, and police walked through the opening like the door was propped open. Broken glass sparkled on the ground in the flashing red lights like the cheap jewelry some of the girls wore at school. Not Hiro, of course. The only jewelry she ever wore was the necklace with a miniature Chicago Police shield on it — or 'star' as they called it in Chicago. It was a Chicago tradition to give a necklace or pin to family members of a fallen officer. She chose the necklace. It was the gift she never wanted, but would never part with either. Gordy thought it was morbid. Almost as spooky as keeping a lock of his hair in her pocket.

A car screeched to a stop in the next parking lot, and a man ran toward the building. Joseph Stein. Frank's partner. He ducked under the yellow crime scene tape and said something to a policeman who tried to block his way. Mr. Stein must have convinced the man he was half owner because the policeman stepped to one side and waved him on. Mr. Stein paused for a moment by the front door, as if wondering if he should unlock it, but then stepped through the door and disappeared inside.

Gordy stretched to get a better view. Was Frank's body still on the floor? Maybe they'd taken an extra apron and covered his face with it. In any case, Mr. Stein was in for a shock.

Gordy ditched his bike and stood next to Hiro. "Okay. Paramedics are here. Nothing more we can do."

She held up a finger, but didn't take her eyes off Frank 'n Stein's.

Gordy watched Hiro. What if Hiro's mom still worked here? She might have been dead too. Gordy wondered if the same thoughts crept into her mind. But right now this place was creeping him out. "Time to go," he said.

Hiro ignored him. Her attention seemed focused on the fringe of the crowd. Gordy followed her gaze.

Great. Neal Lunquist. Just seeing Lunk made Gordy's stomach twist even tighter. Lunk still wore his Frank 'n Stein's shirt, which is one of the reasons they avoided Frank 'n Stein's before 7 p.m. on Thursdays.

Even though there was some kind of truce between them after Cooper saved Lunk's hide, Gordy didn't exactly trust him. To him, Lunk was still the bully that used his size to intimidate. And Hiro seemed ready for a fight whenever he was around, too. She had to, really. Lunk painted a target on her back from the very beginning.

She leaned closer to Gordy. "Look at the creepy looking guy talking to Lunk."

"Got him." Gordy sized the man up. *About six-two. Two hundred and twenty-five pounds. Mid forties.* The guy had a mean look about him. And he looked like he knew how to handle himself in a fight.

She slowly rubbed the shield hanging from her neck between her thumb and forefinger. "He looks suspicious."

"Why? Because he's talking to Lunk?"

"Because he's about the same size and build of any one of those three men we saw. There was plenty of time for him to leave the scene, change clothes, and come back and watch from the crowd. Criminals do that sort of thing all the time. And the man obviously has some kind of connection with Lunk, an *employee*—which would explain how they knew about the safe. What more do you need?"

Gordy shrugged. "A latex mask hanging out of his back pocket would do it."

She folded her arms across her chest. "You're ridiculous. I bet he's got a record."

Gordy didn't care. He just wanted to get away from this place. "We came to see if paramedics were here for Frank. They are—so let's go."

Hiro held up one hand. "Look."

The man stepped closer to Lunk. By the looks on their faces, they were having some kind of argument. Lunk looked like he wanted to tear the guy's head off.

"I need to hear them," Hiro said. "I'm moving closer."

Gordy grabbed her arm. "This isn't a stakeout."

She pulled free and worked her way along the edge of the crowd. Gordy followed, but kept his head low. Hiro's height helped her move close undetected, but Gordy had to work at it.

She stopped behind a small group of people not five feet from where Lunk and the man stood. Lunk's back was turned toward them, and the man didn't seem to notice those milling nearby.

"You got what you came for," Lunk said. "And you've already made a mess of things. Leave me and Mom alone."

The man spit on the ground and snickered. "Is that any way to talk to your father?"

Father? Gordy mouthed the word to Hiro. Now he could see where Lunk got his size.

Lunk clenched his fist. "I'm dead serious."

The man took a step back and held his hands up, palms out. "Okay. I'm done here for now." He turned on his heel and started walking.

Hiro leaned out for a better view just as Lunk turned their way.

Lunk spotted her immediately. He put his index fingers up to the outside corners of his eyes and pulled them back, reducing his eyelids to narrow slits. "What are *you* looking at Hiroko?" He elbowed his way through the crowd toward the yellow tape line.

"Let's go," Hiro said.

Gordy nodded. *About time.* He wouldn't feel safe until he was in his own room. And he certainly didn't want to see paramedics roll Frank out on a stretcher with a sheet over his head ... and Hiro didn't need that either.

Gordy led the way back to the bikes. "Straight to your house."

She looked up at him with a determined half smile. "*Almost* straight home." She motioned her head toward the man walking away from the crowd. "We have a suspect to follow first."

CHAPTER 7

Frank. That was Cooper's first waking thought. The horror of the robbery closed in on him. He felt like he was getting sucked into a bad dream. Cooper's goal Friday morning was a no-brainer. Survive the day without getting caught.

Hiro ran to meet Cooper and Gordy just as they reached the bus stop. Thankfully, the only other kids around gathered at the corner of Fremont and School Street, barely two blocks west. "Did Gordy tell you?"

Cooper looked at his cousin. "Tell me what?"

Gordy didn't look too anxious to tell him anything. "I thought we'd tell him together." He nodded at Hiro like he expected her to take it from there.

"We have a suspect." Hiro fingered the necklace.

"Hold on," Gordy said. "*You* have a *theory*."

Cooper held up his hands. "Tell me later. First we have a new problem to deal with." He had to get this off his chest.

Gordy gave him a questioning look.

"My backpack. I left it under the table at Frank's last night."

Gordy leaned back against the street sign post like his legs couldn't support him any longer. "We're dead."

Hiro groaned. "The police would have found it last night. I'm surprised they didn't pick you up already."

Cooper glanced down the street. Still no sign of the bus. "There was nothing in it to trace it to me. I'd dumped the whole pack on my bed before going out to meet you. The thing weighed a ton."

Hiro looked skeptical. "Your name wasn't on your backpack *anywhere?*"

Cooper shook his head. That was one thing he was sure about.

"No notebook inside? Papers?"

"Just my English book—but I never wrote my name in it."

"You're sure?" Her voice sounded hopeful.

"Absolutely. I stuffed my hoodie in there just before I left, too."

Gordy looked alarmed. "What about your name in your sweatshirt?"

"C'mon, Gordy, what do you think, I'm five or something?"

"Hey," he held up his hands in protest, "some people write their name on things like that."

"I guess we're lucky it was Coop's sweatshirt left behind and not yours," Hiro said. She raised her eyebrows with that "gotcha" look.

Gordy let that one go and stood upright. "Okay. Your name wasn't in your backpack anywhere. So we're good. Right?"

Cooper shook his head. "Not completely. They'll trace it back to Plum Grove."

Hiro said, "That'll narrow the search field."

Cooper slid his old backpack off his back. "For now, I'm using my backpack from last year."

Gordy stepped closer and poked three fingers through a gaping hole in the front pocket. "Physical Science. Seventh grade. I knocked a lit Bunsen burner onto it and burnt a hole in it." He smiled slightly. "And the best part was-"

"Gordy," Hiro interrupted. "We were all there, remember? We need to tell him about Lunk." She stepped closer. "Last night—before I rode home," she eyed Cooper like she wanted to make sure he was listening. "I went back to Frank 'n Stein's. With Gordy."

"Hey," Gordy raised his hands up. "None of this 'with Gordy' stuff. It was your idea all the way."

Hiro ignored him. "We wanted to tell you before the bus gets here."

Cooper felt like the bus just hit him.

Now he felt like *he* needed something to lean on. She rattled off the details, her voice rising in pitch as she did. He just looked at her, trying to listen, but also hardly believing what he heard. *They'd all agreed to lay low.*

"Hiro," he finally interrupted. "Why'd you chance it?"

She looked at him funny. Like it surprised her that he even had to ask. "Frank. I had to make sure he wasn't ... still alone."

He nodded. If he'd thought it would have helped Frank, he'd have done it himself. But it was so risky. "Sometimes criminals go back to the crime scene just for thrills. What if they'd been there?"

"I think they were."

"I tried to stop her," Gordy said. "But *Detective* Yakimoto wouldn't listen."

"I agreed to keep *quiet*," she said. "But I can't hide and do nothing."

They *needed* to hide right now. Stay safe. He shook those thoughts off. "You think you saw them?"

"I saw Lunk. Wearing his work shirt."

Cooper watched as kids lined up to board the bus. "Okay. So Lunk was there. Wearing his work shirt. So?"

"He looked real nervous. Scared. I've never seen him like that before."

Cooper pictured the 15-year-old the only time he'd ever seen him scared—in the back of the police car. The guy who'd made Cooper's life miserable had needed his help; so Cooper had helped. Gordy and Hiro still didn't trust him, but Lunk never bullied Cooper again—and sometimes he actually tried to be friendly with him. The bad blood between Lunk and Hiro had lessened slightly since the incident, but still only slightly.

"His boss was murdered," Cooper said. "That'd shake anybody up."

Hiro told him about the man Lunk argued with—and how they followed him at a safe distance.

"He looked mean," she said. "Creepy mean. He's connected. I know it."

Cooper shook his head. "You followed a mean-looking stranger?"

"A *suspect*."

"You're not a cop. You do know that, right? I know you want to be one someday, but—"

"I can take care of myself." She raised her chin. "Do you want to hear the rest or not?"

Cooper heard the bus round the corner and head their way. *Terrific*. He had hoped the bus would be late to give them more time to talk. "So what happened?"

"We followed him to Lunk's house. The creep is living in the shed."

Definitely strange. Cooper had to admit it. "Okay, so that's weird. But what does it prove, really?"

The bus slowed to a stop and swung open it's doors.

"An inside job," she said. "The man is Lunk's dad."

CHAPTER 8

Cooper led the way to a couple rows of seats near the back of the bus and waited to talk until the bus started moving again. "I never saw his dad around," Cooper said. "I just figured he lived in another state or something."

"Or maybe the state *pen*," Hiro said. "Seriously, he looks like an ex-con. I'm telling you, there's a connection here. Wanna hear my theory?"

The bus slowed, coasted to the curb, and picked up six more passengers. Two of them sat in the row directly in front of Gordy and Hiro.

"Later. When we can talk," Cooper whispered.

She looked disappointed, but nodded in agreement.

Cooper could guess her theory pinned this on Lunk somehow. She'd love that. Lunk made her first day at school miserable when she moved to Rolling Meadows after her dad died. Maybe it was the fact she wore her dad's leather Chicago police jacket to school for weeks—even though it hung almost to her knees. Lunk made fun of the jacket, even when he knew her dad had died. And the more he did, the more other kids stayed away. Not because Lunk was especially popular. It seemed more like kids were afraid they'd be a target if they got too close.

But because all three of their moms were longtime friends, Cooper and Gordy had known Hiro for years. And they ended up being the only real friends she had. Cooper understood her. Most of the time, anyway. Honestly, the girls who locked her out of their tight little circles didn't know what they were missing. That's the way Cooper saw it. She was a great friend. Fiercely loyal. And now the three of them had to stay close and keep quiet.

Cooper sat behind Hiro and Gordy and stared out the school bus window. If only he'd slung his backpack over his shoulder before he went to call Frank. The regrets that kept him awake last night still wouldn't let him rest.

Police cars filled every handicapped parking spot at Plum Grove Junior High. Not a good sign.

Gordy turned in his seat and gave Cooper a wide-eyed look. He'd obviously seen the cop cars, too.

If Cooper had ridden his bike as usual, he'd have been tempted to turn around and pedal home. And he wouldn't have to lie to say he felt sick. His stomach felt jazzed all morning.

But staying home might draw more attention than he wanted. Besides, he'd be ditching his two best friends—and Gordy might need help staying calm. Cooper filed off the bus behind the others, trying to look natural. Gordy looked like a zombie.

"Think they've figured it out?" Gordy fell in step beside Hiro and Cooper.

Cooper eyed the police milling around the entrance. "No."

Gordy tugged on Cooper's arm. "For sure?"

Cooper stopped and let a group of students pass. "If they knew, they'd have already picked us up."

Hiro didn't say a word, but she nodded slightly.

"They're zeroing in," Gordy whispered. "What do we do now?"

Cooper forced his mind to stay logical. Just the sight of all the police had him teetering on the edge of panic. "Exactly what we said before." He willed himself to look calm. *If Gordy knew what was going on inside me he'd totally lose it.* Pushing the thought out of his head, Cooper started walking again. "Just act like nothing is wrong."

One police officer was eyeballing the dozens of bikes poking out of the steel racks. Cooper felt relieved they'd taken the bus after all. Cooper, Hiro, and Gordy mixed in with other students entering the building through sets of double doors. They stayed close together, but Cooper was in his own world.

A handful of police stood just inside the building, watching students enter. The door to the principal's glass-walled office was closed. Principal Shull sat on the corner of his desk listening to several uniformed officers crowded around it. Cooper picked up the pace, and kept his head down. If the three of them could just make it through today without breaking the Code of Silence, there was hope. Then he'd have all weekend to try to figure out what to do next.

Principal Shull made a surprise visit to the first period class—carrying Cooper's backpack. He ducked in, smiled, and pointed at it.

"Anybody lose a backpack with an English book and sweatshirt inside?"

He appeared totally casual about the whole thing, like he was just trying to be helpful.

The man was trolling. Hoping for a bite. Cooper hoped his own act would be as convincing as the principal's. He didn't move.

"No?" The principal smiled again. "Anybody know of another student who is missing one?" He looked directly over Cooper's head at a group of boys sitting behind him.

Cooper turned to look at them too, as did half the class.

Riley Steiner, Walker Demel, and Trevor Tellshow looked totally innocent. They'd looked the same way when the principal came in questioning the culprits behind the *Out of Order-Do Not Enter* signs taped on every *GIRLS* washroom door in Plum Grove school just a couple weeks ago. Rumor had it that head librarian Miss Hoskins had a little 'accident' while running from one bathroom to another—looking for one that was operational. Steiner,

Demel, and Tellshow claimed to be innocent then, too, but they were found out a couple days later. The detentions they served as a result only boosted their hero status among many of the guys—including Gordy.

"Mr. Steiner?" The principal held it a little higher, as if he thought Riley couldn't see the backpack clearly from where he slouched at his desk.

Riley shrugged and shook his head—obviously answering for the whole group.

Apparently satisfied, Principal Shull made a methodical row-by-row visual sweep of the room. Cooper had no worries about Hiro. She could be impossible to read when she wanted to—which drove Cooper nuts. Gordy was another story. Cooper prayed the principal wouldn't read anything on Gordy's face.

"Anybody?" He gave the backpack a little shake.

Jake Mickel raised his hand. "If there's any money in it, it's mine."

It broke the tension, and Cooper laughed right along with the rest of them. Mickel looked pleased with himself, and shot a glance toward the guys in the back.

The principal continued his scanning. Cooper held steady when the man looked at him.

"I'll check another homeroom." Again, the big toothy, "just-trying-to-be-helpful" smile. "If you think of someone, I'll have it in my office. Just stop by."

Right. And the cops will kindly escort you to the police station. Nice try, Principal Shull.

The principal nodded at Mrs. Schmidt, as if to signal the class was all hers again. The man disappeared out the door, closing it behind him.

For the rest of the morning Cooper's heart pumped double-time, while the clock seemed to tick at half speed. When he stepped into Miss Ferrand's fourth period English class, two policemen and Principal Shull were waiting inside. This wasn't good. They stood huddled up by Miss Ferrand's desk like they were planning a raid, or going over their strategy. Obviously the "Gee, did anybody lose a backpack?" plan didn't work. Now they'd moved to Plan B.

Gordy looked like he was going to wet his pants. Hiro sat right in front of Cooper's desk and set her backpack beside her. She locked eyes with him as he passed—like she knew their little masquerade was about to unravel.

This had to be about the English book in his backpack. It obviously led the police to Plum Grove School. The book was only used by eighth-graders, and all the eighth-grade English classes were taught by Miss Ferrand. By process of elimination they were narrowing the field. Fast.

Steiner, Tellshow, and Demel put up a cool front. Talking loud. Laughing. To Cooper it seemed they were trying a little too hard. The fact they deliberately acted like they had nothing to hide made them look guilty as sin. They were in the clear, though. Cooper was sure of that. The police weren't there looking for someone behind another prank. They were looking for him.

Kids still talked, but without the usual volume. Jake Mickel leaned over, eyes wide.

"I heard the cops are here for a drug bust."

If he only knew the truth.

Kelsey Seals, who sat directly in front of Jake, twisted around in her seat. "I heard there might be a bomb threat," she said. "What do you think, MacKinnon?"

Bomb? Like they'd actually keep the students in the building while they checked it out. "I hear they're cracking down on kids doodling in their textbooks."

Jake laughed. "You're an idiot, MacKinnon."

Cooper shrugged. "It's what I heard."

Kelsey turned to share her theory with Eliza Miller—who seemed more than eager to listen.

Miss Ferrand studied the students row by row. Cooper turned to cement when Miss Ferrand's eyes met his. Her eyes held no accusations, just an appearance of deep concern. She kept scanning the room.

Nothing in that backpack pointed directly to Cooper. He was safe, except for the fact that he no longer had an English book. And from the looks of things, he was going to need one. Now.

He looked at the clock. The bell would ring in just over a minute. Cooper didn't dare draw extra attention to himself by leaning forward and whispering to Hiro. He slid his cell out of his pocket and texted her.

GOT YOUR ENGLISH BK?

She jumped slightly, like the vibration of her phone startled her. Fishing it out of her pocket, she read the screen and tapped out an answer.

His phone vibrated with her response.

Y. In b-pack.

Seconds left now before the bell. He texted again.

Hiro read the message and closed her phone without answering. In one smooth motion she slid her backpack behind her chair—right next to his.

The bell rang, and Principal Shull instantly stepped to the front of the class. Punctuality was a big deal with him. One of the policemen joined him.

"Students, I would like each of the boys in this classroom to take out their English book and place it on their desk."

A murmur rose from students. Cooper reached down and slid his hand into Hiro's backpack instead of his own. He found the book easily and slapped it on his desk like it was a "get out of jail" card.

Four boys didn't have a book, and Jake Mickel was one of them. Principal Shull called them forward.

"Hey, I didn't doodle in my book," Mickel said. "I didn't even write my name in it."

Laughter followed him as he shuffled to the front. Seals and Miller exchanged a knowing look.

Principal Shull, along with the police officers, escorted the four boys out of the room. Unless they could pull the book from their locker, these guys would have some questions to answer. Cooper was sure about that. He guessed the police had been doing this each period after the "lost and found" approach bombed, hoping to find the guy without an English book—or an alibi for last night.

Miss Ferrand offered no explanation, and the period passed in a blur. When the bell sounded for lunch, Cooper let out a shaky breath, as if he'd been holding it since he walked into the room. He couldn't get out of there fast enough. Hiro melted into the hallway crowd. Gordy hustled up alongside him and cupped his hand by his mouth. "They're on to us."

"Not here," Cooper hissed. "Split up. See you at lunch." Hiking his old backpack on his shoulder, Cooper picked up the pace and weaved his way through a group of girls.

"MacKinnon," Jake Mickel called from across the hall. He stood in front of his open locker.

Cooper crossed the hallway, dodging kids hurrying to lunch.

"The cops actually wanted to see my book." He pointed to his English book lying on the bottom of his locker.

"Did they check for doodling?"

"Didn't even open it. Just wanted to make sure I had it." Jake shook his head. "Weird, right?"

Grab his book. The thought flashed through Cooper's mind. *Steal it? What was he thinking?* But he wouldn't *actually* be stealing. He'd just borrow it until things cooled down. He slid his backpack off his shoulder and set it in front of Jake's locker. "Maybe it's a new tactic to be sure we do our homework."

He laughed, and turned to stop Kelsey and Eliza, who both approached as kids shuffled past "Did you see the way the cops hauled me out of class?"

This was his chance. Cooper bent down to retie his shoe. The English book stared at him. He glanced up at Jake. His back was turned, and his body blocked the girls' view. His heart thumped harder. With a rush of adrenaline he snatched Jake's book, dropped it in his own backpack, and stood.

Jake was still going at it, but in more detail than he'd shared with Cooper.

Cooper shouldered his pack. "See you, Jake. I'm starving."

"Me too." Jake slammed his locker closed without looking.

"Weren't you scared?" Kelsey asked.

He shook his head. "Not a bit. I had nothing to worry about, right?"

Cooper smiled and jogged toward the cafeteria. *You might have something to worry about now.*

CHAPTER 9

Hiro sat at their usual table and positioned herself where she could watch the cafeteria entrance. Strange how she still felt out of place, even after going here for over a year. Her mom thought the move would be good for her. Mom could be near Gordy's and Cooper's moms — her best friends. And Hiro would have Coop and Gordy — and she'd make new friends. They would be just what she needed. That was the plan.

But all Hiro had wanted back then was to be alone. Her hero died. The last thing she needed was to make friends with a bunch of chirpy girls. All their laughing seemed totally out of place. The whole world should have mourned. The way she saw it, the world tilted a bit more on its axis the moment her dad died. And it was never coming back.

Maybe she pushed the other girls away. But the truth is, they kept their distance, too. She just wished Lunk would keep *his* distance.

As it turned out, it wasn't new friends she needed. It was the old ones that pulled her through. She'd known Coop and Gordy since they'd been kids. And they were the ones who'd really helped her through those dark days.

And Frank had helped her in his own way, too. Why do the good men die? Dads who love their kids and are out there trying to protect people. Business owners who give struggling widows real help and a chance. Frank didn't deserve to die. He gave Hiro's mom more than a job. He gave her hope. Hiro's stomach felt totally messed up. She could feel a lump forming in her throat.

She had to pull herself together. Breaking down in tears wasn't exactly the best way to blend in. She studied the room. To her left the hot lunch line snaked into the cafeteria. She never took hot lunch, and today it smelled like pizza. Long paper banners with the hand painted words "Go Chargers" lined the walls. Right now she'd like to charge right over to the police station and tell them everything.

Candy Mertz, Lissa Bowens, and Katie Barbour sauntered with their trays and sat at the adjoining table. They were deep in conversation — probably about some boy. *Mertz and her flirts.* If they saw Hiro, they didn't show it. It was like she was invisible. *That ought to come in handy when I'm a cop*, she thought.

Hiro watched Coop enter the cafeteria with Jake, Kelsey, and Eliza , but he peeled away when the others stopped to join the hot lunch line. Gordy appeared out of nowhere and walked with Coop to her table, and they sat across from her.

Cooper pulled Hiro's English textbook out of his backpack and placed it on the table. "Thanks for the loan."

"Quick thinking on your part," Hiro said. "But I don't know if our luck can hold.

Coop tapped his backpack. "I picked up another book."

Hero knew exactly what that meant. "You *stole* someone's book?"

Gordy immediately checked his own pack. "Better not have been mine."

"Jake Mickel loaned it to me." Cooper put a finger to his lips. "He just doesn't know it yet."

Gordy snorted a laugh and pulled his sandwich out of his bag. Two sandwiches actually. One peanut butter. The other jelly. They never mixed until they hit his stomach.

Just watching him made Hiro's stomach feel even worse. She pulled out her sandwich and debated eating it or not.

She pushed it away. "Look guys," she said. "The police are going to figure this out. They're not stupid, you know. They've already narrowed their search to our school—and to Miss Ferrand's classes."

Cooper shook his head. "They're fishing."

"They're in the right pond."

He looked over his shoulder. "Like you said. They aren't stupid. Borrowing the book is just buying us time until the police catch the men who did that to Frank."

Gordy shifted a mouthful to one cheek. "They're goons."

"*Goons?*" Hiro shook her head.

He swallowed. "It's a perfectly good word for them. You'd rather I called them *thugs?*"

"Both a little dated, Gordy." She pictured Lunk's dad. "How about we call them *scum?*"

Cooper leaned in. "Goons. Thugs. Elvis. Mr. Clown. Scum. Doesn't matter what we call them. We just need to stay clear of them."

Hiro used her sandwich to hide her mouth. Not that she really thought anybody would try to read her lips, but it certainly worked. "If your cop theory is right, Elvis and the Clown could be right here in the building looking for us." She took a bite and put her sandwich down.

"Looking for *me*," Coop said, "You two got out in time. He was so focused on me, I don't think he saw either of you riding across the street."

"And the principal was looking for a *guy*," Gordy said. "You're in the clear, Hiro."

Hiro took an orange segment out of her lunch bag and tapped it against her lips. "But what if Mr. Clown *did* see us riding off?" She stared off toward the exit. "He'd be looking for three kids sitting together, just like us."

Gordy looked as if he were about to venture into a haunted house—alone. "You think we should split up?"

"What I'd really like is to lock arms together, walk to the nearest policeman and turn ourselves in," Hiro said.

Cooper looked like he wanted to say something, but caught himself. She could see the frustration on his face easy enough.

"I didn't sleep last night—and I don't think I'll sleep tonight," she said. "I've felt sick to my stomach ever since they hit Frank. What if they catch up with us?" For an instant she imagined seeing Lunk's dad show up at her door. Heard his snicker.

"They're looking for *me*," Cooper said. "Just me. I'm the one they saw. The only one."

She looked him square in the eyes. "I'm afraid they're going to find you."

Gordy leaned in close. "You're sure there's nothing to tie your backpack directly to you?"

"If there was, I'd be at the police station by now."

Hiro raised her eyebrows. "No fingerprints?"

Cooper stopped chewing.

"I'll bet the police found some clear ones on that book." Hiro picked at her sandwich.

"What good will that do unless they fingerprint me to confirm a match?"

Gordy looked from Cooper to Hiro. "Can they do that? Can they fingerprint you?" His eyebrows disappeared underneath drapes of straight blonde hair covering his forehead. "We're too young. Right?"

Hiro nibbled at the crust. "They'd have to get permission from a parent."

"So that's it then." Gordy angled the rest of his peanut butter sandwich into his mouth. "Tell your parents not to agree to it."

Hiro gave a little snort.

Gordy's back slumped a little more. He took a bite.

Wiping her mouth with a napkin, Hiro gave Cooper a sideways glance. "And then there's the DNA evidence."

By the look on his face, he hadn't thought of that.

"Your sweatshirt. One piece of hair in that hood and you're pinned to the crime scene. It's probably at the crime lab right now," Hiro said.

Swallowing, Gordy looked from Cooper to Hiro. "But still, they'd have to get a DNA sample from Cooper to match it. Right?"

Hiro reached across the table and plucked a hair from Gordy's head.

"Hey," Gordy said, batting her hand away. "What's that all about?"

"Do you honestly think the police can't get a DNA sample if they really want it?" She looked at Cooper, wishing he'd understand, hoping he'd rethink the whole strategy of staying silent. "You're in danger, Cooper. We all are, but you especially. Our Code of Silence isn't going to keep the things you left behind from telling them everything they need to know."

CHAPTER 10

Ten minutes later Hiro threw up what little of the lunch she ate. Right there at the table. Mertz, Bowens, and Barbour leapt from the adjoining table screaming and pointing, drawing more attention to Hiro. Students clapped and cheered. Hiro hung her head and cried.

Cooper glared at Mertz — huddled together with her two clones. Like they'd never seen someone sick before. They made Cooper queasy just looking at them.

"Let's get you some fresh air, Hiro," Cooper said, holding one of her arms and helping her to her feet. Gordy grabbed all three of their backpacks, stuffed the last of his sandwich in his mouth, and walked on the other side of her. Five minutes outside made all the difference. Even her voice sounded stronger.

"I'm sorry, Coop," she said. "I'm just so scared."

He totally understood the feeling.

Halfway through sixth period, Principal Shull's voice crackled over the PA system. All students were directed to proceed to the auditorium immediately. Any reason to cut class short should have been cause for celebration. Instead, Cooper shuffled along with the herd, keeping his head low.

Climbing to the top row of the bleachers, Cooper sat between Hiro and Gordy. Cops milled around everywhere on the maple gym floor below. Like sentinels at each door, they stood in their blue uniforms, ready to grab their eyewitness, if they could only figure out who it was.

"I don't like it," Gordy whispered. "Do they know something?"

"Yeah," Cooper said. "But not enough." He stuffed his backpack at his feet.

Jake sat two rows down, next to Kelsey and Eliza. It seemed they hadn't stopped talking since they'd started at his locker.

Riley Steiner, Trevor Tellshow, and Walker Demel sat in the front row, which was totally weird for them. For any other assembly they'd be sitting in the back, having their own little party. After the visit from Principal Shull and the cops in Miss Ferrand's class, they obviously knew they were in the clear. They seemed intensely interested in knowing the trouble somebody else was in.

Hiro leaned close to Cooper. "If a violent crime isn't solved in the first 72 hours, the chances of it ever being solved go way down."

Great. Only fifty-five hours to go.

Cooper saw Lunk mount the stairs and head their way. The kid was big enough to be in high school. Actually he *should* be in high school. For some unkown reason he'd been held back before he moved to Rolling Meadows. And it could stay a mystery for all Cooper cared. It wasn't the kind of thing he'd want to ask Lunk about. Being held back didn't have anything to do with smarts, though. The guy was sharp. Like always, he walked alone and wore a black t-shirt and faded camouflage pants.

Lunk kept coming, like he deliberately intended to sit close to them. Cooper felt Hiro tense next to him. When Lunk made eye contact, Cooper nodded and managed a smile.

Sitting on the wooden bench directly in front of them, Lunk turned just far enough to see them. "Hey, Coop." He nodded at Gordy. "Gordo."

"Hey." Gordy hardly looked up.

Lunk grinned at Hiro. "Thanks for the entertainment at lunch. Eat a bad egg roll or something?"

Hiro glared. "No actually, but I saved one for you."

A smile spread across his beefy face. "The lunch lady must have had some too 'cause she heaved all over the table while she was trying to clean up your mess."

Gordy's eyes brightened. "Really?"

"Yeah. She came out with a bucket and a pair of gloves, but before she could even— "

"Stop," Hiro interrupted, covering her ears. She took shallow breaths and squeezed her eyes shut. For a moment Cooper thought she was going to lose it again. Gordy slid a couple of feet away from her.

Lunk's face registered a clear victory. "Did I mention Candy Mertz wasn't looking so good either?"

Hiro pressed her hands tighter against her ears. "No more."

Principal Shull stepped up to the podium. "All right, students, quiet down." He raised his hands in the air.

Within seconds the entire auditorium went silent and still, like they'd been unplugged. It seemed everybody wanted to know why the police were there.

"Thank you." The principal lowered his hands. "This afternoon we have a very serious matter to talk to you about." He paused and scanned the crowd. "I'm going to ask Rolling Meadows Police Detective Hammer to explain. Please give him your full attention."

Hammer marched across the maple wood floor to the podium, his footsteps echoing from bleacher to bleacher. "I'm going to get right to the point," he said, waving a folder in one hand.

Cooper tried to analyze his voice. Did it sound like a DJ? Anybody's would with a microphone like that.

Hammer lowered the folder and scanned the crowd. "Last night a violent robbery took place at Frank 'n Stein's, right in town. One of the owners was brutally beaten. He's in a coma in the ICU at Northwest Community Hospital."

The crowd broke into hushed whispers. Cooper didn't have to fake a look of surprise. *Frank was alive?* He glanced at Hiro. She stared straight ahead, her mouth slightly open. Lunk didn't turn around, but his shoulders slumped.

"We have at least one eyewitness who saw a male, possibly twelve to thirteen years old, fleeing the crime scene on a bike. The boy nearly got hit by a car and admitted to witnessing the robbery."

Cooper held his breath. *Could anyone hear his heartbeat?* It thundered in his ears, and his stomach clenched. Gordy put a hand on his leg and squeezed.

Hammer took the cordless mike out of the podium stand and walked toward the bleachers. "Between the description from our eyewitness and evidence found at the scene, we are convinced the person who fled the diner is a student at Plum Grove Junior High."

A gasp escaped from the student body, and immediately the bleachers were alive with talk.

Cooper couldn't speak, even if he wanted to.

"Hold on." Hammer raised the file folder with one hand until the wave of talk receded. "The police are looking for your cooperation here. If you know anything, if you suspect anyone, I need you to have the guts to talk to one of us. We're looking for a male. We believe he is in the eighth grade. He carries a black backpack. He owns a dark gray zip-up hoodie from Old Navy. He's missing his English book. He may have some fresh scrapes and bruises. This boy rides a mountain bike — the color may be brown or orange."

Again the crowd erupted in excited talk. Kelsey Seals and Eliza Miller huddled close to each other, looking around like they may get attacked.

Cooper's head reeled. They would find him. How could they not? But his bike was silver. That would help. The orange glow from the parking lot lights must have—

"There's something you need to know." Hammer stood with one hand on his hip until the room was silent as a tomb. "The boy who witnessed this is probably scared. And for good reason. He's in real danger." Hammer paused, letting those words sink in. "Maybe it's a friend of yours. You need to help him. Maybe you noticed someone acting strange, out-of-character, or nervous this morning. You come see one of us."

Riley Steiner and his pack actually scanned the room, like finding the witness was a game.

Hammer looked down at the gym floor and then looked at the students again. "You'll be helping us catch a brutal criminal, and you may just be saving your friend's life. The man who put Frank Mustacci in a coma will want to silence an eyewitness as well."

The student body had never paid attention like this for any assembly Cooper had ever seen. Hiro squirmed next to him.

Hammer paced along the front row of the bleachers and waved the folder in the air. "In this folder I have the names of thirty-two boys who may fit one of the key pieces of evidence we found at the crime scene, and we'll narrow that number by at least ten before the day is over."

A list? Cooper wanted to slip between the boards at his feet and hide under the bleachers. Was his name on that list?

"We're talking about a witness to an attempted murder and armed robbery." Detective Hammer paused and scanned the crowd slowly.

Stay calm, Coop. Stay calm.

"We will find our witness. But if you know something, please talk to one of us. To do anything less is really helping the suspect get away with murder ... or attempted murder. Nobody wants to live with that on their conscience."

Cooper felt a tremor pass through Hiro.

Was she buying this nice cop routine? Clown face was wearing a cop uniform. So was Elvis. If police were involved in the robbery somehow, none of them could be trusted.

"Now, we intend to interview many of you. All of you if necessary. Each of you will receive a permission slip explaining the process. The interviews will start Monday and will be conducted by a trained juvenile officer with at least one of your parents present."

Cooper stared at his feet. No way did he want to go through an interview. How would he bluff his way through *that*? And Gordy? He'd never make it.

"I'll sit in on most of the interviews personally," Hammer said. "And I'll tell you right now," he tapped the side of his head, "I have a built-in boloney detector."

The cop paced back to the podium and leaned on it. "Let me say one more thing. We've got fingerprints right now. We're working on DNA samples, and I've got one other piece of evidence that will open the door to finding our witness. It's just a matter of time. I believe he's right here in this gym."

Muffled gasps escaped from groups of girls clinging together all over the bleachers. Like they thought the witness was a criminal, too.

I'm a victim. Cooper felt like his stomach was going to turn itself inside-out. What other piece of evidence? What would open the door? *A key. My house key to be exact.*

"Let me say this directly to the witness: You are holding up a criminal investigation. Not smart. Don't wait for the interviews Monday. See me after the assembly."

Fat chance. The truth was, the police should focus on finding the guys who nearly killed Frank. Or maybe Cooper would have to find a way to find them himself.

Hammer brought the mic closer to his mouth. "And one more thing. You *need* protection. The longer you wait to come forward, the greater the chance you'll be found by the suspect or suspects. That's just plain crazy. I can help you."

The detective was using scare tactics now. Cooper was sure of it. But it was working.

Hammer paused and gave a long hard stare to the crowd as if he was watching for someone to blow their cover with a nervous twitch. "You come see me. Time to give it up." One corner of his mouth turned up in a crooked smile. "Either way, I gottcha, boy."

I gottcha, boy. The words seared Cooper's mind like they were fresh off Frank's grill. The same words the Clown used at the door. *God help me. He's one of them!*

CHAPTER 11

His mind shifted into high gear, but he wasn't gaining any ground. An elbow in his ribs brought him back to reality.

"It's over," Hiro said.

The assembly or their plan to keep quiet? Cooper wasn't sure which one she meant. Students all over the bleachers stood and started filing out. He could hear snatches of excited conversations. Jake, Kelsey, and Emily were talking over each other now, each of them guessing what had happened to poor Frank. Cooper knew exactly what happened, but he didn't dare tell a soul. Gordy sat next to him in stunned silence.

Lunk's face had no more color than Hammer's manila folder with the thirty-two names. Pulling a pen from the corner of his mouth, Lunk turned toward Cooper and Hiro.

"Mr. Mustacci is the nicest man I know," he said, quietly.

And he's alive. Thank God. Cooper nodded. "He always treated us good. Like we were people, not just kids. Hiro's mom used to work there."

Lunk worked the pen between his fingers, turning it end over end. "He gave me a job three weeks ago." Then as if he guessed their question, he went on. "I'm 15, so I can work until seven on school nights. And all day Saturday. Gives me meals, too. All I want."

Normally Hiro wouldn't let an opportunity like that go without a comeback, but this time she remained silent, staring at her shoes. Then again, Lunk only had good to say about Frank. How could she argue with that? Frank's goodness was probably the only thing on Earth they both agreed on.

Lunk kept talking—almost like he was in a daze. "I filled out applications everywhere. Mom didn't want me to take a job, but the rent went up."

Cooper didn't know what to say. Lunk wasn't the type to open up.

"None of the other places even called me for an interview. Mr. Mustacci didn't care that I had no job experience. He gave me a chance."

Goose bumps rose on Cooper's arms. Those were nearly the same words Frank used when the two men forced him to give them the combination to the safe. He had given *someone* a chance—someone who betrayed him and told the wrong people about the safe, and how Frank didn't trust banks.

"How could anybody hurt him?" Lunk's eyes narrowed to slits as dark as his hair.

Hiro finally found her tongue. "Exactly what I was thinking. They'd have to be total jerks. Morons. Scum-of-the-earth, cold-hearted bullies that deserved … "

"Hiro," Cooper interrupted.

She set her jaw and glared at Lunk.

Lunk didn't look offended. "If I find the person who did this, or the witness who is messing up the investigation … " He bent the pen nearly in half and tossed it between the bleacher boards.

Cooper heard the pen clatter against the steel supports on its way down. He had a feeling Lunk would do the same thing to him if he found out he was at Frank 'n Stein's last night.

Like the starting gun at a race, the bell signaling the end of the last period triggered Cooper into action. Leaping to his feet, he stuffed his books in his backpack and slung it over his shoulder on the run. He'd play offense now. Rather than slinking around the halls, afraid of cops questioning him, he could finally get out of the school.

He caught up to Hiro and Gordy. Together they merged into the crowd bottlenecked at the doors leading to the parking lot—and freedom. Policemen stood at every exit handing out neon yellow sheets of paper. Great. The permission form.

Hiro nudged him. "How do we handle *that*?"

Cooper didn't answer. A police interview would change everything. It was one thing not to go to the police—not to *offer* information. It was another thing to lie to them.

The crowd funneled into single file lines at the doors, and the police didn't miss one student. "Have a parent read and sign this," the cops repeated with almost every new student. "Bring it back Monday."

Taking one of the forms, Cooper folded it in half and buried it in his backpack. The pack felt heavier for it. And exactly how was he going to bring the topic up to his parents? Hiro started reading her form as they walked.

Gordy pulled on his arm and stopped him as soon as they had cleared the doors. "Check that out."

Cooper followed the direction of his gaze. The cops were all over the bike rack area. One of the officers held a camera and took pictures of every bicycle.

"Good call on riding the bus today," Gordy said.

Hiro looked up at Cooper. "They'll probably show the pictures to their witness."

The driver that almost hit him.

She leaned in close. "You heard what Lunk said about Frank giving him a chance?"

"Kinda spooky, right?"

Hiro hugged herself and kept walking. "He's part of this. Along with his dad. I feel it."

"But he *likes* Frank," Cooper said.

Hiro gave an exasperated groan. "So he's a good actor."

"Seemed real to me."

When Cooper noticed Detective Hammer, he was almost on them. It was impossible to see his eyes through the mirrored lenses of his aviator-type sunglasses. No accident there.

"Got your permission slip, guys?" Hammer said. The detective still had the manila folder in one hand.

"In my backpack."

The Detective nodded. "Good. You boys in seventh or eighth?"

Cooper felt his face grow warm. He stood taller without trying to look obvious. "Eighth."

"Then you're on my list." Hammer opened the folder. "Names?"

What was going on? "Cooper MacKinnon."

"G-Gordon Digby. But I go by Gordy. Cooper started it, and it just stuck. Even my Mom calls me Gordy now." He talked fast and took a step back.

"There you are." He made a notation in his folder. "I like putting names with faces." He looked directly at Cooper.

For a second Cooper couldn't talk—couldn't breathe. He stared at Hammer's mirrored lenses. All he saw was his own face in each lens looking back at him. *Does he recognize me? He couldn't. It was the guy with the raspy voice that really saw me. Mr. Clown.*

The detective tapped the folder. "Get that permission slip signed."

He turned to Gordy. "You okay Mr. Digby? You seem a bit nervous."

Gordy swallowed. "Perfect." His voice cracked.

Hammer cocked his head to one side. "Trying to test my baloney detector?"

"No sir," Gordy stammered. "I'd never do that."

A smile parted the detective's lips slightly. "Something tells me you could slice up enough baloney to feed half your school."

Hiro slid between Cooper and Gordy and hooked their arms.

"And I'm the lucky girl who has these phony baloneys for best friends." She rolled her eyes and tugged the boys toward the curb. "And if they make me miss the bus, I'm really going to turn them into dead meat."

Hammer's head rocked back with a burst of laughter. "Better get going, guys." He motioned them toward the line of buses along the edge of the parking lot. "She's tough."

Still holding them by the arms, Hiro whisked them away toward the buses.

"Nice save, Hiro," Cooper said.

"You're welcome. But we need to talk. This isn't over—you know that, right?"

Cooper stopped outside their bus. "Yeah. We're on the list." He glanced back toward the school entrance. Hammer was still standing where they'd left him—watching them.

"And after the way Gordy acted so nervous," Hiro said, "I think you two just moved to the top."

CHAPTER 12

Cooper didn't dare say a word about it on the bus ride home. What if somebody else overheard him? Thanks to Hammer's little speech in the gym, kids were on high alert, suspicious of anybody but their closest friends. Kids on the bus huddled close together and talked, sometimes pointing to other riders.

He had to think. The situation had heated up a lot faster than he expected it would. He'd convinced himself that all he really had to do was keep quiet. Stick to the Code. But that wouldn't be enough anymore.

Cooper tried to push that thought out of his head. The important thing was that they made it. They got through day one. And Frank was alive.

The three of them left the bus together and stood watching it pull away down Fremont Street.

"We need to talk about this," Hiro said.

Cooper started walking toward his house. "There's nothing to talk about."

Hiro caught up to him. "Really? Well, maybe I have one of those baloney detectors now, because I can tell you're full of it."

Gordy jogged a few steps ahead, turned around and walked

backwards. "Look, let's just forget about it all for awhile. This is Friday. Tomorrow is Saturday. And then we have Sunday."

Hiro put her hands on the sides of her head and shook it in obvious frustration. "And what comes after Sunday, Mr. Calendar?"

Gordy fell in step alongside them. "Monday?"

"Right. And your own personal interrogation by a juvenile officer."

Gordy groaned. "Did you have to bring that up?"

"We need a plan," Hiro said. She picked at her braid. "We have to *do* something."

For a second Cooper had that feeling they were being watched. He glanced up and down the street, but didn't notice anyone. Not even a car. "Look," he said. "You're right. Meeting one-on-one with the police could be disastrous."

"*Could* be?" Hiro cocked her head to one side.

"Maybe we could call in sick Monday," Gordy said.

"You're smarter than that." Hiro tapped Gordy's forehead. "And that won't look suspicious?"

Gordy mumbled something, but Cooper couldn't quite make out what he said. It wouldn't be hard to guess.

Cooper sat on the curb. Hiro and Gordy sat beside him. For a minute nobody said a word. He figured they were both waiting for him to speak. He felt their eyes on him.

"What if..." he tried to focus his thoughts, "What if we try to figure out who the robbers are ourselves?"

Hiro looked at him. "And how would we do that?"

"The back-up hard drive."

"You mean look at the surveillance tape?"

"Why not? If there's a camera in the office we may get a look at Mr. Lucky's face."

Hiro stood. She fingered her necklace like it was a source of investigative inspiration. "Or maybe the other two had their masks off while they worked on the safe."

"Hold on," Gordy said. "What are we supposed to do if we *do* get a clear view of them?"

Cooper took a deep breath and let it out slowly. "Maybe we could burn a DVD, just that portion of it, and mail it to the police."

"And if the police see any one of their faces," Hiro said, "maybe they'll call off the whole interview thing Monday and concentrate on finding the real guys."

Gordy looked hopeful. "Yeah. That could work. Then we'd be in the clear. Right?"

"And," Hiro said, "we'd actually be *helping* with the investigation."

Cooper stood and the three of them walked toward Cooper's house. "It beats waiting for them to find *us*."

"When do we start?" Hiro said.

"Tomorrow. We'll use my dad's laptop. We can bring it out to the shed."

Hiro looked up at him and smiled. She hadn't done that since agreeing to the Code.

"Hey, Coop." Gordy pointed. "Check out your fence. It looks like somebody drove through it into your backyard."

Cooper stopped dead and stared. Two sections of cedar fencing stood propped against the garage door, along with a single post. A trail of plywood and boards lined the ground all the way from the driveway through the opening in the fence It looked like a path laid out as if to protect the grass from getting deep ruts.

"The surprise," Cooper said. He'd totally forgotten about it. "Mom said Dad was bringing something home today. Mattie is totally convinced she's getting a pony."

"Every girl's dream," Hiro said. "Whatever it is, it must be heavy."

Gordy trotted toward the driveway. "Like a horse trailer?"

Cooper jogged alongside him. "No—it can't be."

"Oh yeah," Gordy snickered. "Mattie got her pony."

Almost on cue, the silver nose of the pickup poked through

the opening of the fence. Cooper's dad pulled the F150 onto the drive. He wasn't pulling a trailer. The driver's window was down, and Dad waved.

"Wait," he called. "Don't go back there yet." He parked the truck and jumped out—a blur of faded blue jeans and a denim shirt. "Hey, Gordy, Hiro. Glad you're here too."

Fudge loped out from the backyard and slammed against Cooper. He bent over and tussled her ears. She nuzzled his hand and wriggled against Hiro's legs like she couldn't decide who she wanted to be with. Hiro knelt down and said something to her. Fudge leaned into Hiro, like she was eating every word.

Hustling over, Dad put a hand on each of Cooper's shoulders. "I got it." He had Christmas in his eyes.

Cooper looked up at his dad, a feeling of doubt nagging at him, but he didn't want to disappoint him. "Got *what?*"

Dad threw an arm around Cooper's shoulder and started walking towards the gap in the fence. "I'm going to show you—and you're going to love it."

A school bus lumbered down Fremont, lights flashing as it coasted to a stop at the end of their driveway.

Dad stopped. "Let's wait for Mattie to get off the bus."

When the doors swept open, Mattie hopped to the pavement, her ponytail bobbing happily. "Daddy!"

She ran to him and threw her arms around his waist. "I missed you."

Dad bent down and kissed the top of her head. "I missed you too, Squirt. And I have a really great surprise in the backyard."

Mattie squealed. "Can I ride it?"

Gordy snorted and laughed.

Dad started for the backyard again. "We'll all go for rides, lots of them—when it's fixed."

Cooper could see his dad watching him as they approached the corner of the house. Dad obviously wanted to see his expression the moment he saw it.

Cooper stopped and stared. A boat. A very big and worn-out looking boat.

"Hokey smokies!" Gordy shouted. "That thing is huge."

More than huge. It looked like Noah's Ark had been discovered and now rested in their fenced-in backyard.

Dad gripped Cooper's shoulder and gave him a shake. "Can you believe it? Look at this baby."

"I'm looking," Cooper said. "But I don't believe it." *Big, beat, but beautiful.* "Whose is it?"

Mom stood with her arms folded across her chest in the shadow of the trailored cabin cruiser, her five foot two inch height barely a head above the dull blue waterline stripe. She looked like she'd rather have a pony.

Cooper's dad put an arm around his shoulder, pulled him close and grinned. "Ours."

"No way!" Gordy slapped Cooper on the back.

"Ours ... to keep?'

"Uh-huh." Dad rushed ahead. "It was my uncle's." He gave mom a hug, then stood next to the boat and grinned. "I spent the best parts of my summers on this boat as a kid. Lake Geneva, Wisconsin. I loved that place."

Cooper shielded his eyes from the sun and looked up at its full height. On the trailer, it had to be twelve or fourteen feet high to the top of the searchlight mounted on the canopy over the bridge. "But this is *really* your uncle's?"

"*Was* my uncle's. *Was.*" He wrapped his arms around Mom and lifted her off the ground. "It's ours now, right babe?"

Mom didn't look too thrilled—but Cooper's pulse definitely spiked as the truth set in. "So we *own* it now?"

"Completely." Dad looked like the next door neighbor when they'd brought their newborn baby home from the hospital. "He gave it to us. GAVE it to us. A 1956 Chris Craft Futura cabin cruiser—*FREE.*"

Mom shook her head. "But it's going to cost us now."

"Only as we can afford it," Dad said.

Cooper stepped close to the boat and ran his hand along the white painted planking. Chips of paint crumbled under his fingertips and spun to the ground.

Dad reached over him and pulled off a pancake-sized peel of the old paint and thumped the wood underneath with his knuckle. "See? It's solid. This thing was built like a tank. All we have to do is sand and repaint it."

Cooper traced his hand along the side all the way to the front. The bow looked like it could slice through any wave.

Dad followed right behind him. "What do you think?"

Cooper turned to face his dad. "It's gorgeous. How could he just give this away?"

"His wife finally talked some sense into his head," Mom said.

Dad laughed. "He's been in a nursing home for some time now. The boat's been in his backyard for years. All I had to do was pull it out of there."

"Uncle Carson," Gordy said. "Will this thing actually work?"

Dad squatted down and pointed underneath. "Take a look toward the back and tell me what you see."

Cooper bent down next to Gordy and looked at the copper-bronze colored bottom of the boat. A darkened brass rudder hung down, flanked on either side by a big four-bladed propeller.

"Has this thing got two motors?" Gordy asked.

"Bingo," Dad said. "Twin hemi V–8's. They'll need a little work, but we'll have this thing on the water by next spring." Standing, he put his hands on his hips. "You should see the wake it throws. It looks like it's dragging the lake."

Cooper could envision it. The roar of the engines, warm breeze in his face, and a white frothy wake churning away from the back of the boat. "Are we going to name it?"

Dad smiled and motioned toward the back end of the boat. "It already has a name. It's painted on the transom. See what you think." Dad pulled back a faded green tarp that draped over the back of the boat.

The varnished mahogany planking served as a backdrop for large script letters in white and black paint angling upwards. *The Getaway*. Cooper smiled. The name fit.

Dad stood beside him. "And it always was a getaway for me as a kid."

Cooper thought his dad looked like a kid right now. There was a part of him that wanted to lose himself in the boat. Explore every inch of it. Find out all its secrets. But that would be a lot easier if he didn't have some secrets of his own he was hiding.

"The swim platform on the back was added somewhere along the way. But it sure makes it easy to get in the boat." He hiked himself up onto the platform.

"What do you think, Mattie?"

Cooper looked at his little sister. Somehow she seemed to have the opposite reaction to the whole thing as he did. Hiro slung her arm around her, and it looked like Mattie was ready to cry at any moment.

"Are we keeping it here?" Mattie's eyebrows were crumpled the way they always did when she was upset.

"Well, yeah, Squirt," Dad said. "For now anyway."

Mattie frowned. "Where are we going to keep my pony?"

"Pony?" Dad looked confused. "We're not getting a pony—that would be way too much work."

Mattie turned away and buried her face in Hiro's shirt.

"C'mon, Squirt," Cooper said. "This is way better than some *dumb* pony."

Mattie whipped around. "Ponies are smart." A tear found a path down her cheek.

Hiro smoothed it away. "How about sometime we'll pretend the boat is our ship. And you can be the mermaid. How would you like that?"

Mattie sniffed.

Hiro leaned in close. "You'll be the prettiest mermaid anybody ever saw."

She smiled just a bit.

"But you'd better watch out for the octopus." Cooper held out his arms and waved them around slowly. "They like to tickle mermaids," Cooper said, darting his hands under her arms and tickling her. "And they have so many arms you can't possibly stop them."

Mattie dropped to the ground and rolled side to side on her back, laughing and kicking and swinging her hands. Fudge barked and tried to nuzzle in between them.

"All right, Cooper," Mom said, tussling his hair. "Leave the little mermaid alone."

Cooper got up, and feigned another attack.

Mattie squealed and balled up on the ground.

Cooper glanced at Hiro and for a moment saw her look at him with the way she used to, before the Code. "Okay, I'll let you go *this* time." He reached out to Mattie, and she grabbed his hand and he pulled her to her feet.

"Mattie," Mom said, "how about you and I go in and work on dinner while they keep exploring the boat? I could really use a taste-tester."

Mattie nodded and followed her mom toward the back door. Fudge trotted behind them, tail swinging like she knew she'd get samples too.

"I'd better get home," Hiro said.

"Don't you want to see inside?" Dad called out.

Hiro glanced at Cooper's mom with a pleading look.

"Why don't you just show the boys for now," Mom said. "Believe it or not, some people may not be quite as excited about *The Castaway* as you are."

"The Getaway," Dad said. "It's *The Getaway*."

Hiro giggled. "The boys can show me tomorrow—but I really have to go. Congratulations on your new boat. It's a real prize."

Dad smiled. "Blue ribbon stuff all the way."

Cooper watched Hiro leave. She turned and waved just before going around the corner of the house.

"C'mon up here, guys," Dad said. "Wait'll you get on deck and see inside."

Dad led the way, with the boys on his heels. Cooper and Gordy hoisted themselves onto the swim platform, then up to the top of the transom and over the stainless steel rail. The three of them stood on the weathered teak floorboards of the open deck area at the rear of the boat.

"I love it," Gordy said.

Cooper knew the feeling. He still couldn't believe it. This was really theirs now? He looked toward the bow and held his breath.

"This is the bridge — the place where you pilot the boat." He pointed to two captain's chairs standing side by side on tall pedestals behind a huge windshield. Unlike a car, the steering wheel was in front of the seat to the right. The dashboard had a cluster of gauges and controls.

Cooper climbed behind the controls and sank into the cushioned seat. Gordy climbed onto the captain's chair next to him. The extra height gave a perfect view through the windshield and out over the bow. Side windows worked as a wind and spray shield, but the back stayed open. Perfect.

"I'll be sitting here," Cooper said grabbing the wheel. "And Gordy will be there ... so where will you sit, Dad?"

Dad laughed. "Don't worry. You'll both get chances to drive. And wait 'til you feel ... and *hear* the rumble of those engines. There's nothing like it." He pointed to a pair of doors built into the deck floor. "They're mounted below those doors. We'll check them out in a bit."

Cooper stood, imagining the pitch and roll he'd feel on deck when this was out in the water. "Dad, I can't believe this."

Dad smiled. "Welcome to *The Getaway*." He walked to the side rail and ran his hand along its smooth surface. "This boat is magic, you know."

"Magic?" Cooper and Gordy spoke at the same time.

"Uh-huh." He slid onto one of the captain's chairs and turned with one arm hanging over the back. "This boat can take you places without even leaving the yard."

Digging in his pocket, he pulled out a ring of keys and nodded toward the locked mahogany hatch leading to the inside cabin. "Ready to do some serious exploring guys?"

At a quick glance, the keys looked almost exactly like the ones from Frank 'n Stein's. Cooper's elation suddenly deflated as the memory of fishing for the keys in Frank's pockets flashed in his mind. For a couple minutes, he'd forgotten the robbery. And the police. And Frank in a coma.

"Coming, Coop?" Dad already had the hatch off.

"Definitely." Cooper stepped over the threshold and ducked inside the cabin behind his dad. Light streamed in from a series of oval shaped windows on either side of the room. The cabin looked compact and efficient. A small kitchen sink with cabinets above and below stood just to the left—a built-in table with booth-like benches on either side to his right.

Unlike the outside of the boat, the interior looked new. Richly varnished mahogany hardwood trimmed out the cabin. All it needed was a good cleaning.

"And up here in the bow," Dad said, "sleeping quarters."

"How great would it be to sleep in here, right Coop?" Gordy sat on the edge of one of the beds.

Cooper nodded. A great place to hide, too. Something about being inside the boat gave him a sense of safety. He could only imagine how much more safe he'd feel if it were anchored in a lake somewhere instead of parked in his backyard.

Cooper's dad lifted the top off one of the seats flanking the table. "Check this out." A storage compartment underneath held several orange horse-collar type life vests and an old Fremd Vikings gym bag.

He tugged the bag free and unzipped it. "It's still here. Just the way I left it."

Cooper stepped forward for a better view as his dad pulled a black mask, fins, and snorkel out of the duffle.

"I spent as much time *under* the water as I did *on* the water." Dad slid the mask over his head and grinned. "I loved diving."

Gordy picked up one of the fins. "Snorkeling or scuba?"

"Both. Always looking for treasure." He dug deeper into the duffle and pulled out an industrial-looking magnet with a nylon cord tied around it. "When I was really young we'd drag this from the boat just to see what I could pick up on the bottom."

"Ever find anything valuable?" Gordy inspected the magnet.

"Lots of things. They were treasure to me, anyway."

Cooper pulled a black notebook from the duffle. A red diver's flag sticker clung to the cover, peeling up on the corners.

"That's my diving log book," Cooper's dad said. "Used to write down the details of each dive."

Cooper flipped it open. Dates, depths, and temperatures were recorded. Visibility and details of things he found on the bottom were all there. The idea of strapping a scuba tank on his back and disappearing under the surface of the lake sounded like the perfect escape. No police. No robbers. No lies.

Dad rummaged through the duffle and pulled out a black metal flashlight, unscrewed the end and shook two very corroded batteries out of the handle. "Should have never left the batteries in." He inspected the contacts inside the handle. "I'll get this cleaned up first thing. It should be okay." He jammed the flashlight in his back pocket.

"What's the coolest thing you ever found?" Gordy angled himself to look at the dive log with Cooper.

"All sorts of stuff. Old bottles. Tools. Money."

"Money?" Gordy smiled. "How much?"

Cooper's dad dodged the question. He loved to draw out the suspense. "The lake is full of secrets ... you just have to keep searching for them. I found parts of boat wrecks, an ice fishing shack, and bones ... just to name a few."

"Bones?" Cooper hadn't heard this story.

Gordy looked at him wide-eyed. "Were they in the ice fisherman's shack?"

Cooper's dad smiled. "I'll tell you all about them. And plenty more ... another time. Right now we've got more exploring to do before dinner. Who's up for a look at the engines?"

Cooper set the notebook aside. But he made a mental note to spend some serious time looking through it when things got back to normal.

Over the next hour Cooper got to know *The Getaway* as well as he knew his own bedroom—and he loved it just as much.

Dad looked at his watch. "Almost dinner time." He swung a leg over the back rail and dropped onto the swim platform below. "I'm starved."

Gordy followed, but Cooper hated to leave. He wished the boat was on Lake Geneva right now with a full gas tank. They could cruise the lake until things calmed down in Rolling Meadows. He stepped on the engine hatch and bounced a bit to make sure it was closed tight. From this vantage point he could see over their fence into their neighbors' yards on either side of them.

"Cooper," Mom called. She stood in the doorway, motioning him over. "I just heard on the news that something terrible happened at Frank 'n Stein's last night. The story is up next—hurry."

Cooper's heart dropped like an anchor—and the magic of the boat sank with it.

CHAPTER 13

Cooper dragged behind, rehearsing his part in the imagined conversation he might have with his parents. Mom sat on the couch and turned around as soon as he stepped into the family room.

"It sounds awful." She patted her leg and motioned Mattie to climb on her lap. Fudge padded over and curled up at Mom's feet.

Dad grabbed the wooden rocker, pulling it close and off to one side of the TV. Gordy sat on one arm of the couch, but Cooper swung a kitchen chair into the room behind everyone else. He didn't want his face to give anything away during the news report. He wished Gordy had done the same thing.

Positioning the chair backwards, Cooper straddled the seat and rested his arms across the back of it. The story showing up on the news wasn't something he figured on. With all the things going on in the Chicago area, why would they pick this story?

His stomach clenched the moment a live feed from Frank 'n Stein's flashed on the screen. A reporter stood in the foreground holding a microphone.

"I'm standing in front of Frank 'n Stein's Diner in Rolling Meadows, the scene of a brutal robbery shortly after closing last night," the reporter said.

The camera zoomed in on the front of Frank's. Yellow POLICE

LINE DO NOT CROSS tape stretched across the front of the building announcing to the world that something evil had happened there.

"Frank Mustacci," a smiling picture of the man flashed on the screen, "was found beaten last night in his restaurant shortly after closing."

"No!" Cooper's Mom hugged Mattie.

Cooper felt Frank was looking right at him. Wondering why Cooper didn't hop over the counter and help him. *How could I have let them hurt him like that?*

Gordy looked back over his shoulder and caught Cooper's eye. Cooper could read his cousin's face as clearly as if he'd actually spoken the words. *What are we going to do now?*

The camera returned to a head and shoulder view of the reporter. "There is speculation that this robbery may be gang related, although authorities are not commenting on that," the reporter said. "A boy approximately twelve to fourteen years old was witnessed fleeing the crime scene on a bike."

Cooper's mother gasped. "He could be your age."

He is my age—to the exact second.

Dad reached for the remote and turned up the volume.

The camera zoomed back to show a stocky man wearing a green Frank 'n Stein's polo shirt standing next to the reporter.

"I'm joined here by Joseph Stein, Frank's partner and co-owner of Frank 'n Stein's."

Mr. Stein gave a slight nod.

Cooper had seen him plenty of times working the order counter at the diner. Now he looked quiet and sad, nothing like his usual outgoing self.

"Mr. Stein," the reporter turned from looking at the camera to directly face the man. "Does it surprise you that a teenager may have been involved in this?"

"Frank is a really, really nice guy. What shocks me is that *anybody* could have done this to him—especially a kid. Frank loved when kids hung around." Stein bit his lip like he was trying to keep from breaking down. "Honestly, unless it was some kind of gang initiation or something, I don't think a kid had anything to do with this."

Cooper wanted to scream, "*Mr. Stein* is *right. There were three of them, and none of them were kids!*"

"My understanding is the boy seen fleeing the crime scene is a possible *witness*," Stein explained, "not a suspect."

"Do you have surveillance cameras?" the reporter asked.

"Absolutely. All the cameras feed into a single unit, which was destroyed by whoever did this. There's an auxiliary hard drive that stores all the data, but the person who did this was smart enough to take it with him," Stein said.

"Do you think this was done by professionals?"

"The police told me they have good prints and some other evidence left behind by whoever did this." Mr. Stein shifted his weight. "That doesn't sound too professional to me."

"What type of evidence?" The reporter moved the mic closer.

Cooper's stomach twisted. He could answer that question.

Mr. Stein put his hands up in front of his chest. "I'm not sure I should be saying anything more. I don't want to do anything that may mess up the investigation."

"Of course," the reporter agreed, but Cooper sensed a bit of disappointment in her voice. "Have authorities given you any indication how long they expect the investigation to continue?"

Mr. Stein shook his head. "Specifically, no. But they seemed confident they'd have a suspect in custody within just a few days."

Cooper tried to think. The cops have prints. That made sense. They could have picked up his prints on the door, the knife — all over. But that won't do them any good unless they have something to match them with. Or unless the police intended to start taking fingerprints at school. He made a mental note to take a closer look at the permission slip. But Elvis and the clown wore gloves, so none of the prints were going to lead to the real robbers.

"And we'll open for business as usual tomorrow," Stein said. "It's the way Frank would want it. We'll be taking donations for Frank's medical bills—so please ..." His bottom lip quivered and he lowered his head.

The reporter put on a sympathetic face. "Thank you for taking the time for the interview. I know this must be a hard time for you."

Mr. Stein bowed slightly, and backed away. The camera quickly cropped to a tight head and shoulder shot of the reporter.

The reporter had a gleam in her eyes. Either she really loved being in front of the camera delivering terrible news, or she had some juicy tidbit she'd been dying to reveal to her television audience.

"There is strong evidence to suggest the mystery witness attends this suburban junior high school. This tape was filmed earlier this afternoon."

Mom sucked in her breath. "Carson! That's Plum Grove."

Cooper's dad didn't take his eyes off the screen. Leaning forward, he turned the volume up even more. Cooper's stomach swirled. He'd have a lot more explaining to do than he'd bargained on.

The newscast cut to a video of Plum Grove at the end of the school day. Students were flowing out of the doors and cops were everywhere. "We interviewed Rolling Meadows Police Detective Hammer earlier today about the incident."

The screen showed a clip of the same reporter standing in front of Plum Grove School as the last of the buses pulled away from the curb. Hammer stood next to her wearing the sunglasses with the mirrored lenses.

"Detective Hammer, are there any similarities to the 1993 slayings at Brown's Chicken in nearby Palatine?"

That was it. The infamous Brown's Chicken robbery. Seven people murdered in the walk-in freezer. No wonder they were giving this air time. Even though it happened years before Cooper was born, the massacre at Brown's was told and retold like a local ghost story. Cooper tried to refocus on the news report.

" ... other than that, no similarities at all," Hammer said.

"There was a lot of police activity here at Plum Grove Junior High today," the reporter said. "Do you believe one of the students is involved?"

"I believe one of the students witnessed the crime."

"But that witness hasn't come forward?"

"Not yet." Hammer gave a half-smile. "But he will. Or I'll come to him."

Cooper shuddered. *Even if you have to try that key in every house in town.*

"Will the fact that Frank Mustacci's brother-in-law is the Mayor of Rolling Meadows have a bearing on the efforts put into this investigation?"

Cooper held his breath. Frank was related to the Mayor? How had he never heard that? Of course it would put pressure on the police to solve the crime—*or pin it on someone.*

"Absolutely not," Hammer said. "We give 100% to every criminal investigation. This one will be no different."

"Detective, the Brown's Chicken robbery and murders baffled investigators for ten years and may never have been solved if an angry girlfriend hadn't spoken to authorities." The reporter paused. "Do you feel the Frank 'n Stein's investigation will run into similar problems?" She held the microphone in front of Hammer for his response.

"The Brown's Chicken investigation had its own unique challenges and the trail got cold."

"So you feel confident you'll get your man—or teenager as the case may be."

"Oh yeah. We'll get him." The cameraman zoomed up slowly on Hammer's face. "This trail isn't cooling down for us. It's getting warmer."

Cooper could feel the heat. Licking dry lips, he tried to swallow.

"Thank you, Detective Hammer," the reporter said. The camera moved in tight on the reporter's face. "Frank Mustacci remains in a coma at Northwest Community Hospital."

The reporter signed off, and Dad muted the TV. Turning slowly, he looked directly at Cooper—or through him.

"You knew all about this, didn't you Cooper?"

CHAPTER 14

How much could Dad know? Maybe parents had an instinct about their own kids, or Dad had a baloney detector of his own. But if he acted like he was holding anything back, Dad would be all over it. Cooper swallowed. "Yeah, isn't it awful?"

"You never said a thing about it when you got home." He glanced at Gordy. "Neither of you did."

Gordy stood — and Fudge yipped and scrambled away. "Oh, sorry, Fudge." He jammed his hands in his pockets.

Cooper had to say something before Gordy did. "I-I guess it was the boat."

Mom shifted Mattie off her lap. "What?"

"Yeah," Cooper said, relieved he had a trail to lead them down. "The whole surprise of the boat. We were talking about the robbery on the way home, then we saw part of the fence down and then there you were, Dad, driving out of the backyard with the pickup."

The explanation just kind of gushed out. Cooper was getting some real traction now. "And once I saw the boat, I didn't think about what happened at school today until you called us in to see the news."

Dad moved over to the couch and sat on the arm. "I guess I

can understand that." He nodded like he was thinking. "But still ... we're talking about Frank here."

Taking a deep breath, Cooper forced himself to slow down. He couldn't afford a mistake now. "Detective Hammer, the guy they showed on TV, talked to the students at an assembly today. Said Frank is in ICU at Northwest Community Hospital." He paused. "He's in a coma, just like the reporter said."

Cooper's mom wiped back tears. "This is going to hit Hiro's mom hard."

"Hiro thinks Lunk might be wrapped up in it somehow," Gordy said. "He works there part time now, you know."

"Neil Lunquist." Mom stood and started toward the kitchen. "I still have a hard time trusting that boy."

"Which is why that doesn't make sense," Cooper said. "I mean, how obvious would that be? I'm sure the police would check out every employee's story."

Stopping, she turned to look at Cooper. "Those sirens we heard last night. That must have been what it was all about. I told you something terrible must have happened."

Mom didn't know the half of it. Cooper pushed the images out of his mind. "They gave us a form for you to sign." Volunteering this information hadn't been part of his plan. He'd hoped to stall the whole thing off. But not mentioning it now might only make them suspicious when they did find out.

"What kind of form?" Dad looked right into his eyes.

Cooper kept his gaze steady. "Some kind of permission form so they can set up interviews with the kids."

"I'd better take a look at it," Dad said.

Cooper needed to breathe. All he wanted to do was get out of the room. "I'll get it right now." Hurrying into the kitchen and down the hall toward the front door, he pulled open the closet and knelt down beside his backpack. The form wasn't hard to find, and when he turned around his dad and Gordy were headed his way.

"Did the police say why they felt the witness is a Plum Grove student?"

"Uh-huh." Cooper pulled the English book from his backpack that he'd "borrowed" from Jake Mickel. "This. Someone left a book in the dining area."

"And that led them right to Plum Grove." Dad nodded.

And by showing the book, Cooper hoped he'd effectively lead his dad from shifting any suspicion his way.

Mom came around the corner from the kitchen. "I'm just glad you rode bikes in the park." Shuddering, she stepped over and hugged Cooper. "If you had gone to Frank 'n Stein's like you'd planned to, you might have been there when they got robbed." She squeezed him tighter. "I probably shouldn't have said that, because now you might get bad dreams."

Might get bad dreams? Cooper squirmed just a bit. Last night his dreams would have terrified a horror film fan.

"You were going to Frank 'n Stein's last night?" Dad raked his fingers through his hair. "Thank God you didn't go. What made you change your mind?"

Cooper hesitated. "Well, uh, we started heading that way, but, um—"

"I wasn't hungry," Gordy interrupted.

Mom laughed. "*You* not hungry?"

"And so we rode around a bit until I did get hungry."

Cooper had to stop him. If Gordy kept on going, he'd blow everything.

Dad looked confused. "So then you did go to Frank 'n Stein's when you got hungry?"

"No." Gordy's eyes darted to Cooper. "I sort of had an accident and fell into the creek. So we couldn't go to Frank 'n Stein's. I got all wet and muddy. Real muddy. My shoes were loaded with it."

Dad glanced at Gordy's feet. "Shoes sure cleaned up nice."

"I *wish*," Gordy said. "These are my old ones."

"Did either of you boys see anything that might help the police?"

Cooper shrugged. "It was dark." He needed to get the focus off last night. *The permission slip.* "Here, Dad." He held out the bright yellow form.

Cooper's dad took the form and frowned as he read it. Mom stood behind him and read over his shoulder.

"They may ask for DNA testing?" Cooper's mom said. "Isn't that a bit extreme?"

Cooper's dad kept reading the form. "They intend to find out who the witness is, whether he wants to offer the information or not."

"Do we sign it?" Cooper's mom look concerned.

Carson MacKinnon nodded. "I don't see why not. One of us will be there. We need to do everything we can to help. We've got nothing to hide."

Maybe you don't. Cooper watched his dad sign the form. *But I sure do.*

CHAPTER 15

How Cooper fell asleep, he had no idea. Long after everyone went to bed he lay there thinking about the man wearing the clown mask. He slipped down the stairs and double-checked the dead bolts on the front and back doors. He even left the hall light on and jammed his desk chair under his bedroom doorknob. Fudge curled up next to the bed. His baseball bat went under the covers with him. Flat on his back and eyes wide open, he watched the fish in his tank and listened to the house creak and snap in the cold night air. That was the last thing he could remember.

Saturday morning Cooper dug out the hard drive and climbed onto the faded teak deck of *The Getaway* to meet Gordy and Hiro. He didn't have to wait long. By the time he flipped open his dad's laptop Gordy walked through the opening in the fence with Hiro at his side. Gordy grinned and waved, then trotted to the ladder propped against the stern of the boat. Hiro looked like she'd had a rough night, too.

Gordy swung a leg over the railing with Hiro right behind him. "I caught Hiro up to speed with what happened here last night."

Cooper hoped she'd be impressed. He held to the Code. "I guess my dad's baloney detector was out of commission."

"Because he *trusts* you," Hiro said.

The words burned a hole in Cooper's gut. He ducked inside the cabin, set the laptop on the table, and slid onto one of the benches.

"I can't believe you didn't just tell him."

Cooper stared at her in disbelief. "We agreed to the Code, remember?"

"We agreed to keep quiet."

"That's what we're doing."

Hiro shifted. "We're lying."

Cooper instantly felt his face heat up. He didn't like being dishonest with anyone, especially his parents. He liked being reminded of it even less. Lying was wrong. He knew that. But this situation made it different. It had to be done.

Her eyes bored into him. "Doesn't that make you feel just a little bit guilty?"

"No," Cooper lied. "I'm doing him a favor. I'm doing all of us a favor."

She tossed her braid over one shoulder. "How do you figure?"

"I'm protecting them." Cooper pulled the hard drive from the pocket of his cargo shorts and connected it. "Look. I thought we were going to do some detective work together." He tapped the hard drive.

She nodded, her mouth formed one tight line. She didn't look convinced, but she didn't argue either.

He'd take what he could get. "Let's get on with it."

Hiro didn't speak for a moment. "You're not going to bring this to the bell tower Sunday night, are you?"

"Not unless I bust it in pieces first."

She seemed satisfied with that.

Cooper focused on the laptop screen. The computer recognized the external drive immediately. Thankfully the fall didn't damage it. A part of him dreaded the images he might see.

"Uh-oh."

Gordy leaned in closer to see the screen. "Uh-oh, *what?*"

"I can't open the file."

"Click on it again."

Cooper gave it another shot. A window popped up for Silent Sentry Surveillance Systems with a $1500 introductory offer for the program. *Dead end.*

Hiro groaned. "We need the program. We're never going to get these files open without it." She slumped back in the booth. "*Now* what?"

It didn't exactly sound like a question. More like a test question.

Cooper unhooked the hard drive and tucked it back in the pocket of his cargo shorts. "I'll bury this again. And for now, we stick to the Code."

"And do *nothing*?"

"Sticking to the Code is something."

Hiro stood, threw her arms in the air and slapped them down at her sides. "The police are closing in. Maybe those scumbags are too. We have to *do* something. Get help. Tell somebody."

"So you think we should just lock arms and skip into the police station and tell them what we've seen?"

"Maybe we should." She raised her chin and gave a slight nod.

"And what if Elvis *is* Hammer—or one of the other Rolling Meadows cops?"

"That makes no sense. Why would a police detective rob Frank 'n Stein's?"

"I have no idea."

Hiro stood. "And I say Lunk is part of this. Or his dad."

Cooper shook his head. "That theory has just as many holes. I say we wait this out."

Hiro put her hands on her hips. "We need protection. We have to go to the police."

"Listen," Cooper said. "They have my house key. Fact. Said they'd find me if I talked. Fact. It's not just me I'm worried about. I lay in bed at night thinking about some guy in a clown mask hauling off and hitting my mom. Or Mattie."

Hiro folded her arms across her chest and sat back down. "I know. I get it." Her voice softened. "But we have to do something."

"I just can't go to the police. When Hammer used those same words—*I gotcha boy*, I just got chills, you know?"

"You think it really could be him?" Gordy spoke nearly in a whisper.

"It's possible. And when he talked about having some other piece of evidence—something that could *open the door* to finding the person at the crime scene, also known as me—what do you think popped into my mind?"

"The key," Gordy said.

Cooper shrugged. "Exactly. I felt like he was sending me a message." Cooper pictured Detective Hammer's face in his mind. It would be a perfect cover, wouldn't it? Who would question a detective? And who would be able to steer the investigation away from himself any better than the guy who gave the orders? He turned to Hiro. "Until we can be sure the police aren't involved, I think we need to stick to the Code. Let's give this a little more time. Okay?"

Hiro held out one hand. "Let's think. On the one hand we hide the truth, but we stay safe." She held out her other hand. "On the other hand, we come clean and may get killed as a result." She shrugged. "We lie or we die. I just can't make up my mind."

"I'll take that as a yes," Cooper said.

She nodded. "But for how long? The truth always comes out—and when it does we may be in a lot more trouble." She looked from Cooper to Gordy. "This is too big for us. You know we won't make it through the police questioning Monday, right?" She looked directly at Gordy.

Cooper didn't answer. She had a point. A good one. But if they could just keep this whole thing quiet a little longer, buy some time, maybe they could find some other way. Why say anything until they were absolutely sure they couldn't keep it a secret any longer?

"Okay," Cooper said. "If we don't figure out a way out of this by the time they start the interviews, we'll dissolve the Code and we'll spill to the police. Agreed?"

"You mean that?"

Cooper nodded and saw the flicker of relief in her eyes. He wished it made him feel that good. But the whole idea of breaking the Code started something ugly churning in his stomach. There had to be another way.

The Code of Silence was their ticket to safety. Their *Getaway*. A boat that would bring all of them over the rough waters of the mess they were in. They just had to keep it afloat until the storm passed by.

CHAPTER 16

Cooper pulled the hood of his old pullover sweatshirt up while the three of them biked through downtown Rolling Meadows. His zippered hoodie was probably still in the crime lab somewhere. Cooper missed riding his newer bike, too, but he wasn't going to take that out of the shed until everything cooled down. Like maybe next spring.

They rode single-file along the edge of the road, giving Cooper time to think. He'd lied to his parents. He told himself it was all about keeping them from getting too suspicious. And it was really the courageous thing to do. A way to keep them safe. But still ... he deliberately deceived them. That didn't exactly sound heroic.

When Frank 'n Stein's came into view he slowed a bit. Cars filled the parking lot. True to his word, Mr. Stein was open for business. Not that Cooper had any intention of going there.

"I guess we won't be going back there for awhile," Gordy said, almost as if he'd been reading Cooper's thoughts.

Hiro pulled up alongside Cooper. "And how would that look?"

"What?"

"We go to Frank 'n Stein's two or three times a week," Hiro said. "Now suddenly we don't show up. Wouldn't that look a little suspicious?"

"You think too much." Gordy waved her off with one hand. "Nobody will even notice."

Cooper stopped pedaling and coasted along the sidewalk. "Hiro has a point."

"*Hiro* has a point?" Gordy said. "What about me?"

Hiro shrugged. "All I'm saying is that if we do go, it shows we have nothing to hide."

Cooper slowed to a stop. The Code wasn't just about keeping quiet. It was also about not looking guilty. About keeping suspicion away from them. "Actually, that makes sense."

"That's crazy."

"And I'm not crazy about going," Cooper said.

"So don't." Gordy wheeled his bike around and pointed it up the street. "I say we go back to Taco Bell, order some of those cinnamon twisty things, and drain the pop machine with our free refills."

"Hey," Hiro said. "We're all a little spooked."

"Spooked? Me? I just feel like Taco Bell right now, that's all."

Sometimes the easy way wasn't the best way. Cooper knew that. He also knew the longer he waited, the harder this was going to be. "I'm going to Frank 'n Stein's." He hoped by saying it out loud he'd feel as confident as he sounded. Not this time.

"I'll go too," Hiro said. "Maybe we can find out how Frank is doing."

"Have a great time." Gordy circled around them once. "Count me out."

"Sure you don't want to come with us?" Cooper pulled a quarter out of his pocket. "I'll show you those moves."

"I'm going to Taco Bell." Gordy didn't smile. "If you're smart you'll come with me." He jerked his bike toward the fast food restaurant and stood on the pedals.

Cooper watched for a minute, hoping he'd turn around. Gordy never even looked back.

"You changing your mind?" Hiro said.

"Uh-uh." Cooper started pedaling for Frank 'n Stein's. "I just thought he would."

They coasted into Frank'n Stein's parking lot and propped their bikes against a pole.

"You ready for this?" Hiro practically whispered.

"Sure," Cooper lied. A sheet of particle board replaced the broken window in the door. Chips of glass winked at him from cracks in the asphalt like they knew his secret. He reached for the door and tried not to think about the last time he stood in that spot.

The familiar smell of seasoned beef and Chicago hot dogs charring on the grill welcomed him in.

"Hiya, kids." Mr. Stein stood behind the counter and smiled. "What can we get you?"

Cooper ordered a chocolate Monster shake and wiped sweaty hands on his cargo shorts before handing Mr. Stein the money. Stein took one of the dollars and stuffed it in a giant pickle jar on the counter nearly half filled with coins and dollar bills. A hand-printed sign taped to the rim of the jar read "Hospital fund for Frank Mustacci." A picture of the co-owner flipping a burger on the grill was clipped to the sign. Cooper's throat burned.

Mr. Stein did the same with the money Hiro handed him for her iced tea.

"How is he?" Hiro whispered.

Stein's smile faded. "Still in a coma." He grabbed a rag and wiped off the counter. "But when I saw him this morning, his color looked better."

"That's good." Hiro tapped two straws out of the dispenser and handed one to Cooper. "Think I could go see him?"

Cooper's heart slammed into his chest.

"You'd be like an angel to him if you did." Stein leaned across the counter toward Hiro. "You a churchgoer?"

Hiro nodded.

"You say a prayer for our friend, will you?"

"I have every hour since it happened."

Mr. Stein's smile returned. "Atta girl. Say one for both of us, eh?" He turned to the drive-thru window.

Hiro reached in her pocket, pulled out some cash, and added it to the pickle jar. She looked at Cooper as if she totally expected him to do the same.

He pulled out the only money he had—his emergency "snack buck." He took one last look at Washington's face with the black marker mustache and glasses he'd added and dropped it in the jar.

Hiro nodded her approval. "He needs all the help he can get."

Cooper glanced into the kitchen—all the way to the back door. It was still a crime scene to him. The mop and bucket stood against the side wall. Had they used it to swab up Frank's blood? The creepy feeling gnawed at him.

"Chocolate shake, iced tea, large fries?"

Neil Lunquist held the cardboard tray out to them over the counter.

"Oh, hi, Lunk." Cooper took the tray. "We didn't pay for fries, though."

Lunk mouthed for him to stay quiet. "I take care of friends. Take it."

"But—" Cooper glanced at Mr. Stein working the drive-thru window. His back was turned, and it was obvious he hadn't seen a thing.

Lunk jammed his hand in his pocket and pulled out a couple of singles. "Here." He stuffed the money in the pickle jar. "Feel better?"

Cooper nodded. "Thanks."

Cooper took the tray and turned. Mr. Stein had decked the whole dining area out with Halloween decorations. Like some kind of haunted castle—only this one was for real. Normally Cooper would grab their booth in the back. Today? He just wanted out of here.

Hiro nudged him. "Picnic table outside?"

"Perfect."

Hiro seemed as anxious as he was to leave. She grabbed a couple of napkins and filled a small paper cup with ketchup.

He'd done it. He showed his face. It felt good to face his fears, to push himself. It felt even better to push back out the door.

Hiro didn't say a word as they walked to the table. She swung a leg over the bench to face the creek. Cooper didn't feel right about Frank 'n Stein's being behind him where he couldn't see it—like he expected Elvis or the clown to rush out the door at any moment. That was crazy. Still, he positioned himself on the bench opposite of Hiro so he could keep an eye on things.

"Glad to see your conscience still works," Hiro said.

"What?"

She picked up a fry and dangled it in front of him. "The fries?"

"Oh, that." Cooper pulled the lid off his shake and poked the straw in deep. "I didn't feel right about it." He drew in a cool mouthful of the shake.

Hiro sipped at her tea and pulled her braid over her shoulder. "It was nice to see the old Cooper for a change."

"What's that supposed to mean?"

"Don't play dumb."

Cooper grabbed some fries and avoided looking at her. Why couldn't she just leave it alone? Give this a little time to work itself out? Then the lies would stop. All of them.

"I don't know how he can still work there," she said.

"Lunk?"

"Uh-huh."

"He couldn't have been one of the guys at that robbery."

Hiro shrugged. "He's in it somehow. And I'm going to figure it out."

"Give it a rest. Lunk isn't all bad."

She raised her eyebrows and cocked her head to one side. "Is he changing—or is it you?"

"What?"

"I'm praying for you, Cooper." Hiro said it so quietly, as if she hadn't intended him to hear.

But he heard it so clear that his ears burned. "Look." He bounced his straw up and down in the thick shake. "You should be praying that Gordy doesn't blow it, or that those men don't find us, or that they get caught somehow."

Hiro didn't say anything. But her eyes went right through him—like she was reading his mind. She looked down suddenly, like she didn't like what she saw.

"Do you think Frank will make it?"

Cooper thought on that a minute. "If his color is better, that has to be good. Are you really going to see him?"

Hiro nodded and bit her lower lip.

Truth was, he wished he could too. But how could he face him, even if he was in a coma?

A Rolling Meadows police car wheeled into the lot and pulled into one of the parking spaces.

A knot tightened in his stomach. A police car at a fast food restaurant wasn't an unusual sight, but Cooper wondered if the cop was there to get a meal or to work on the case.

Cooper held his breath for an instant while a policeman opened the door and stood. Detective Hammer. *Perfect.*

Hammer scanned the lot like a man in the habit of looking for potential trouble. When his mirrored sunglasses turned Cooper's way, he smiled and strode toward the picnic table.

"Oh no." Cooper groaned, covering his mouth with one hand. "Hammer is coming this way."

Hiro's eyes grew wide, then instantly closed tight.

Was she praying?

When Hiro opened her eyes, she looked normal. Relaxed.

Cooper hoped he looked as natural.

"Cooper MacKinnon, right?" Hammer, still wearing the mirrored sunglasses, stopped at the table and hiked one foot on the bench. "Plum Grove School."

"Hello, detective."

"Where's your friend?"

"Gordy?" Cooper pointed down the street. "He went to Taco Bell instead."

"Any reason he would want to avoid Frank 'n Stein's?"

"Uh-uh." Cooper shook his head. "He just wanted those cinnamon twist things."

Hammer gave a single nod. Without seeing the cop's eyes, Cooper couldn't tell if he believed him or not. He started back toward Frank 'n Stein's. He stopped and turned just as he reached the parking lot. "Come here often?"

Cooper nodded and raised his cup. "I love their monster shakes."

"Did you have one Thursday night?"

His arm froze. "Huh?"

One corner of Hammer's mouth turned up. "Anything you want to tell me?"

Cooper held his gaze. Lying was an art. To master it you had to know when to stop talking and how to divert a direct question. "Yeah. You should try the monster shakes." He sucked on the straw and kept his focus on Hammer's sunglasses. To look down, or anywhere else would be as good as admitting he was hiding something. He held up the shake. "The chocolate is best."

"Maybe I will." Hammer smiled. "We'll have plenty of time to talk at school Monday. Did you get that permission slip signed?"

"Already in my backpack."

Hammer nodded. "Monday, then." He turned and walked to the front door, stopping only briefly to inspect the bikes.

"He's on to you."

Cooper's leg bounced under the table. "He was baiting me. Looking for a reaction. He doesn't know anything."

"You don't think he suspects?" Hiro shook her head. "He asked if you had a shake *Thursday* night."

She looked surprised for an instant. Like something just clicked into place. She reached up and started fingering the police star necklace.

"Hiro?"

"What *did* you do with your shake Thursday night?"

Cooper thought for a moment. "I left it on the table."

"With the backpack," Hiro said. "That means they have your DNA for sure."

He didn't need Hiro to tell him what that meant. Fingerprints and DNA. All the police needed to do was get a sample from him.

Cooper poked at his shake with the straw. He felt like he was locked back inside Frank 'n Stein's, unable to escape. How was he going to get out of this? The surveillance tapes were a dead end. But he had to do something. He couldn't just sit here and hope he didn't get caught. He had to search for the robbers as hard as they were probably searching for him. But how on earth was he supposed to do that?

Gordy flew into the parking lot holding a Taco Bell bag along with the handle grip. He didn't pull on the brakes until he hit the grass near the picnic table. The bike skidded one way, then the other before slowing enough to hop off. He dumped the bike on the grass and strolled over.

"Eating outside." He jerked his thumb toward the police car. "Good idea." Gordy dropped his half-empty bag on the table and grabbed some of Cooper's fries. "Wonder what that's all about."

"It's Hammer," Hiro said. "He was asking about you. Said he'd already been to your house."

"W-what?" Gordy took a step back, eyes wide open. "What does he want?"

"Nothing," Cooper said. "Hiro's messing with you."

Gordy glared at Hiro and looked over his shoulder at Frank 'n Stein's. "Let's get out of here."

Cooper couldn't agree more. The thought of the detective coming back with more questions made him uneasy. He stuffed the last few fries in his mouth and crumpled up the bag. He swung one leg over the bench and stopped. Hammer walked out the front door—and headed their way.

CHAPTER 17

"There's your friend."

Gordy heard Hammer's voice behind him. *Now what?* He turned just as Hammer strolled up, monster shake in hand. Hammer stopped to inspect Gordy's bike, and then walked right up to him. The cop stood close. Way beyond the comfort zone.

Gordy felt as stiff as the Frankenstein mascot himself.

"How was Taco Bell?" The detective's face showed no emotion. The mirrored lenses didn't give anything away either. Gordy imagined a cold stare behind those glasses. Dark eyes. Elvis eyes.

"Mucho bueno." He held up the bag of twists. "I think that's Spanish for very good."

And it would be *mucho bueno* to get away from Hammer. He should have just stayed at Taco Bell.

"I tried the monster shake." Hammer stirred it with the straw. "Cooper here was telling me how much he likes them."

"Gets one every time we come in," Gordy said.

"Comes here a lot, does he?" He took a sip and waited for his answer, probably enjoying the way he could make people sweat.

"Well, yeah, sometimes. We all do." Gordy glanced at Coop. Did he just say too much? "It's been awhile though."

"Couple days, maybe?"

Gordy took a step back. He could use a little help here.

"Detective Hammer." Hiro held onto her necklace as she spoke. "Would it help if I bike to Gordy's house and bring back his signed permission form for you? I mean, then you could question him legally."

A slight smile creased the officer's face. He took a long draw from his shake. "I can't wait until Monday. You boys are officially at the top of my list. Congratulations."

"Look, " Coop said, pulling a pen from his pocket and writing his phone number on his napkin. "Here's my phone number. Call my parents right now if you want. Then you can ask me anything you want. I have nothing to hide. None of us do." He handed Hammer the napkin. "Frank Mustacci was good to us, and I want to see whoever did this to him caught and put away for good."

Hammer took the napkin, looked at it for a moment, then folded it and slid it in his pocket. "I think I can wait until Monday." He held up the monster shake and saluted with it. "Thanks for the tip on the shake."

Gordy wanted to give him a couple tips of his own.

Hammer headed back to his car, climbed inside, and started the engine. Gordy didn't want to stare. He turned his back on the parking lot and listened for him to back out, but he didn't leave. Maybe he was on the radio or something. Or maybe Hammer was just trying to rattle him.

"We all should have gone to Taco Bell," Gordy whispered. He'd tried to keep them all clear of Frank's. He stuck to his guns, even though it killed him that Hiro and Coop didn't change their mind and follow him. He'd been so sure they would. They had to stick together—even in little things like this. "Thanks for bailing me out. That guy could make a dummy sweat."

Hiro looked at him and raised her eyebrows. A smile surfaced and it looked like she was about to dish out a zinger.

Gordy knew what she was thinking—and what she was probably about to say. He held up his hands to stop her. "A dummy—you know, a mannequin—like our friendly greeter at Frank's."

"Ohhh." She gave a slow nod. "You're not sweating, though, are you?"

He fished a handful of the twisty cinnamon things out of the bag. "You just love yanking my chain, don't you?"

She nodded and smiled. "Every bit as much as you love yanking mine."

Coop gave another slurp on his shake, obviously hitting bottom. "Let's not talk here—just in case the detective can read lips. Let's meet at *The Getaway*." He started toward the garbage can.

"Coop, don't," Hiro said.

"Don't what?"

"Don't toss your cup in the garbage. Bring it with you and throw it out at home." She nodded toward the police car but kept her head down. "What if he's waiting for you to drop that in the garbage can so he can get another DNA sample?"

Cooper stopped and his eyes got wide.

"Whoa," Gordy said. "They'd match it to the one you left on the table." Gordy didn't know if he could take this much longer.

Cooper nodded.

Gordy's legs felt shaky. *Yeah. What if?* Hammer would have all the evidence he'd need to make an arrest—or a surprise appearance as Elvis. How could they hold up this charade? Gordy wanted to stick with the Code, stick with Cooper, but Hiro was obviously wavering. And Gordy felt like he'd accidently spill everything if Hammer so much as turned his head toward him. How would he ever get through Monday? Even Cooper would have messed up royally if Hiro hadn't stopped him.

Hiro was definitely super perceptive. She had sensed danger at Frank's the other night before either one of them. In a flash, Gordy heard her voice in his mind. "Let's go. Please! I have a bad feeling!" Gordy wondered if Hiro was getting a bad vibe right now.

Cooper stuffed the empty cup in his backpack. "How did you even think of that?"

Hiro smiled. "It's what I'd do if I were him."

Cooper mounted his bike. "You're going to make a good cop someday, you know that?"

"Better believe it."

CHAPTER 18

The three of them rode back to Cooper's house in relative silence. Hiro's mood seemed to shift on the ride. By the time they climbed up the ladder and over the stern, she turned quiet.

Instead of going inside the cabin, Cooper led them to the bow. He sat at the very front and let his legs dangle over the side.

"We need to talk about that surveillance hard drive." He could hear the raspy voice in his ear. *Sunday night. Or else.* He rubbed the back of his neck. He could almost feel the man squeezing.

Gordy eyed him. "You're not thinking of delivering it to the bell tower tomorrow night, are you?"

"No. But I've got another idea. I just need to process it a little. We won't be able to talk at church. Wanna meet here after lunch?"

Gordy shrugged. "Works for me."

Hiro seemed off in another world. Cooper waved his hand in front of her eyes. "Hiro?"

"I'll be busy in the afternoon. But I can make it here after dinner, I guess."

"Okay. What's wrong?" He hated to ask the question — because he wasn't sure he wanted to hear the answer.

"Twenty minutes ago I threatened a police detective." Hiro fidgeted with her braid. "I'm supposed to be a policewoman someday, and I confronted the man on his police ethics. *We're* the ones who are wrong here."

Cooper didn't know what to say. She'd just bailed them out of a jam—at her own expense. In some other situation that may have made him proud or especially grateful. Right now it made him feel dirty. Like he'd stepped in the mud and wiped his shoe on her jacket.

She rubbed the necklace. "Maybe you should have said something."

"Like what? Oh, by the way, we *were* here the other night. Saw the whole thing. Elvis and his clown pounded Frank and robbed his place. Honest. Oh, and by the way, are you Elvis?"

Gordy snickered, but he looked a little spooked.

"I mean, come on, Hiro. What if Hammer is one of the guys? If I say something to him, I could be playing right into his hands."

Her eyes filled with tears. *Great.*

"My Dad would be ashamed of what I just did. Of what I'm doing. I've dishonored him."

Ouch. "What do you expect me to do?" Cooper asked.

"Fight for the truth. Like you always used to do." Hiro crossed her arms across her chest. "Can't you see this is going to backfire on us? They're going to find out, and when they do, we'll look a lot worse than if we'd just come forward with it."

"But we didn't do anything wrong," Gordy said. "Right, Coop?"

Cooper nodded. "You make us sound like we're criminals or something."

"We're *lying* to the police. We're holding back *evidence* with that surveillance hard drive. That *does* make us criminals."

"C'mon, Hiro. You're looking at this all wrong."

"Am I?" She stood and took a step toward him. "Your only concern is protecting yourself."

"What?"

"You don't care about anyone else."

Her words knocked the wind out of him just as if she'd caught him off guard with a fist to the stomach. Didn't she get it? The Code of Silence was about protection—*for all of them.* Why did she think he went all the way to the back of Frank 'n Stein's kitchen to grab the keys? To protect them. If he didn't they'd likely have been caught.

"That's not true." He wanted to explain it to her. To show her how wrong she really was. But he stopped. He wasn't so sure she'd hear him if he tried. And if she didn't, the wall between them would get a little higher. *The wall.* Sometimes it *did* seem like this thing was turning into a wall.

Then again, maybe she was just thinking about *herself.* How lying to the cops might mess up her chances of becoming one someday. Cooper could feel his own steam rising at that thought.

"When are we going to visit Frank?" she asked.

Where did *that* come from? Cooper wanted to say something about "lying low" again, but she looked dead serious. "I'd like to," Coop said.

"But you won't." Her voice had an edge to it.

"I just think it might be a little risky."

She shook her head. "Like we'll look suspicious somehow if we visit?"

"Well, yeah, something like that."

"I'm with Cooper," Gordy said. "Visiting Frank is crazy."

"Crazy?" Hiro raised her chin just a bit. "Frank is a friend. And friends visit. You don't think it looks crazy if we *don't?*"

Gordy looked as uncomfortable as Cooper felt. "Maybe we could just send a card. We could all sign it, and, uh ..."

Always trying to keep the peace. Cooper loved that about his cousin. But the card idea wasn't going to fly with Hiro.

A quiet settled over them. Cooper needed options. Trouble was he didn't have any. He took in a deep breath and let it out slowly.

"Okay." Cooper finally broke the silence. "The way I see it, we're running out of road here. But I still say we wait until the last second to tell what we saw."

Neither of the other two spoke for a moment.

Cooper felt they were waiting for him to say something. "We'll come clean before any one of us goes into Detective Hammer's interrogation."

Gordy thumped his fist on his chest. "I can bluff my way through with Hammer. I'm for sticking with the Code."

"And what about his baloney detector?" Hiro said.

"I'll be like a rock. Nobody will get anything out of me."

Cooper held up his hands. "Hold on, Gordy. We can't take a chance with the interrogation, no matter how sure we are about sticking to the Code."

Hiro nodded. Gordy looked like he was ready to say something, but Cooper held up his hand to stop him. He had to finish this thought. "But we can't just go to school Monday morning and spill to Hammer either. Not alone."

Gordy nodded. "Exactly. If he really is Elvis, we're toast."

"Sooo," Hiro's eyes narrowed. "What are you saying?"

"If we don't hear they've caught the robbers by the evening news on Sunday night, I'll tell my parents everything. We can go to the police together if you want."

"If we go as a group," Hiro said, "we'll be safe. I'll bring my brother too."

Cooper shrugged. "Why not? The more of us that go to the police station, the better. They can't get all of us."

Hiro smiled. It was just a quick one. A flash of teeth and then gone again. But it was enough for Cooper to know the old Hiro was still there. Still loyal. He didn't know what he'd do if that ever changed.

"Why wait until Sunday night?" Hiro pleaded. "Let's get this *over* with."

"Because I'm praying the robbers will be caught before then and we won't have to get involved at all." *Praying?* Why did he even use that word? He'd been *worrying* plenty, but praying was a different story.

Hiro looked like she was wrestling with something. Like how to convince Cooper they should turn themselves in right now.

"Okay. I'll wait." She folded her arms across her chest.

Gordy shot her a suspicious look. "Why the sudden change of heart?"

"We're only talking twenty-four hours." She nodded. "It will be here before we know it."

That's what Cooper was afraid of.

CHAPTER 19

"Just talk to him, Hiroko. Like you would at the diner."

Hiro looked at her mom, and then back at Frank Mustacci. Oxygen tubes in his nose. IV's trailing into his arm. Wires running to monitors with printers graphing his vitals. It was a little hard to imagine talking to him like this at Frank 'n Stein's. He needed to be wearing his white apron instead of the hospital gown. And his hands needed to be doing something. Loading relish on a dog. Piling beef on a bun. Something. She'd never seen his hands so still. Now that she was here, she had no idea what to say.

Maybe her mom sensed it. She had a way of knowing what people were thinking. Mom also had a way of not pushing. She cradled one of Frank's hands in her own and stroked it gently.

Hiro wanted to do the same. But she couldn't. She pictured him laying on the floor of the diner. When she thought he was dead. He didn't look any more alive than he did that night.

"Do you remember how confused I was when I first worked for you?" Her mom's voice was soft. Soothing. "I mixed up orders. Gave customers fries when they ordered onion rings. Put hot peppers on their beef when they ordered sweet. But you knew it was the grief, didn't you? Remember what you told me?"

Hiro looked for any sign of understanding on his face. Eyelids flickering. Maybe a twitch. She saw nothing.

"You're in a tunnel, Katsumi. It's dark and scary, and you think it will always be this way. But you'll get through. You'll see." She squeezed his hand. "And you were right. God led me out of that horrible place. And he put you in my life like an angel in an apron, encouraging me all the way."

Hiro wanted to talk to him that way. Wished she could tell him how she missed his grandfatherly advice. The way he checked up on her. Watched out for her.

"And now *you're* in a tunnel. It's dark. It's scary." Hiro's mom leaned in close. "But you're going to find the way out. Our Jesus will show you when the time is right."

They were *all* in a dark tunnel. Her, Coop, Gordy ... all three of them. Only their tunnel was made of lies and deception. And they needed to find a way out. She wished they were here right now.

They weren't able to talk at church this morning, and they probably wouldn't talk until they met at *The Getaway* to work out their plan for the surveillance hard drive and the bell tower.

"How about we pray with you, Frank. Would you like that?" Hiro's mom talked to him like she really believed he could hear her.

When her mom started praying, Hiro's throat burned. She held her own hand and prayed at the same time. Prayed her own silent prayer. *Don't take him away from us, Father. Bring him back. Please. Bring him back.*

She didn't realize her mom had stopped praying until she felt her hand on her shoulder.

"We'll let him rest now."

She didn't want him to rest. She wanted him to sit up and get out of this place.

Her mom placed his hand back on the bed. "We'll be back, Frank. I promise you that."

And I can promise you something, too. Hiro stood. *I'm going to find the person who did this to you.*

Her mom walked out of the room. Hiro hesitated, then reached out and touched his hand. It felt warm.

CHAPTER 20

Gordy could see everything from the table he and Hiro shared outside Dunkin' Donuts. Coop approached the bell tower on foot from the opposite direction—from the west. Cargo shorts. Sweatshirt. Backpack. Even *he* didn't recognize Coop with the hood pulled so far forward. His entire face was lost in the shadows, even when he passed under a streetlight. The darkness made for a perfect cover.

Gordy kept his eyes on everything west of them. Hiro had everything to the east, which was tricky because of the McDonald's and the size of the parking lot for the Jewel-Osco grocery and drug store.

Hiro also had the phone. If they saw anybody watching him, or heading his way, he'd get a call, and put into play one of the escape plans.

"He's at the bell tower," Gordy said. "Duct tape is out. Aaaaand he's taping the note to the bell tower. Kaboom. Message delivered."

"Cut the commentary and keep your eyes open," Hiro whispered. "If anybody is watching, Coop's in the danger zone now."

Gordy grabbed a donut. "Just like a real stakeout, eh? Donuts and everything." If he didn't do something to try to keep things light he'd go nuts. He felt jumpy enough as it was already.

Coop stayed on the sidewalk and picked up the pace, walking directly past them without even glancing their way. Gordy watched to make sure nobody trailed him.

They'd hammered out the plan on *The Getaway* after dinner. Gordy still didn't like the idea of Coop making the drop alone—or even leaving the note in the first place. Hiro gave it her vote, though. Felt they'd be doing something. Which really meant she wanted to play detective. At least they decided to wait until after dark.

Hiro even brought her pocket digital camera. Not exactly the high-tech surveillance equipment the police had, but hey, it had a 10-to-1 power zoom. Which is why Gordy figured this was all about Hiro wanting to find the robbers herself.

Gordy wished he'd been the one making the drop. Once he got on his bike, no way those guys would catch him. "You think those goons are watching?"

Hiro didn't answer. She nibbled on a donut and kept her eyes on Coop and the parking lot.

The silence made him jumpy. "I can't believe you really went to see Frank."

"The real shocker is that you two didn't."

Gordy winced. He had a hard time with that too, but he wasn't about to tell Hiro that. She'd be all over him to go see Frank. Time to change the topic.

"Okay. If the robbers *do* pick up the note, think they'll buy the part about the hard drive being buried and that nobody will get it—not even the cops?"

Hiro didn't answer, but kept focused on Coop. "He's going around the McDonald's now," she said. "Let's move."

The plan called for a casual walk over to McDonald's so they could keep an eye on Cooper from there. Hiro's pace seemed anything but casual. Which was okay with Gordy. The moment Cooper dropped out of his line of vision, the more Gordy didn't like this plan.

They went inside McDonald's and hurried to the windows just

in time to see Coop walk into the grocery store. About a hundred yards of parking lot separated them. Gordy checked his watch. He'd allow him thirty seconds to get to the washroom. Ninety seconds to change and stuff his shorts and hoodie in the backpack. Thirty seconds to get out.

Hiro stood at the window and watched. Gordy paced.

"Are you ready to order?" The uniformed order-taker lady smiled at him.

"Oh, uh, no." Gordy checked the Jewel exit again. "Still trying to decide between one of those smiley meals with the cool prize and a jumbo hotdog." Anything to get her out of his hair.

The lady cocked her head to the side. "We don't serve hotdogs."

"Oh, yeah. Sorry."

He checked his watch. Five minutes. *Too long.* Hiro must have had the same thought. Without a word they headed for the doors.

Hiro had her phone out by the time they'd rounded the building.

"There he is," Gordy said. Coop walked out the doors on the pharmacy side of the building. Jacket. Blue jeans. Baseball cap. Only the backpack looked the same.

Gordy slowed the pace and let out a deep breath. "Finally."

Cooper's bike stood waiting for him right where Gordy locked it up on his way to Dunkin' Donuts. Hiro's bike was locked next to it. She would follow Coop at a distance. Gordy would walk home. That was the plan. So far, so good.

If Coop felt nervous, he did a good job of hiding it. Within seconds he mounted the bike and casually pedaled due east toward Meadow Drive before disappearing around the far corner of the grocery store.

Gordy scanned the lot, all the way out to the cars backed into the stalls along Kirchoff Road. *Almost there.*

A dark SUV pulled out of it's parking slot, turning on its headlights as it rolled forward. Head*light*. "Hiro!"

"Got it." She punched in Cooper's number on her phone and raised it to her ear.

The SUV plowed through the lot—passed the easy exit onto Kirchoff and headed right for the side exit onto Meadow. Even with the overhead lights blazing in the parking lot, Gordy couldn't make out the driver—but the goon had definitely seen through Cooper's disguise. The bell tower wasn't even visible from here. Elvis or the clown must have been positioned where they could see the bell tower—and they phoned their partner in the SUV. There was no other way this driver could have spotted Coop.

"Pick up, pick up, *pick up*!" Hiro shouted into the phone, running between parked cars for her bike.

Gordy sprinted for the corner of the building. *This can't be happening!*

CHAPTER 21

Cooper felt the phone vibrate in his pocket and had it to his ear after the second ring.

"You've got a tail," Hiro shouted. "One headlight. *Move!*"

He dropped the phone in his pocket, made a hard left to cut down the alley behind the Jewel, and stood on the pedals.

He spotted the SUV out of the corner of his eye. And the driver obviously saw *him.*

Tires squealing, the vehicle turned off Meadow and barreled into the alley behind him.

Building to the left. Six-foot cedar fence to the right. Kimball Hill Park straight ahead. If he could make it into the park he'd lose them. *God help me. God help me.*

Even with the wind rushing in his ears he heard the SUV driver gun the engine—gaining on him. They were going to run him down. He chanced a quick shoulder check. The SUV was closing fast. *Too* fast. He wasn't going to make it!

Cooper hit the brakes, skidded, and jumped off the still rolling bike. Leaping for the fence, he clawed his way to the top even as the SUV skidded to a stop behind him.

CHAPTER 22

Hiro dropped the lock on the ground and mounted her bike on the run. Banking the front corner of the store, she spotted Gordy sprinting along the side of the building. She pumped harder and passed him just as they reached the alley.

The vehicle was stopped, driver's door open, about three quarters of the way down the length of the building. A shadowy figure pitched Cooper's bike in the back and slammed it shut.

"Noooooo!"

The man dashed back into the SUV, hit the gas, and peeled out—sending gravel pinging off the pavement toward her.

He must have thrown him in the back seat. "COOP!"

In seconds the car disappeared around the corner. She didn't even catch the number on the plates.

She clamped on the brakes and stopped, dumping her bike as she did. *Too late for the camera.* Hands trembling, she fumbled for her phone as Gordy pounded up.

He bent over, hands on knees gulping for air. "Gotta—help—Coop. 9-1-1."

She was on it, if her hands would stop trembling enough to hit the right keys.

Her phone rang instead, startling her. *Coop!*

She connected and swung it to her ear. "Are you okay?"

"Where is he?" Gordy reached for the phone.

Hiro pulled away. "Over the fence?" She looked down the alley. "He got over the fence. He's on foot. By the playground behind Kimball Hill School."

"Tell him to hide," Gordy said, already running for the fence. "We'll come to him."

CHAPTER 23

Hiro sat a couple rows in front of Coop and Gordy on the bus ride to school Monday morning. Any closer and she might have hauled off and hit one of them. Somebody needed to knock some sense into those boys.

Coop tried to discount the incident in the alley. He was spooked — she could tell. But he tried to cover it up — just like he'd been doing with everything else since they agreed to the Code. The problem was, Coop was getting away with it. His parents thought they went to Frank'n Stein's, just like he'd told them he was going to do. How he was going to explain the missing bike, she had no idea. But knowing Coop and his new talent for lies, he'd come up with something convincing.

Hiro stepped off the bus ahead of Coop and Gordy. The school parking lot Monday morning proved to be every bit the circus it had been last Friday. Only this time it wasn't just the police. A mob of angry parents milled around the entrance.

The whole interview process had been totally derailed — by Lunk's mom. Rather by Mr. Slimhall, her attorney. Which made Hiro fuming mad.

The slick lawyer and his staff called every parent of the Plum Grove student body over the weekend. The moron told her mom how "innocent kids often get fingered for the crime by some grudge-wielding classmate."

That didn't worry Mom. The thing that caused her to agree not to sign the form was when he reminded her that a witness would be called to testify against some pretty desperate criminals—possibly with underworld connections, who may want a little payback.

Apparently the tactic worked on enough of the parents to raise a significant protest. No interviews would be conducted until the whole thing got sorted out legally, and that could be days. Mom had gotten a call back from the attorney with the news while Hiro was wrapped up in the bell tower stakeout fiasco.

Coop got the word and loved it. It meant they didn't have to break the Code yet. That's the way he saw it—and he definitely *wasn't* seeing this thing with 20/20 vision. Coop said something like, "Now that the police won't be tied up interviewing students, they can throw all their efforts into finding the real robbers." *Ridiculous.*

Detective Hammer stood in front of the group, wearing his mirrored sunglasses, waving his hands like he was trying to quiet them down. The police were so busy with the grumbling parents they didn't seem to pay any attention to the students—which probably explained the matching grins Coop and Gordy wore.

They caught up to her and walked into school together. Honestly, the two of them looked better than they had in the four days since the robbery, even after the incident last night. That ticked her off a little, too. Hiro felt like she was going to explode. The way she saw it, she and Coop were at polar extremes. She wanted to go to the police and spill. He wanted to avoid them at all costs. Even if that meant more lies. What was happening to him?

And Gordy sort of bounced between the two of them. Trying in his own way to be loyal to both. Trying to bring them together. She could see that. It was one of the things she loved about him. But sometimes it made her want to kick him, too.

The three sat at a lunch table at the back fringe of the cafeteria. The adjacent table stayed empty this time. Apparently Mertz and her flirts weren't taking any chances that Hiro might lose her lunch again. Hiro smiled. That suited her just fine.

Gordy sat across from her and tore into his lunch like he hadn't eaten in days. Coop sat next to her and acted like he didn't notice anything was bothering her. So if he wasn't going to bring up the topic, *she* would.

"You broke your word to me," Hiro said. And that was the issue, wasn't it? He'd lied. To *her*. She looked him in the eyes. "You said if the men weren't caught, and if we didn't hear a report on the Sunday night news, we'd break the Code. We'd tell our parents and go to the police."

"But it was only because of the police interviews today. When those got delayed-"

"You're in danger, Coop," she interrupted. "We all are. Some very bad people are looking for us. And we're hiding the truth from the ones that *can* help us."

And they needed help. Last night she thought she'd lost him. It terrified her. And he might not be so lucky next time.

Coop looked around the cafeteria like he worried somebody might overhear. "Believe me, I'm with you on that. That's all I could think about last night. And I got an idea." He leaned forward. "I've got a plan."

Hiro groaned and shot him a skeptical look. "The last one didn't turn out so hot."

"It's a whole new ball game now."

"A game? This is a game to you?" Hiro said.

"That's not what he said, Hiro. C'mon." Gordy picked up his carton of milk and started to chug it.

"That's exactly what Coop thinks this is," Hiro said.

Gordy kept guzzling the chocolate milk.

She looked from Gordy to Coop. "I think *both* of you think this is a game. Gee, why don't we play 'cops and robbers' while we're at it?"

Gordy hunkered over in a choking laugh. Milk ran out of his nose and dripped on the cafeteria table.

Coop handed him a napkin.

They *were* playing cops and robbers weren't they? Only this wasn't some game. The robbers wanted to silence Coop, and the cops were trying to make him talk. Somehow she had to convince Coop they needed to end the Code of Silence. If Coop agreed, Gordy would follow.

Gordy mopped himself up. He thumped his chest with his fist and cleared his throat several times.

She hardly dared to pin her hopes on his new plan. She thought about the strategy *she'd* been turning around in her head last night when she couldn't sleep. Coop would hate it. But she'd made up her mind to put a plan of her own into action. And she had no intention of telling him. Not yet.

But she did want to hear about his idea. "So what *were* you going to say?" Hiro looked at Coop. "Your plan?"

He looked around as if he wanted to be sure no one was close enough to listen in. She followed his lead and checked to be sure nobody approached from the other direction. The steady noise of the cafeteria actually gave them a decent level of privacy. "I've got a plan to help the police find the robbers."

Hiro would love it if that was true. But she wasn't ready to hire a band and start a parade down the cafeteria aisles. "Like what?"

"Not here. Meet at *The Getaway* after school."

Was he stalling her? She locked eyes with him. "I hope it's more than *stay quiet and keep under the radar.*"

"Way more. I think I've found a way out of this. And for once it involves *talking* instead of being silent. But that's all I'm going to say here."

"More *lies?*"

"Uh-uh. The opposite. It's a way for us to tell the truth without getting caught. Interested?"

She gave him a single nod. "Very." She wanted to trust him.

Wanted things to be the way they were. She felt the tension between them ease a bit.

Gordy grinned. "This is more like it."

Obviously he felt it too.

"How about we get off the bus a couple stops early to hit the mini mart on the way home." Gordy looked from Hiro to Cooper. "We can fuel up for our meeting."

When he was happy, the world was a sunny place … and Gordy liked to eat. Hiro hit the fridge when the shadows closed in.

Cooper shrugged. "Why not?"

Out of the corner of her eye she saw Lunk approaching with a food tray in hand. She braced herself.

"Is this saved?" Lunk nodded toward the empty space on the bench next to Gordy. He slid his tray on the table and sat without waiting for a response.

"Well, I imagine you must be proud of yourself, Mr. Lunquist," Hiro said.

Lunk's eyes narrowed. "What's that supposed to mean?"

"Stopping the police investigation. Your mom is the one who started the whole attorney thing. Mr. *Slimeball*, I think. Right?"

"Mr. Martin Slimhall." Lunk took a bite of his hamburger and nodded. "She got the ball rolling. Yeah. But she's not the only one. You saw the people out front this morning."

"And what was that little act in the gym last Friday, about you wanting so badly to see the person responsible caught?"

Lunk looked at her like she was crazy. "I do want them caught. In fact, I'd like to catch the scumbag myself and have ten minutes alone with him before I call the police."

He didn't care what she thought. She wasn't much more than an annoyance to him. She could see that in his face. Like she didn't bother him. Like she was a mere bug to be swatted away. Dismissed. Well if she was a bug, she'd be a mosquito—and she'd draw blood. "Then why slow down the investigation?"

"I'm not *slowing* it down." Lunk wolfed down another bite.

"Right. The cops are out writing speeding tickets today instead of tracking down leads here. I wouldn't call that progress."

Lunk's face grew red.

Gordy cleared his throat. "Gee, Halloween is just three days away. What are you going to be, Hiro?"

She glared at him. "Don't even try to change the subject, Gordy." Honestly, she appreciated the way he always tried to be a peacemaker, but if he got in between her and Lunk ... look out.

"Admit it, Mr. Lunquist." Hiro raised her chin. She was proud to be a mosquito. "You *say* you want justice for Frank, but your actions tell a different story."

"I'm just making sure the cops don't get over anxious and put the finger on the wrong person."

"Like yourself?"

"They've done it before." He glanced at Coop.

Maybe he expected Coop to back him up on that point. Maybe he just wanted to read his face to see if he shared Hiro's opinion. Cooper just sat chewing his sandwich and staring at some spot on the table like he was fascinated by it.

"Look," Coop said. "You're both making good points."

Lunk looked at him with suspicion in his eyes.

Hiro felt the same way. Now *Coop* was trying to be a peacemaker?

"Okay", Coop said. "Both of you want to nail the guy who did this to Frank. Right?"

For an instant she saw Frank the way he looked in the hospital bed. Her eyes burned and she blinked back tears. "You know I do."

"Lunk?"

He stared at his plate. "Yeah, as long as it's the right one."

"Then like it or not, you're both on the same side. Try acting like it."

Lunk shifted on the bench. He looked at Coop for an instant, then reached for his burger and took another bite.

Hiro fingered her braid, but didn't say a word. *Lunk on the same side as us? What about Lunk's dad? Lunk had never been on her side. For anything.*

They ate in silence for several minutes—which seemed like forever. Hiro tried to think of some safe topic to bring up, but right now every thought centered on the robbery, or Frank, or how the Code of Silence put a chokehold on Coop. And while she hated the fact that they hadn't broken the Code of Silence yet, maybe she should be thankful. Police interviews weren't really going to do more than flush the three of them out of hiding. It probably wouldn't help them find the real robbers, and the case was getting colder by the minute.

"Sometimes I think the police suspect some junior high punk did it," Lunk said. "Oh, they're not saying that. Not officially. They say they only want some eyewitness. But if you ask me, they haven't ruled out the fact that whoever left that backpack there may have been involved." He kept his head down like he was talking to his plate. "I'll tell you this, more than one person is involved. Frank would never let one guy take him down."

Kids started getting up from their tables. Carrying trays to the garbage. Hiro watched Candy, Lissa, and Katie pass.

Coop leaned in. "What makes you say that?"

"He fought in Vietnam in '69 or '70. I saw a picture on his office desk."

Hiro's antenna went up. So Lunk *had* been up in Frank's office. That means he knew about the safe. What if he told somebody about it? The wrong kind of somebody?

Hiro shot Coop a glance to see if he caught it.

She wanted to keep Lunk talking. "That was a long time ago."

"But a man doesn't forget how to fight. It becomes instinct."

Hiro tried to picture Frank in a uniform. She couldn't imagine him trim and young. In her mind she pictured Santa packing an M16. Definitely not the type of thing you'd see on a Christmas card.

Lunk shoved his empty tray to the center of the table. "He can still handle himself. I helped him unload a delivery truck. He carried thirty-pound boxes of hot dogs to the freezer like they were shoe boxes."

Hiro smoothed her napkin and placed it on her plate. "I'd have never guessed that by looking at him."

"Looks can be a real fooler," Lunk said.

"And you want to find the people who did this to him," Coop said. "Exactly how do you plan to do that?"

Good question,Coop.

Lunk shrugged. "Watch. Keep my ears open. Think. I'll come up with something."

What was that supposed to mean?

The bell rang and interrupted her thoughts. Students stood all over the cafeteria, and the noise level rose with them. Lunk grabbed his tray and left without another word.

Gordy let out a sigh of relief.

"I don't trust him," Hiro said. "He's trouble. He'll never change."

"Hiro's right," Gordy said. "And he had to know about the safe. Did you catch that bit about Frank's office?"

Coop nodded, like he was questioning things himself. "He sure *acts* like he wouldn't have had anything to do with it, like he wouldn't have given his dad some inside information."

He crumpled his lunch bag and stood. "But then again Lunk said it himself. Looks can be a real fooler."

CHAPTER 24

Coop dreamt of being a fireman. Hiro? A cop. But Gordy had bigger plans. He'd own a diner like Frank's someday. Or a mini-mart like the one they were in. Either way, by being his own boss he'd never have to worry about hunger pains. Which was exactly what he felt now.

He juggled three bags of chips, a couple of candy bars, and a 20-ounce soda. Coop picked up a sack of bite-sized powdered donuts and chocolate milk. Hiro held a bottled water and an apple.

"Gee, Hiro, really going hog-wild, huh?" Gordy said. "Not exactly my kind of picks."

"I'm not surprised." She raised her eyebrows. "This is brain food."

"Ooooh." Coop laughed. "Direct hit."

Gordy managed to grab another candy bar on his way to the checkout counter. A man stood at the register ahead of them. Dozens of lottery tickets covered the white countertop in loose coils.

"I'll take ten 'Lucky Picks', a dozen 'Lucky Duckies', and … let's see," the man paused to let the clerk catch up. " … hit me with about twenty of the 'Cash Cows'. That should do it."

Gordy had never seen anyone order that many lottery tickets at one time. The man looped the tickets around his neck like

Hawaiian leis. A mound of cash lay on the counter—and right on top was Cooper's "snack buck" ... the one he'd donated to Frank's hospital fund.

The man turned. *Mr. Stein*. He'd just spent the money for Frank on *lottery tickets*.

The co-owner of Frank 'n Stein's recognized them instantly. His face lit up in a friendly smile. "Look who I caught buying after-school snacks! Your parents know about this?" Stein winked.

Gordy's eyes went back to the dollar with the moustache drawn on Washington's face.

Mr. Stein must have picked up on that. He held up the empty jar with Frank's picture on it. "We collected $110 and change. Not bad for just a few days. Of course, I knew that a hundred bucks wouldn't do a thing to Frank's hospital bill." He shook the lottery tickets. "But these babies can change all that."

"You spent the entire hospital fund on *lottery* tickets?" Coop put his donuts and chocolate milk on the counter and picked up the emergency snack dollar he'd kept in his pocket for as long as Gordy could remember.

Mr. Stein stepped aside. "Uh-huh," he said. "A smart investment. Now we have a chance to do something really big."

Gordy had to agree ... a hundred dollars wouldn't do much for Frank. "What if you only make twenty bucks or something?"

"Then I'll make up the difference. But look at all these." He shook the leis. "I'll bet we've got some real winners in here."

The clerk rang up Coop's snacks, took his twenty, and gave him back his change, including his snack buck. Coop looked glad to get it back.

"Why don't you kids stop by later and help scratch these off," Stein said. "See how we did."

Gordy glanced at Coop and read his face instantly. *Fat chance on that idea.* Which suited Gordy just fine.

"Any change with Frank?" Hiro asked.

"I think he looks better, but then that may be wishful thinking."

Mr. Stein sighed. "No signs of rousing, though, if that's what you mean." He stepped to one side while Gordy lined up his snacks on the counter. "Are you keeping up with your prayers for Frank?"

"Every time I think of him," Hiro whispered.

Stein reached one arm around her and patted her shoulder. "Good girl. I knew you were lucky the moment I met you."

"Lucky?" Hiro asked as she placed her food on the counter.

"Yep. Frank is lucky to have you for a friend. And I'd like to consider you my friend too." He held out his hand.

Hiro hesitated for a second, then gripped his hand and pumped it once.

"Whoa," Stein said with a chuckle. "Nice grip."

Hiro's face reddened, and she looked down at her feet.

"Ever think about stopping by the hospital and visiting Frank?"

Hiro looked at him. "I went yesterday. With my mom."

Gordy was glad Mr. Stein hadn't asked him the same question.

"There, see? I told you Frank is lucky to have a friend like you. I think you visiting Frank may be the best medicine he can get."

The clerk put Gordy's treats in a bag and handed him his change. Hiro stepped up to pay.

Mr. Stein started for the door. "You three come by the diner anytime." He put his hand by his mouth and whispered. "I'll make sure you get a little healthier snack than you're getting here."

Gordy liked the sound of that. "Like shakes and fries?"

Mr. Stein laughed. "Exactly." He pulled open the door and stepped outside. A few minutes later, Coop, Gordy, and Hiro started toward home.

Coop opened the bag of powdered donuts and snagged one. Gordy darted his hand in the donut bag and pulled out two.

Hiro walked beside them and took a bite of the apple. "How do you two feel about him spending those donations on lottery tickets?"

Gordy shrugged. "Did you see all the tickets he had? He's sure to win something. I think it was a good idea."

"It didn't bother you that he used money that didn't *belong* to him?" Hiro asked.

"He's still using the money for Frank," Gordy said.

She sighed and shook her head. "But what about the *principle* of the thing?"

"Oh, here we go." Gordy didn't want to think that hard. All he wanted was to snack a little and—

"Are you telling me it's right to spend somebody's money without asking them?"

"Like Frank is really going to know."

Hiro's eyes narrowed to tiny slits. "Gordon Digby. That was an awful thing to say,"

Gordy held up his hands. "I'm sorry. That *was* awful."

Hiro looked at Coop. "Do you share Einstein's opinion?"

Coop thought for a second. "Mr. Stein sure didn't see anything wrong with it."

"I'm asking what *you* think."

"I don't like it."

Hiro looked satisfied with that.

"If he wins big, it could do some *serious* good," Gordy said.

Hiro snorted. "Remind me never to let you hold my wallet."

Coop didn't comment, but looked like he'd drifted off into another world. Maybe he was working on his plan. Gordy gave him space.

"Let's walk by the bell tower," Coop said.

Gordy eyed him.

"See if the note is gone."

Gordy did *not* want to go near there. "It's out of our way."

"Not much."

Gordy hustled a few steps ahead, turned around and walked backwards so he could face them. "What if they're *watching*?"

Coop shook his head. "They're looking for one boy, not a group of three." He looked beyond Gordy. "I just want to see if they picked it up."

Gordy looked behind to make sure he wasn't going to trip over a curb or something. "Okay, so let's walk home, I'll get my binoculars, and we can take a look from a hundred yards away. I vote no to getting any closer than that." He turned and fell in step alongside them. "Hiro, you've got the deciding vote."

She thought for a second. "I'm with Coop on this one."

"*What?* C'mon, Hiro. Have a little more of your *brain* food. They were watching the bell tower yesterday. Just waiting for Coop to step into their trap."

"We'll stay on the opposite side of the street," Hiro said. "And whether or not the note is there, we don't stop. We don't even slow down."

"Right," Coop said.

Gordy didn't like it. Not even a little bit. "Now I wish we'd stayed on the bus." He twisted off the cap of his soda and chugged nearly half the bottle. But at least Coop and Hiro were working together. The tension between them was really getting to Gordy. The last thing Gordy wanted was for them to be fighting. They needed to stick to the Code, right? Somehow, the fact they were in it together made sticking to the Code okay. If they fought, lost their unity, well then... Gordy didn't want to think about that. He dug out another candy bar and ate the whole thing at once.

"When we get close," Hiro said, "why don't I do the looking for all of us. If someone is watching us, they'll be paying more attention to you guys than they will me."

"Good call, detective," Coop said. As they got closer to the bell tower, Cooper held the bag of mini-donuts out toward Gordy. "Let's keep our eyes focused on the bag as we go by," he said.

Gordy grabbed a couple and stuffed them in his mouth as they walked. "What if they left a note for *you?*"

Coop thought for a moment. "No way are we going to get it. We tip the police."

Hiro slipped in between them and hooked her arms in theirs. "Exactly."

She kept her arms locked with theirs as they approached the tower.

"Okay," Hiro said. "Definitely no note ... but there's something weird ... " she sucked in her breath and clutched onto his arm tighter. "O God," she whispered. "Dear Jesus."

Gordy looked at the base of the bell tower and immediately saw a bike. Coop's. Mangled, crushed, and folded nearly in half. *No.* They didn't leave a note, but they definitely delivered a message.

"Don't stop. Keep walking," Hiro said. Her voice sounded tight. "Keep walking. Keep walking"

She didn't have to tell him to keep walking. He had no plans to stop. In fact right now the only thing he really wanted to do was *run.*

CHAPTER 25

To Cooper, the walk home seemed strangely quiet — which gave him the chance to sort things out in his head. Gordy seemed to do as much checking over his shoulder as he did looking ahead. And Hiro was likely building a case for breaking the Code. They took a roundabout way to their street, doubling back more than once just to be sure they weren't being followed.

Fudge bounded to meet them the moment they walked into the backyard. She zeroed in on the mini-mart bags, sniffing and poking them with her nose. She barked when Cooper headed up the ladder. He grabbed a powdered donut from his bag and held it up for her to see.

Ears alert, she focused on the donut in his hand.

Cooper feigned a throw. Fudge bounded after it, but quickly turned back. He threw again, but this time with an easy, underhand pitch. Fudge caught it and wolfed it down without chewing at all. She pranced back happily and stared at him, hoping he'd throw again. As if she didn't have a care in the world. Cooper couldn't imagine how nice that must feel.

The day was too perfect to be indoors, even if it was in the cabin of *The Getaway*. Cooper found a seat on the bow and the other two followed. Both of them looked at him, waiting for him to begin.

"Okay," he said. "Elvis and the clown are still in town, and they're serious."

"Seriously demented," Gordy said. "They twisted your bike like a pretzel."

More like the knot in Cooper's stomach.

"We need protection, Coop," Hiro said. "If they'd caught you last night we'd have found *you* under the bell tower. You know that. Right?"

He nodded, but Cooper had no intention of ever being that close to them again. "There is one good thing about them still being in town," he said. "The police can still catch them."

Hiro nodded slightly. "True."

We've been able to stick to the Code for four days, and we just caught a real break with the whole police interview thing."

"A *break*?" Hiro took a sip of her water. "There's more than one way to look at that. And if they have a solid reason to do it, they can still pick you up for questioning."

She was right.

"Anyway, we can't just sit around and hope the police nab the robbers."

Gordy twisted open the cap on his soda. Fizz streamed out, and he held it over the edge of the bow so it dripped down to the ground below. "So what do you think we should do?"

Cooper looked from Gordy to Hiro. "Help with the investigation."

Hiro looked at him for a long moment. Like she was trying to visually test the sincerity of what he just said. "How?"

Cooper glanced at the house for a moment. The bow of *The Getaway* was a perfect spot to talk. He could see anybody coming long before they got within earshot. "The police are spending too much effort looking for their mystery witness." He pointed to himself.

"They may not have any other leads," Gordy said.

Cooper leaned forward. "So we have to find a way to steer the police in the right direction, without blowing our cover."

Hiro slumped back. "Are we just going to rehash our situation, or do you have some way to accomplish this impossible task?"

Cooper smiled. "I have a plan. And I think it will work."

"I'm listening."

"Okay. I type a letter to the police telling them what happened. They're only sure about one of us being there, so I won't mention anyone else but me. I tell them about the guys who did it. The ones they *should* be looking for."

"Wait a second," Gordy said. "If you do that, and the cops did it, they'll really be out to find you. They'll figure you're going to talk."

Cooper shook his head. "I'll make it really plain that I can't identify the men."

Hiro looked deep in thought. "Why would they believe it? They may have gotten dozens of letters from people claiming to have been there. People do that, you know."

"I've already got that worked out." Cooper pulled a powdered donut from his bag and stuffed it in his mouth. He twisted off the cap of his chocolate milk and gulped down a couple of cool mouthfuls.

Hiro jabbed him. "Are you going to tell us, or what?"

"I give them some details only I would know."

"Like what?"

"Where Frank was laying. How he was laying. That a stool was used to break the glass door. That the register change drawer was on the floor. That Frank's glasses were on the floor by the feet of Frankenstein. Things like that."

Hiro thumped him on the back. "Brilliant!"

"Almost as good as coming clean and telling the truth?"

Hiro smiled. "Almost."

It was good to see her smile at him again. And there was something more. Respect. "Well, it's as close as we're going to get."

Gordy wiped his mouth with the back of his hand. "Sounds good to me. Then we just drop it in the mail?"

"Yeah," Cooper said. "The bad thing is we'll lose a whole day or so before the police get it."

"Why don't we deliver it ourselves?" Hiro said.

Gordy snorted. "And risk getting caught?"

"No, not at the police station." Hiro stood and paced the bow. "The night drop slot at the library?"

Cooper thought about that for a moment. "We address the letter to the police. The librarian will get it in the morning and call them. They'll probably send a squad car right over." He nodded. "Great idea. What do you think, Gordy?"

Gordy didn't look so convinced.

"What if the librarian doesn't call the police? The mail is safer."

"But slower," Cooper said.

Hiro shrugged. "Why not do both?"

"Perfect." Cooper threw a powdered donut to Fudge. "If the library idea works, the police will get a head start on finding the men. If the library sits on it, the police still get the letter in the mail."

Hiro stopped pacing and leaned against the rail. "One problem."

Cooper popped another donut in his mouth and looked at her.

She fingered her necklace. "It might actually make things worse. I mean, if I were a cop—"

"But you're not," Gordy interrupted.

Hiro glared at Gordy.

Cooper held up one hand. "Let her finish."

"If I were a cop—" she glared at Gordy as if daring him to interrupt again "—this letter would make me want to question whoever wrote it. Maybe I'd find out even more details if I questioned the witness in person. Right?"

"Well that's not going to happen," Cooper said. "They'll have to be satisfied with the letter."

"But they won't be. Not unless they can talk to you."

Cooper thought about that for a second. "And if they really want to talk to me, they may try even harder to find me."

"And," Gordy said, "the letter may give them some clue as to who you are."

"Great." Cooper twisted off the cap of his chocolate milk and took a long drink. "We're back to square one."

Hiro sat back down between them.

"What if I put a phone number in the letter?" Cooper said. "We could pick up one of those disposable phones at Walmart."

Hiro's eyes brightened. "We buy the phone with cash and there's no record of who owns the phone!" She clapped him on the back again. "Let's do it."

"I feel like a spy or something." Gordy smiled. "So when do we get this letter out?"

Cooper looked at Hiro, then back at Gordy. "Tonight."

CHAPTER 26

Cooper felt energized. He was playing offense now. The three pooled their cash for a phone. Hiro and Gordy left on their bikes for Walmart. Cooper stayed back to write the letter.

He worked at the computer right in the family room. It was either that or the library—which didn't seem like the best idea. Every time his mom walked through the room, his heart pounded out a warning. He wanted to work fast, but he had to be careful with every word. He had to give enough information to prove he was at the scene of the crime, yet not give away his identity while he was at it.

"Homework?"

Mom's voice startled him. Cooper whirled around in the desk chair. She walked toward him, her eyes on the screen. Cooper stood, blocking her view.

"Yeah, I'm trying to get this done so I can go riding with Gordy and Hiro later."

Lies and deception. They came easy now. Cooper pushed the thought out of his mind.

"Need any help?" She moved her head to one side as if trying to see the screen.

Cooper reached over and gave her a hug. "Thanks, Mom."

"What brought this on?" Mom hugged him back. She seemed pleasantly surprised. And distracted.

"Let me finish this up, and maybe I'll have you proofread it when I'm done."

"Okay." She gave him a squeeze. "Just let me know when you're ready."

Cooper didn't sit until she left the room. He banged out the letter, printed three copies, and had another thought. He made some quick changes, printed one copy, then deleted the file. He found envelopes in one of the desk drawers and printed those too.

He didn't start to relax until the letters were safely tucked away in his backpack.

Now all he had to do was add the phone number and wait until dark.

Cooper met Hiro and Gordy in the cabin of *The Getaway* after dinner. Cooper laid the copies of the letter and the four envelopes on the small built-in table.

"Don't touch them," Cooper said. "If they dust them for fingerprints, we only want them to find one pair."

"Good thinking," Hiro said. "Maybe you'll make a good cop yourself."

Cooper didn't want to be a cop. He wanted to get as far away from them as he could.

Gordy counted the envelopes. "Why the extras?"

"One copy for me to keep. One for the Daily Herald."

"The Herald?"

"I was thinking." Cooper picked up the envelope and slapped it on his open palm. "If the police don't take the letter seriously, maybe the paper will. I just had to make some changes to this copy."

"I'm impressed," Gordy said. "Looks like you've covered all the bases."

Cooper printed the phone number on the police copies of the

letter and added "Between 3:30 and 4:30 p.m. ONLY." He didn't want anyone trying to call him while he was at school or at the dinner table. He wrote slow and neat. If the police showed it to any one of his teachers, they definitely wouldn't recognize the writing as being his.

"Maybe we should say something about Lunk," Hiro said.

"And if they find he's not involved they'll *really* think we're trying to mess up their investigation," Cooper said.

"You still think he had nothing to do with it. I think that's a problem."

"Let's just say I'm not convinced. Besides, I'm not going to risk retyping this."

Hiro didn't argue, but she didn't look happy either.

"What about the printer?" Gordy pointed at the envelopes. "Can they trace it back to you by looking at the text under a microscope or something?"

"We're okay," Hiro said. "The police have his fingerprints and DNA. If they suspect him enough personally to bring him in for questioning, they won't need the printer to tie him to the crime scene."

She pretty much summed it up. Not exactly a comforting reminder. They hung around *The Getaway* until just after the library closed. Cooper felt a strange mix of excitement and fear when he pulled his new bike from the shed, like he was on some kind of secret mission. The fear? He just might be dismantling part of his cover at the same time.

Gordy led the pack on the bike path through Kimball Hill Park and under Kirchoff Road. He looped around on the other side. Hiro followed next and Cooper took up the rear. Frank 'n Stein's sat deathly still. The neon in the windows reminded him of last Thursday night, only four days ago. It seemed way longer than that.

They approached the library from the backside. Several cars were in the employee lot, but the regular lot sat empty. The lines between the spaces gave an eerie glow in the moonlight. For some reason it made Cooper think of a graveyard. He was glad Gordy and Hiro came along. He pedaled harder. *Let's get this done.*

Gordy coasted to a stop in front of the library and took lookout duty. Hiro dropped off far enough from the entrance to stay off to the side just in case the library had a camera mounted to monitor the area. Cooper left his bike with her, pulled up his hood, and hustled up to the glass double doors.

Lights were on, but everything looked still. He fished the envelopes from his pack.

"Give to the Rolling Meadows Police. Urgent." Cooper whispered as he read aloud. He opened the book return night drop and hesitated for a moment.

"What are you waiting for?" Hiro motioned for him to hurry.

Cooper dropped the letter in the book return and closed the door. He heard the faint whoosh as the letter slid down the incline. No turning back now. He did the same with the envelope addressed to the Daily Herald.

"Let's go," he said.

Hiro nodded.

Biking back seemed shorter. They cut over to the post office to drop the other police letter in the mail box, then biked through the park like three ghosts. The wind felt cool and clean against Cooper's face. The wind rushing in his ears soothed him in its own way. Adrenalin still pumping, he felt like he could ride all night, but he knew he'd better get back before his parents started asking questions.

"Great night, Coop." Gordy rode up alongside him. "I gotta get back." Gordy gave a quick wave and peeled off toward his house.

He was right. It felt good to fight back, even if it was in a small way.

Cooper rode alongside Hiro to her house and coasted to a stop. He put a foot down and looked at Hiro. "Are you okay with me?"

"Getting there." She smiled.

"*Getting* there?"Cooper had expected something more. Like a little more gratitude. He took a risk for all of them. The letter may not have been a huge thing, but at least it was a step in the right direction.

Her smile changed. A sad smile. "I hope this works. I really do. But even if they catch those scumbags, I don't think I can be truly happy until we come clean. To actually go, like in person, to the police, or our parents, or *somebody*."

The good feeling he'd enjoyed melted away. "Look. I'm doing what I can. I want those guys caught too. But I'm not going to risk you or Gordy or my family to do it."

"Or you. You left yourself out of it," Hiro said. "A lot of this has to do with protecting *you*."

"Okay. Yeah. But *I'm* the one they saw. It's *my* house key they have."

Hiro nodded—like she agreed but not totally. "If you're wrong about police being involved—what then?"

"You seem to have all the answers. Why don't you tell me?"

Hiro paused. "You're risking all of us to protect you."

"What?" He felt his face heat up instantly. "That's crazy. I'm trying to protect all of us."

"But you can't. Don't you see that? We need police protection. We need our parents involved. You may think you're some kind of protector here, but you're putting all of us in danger—and that's the truth."

"The *truth*?"

"Yeah," Hiro said. "There was a time that meant something to you."

He didn't want to hear any more of this. Not another word. Cooper pushed off and started pedaling. "G'nite, Hiro." After the effort he'd just made, he didn't want to be told that it wasn't enough—or that it was all about protecting *him*.

"Coop!"

He didn't turn around.

"C'mon. Don't be mad. Friends are supposed to be able to talk."

Friends. Right. He pedaled harder. He wanted to get away from her. From everyone. But the faster he went the more miserable he felt. Riding off like this had to hurt her. Something he never wanted to do. He turned the corner and slowed his pace. Her words echoed in his head. He couldn't stand the thought of being around her right now. Couldn't stand the way she looked at him—like he wasn't doing enough. But the thought of not being with her was worse.

The adrenaline high he'd gotten from delivering the letter was long gone. He felt drained. Empty. He pedaled and coasted. Pedaled and coasted. The darkness surrounded him. Went through him. Suddenly, in his world of lies, the truth came to him. It wasn't Hiro he'd wanted to get away from. It was himself.

CHAPTER 27

Cooper woke with a heavy sense of dread in his stomach. He lay in bed and checked the clock. The alarm was due to ring in just a few minutes. Normally he'd roll over and wait for the alarm to ring. And hit the snooze button when it did. Instead, he turned off the alarm and stared at the ceiling.

Fudge sat up and laid a groggy head on the edge of his bed. He worked his hand under her collar and gave her a good scratch. Why hadn't he just turned around when Hiro called him? Maybe he wanted to punish her. Make her feel really bad. But he ended up doing a number on himself at the same time. *Stupid.*

The first chance he could, he was going to make it right. He'd see her at the bus stop and say he was sorry the moment he saw her. Cooper imagined the scene in his mind. It made him feel a little better, but the dread still hunkered down in his stomach.

He knew the incident with Hiro was only part of the problem.

It was the lies. The deception. Enough to fill a backpack. And when he woke up every morning he put the pack on and carried it until he drifted off in sleep. The pack felt heavier today.

He forced himself to think of the letters to the police and the newspaper. It was a good move. Even Hiro admitted that. It was also a step toward detection. He reached under his pillow and pulled out the phone Hiro and Gordy had picked up.

Would the police or the newspaper actually call today? He hoped not. The letter should be enough for the police to go on. The newspaper too. The details about the robbery should be enough to prove he was actually there. But what if they called to try to get more information? Could they put a trace on a cell phone? Would they try to keep him on the phone long enough so they could track him down?

"Hello. Hullo." Cooper tested his phone voice. What if Hammer recognized him?

Cooper sat up and swung his legs over the side of the bed. One thing was certain. He would keep the phone off until after he was out of school. Until 3:30, just like he put in the note. He stepped over to his desk and slipped the phone in his jeans pocket. And he'd be sure to be in Kimball Hill Park before he turned it on. Someplace far enough from the house in case the police *were* able to trace the call.

He'd need some way to disguise his voice. Cooper shuffled into the bathroom. The toilet paper roll was nearly empty. He changed out the roll and stuffed a wad of toilet paper in the tube.

Fudge stood by his bedroom door and looked at him.

He put the tube to his mouth like a bullhorn. "Want to go out, girl?" The words sounded muffled and echoed through the tube.

She cocked her head and wagged her tail.

"Wish I could stay here with you today," he whispered, pocketing the tube. "Or maybe just hide out in *The Getaway* all day."

Only Gordy met him at the bus stop. Hiro still hadn't showed up when the bus lumbered around the corner. She'd never missed the bus as long as Cooper knew her. Maybe she was sick. Sick of him. He hated the thought that he couldn't straighten things out with her. That he couldn't apologize for getting mad at her the night before. But she'd asked for it, hadn't she? Why did she have to keep pushing him to break the Code?

Hiro didn't show for class either. Maybe she really *was* sick. Cooper's stomach wasn't feeling so hot either—but he knew it had nothing to do with a bug. Now he'd have to wait until after school to make it right with Hiro.

He felt the phone in his pocket. He'd hoped Gordy and Hiro would both be with him if a call came after school. Now it might be just Gordy.

Cooper tried to function with a mind that stayed divided all morning. Even while in class, he kept checking the clock. The library opened at 9:00 a.m. By 9:30 he figured the police had his letter. They'd be checking out the details.

And waiting to call him.

No. He pushed the thinking out of his mind. Not waiting for anything. The police would start looking for Elvis and the clown and Mr. Lucky. Why would they waste their time trying to talk to him?

By the time he made his way to English, the idea of a call from the police consumed him.

He walked alongside Gordy and spoke quietly, the noisy halls providing a place to talk without being overheard. "What if they record my voice and analyze it somehow?"

"Count on it," Gordy said.

"Great."

"Just disguise your voice."

"I'm already on that. I'm just not sure if I should speak in a high or a low voice."

Gordy shook his head. "Not good enough. If they record you, and they will, they'll be able to play it back at different speeds to nail your normal voice."

"I plan to muffle it too."

"Yeah. Talk with your mouth full. I do it all the time."

Cooper smiled.

The smile slid off his face when he entered the classroom. A copy of the Daily Herald sat on Miss Ferrand's desk. There, on the front page, was a picture of Frank 'n Stein's and a headline that read, "Witness Letter Raises More Questions."

Gordy must have seen it too. He nearly came to a complete stop.

"How did it get in the paper already?"

Exactly Cooper's thoughts. The paper gets delivered early. Before the library opens.

The bell interrupted his thoughts, and Miss Ferrand wasted no time getting down to business. She shut the door and walked back to her desk. She picked up the paper and held it up so everyone could see it. The class quieted down almost immediately.

"According to today's Daily Herald, last night somebody slipped a letter addressed to the police and another one addressed to the paper in the library night drop." She sat on the edge of her desk. "Someone in the library emptied the drop box before they went home for the night and found them."

That answered the timing question.

"I'm going to read parts of the article to you." She looked around the room. Slowly. Stopping to get eye contact with each of the boys.

Hiro's empty desk in front of him made him feel way more exposed than normal.

"The police believe that the person who wrote the letter is in one of my eighth grade classes."

The room erupted in excited chatter. Girls leaned across the aisles talking to each other and shooting the boys suspicious looks.

Cooper reached in his backpack and put his English book on his desk. Actually, Jake Mickel's book.

Kelsey Seals turned around and looked at Cooper's desk, then at Jake's behind her. "Where's your English book today, Jake?"

"I don't know," he said. "Somebody must have swiped it."

She cocked her head to the side just a bit—her distrust obvious. Eliza Miller stared at Jake, eyes wide.

Jake turned to Cooper. "Honest. I had it in my locker."

"It'll turn up," Cooper said. *But not until this is all over.*

Miss Ferrand stood and slowly walked between the rows of desks. She kept talking and focusing on the boys, but Cooper wasn't following. He tried to figure out what he was going to do when she looked at Gordy. Or at him.

When she came to Gordy, Cooper watched him as intently as Miss Ferrand did. He looked guilty as sin. Cooper knocked his book on the floor.

"Sorry," he said.

"You're a klutz, MacKinnon," Jake Mickel said.

Riley Steiner and his pack laughed, but it was just enough to do the job. She locked her eyes on him as if she knew the book had been a diversion. He forced himself to look right into her eyes. Any wavering and he'd be giving himself away.

She looked at him longer than anyone else in the room so far. Her eyes were light blue. Gray, really. Weak looking eyes. Cooper had to stay strong. He tried to look right through her eyes into her head. Finally she turned away to look at the next suspect.

She continued through the room, but never went back to Gordy. After her little staring game was over, she made some notes on a legal pad on her desk, then folded the newspaper so she could hold it with one hand without it flopping over.

*"Dear Daily Herald,"*she read, then paused and looked up as if to make sure everyone in class was listening.

The entire class sat stone still. Apparently satisfied, she sat on the corner of her desk again and focused on the newspaper.

"The police are looking for a boy in junior high in connection with the robbery at Frank 'n Stein's last Thursday night. I was there. The way they're pushing, sometimes I wonder if they think I'm the one who robbed Frank Mustacci. That isn't true. I didn't rob the diner or hurt Mr. Mustacci. Frank let me stay while he cleaned up. When I was ready to leave, the front door was locked. I called for Frank because I figured he had the keys. I think he was taking a load of garbage to the dumpster.

I was at the front counter when the back door burst open—and somebody pushed Frank inside. I hid behind the counter and two men beat Frank and forced him to give the money from the cash register. Then they said they knew about his safe and made him give the combination. Frank went for a knife, and the two of them beat him again.

While they were opening the safe, I escaped using Frank's keys. He was lying on his back behind the counter, with his head toward the dining area. I thought he was dead. Honest."

A collective gasp escaped from the room. Ferrand paused and nodded, obviously pleased by the reaction. She scanned the room. Maybe she hoped to see one of the boys unmoved by it all, or nervous. Cooper let his jaw go slack, his mouth hang open as if in total disbelief of what he was hearing. Her eyes caught his for a moment and then moved on.

She went back to reading the paper.

"The men heard me escaping and started after me. I barely made it out the front door and turned the lock in time. I didn't get a good look at them. They were wearing masks. One wore a clown mask. One wore an Elvis one. The clown had a hoarse-sounding voice. Elvis sounded like a DJ. They both had cop pants on. They talked to a third guy, but I never heard or got a good look at him. He was the driver, I think. He came in after they beat up Frank. They called him "Mr. Lucky."

That's why I'm not going to the police in person. I don't know who I can trust. I can't identify these guys anyway, so the police can stop looking for me. They need to find out who did this and stop wasting their time chasing after me.

The one guy got a pretty good look at me. And he threatened me. So don't even try to get me to say anything more. I have nothing more to say. He pulled the surveillance camera hard drive, which I grabbed on my way out. It won't help anybody to have it, but it may hurt me. I was in plain sight of the camera. The hard drive will prove I didn't do anything wrong, but it will also identify me. So it stays with me. That's everything I know about the robbery.

I am going to write a cell phone number on the bottom of this letter. I will answer the phone between 3:30 and 4:30 pm to answer any question you may need to ask for me to show this isn't some prank. I can prove I was there. I can tell you exactly where Frank was laying. I can tell you what was on the floor in front of the counter. I can tell you what they used to break the front window to get at me. I can tell you what I left behind at one of the tables. Find the real robbers. Nail the monsters that did this to Frank Mustacci. Stop looking for me.

Sincerely, "Silence is Golden"

Cooper glanced around the room. Girls sat like zombies with pale faces and wide-eyed stares. Kelsey Seals turned, mouth partially open like she wanted to say something, but couldn't figure out how. Probably a first for her. Eliza Miller, biting her lower lip, stared at Jacob Mickel like she already had the mystery witness figured out.

The boys' eyes were on fire. Like they *wish* they'd written the letter. They had no idea what they were asking for. Cooper tried to mirror their faces.

Miss Ferrand looked up. "The article goes on to speculate on different theories. The paper believes the note may be legitimate, and they intend to follow up. According to some unnamed source in the police department, the police share a similar opinion. Which brings me to the next point."

She walked up and down each aisle. Slowly. So slowly. Ignoring the girls, but deliberately looking at each of the boys as she did. "The writer of this letter did a very brave thing. And he has every right to be scared right now." She looked directly at Cooper.

He crumpled up his brow and tried to muster up a confused expression. He looked behind him and then back at her. She moved on.

"I want to send my own message to this person." She went to the white board and wrote a phone number with a red marker. "This is the school phone number. I have a mailbox just like every other teacher. You call me. Leave a message. I can help. I'll check my messages right up until when I go to bed. Questions?"

Cooper had some questions for her. Like, was she crazy? Did she really think he would open up to her?

Kelsey Seals raised her hand. "What will you do?" Obviously she'd found her voice.

"I'll go straight to the top," she said. "The principal is very good friends with Detective Hammer. We'll make sure the witness is protected."

Cooper slouched down in his seat. She *was* crazy.

"Like the witness protection program or something?" Jake Mickel blurted it out. One of the jealous boys.

"I don't think so. But he'll be safe. Trust me on that."

Trust *her*? The one who gave pop quizzes with trick questions? Right.

Eliza Miller raised her hand, cautiously, like she wasn't sure she should. "What if, like, somebody suspects somebody else in the class?" Her eyes darted toward Mickel for an instant. "What should we do?"

"Talk to me and tell me why," Ferrand said.

This thing could turn into a real witch hunt. Nice move, Miss Ferrand.

More hands shot up. More mindless questions. Cooper tuned most of them out. His mind snapped back to Hiro. Did the Yakimotos get a paper? He imagined her absorbing the article. At least she should be happy the plan worked.

"Paper and pencil out, everyone."

Miss Ferrand's voice pulled him back into the classroom. "I want each of you to write my number down right now." She pointed at the board. "And you call me. Understand?"

Maybe the principal put a bounty on his head.

The noise level went up as kids scrounged in backpacks for something to write on. Cooper fished out a scrap of paper. He looked up at the number like he seriously intended to write it down. Instead he wrote *fat chance* across the paper, folded it and slipped it in his pocket.

He watched Gordy hesitate for a moment, then write something on the paper. He looked at the number on the board again and checked his paper as if to be sure he got it right. Gordy put on a convincing show of it—and hopefully that's all it was.

"Or if you want to talk after class, I'm here for you. Understand?"

Heads nodded all over the room. Cooper nodded his head too. He understood all right, but he'd stick to the Code of Silence, thank you very much.

Miss Ferrand made another notation on her legal pad, then looked directly at Cooper. "Does everyone have my number?"

Cooper nodded again, but had the uneasy feeling she was especially concerned that he wrote it down. That whole "women's intuition" stuff was spooky. Something nobody could really explain or understand. Hiro had an extra dose of it.

Miss Ferrand looked at him again, picked up her legal pad, and started toward him. Maybe she didn't want to take a chance on whether he'd stay and talk or not. She looked like a reporter on her way to a juicy interview.

The bell rang, and the kids erupted into excited talk like it had been bottled up inside them for days, and they couldn't handle the pressure anymore.

Girls jumped up in the aisles and hovered around Miss Ferrand as if they needed protection somehow. Seals and Miller led the charge. Which was just fine with Cooper. He slipped by her in the confusion and made a beeline for the door with Gordy right on his heels.

"Cooper MacKinnon!"

He heard her call just as he rounded the corner into the hall, but acted like he didn't hear a thing. Out of her line of sight, he took off at a run. He figured he had five or six seconds before she'd break free from the girls in class and make it to the hallway.

Kids burst out of other classrooms and filled the halls. Cooper kept count of the seconds. Three, four, five. He ducked in front of a herd of seventh graders piling out of Mrs. Brittain's class and stopped running. Gordy scooted in right next to him.

"Don't look back," Cooper said. He kept his head down and walked fast, hoping she wouldn't spot him.

Maybe Hiro had the right idea. Taking a sick day might be good for his health.

CHAPTER 28

"This is nuts," Gordy said, hustling to keep up with him. "Think she suspects us?"

"Not us. Me."

"Why just you?"

"The letter made it sound like I was alone. She's looking for only one person."

"Think you're at the top of her suspect list?"

Cooper chanced a look over his shoulder to make sure she wasn't following. "I don't know why, but by the way she looks at me ... yeah."

"Top of Hammer's list. Top of Ferrand's list. Ditching her won't help any."

"Thanks for the reminder. I only need to buy some time."

They hustled into the cafeteria side by side. Cooper stopped and pulled a sweatshirt from his backpack and pulled it over his head.

Gordy gave him a questioning look. "What are you doing?"

"Changing how I look a bit. I wouldn't be surprised if Miss Ferrand comes looking for me during lunch."

"Tell me you're not going to pull the hood up."

Cooper smiled and kept walking.

"I wish Hiro was here," Gordy said.

Hiro. Cooper's heart sunk. "Me too."

"Ferrand will expect us to sit together. Think we should split up?"

"Might help." Cooper scanned the lunchroom. "See you on the bus."

Gordy nodded and headed for the hot lunch line. Cooper pulled his bag lunch from his backpack and looked for someplace to sit. He wanted to find a spot all to himself so he could think. And keep an eye out for Miss Ferrand. But sitting alone somewhere was a little obvious. The smart thing would be to sit somewhere he wouldn't normally consider sitting. Like *under* a table.

A burst of laughter from a table full of girls caught his attention, and probably every other person in the cafeteria. Julie VonMoose had an empty spot next to her, but he didn't feel *that* desperate.

Cooper looked over his shoulder and checked the entrance. Still gobs of kids piling in, but no Miss Ferrand. He couldn't keep standing in the middle of the aisle. If she walked through the doorway he'd be dead.

Steiner, Tellshow, and Demel pushed through, talking loud and tough. Clearly wishing they were a part of the unfolding drama around the robbery, and trying to make up for the fact that they weren't.

Cooper started toward a table at an opposite corner of the cafeteria than he usually sat. He'd get a good view of the cafeteria, and an exit door was just a matter of feet away. There were several empty spaces. Cooper swung a leg over the bench and sat quickly, keeping an eye on the entrance. He pulled out his sandwich and took a bite.

"Hey, MacKinnon. Have a fight with Gordo or something?"

Lunk's voice. Cooper's stomach tightened. He hoped he would just keep going.

No such luck. Lunk swung a leg over the bench and sat across from him with a tray loaded nearly as heavy as Gordy's normally was.

Lunk eyed him through shaggy black hair. "So why aren't you sitting with Gordo and Yaki-dodo?"

"Yakimoto. Hiroko Yakimoto." Cooper chomped another hunk of sandwich. "Hiro isn't here today. Must be sick."

"She's *always* sick." Lunk smiled. "Wants to be a cop. Right? Definitely something sick with that girl."

Cooper looked past him. Miss Ferrand stood just inside the cafeteria doors scanning the room.

Lunk followed Cooper's gaze, then studied him, eyes squinting just a bit. "Waiting for someone?"

"Uh-uh." Cooper lowered his head just a bit and focused on his peanut butter sandwich.

Miss Ferrand started walking. Slowly, like a prison guard pacing the cell block, watching the inmates. He could see her scanning the tables. Not a routine, making sure everything is under control type scan. She was looking for someone. *Him.*

Lunch wasn't even close to being over. Was she going to walk around the entire perimeter of the room like this? She reminded him of a cat he'd seen stalking a bird in their backyard. The cat moved slowly. Deliberately. Getting closer and closer to the little chickadee that was busily tearing into bread Mom had thrown out in the yard. Cooper envisioned the cat pouncing on the unsuspecting bird at any moment. He'd pulled off his shoe and threw it at the cat just in time.

Cooper saw Gordy come out of the hot lunch line. He walked to the usual table with his tray in front of him and sat down. Ferrand was on him like the paparazzi. Gordy shrugged and looked around the room, while he talked to her. Miss Ferrand nodded briefly, and resumed her search. Whatever Gordy told her must have worked.

Miss Ferrand got closer. Arms folded across her chest, her claws painted red. A cat on the prowl. And Cooper was the bird.

"*Avoiding* someone?" Lunk leaned in closer. The corner of his mouth turned up in a smile. The kind of smile that said he knew.

Hammer had singled him out. Ferrand was zeroing in. Now Lunk. Was everyone psychic or was he that easy to read?

Cooper ignored Lunk and tried not to look at Miss Ferrand.

He couldn't help but steal a glance. She'd rounded the corner and slowly patrolled his way. He needed a shoe.

"You in some kind of trouble?" Lunk's voice was low.

Cooper didn't answer. He needed some quick, witty remark. A comeback that would get him off the hook. But he couldn't think. His brain seemed as mushy as the peanut butter sandwich in his stomach.

"I'm taking that as a *yes*," Lunk said. He looked down the aisle. "You want to get out of here?"

Cooper stared at his lunch bag. What's the worst that could happen if Miss Ferrand had a little talk with him? She'd ask some questions. He'd hatch more lies. He was getting pretty good at avoiding the truth. The real issue was whether she would see through him. And if she did, would she talk to the principal, or Detective Hammer? All the Detective needed was a decent reason to single him out for questioning. Ferrand might be able to supply that if she could get him one-on-one.

The course seemed clear. *Avoid the talk*. Stall it off. No good could come of it, and her snooping around could threaten the Code.

"Not in a very talkative mood, are you, MacKinnon?" Lunk said.

"My stomach," Cooper said. "A little messed up."

"Anything to do with Ferrand?"

Cooper glanced over. She couldn't have been more than thirty feet away. She'd stopped walking for the moment, giving the room another visual sweep from that vantage point. She still didn't see him, but it was only a matter of seconds now. He braced himself. Told himself to relax. Stay calm.

"I'll distract her," Lunk said.

"What?" Cooper looked at him.

Lunk nodded toward the side exit. "Hit the washroom around the corner until the end of the period. You'll be safe there."

Without waiting for a response, Lunk stood and grabbed his

tray. He plowed past some students standing in the aisle—and right into Miss Ferrand.

His tray crashed to the floor, the sound echoing off the cinder block walls. Miss Ferrand stood with her hands out to her side looking at ketchup blotches on her clothes.

Kids jumped up from their seats for a better view. Riley Steiner and his boys stood on a bench leading the entire cafeteria in whistles, claps, and cheers.

"Sorry, Miss Ferrand." Lunk's voice sounded sincere over all the other noise.

Cooper jumped from his seat, and stumbled over his backpack. A black permanent marker spilled out. And the phone. He shouldered the pack, scooped up the phone and marker and jammed them in his pocket as he hustled for the exit. Once around the corner he ran for the men's room. He kept running until he locked himself in the handicapped stall.

Had Miss Ferrand seen him scoot out of the lunchroom? What would she think now? If she did see him, he'd be on her most wanted list for sure. And what about Lunk? He owed him some kind of explanation—but what?

Cooper hung his backpack on the hook behind the door. Pulling the phone from his pocket, he turned it on. The phone came to life. A little part of him wished it didn't. If it was broken, he wouldn't have to worry about getting a call from the police. He turned the phone off as quickly as he could, fearing the police might try calling early.

He wondered what Miss Ferrand was doing now. Mopping herself up in the ladies room? Escorting Lunk to the office? Either of these would keep her distracted. What if she was talking to Gordy? Pumping him with questions. Watching his eyes.

Hiro picked a lousy day to stay home. She'd abandoned them. If she'd been here, at least he wouldn't have to worry about Gordy taking on Miss Ferrand by himself.

But he'd escaped another potential trap. Barely. This was crazy.

He leaned against the stall and waited for the period bell to ring. He was innocent. He hadn't done anything wrong, yet here he was hiding in the bathroom. He wanted to shout it out loud. Over the school PA system. Tell everyone he didn't do anything wrong.

The stall partitions had been painted over who knows how many times, erasing brainless messages guys wrote. The current paint was about the color of buckskin. Not the smartest shade to discourage guys who were into graffiti. Cooper had never written on a wall before. He stared at it. And pulled the permanent marker from his pocket.

When the bell rang, he stepped back and looked at the inside of the wall like he was seeing it for the first time. Written in three inch black letters were the words "I did nothing wrong! I didn't do it!"

What was I thinking? Cooper grabbed a piece of toilet paper and rubbed one of the letters. It didn't even smudge. *Idiot.* He grabbed his backpack, slung it over his shoulder, and used the toilet paper to open the latch.

The outer door of the bathroom opened. He heard voices. Cooper hurried to the sink to wash. Two guys walked in, but didn't even look at Cooper. Lunk was right behind them.

Cooper saw him in the mirror. Lunk looked at him, and then at the stall door yawning open. Cooper wanted to say thanks, but the words didn't come. Instead, he stepped away from the sink, and without bothering to dry his hands, went for the door.

He totally expected Lunk to follow him. When he sensed that he was pushing through the door alone, he felt a measure of relief. Cooper glanced over his shoulder and tensed. Lunk disappeared into the handicapped stall.

CHAPTER 29

Cooper didn't see Miss Ferrand for the rest of the afternoon, but he kept his head down in the halls between classes, just in case. Maybe she went home to change. The final bell rang, and he hit a set of side doors and circled around the outside of the building. He wasn't going to risk the main doors. He had to focus on other things now—like the fact he might get a call from the police on the cell in his pocket. He had to handle it right. Quick. Disguise his voice. And not give anything away.

The safest thing would be to walk home. Explain to Gordy later. To get on the bus was to potentially walk into a trap; but if he walked, he might not make it to the park before the phone call came.

Cooper stayed in the front of the building, but stalled getting on the bus. He'd hop aboard just before it left. If Miss Ferrand or the principal came looking for him, he'd be a sitting duck on the bus.

Gordy found him easy enough.

"Miss Ferrand ever find you?" Gordy said.

"No."

Gordy looked at him. "Just how do you plan to avoid her in English tomorrow?"

"Great question," Cooper said. "I don't know. I just have to make it through today first." He scanned the mass of students gushing out of the school. A couple of teachers were supervising by the bus lines. But no Miss Ferrand.

Lunk pushed through the crowd and headed their way. *Great.* Dread settled in Cooper's stomach.

"Hey, MacKinnon."

Lunk's voice sounded casual enough, but he had an intensity in his eyes.

Gordy took a step back.

Cooper looked past him toward the exit doors. "Thanks for what you did at lunchtime."

Lunk gave a half smile. "I enjoyed it. You want to tell me what is going on?"

A direct question. One Cooper didn't want to answer. Something about Lunk's eyes said he had a pretty good boloney detector himself.

"It was stupid," Cooper said. He brushed on a smile. "I overreacted to something she said in class. I had a feeling she wanted to talk to me about it."

"Just wondering." Lunk pulled out a pocket spiral notebook. "Either of you have a marker I can borrow?"

The question sounded innocent, but warnings went off in Cooper's head. Did he really need a marker, or did Lunk want to see if Cooper had one?

Gordy shrugged. "Not me. Cooper always has one in his pack. Right, Coop?"

Cooper cringed inside. "Yeah. I, ah, should have one somewhere." He lowered his backpack and hovered over it, making a show of checking each compartment. All the while he knew the marker was in his jeans pocket.

The crowds of students thinned, forming spaghetti lines onto the buses. In a minute they'd have to get on the bus or risk being spotted too easily on the sidewalk. Could he stall that long?

"I need black," Lunk said. "Permanent."

"That's the only kind he carries," Gordy said.

Great, Gordy. Cooper stood and shrugged. "Must have lost it."

Gordy pointed. "How 'bout your pockets?"

Cooper wanted to glare at Gordy, but Lunk's eyes were locked on him. He checked his pockets, slowly. He hoped Lunk would tell him to forget it. Tell him he didn't need it anyway. He felt it in his right front pocket. Should he pull it out?

Lunk kept his eyes on him. He didn't look like a guy who was going to let it go. Cooper pulled the marker out. "Will this work?" He handed Lunk the marker.

Lunk pulled off the cap and looked at the tip. "It looks perfect."

"We gotta go," Cooper said. "Keep the marker until tomorrow. We'd better catch our bus." He shouldered his pack.

Gordy started trotting toward the sidewalk. Cooper followed, but Lunk called after him.

"Tell me, MacKinnon. Exactly *what* didn't you do?"

"Ride my bike. So if I miss the bus, I'm toast. We can talk tomorrow."

Lunk stood there, his weight settled mainly on one foot. The look on his face said he intended to follow up.

And if he did, Cooper really *was* toast.

CHAPTER 30

Cooper felt weak when he dropped onto the seat beside Gordy.

Gordy frowned. "What happened to you?"

"I think Lunk is on to me."

"You sure?"

"He knows I'm hiding something. He just doesn't know *what*."

Gordy twisted to look out the window as if he thought Lunk might be watching them. Reading their lips. "What did you tell him?"

"Nothing. Thankfully we had to get on the bus."

The bus door closed and the driver eased away from the curb.

Gordy gave a low whistle. "Close call."

"Too close." He'd made it through another day, but they were getting harder. And it wasn't over yet.

He checked his watch. In thirty minutes he'd be turning on his phone, and the thought of that just added to his mounting concerns about Miss Ferrand and Lunk. And *Hiro*.

Gordy didn't speak until the bus pulled out of the parking lot. "Think the police will call?"

"I'm sure of it." As much as he dreaded it, he also knew this was his chance. It would be worth it if he could get the police to stop looking for him and put all their efforts into finding Elvis, Mr. Clown, and Mr. Lucky. Then he'd straighten things out with Hiro.

"I'm glad *I* don't have to talk to them," Gordy said. "Think Hiro will show?"

"Hope so." Cooper felt more confident when she was around, and if a call came from the police, he'd need all the help he could get. But most of all he wanted to make things right with her about last night. He wanted her to know he was sorry about riding off angry.

The bus swayed down Plum Grove Road, picking up speed. Cooper reached in his backpack and pulled out the cell. Holding it in his hand, he stared out the window. *Did the letter really help the police? Were they any closer to finding the men who put Frank in the coma?* Cooper's knee started shaking.

By the time the bus reached their stop, Cooper felt like his whole body was shaking. The two boys hustled off the bus.

Gordy started across the street as soon as the bus passed. "Meet you in five minutes?"

"Right." Cooper jammed the cell in his pocket and took off at a run for his house. The front door was locked, so he circled around to the back. Peering through the glass on the back door, he saw Mom with her back to him working at the kitchen counter. The fact that she wore the black apron meant she'd been baking. He tapped on the glass. Mom turned and smiled. Fudge bounded into the kitchen barking her security dog bark, which turned into a tail swinging "let's go out and play" bark the moment she saw Cooper.

His mom pulled open the door and gave him a hug. He was only slightly taller than her, but just enough to look over her shoulder at the microwave clock. He had to get moving.

She kissed him on the cheek. "Still didn't find your key?"

"Nope. Did you talk to dad about getting the locks changed?"

"No." She opened the refrigerator door. "Dad figures it will show up. Nothing to worry about."

That's exactly what worried Cooper ... that the key *would* show up. In the hands of Elvis. Or the clown. Or Hammer. His mind flew back to the stool crashing through the window the night of the robbery. Changing locks wouldn't stop these guys anyway.

"What would you like for a snack?" Mom said. "Peanut butter sandwich? Cookies? I just baked a fresh batch."

The five minutes had to be nearly up. "Not right now. I have to meet Gordy. He's probably out front waiting for me."

"There's always time for a snack. I'll get one for Gordy too." Mom disappeared toward the front door.

Cooper followed with Fudge right at his side. Mom opened the door and swung open the screen. Gordy stood in front of the porch holding his bike. The surprise on his face was obvious.

"How about a little snack, Gordy?"

Gordy glanced his way, and Cooper shook his head slightly.

"Aw, thanks, Aunt Dana. Maybe later."

"Gordon Digby, you never turn down a snack." She looked back at Cooper, suspicion in her eyes. "What are you boys up to?"

"Just riding bikes, right Coop?"

Cooper nodded.

Mom didn't look convinced. "You're not planning to shoot that potato gun are you?"

"No. Honest, Mom. We're just going to ride around a little. Maybe play some ball."

"Then you can take time for a snack." She walked past him into the house.

The way she said it, it was almost like a test. If he didn't have a snack, she'd know they were up to something. Then there'd be more questions. More lies.

"I guess a snack would be a good idea," Cooper said. He motioned for Gordy to follow.

"What would you like?"

"Cookies," Cooper said. It would be quicker.

Mom pulled out the chocolate chips and set them on the table. Gordy started right in and sat down like he had no idea what time it really was. Cooper grabbed one too, sat across from him, and ate fast. Fudge laid her head on his leg.

Mom opened the freezer and shifted things around on the

shelves. "I have some vanilla ice cream in here somewhere. How about I make an ice cream sandwich with those cookies?"

Gordy's eyes lit up. "Excellent!"

Cooper kicked him under the table and pointed at his wrist.

"How about you, Cooper?" Her voice sounded muffled by the freezer.

"The chocolate chips are perfect just like this." He broke off a piece and fed it to the Hoover under the table. Fudge sucked it up and swallowed it without even chewing.

Mom nodded and pulled the vanilla ice cream from the freezer. Cooper felt the phone in his pocket, thankful he hadn't turned it on yet.

The doorbell rang, and Cooper jumped to his feet. Fear-charged adrenalin. *What now?* If it was Miss Ferrand he might as well give it up. Trotting down the hall, he recognized the silhouette framed in the screen door. "Hiro."

"Ask her if she'd like a snack," Mom called after him.

Cooper swung open the door. "Where were you today?" Fudge bounded out and greeted her with a wagging tail and happy whimpers.

She bent down and kissed Fudge on the top of her head. "I'll explain later."

Her voice sounded fine. If she was sick, it wasn't a cold.

"Shouldn't we be leaving?" Hiro said.

"I'm trying."

Mom came around the corner wiping her hands on a towel. "Can I get you something, Hiro?"

Gordy followed her, holding the cookie ice cream sandwich like a Whopper.

Hiro smiled. "It looks really good, but we have to run. We're supposed to be at the park right now meeting someone."

Cooper's mom put her hands on her hips and eyed him. "First you were playing ball. Now you're meeting someone?"

Not good. Cooper hesitated, but only for an instant. "I can explain. Later."

"You can explain now, too."

She didn't look like she was going to budge.

Cooper sighed. "We *are* going to play a little ball. But there's also someone I've got to talk to. Just a guy I'm trying to help out a little—and I'm not even sure he'll show up. But I'm supposed to be there by 3:30—and if I don't leave now I'll be late."

Cooper's mom looked at him like she was trying to make up her mind.

Hiro cleared her throat. "Actually I've been the one trying to encourage Coop to talk."

Mom's shoulders relaxed and she gave Hiro a hug.

Cooper leaned over and gave his mom a kiss on the cheek. "If there's anything to tell, I'll fill you in later. Okay?"

She gave him a kiss back. "You'd better."

"If he doesn't," Hiro said, "I will."

Cooper had a feeling she really meant it, too.

Mom smiled. "Have a good time."

Minutes later Cooper left the residential section and wheeled his bike across Campbell Street and into Kimball Hill Park. Hiro still rode right next to him. It felt good to be on his new bike again. It felt better to be riding next to Hiro. He held his bat along the handlebars and a ball in his pocket. They rode in silence. She didn't offer any explanation as to why she missed school today—and he wasn't sure he wanted to ask.

What he really wanted to do was tell her how sorry he was for the way he acted last night. But it would have to wait. He had to get the phone call done first. He checked over his shoulder. Gordy lagged several houses back, trying to eat the ice cream sandwich as he rode.

The bike and jogging path ran between a small pond to the left and Salt Creek to the right. Ahead, a footbridge crossed the creek to connect with the bike path on the other side. Eventually the bike path on the other side of the creek led under Kirchoff Road to

Frank'n Stein's. Cooper wished he was heading there for a monster shake and fries right now.

"Hello. *Hello.* Hullo." Cooper practiced disguising his voice. His high voice sounded wimpy. Talking really low tickled his throat.

The park was the perfect place to field a call. He didn't want it too near his house, just in case the police were able to trace the cell. A public place was best, especially one like this where they could see police approaching from a good distance away. Far enough to allow them a chance to escape—and from the park they could take off in any direction. Campbell Street and Kirchoff Avenue ran parallel to each other, with Kimball Hill Park sandwiched right between them.

Cooper coasted the last twenty yards to the bridge and braked the moment he crossed. He ditched his bike and the bat in the tall grass next to the footbridge. Crouching, he worked his way down the embankment just a bit.

Hiro took her post on the top of the bridge, keeping an eye on things to the south. Kirchoff Road was clearly visible. A moment later Gordy stood opposite of her, keeping an eyeball peeled toward Campbell Street, in the direction from where they'd just come. From this vantage point they'd be able to spot any police cars in the area.

Cooper checked his watch. 3:35. He sat nearly under the bridge so he wouldn't be seen by anyone scoping out the park. If the police were patrolling the area, all they'd see was Gordy and Hiro standing on the bridge—and neither of them holding a phone.

Reaching in his pocket, Cooper pulled out the phone and pressed the power button. The phone came to life, and Cooper's heart picked up the pace. He fished out the toilet paper tube and made sure the wadding was still inside.

Hiro leaned over the railing. "You ready for this?"

Cooper nodded. Another lie. The truth? He was ready to chuck it all. Get away from it somehow. Escape. Be done with this. But just maybe the phone call was his ticket.

"Are you going to say something about Lunk?"

Cooper stared at her. "Like what?"

"Just ask them to check him out. Check his dad out."

"We'll see, okay?" It came out too forceful, too harsh.

Her lips disappeared in a tight line.

Great. He'd upset her again. Why couldn't she leave it alone?

"How long do you think we have before they can trace this thing?" Cooper wobbled the phone in his hand, trying to get her mind off the comment he'd just made.

Hiro shook her head. "Cell phone? No idea. Keep it short to be safe."

Right now he wished he hadn't given the police a phone number at all. He looked at his watch. "What time do you have, Hiro?"

"3:37."

"Maybe they won't call."

"Give 'em time." He hardly dared hope they wouldn't.

The phone chirped almost on cue.

Cooper's heart lurched. He cleared his throat, and before connecting, practiced saying hello several times, changing his voice a bit more every time he did.

"Grab it," Gordy hissed.

Cooper nodded, put the tube to his mouth, and pressed the button. No turning back now.

"Hello." He used the high voice.

"This is Rolling Meadows Police Detective Richard Hammer. Are you the one who wrote the letter?"

"Yes."

"What do I call you, friend?"

"Let's leave it at that."

"What?"

"Friend."

Hammer paused slightly. "Okay, *Friend.*"

Cooper sunk lower in the grass. "What do you want from me?"

"Your full cooperation."

"That's why I wrote the letter. You need to find those men."

"I want you to come in and talk."

"No."

"What are you afraid of?"

"I told you in the letter. Two of the men wore cop pants. I go to the police, and maybe I end up talking to one of *them*."

"Ridiculous."

"I won't take that chance." He glanced up at Hiro and Gordy. Both of them were on the same side of the bridge watching him and listening. So much for the lookout plan.

Hammer sighed. "Get a chest."

"What?"

"Get a chest. Be a man. Come to the police station and help us find these men."

Cooper felt his cheeks burning. He wished he'd gone with the low voice. "It's the phone or nothing. And you're almost out of time."

"Okay," Hammer said. "You say you were at Frank 'n Stein's during the robbery. How is it that they didn't see you?"

"I hid behind the counter. I told you that in the letter."

"Were you alone?"

Cooper looked up at Hiro and Gordy. "Yes. Just me."

"And you were the one on the bike at the Dunkin Donuts drive-thru?"

"Yes."

"If you're innocent, why did you take the hard drive for the surveillance cameras?"

"The guy they called Mr. Lucky disconnected it. I was afraid they'd be able to identify me."

"Do you still have it?"

Cooper hesitated. "Yes."

"Where is it?"

"Hidden where you'll never find it."

"I need that hard drive."

"I looked right into the camera. I can't give it to you."

"Can't or won't?"

Cooper could picture him with the mirrored lenses. "Won't."

Hiro motioned from above him and mouthed Lunk's name.

"Listen good," Hammer said. "I think you're wasting my time. You didn't describe anything to me that someone couldn't see through the window. So you rode your bike to Frank's and looked in the window before the police came. You saw him laying there and thought you'd get some thrills with your crazy story about men wearing latex masks."

Cooper fought back panic. "Know what I think? You might be the man in the Elvis mask."

Hammer didn't say a word. Cooper took it away from his ear for a second and checked the screen to see if the man disconnected.

Hiro pointed at her watch.

"Unless you give me that surveillance camera hard drive, how do I know there are any men at all? Maybe you don't want me to have the drive because there *were* no other men. Just you. Maybe a couple of friends, too. And you guys got in over your heads."

"No, no that isn't what happened at all."

"Only one way to prove that."

"Look, you just have to believe me. It's all true. You need to find those men"

"How can you prove to me you were really there—that you really saw all you claimed to have witnessed?"

Was Hammer really questioning whether he was there, or was this a stall tactic? Or an attempt to get him even more nervous so he'd mess up?

"I was there." Cooper's voice sounded more shrill.

"Give me proof."

Gordy motioned with both hands and drew one finger across his throat. "Cut it," he whispered.

"What more proof do you need?" Cooper said.

"Hard drive."

"No deal."

"I thought you wanted to help us?"

"They wore *masks*. I didn't. The hard drive won't help you find the robbers, just me. Forget it."

Using a high-pitched voice to stand up to a cop seemed incredibly stupid. Like robbing a bank with a squirt gun.

"Then I'm going to figure this is all some kind of elaborate joke on your part. You weren't even there. So I'm going to keep looking for the kid who was really there. And I'm going to find you, too."

Hiro tapped on her watch furiously. She scampered off the bridge and down the embankment. "Get out," she whispered.

He's stalling me. Cooper looked around, half expecting to see police cars roaring up to the park. "I'll send you more proof."

"When?"

"Tonight."

"What kind of proof?"

He *is* stalling.

"You'll see." Cooper pushed the disconnect button and sat there wishing he hadn't agreed to send more proof.

Hiro ran toward him the instant he put the phone down. "You should have mentioned Lunk's dad."

Cooper didn't want to go there. "He kept firing questions at me."

"What happened?" Gordy hustled off the bridge and slid down next to him.

"He wants more proof." He looked at Hiro. "How long was I on?"

Her eyes were open wide. "Too long. We should get out of here."

The phone rang again. All three of them jumped. Hammer calling back, no doubt. Or maybe it was the Herald. Cooper turned off the power. He wasn't sure how it all worked with cell phones, but what if they could still track him as long as the phone was on?

"Get down," Gordy shouted. "Police."

The three dropped as low as they could. Cooper peered through the tall weeds and grass. A Rolling Meadows Police car prowled down Campbell Street and pulled to the side of the road a couple hundred yards away, effectively blocking the most direct way home.

CHAPTER 31

"Think he saw us?" Cooper strained to see.

"I don't know," Gordy said. "What's he doing there?"

"Calling for backup?" Hiro's voice sounded as tiny as she was.

"Great." Cooper hugged the ground. Smelled the cool earth below his face. Wished he could burrow in somehow. Tunnel his way home.

Gordy shifted. "What now?"

"Keep still," Hiro said.

The police car didn't move. Was he watching them? If backup arrived, their chances of getting away would go way down.

Cooper raced through his options. If they took off now, there was only one cop to chase them, but then again maybe the cop wasn't even looking for them. To make a run for it now may tip him off. Sit tight and wait might be the smarter thing to do. But that didn't make it any easier.

Only a handful of people were in the park. If the three of them took off together, they'd certainly be noticed.

"Listen," Hiro said. She cocked her head in the direction of Kirchoff Road behind them.

A siren.

Cooper turned to get a visual. A squad car raced down the busy street, lights flashing.

Coincidence? Or maybe this was backup on the way. If he stopped on Kirchoff, they'd be blocked to the North *and* the South.

"What do we do?" Gordy poked his head up like a gopher. "They're going to box us in here or something."

"What do you think, Hiro?" Cooper regretted asking her the moment the words left his mouth. He knew what she wanted. A white flag.

"If we try to run, they'll catch us," she said.

Cooper army-crawled his way partially up the embankment for a better view. Gordy and Hiro's bikes were propped against the bridge. His lay on its side. Hugging the ground like it was trying to find cover too. His bat lay next to it. The police car on Campbell hadn't moved.

"Okay," Cooper said. "Plan B." He dug the baseball out of his pocket. "We go up there and play a little ball. I'll bat, you two field."

Hiro didn't say anything, but the way she played with her braid he figured she was working out the pros and cons in her head.

"We hide in plain sight," Cooper said. "We won't look as suspicious as we would riding away on our bikes."

Gordy grabbed Cooper's leg like he didn't want to be left behind. "How do we explain why we were down here by the creek?"

Cooper held up the ball. "Fishing the ball out." He looked at each of them and hoped he didn't look as scared at they did. Gordy had that wide-eyed guilty-as-sin look. "Ready?"

Cooper turned a shoebox-sized rock over and scooped out a hollow in the cool earth under it. He fished the phone out of his pocket, placed it in the hole and shifted the rock back in place. If he did get stopped and questioned, the phone might be his death warrant. Literally.

"Here we go." Cooper said a silent prayer, took a couple of deep breaths, and stood up. He fought the urge to look at the police car. His periphery vision would be enough to warn him if the car made a move.

Strolling up the embankment slow and easy, he picked up his bat and shouldered it. "C'mon you two," he called. The police car didn't move, but he could feel the cop watching him.

Gordy and Hiro climbed the embankment at the same time.

"Take the field." Cooper pointed with the bat like he was Babe Ruth. "Hurry."

Gordy and Hiro took off at a jog, and Cooper batted one over their heads. The smack of the bat worked like a starting gun, kicking Gordy into his competitive mode. He opened up the throttle and took off after the ball.

Gordy relayed it to Hiro, and she tossed it back to Cooper.

He took another swing, and sent the ball on another flight. Leaning on the bat, he watched Gordy hustle for the ball.

"We have more company," Hiro said. "This one has its lights flashing."

Cooper forced himself not to turn around. Told himself to act normal. He wiped slick hands on his jeans to get a better grip, and knocked a half dozen more out into the field.

"They're gone," Hiro said.

Cooper dropped the bat and leaned his hands on his knees. Gordy and Hiro hustled up.

Gordy's face looked as white as the baseball. "Where do you think they went?"

"My guess?" Hiro put her hands on her hips. "They're cruising the neighborhood."

Gordy looked toward Campbell Street. "Maybe we should stay here awhile."

Cooper nodded. "Then I need to write another letter to Hammer." He gave them a quick rundown of the conversation with the police detective.

Hiro and Gordy hustled back to field more balls. It gave Cooper time to think. After nearly fifteen minutes he motioned them back.

"So what's the plan?" Gordy handed Cooper the baseball. "How are you going to give them more proof without the hard drive?"

"More details, for starts." Cooper said. "What was in Frank's pockets. The name of the book in my backpack." He watched Hiro. "Then I'll tell them that my prints should be on the knife that was laying on the floor with the coins from the change drawer."

"Which," Hiro said, "should be all the proof they'll need. All they'll have to do is match the prints on the knife handle to the prints all over the letter."

"Exactly," Cooper said. "And just to make sure they don't come back and ask for proof again, I'll give them the clincher."

Hiro gave him a sideways glance.

Cooper smiled and looked from one to the other. "When I left Frank 'n Stein's that night, I still had Frank's keys."

Gordy's eyebrows went up as he nodded. "You locked the door."

"So," Hiro said. "You'll write that you have Frank's keys." She pushed her hands in her pockets. "All they have to do is ask Mr. Stein and he'll verify the keys are missing. That will prove you were really there, *in* the diner."

"Then the cops can concentrate on finding the robbers." Cooper glanced at Hiro. He hoped she'd smile at him. Show some support. Approval. Her face didn't give him a clue as to what she was thinking. He still hadn't straightened things out from last night. Then again, until the robbers got caught, how could he really straighten any of this out?

"If I were a cop," Hiro said, "and I knew you were going to write another letter tonight, I'd stake out the library."

Gordy whistled. "You think the cop asked for more proof just to set a trap?"

She reached up and held the police star necklace. "Could be."

"Great," Cooper said. He imagined himself dropping the letter in the book depository and police swarming in from all over. Or worse yet, maybe just a couple cops—wearing latex masks. "So we'll pick a new drop spot."

"Yeah," Gordy said. "Throw 'em off guard. Any ideas?"

Cooper shook his head. "But we'll think of something." He picked up his bike, crossed the bridge, and started walking toward the edge of the park like he was in no hurry at all. Gordy and Hiro did the same. Only when they reached Campbell Road did he mount his bike.

Cooper rode between the two of them as they headed back. They decided a slow ride would look less suspicious. Gordy struggled with it. Riding ahead, circling back. Getting ahead again. Cooper thought about taking this chance to talk to Hiro. To tell her he was sorry about last night. But the thought of writing the new letter kept getting in the way.

"I went to see Frank again today." Hiro said it so quietly it almost sounded like she was talking to herself.

Guilt settled in immediately. She'd been to see Frank twice. He hadn't even gone once.

"So you weren't sick at all?" Gordy glanced at Cooper.

"Sick of worrying somebody is going to kill Coop, or one of us. Sick of the lies." Hiro didn't make eye contact with Cooper. "I didn't feel like going to school."

Cooper coasted to a stop. "And you think I did?"

Hiro braked and put one foot down. "I don't know, Coop. It seems like lies aren't bothering you much these days."

Her comment stung. Who was she to judge him? She'd ditched them at school today. Wasn't there to help. Maybe she deserved the way he treated her last night. "Your mom let you stay home from school even though you weren't really sick?"

Hiro studied the pavement. "I just told her I was sick. And after she left for work I biked to the hospital."

Cooper tried not to let his frustration show. "And they let you see him by yourself?"

"Yes." She nodded, but had a distant look in her eyes like she was still in the hospital room.

Gordy was quiet, but after a moment, he whispered, "How did he look?"

She shook her head slightly, like she was forcing herself out of a daze. "The same."

Cooper saw the scene in the reflection of Frank 'n Stein's window all over again. Frank getting beaten nearly to death. He pulled the baseball out of his pocket and picked at the stitches. "Did they say anything? The nurses?"

"Not to me. But they *act* like he's going to get better."

"What makes you say that?"

"They talk to him."

"Really?"

"Yeah. Whenever they came into the room they'd say things like, 'Hiya, Frank. You're looking good, honey. You ready to get up soon?'"

Cooper had it pictured in his mind. "Did he move or anything?"

"Nothing."

"Whoa," Gordy said. "Like he's in a coma or something."

Hiro tapped him on the forehead. "He *is* in a coma."

Gordy's face got red. "Well, yeah, I *know* that."

Something surfaced in Cooper's mind. Hiro was operating on her own now. She didn't show up at school. She visited Frank. Doing everything without letting Gordy or him in on her plans. Wouldn't the police want to question anyone that came to visit him? Had she even considered that before she went there?

"Maybe *I'll* stay home from school tomorrow," Gordy said.

"Great," Cooper said. "So you're going to ditch me too, eh?"

"*Ditch* you?" Hiro's chin went up. "Is that what you think I did?"

"Yeah. That's *exactly* what you did."

"Look, I'm still sticking by that *stupid* Code of Silence. If I abandon you it will be more obvious than taking a day off school. I'll break the Code and tell the police myself."

Cooper felt his face get warm. Did she just give him a threat?

Hiro looked down at her feet. "I want to feel safe again. I pray and pray for God to protect us. Then I go right back to living a total lie. How can God respect that? I don't trust him enough to tell the truth?"

"The lies will stop."

"Only when we come clean. But until then we're *living* a lie. I was trying to tell you last night. This is too big for us. We need help. Because of the Code I haven't told anyone except God. And how can I expect his help when I hide the truth?"

"You think it doesn't bother me?" Cooper whispered.

Her head snapped up and her eyes bore into him. "Not anymore. Lie, lie, lie. That's all you seem to do."

"Really?" Cooper clenched his jaw. *Stop. Don't say another word. Cool down before you say something you'll regret.*

"Yes, *really*." She leaned forward. Like she needed to put every bit of her weight behind her words. "There was a time when you would have felt terrible if you lied. Now you don't seem to feel anything at all."

Her eyes. Cooper couldn't get past her eyes. Something different there. Missing. The respect was gone. All he saw was disgust. Contempt.

Her look hit him in the gut just as real as when the robbers wailed on Frank. And it hurt with a kind of pain he'd never felt before.

How dare she say he didn't feel *anything*. She had no idea how he felt. He opened his mouth to lash back. To sting her like she'd just done to him. He looked at his feet and clamped his mouth shut instead.

"Go ahead and say it, Cooper MacKinnon." Hiro got in his face. Taunted. "You were going to say something. Get it off your chest."

Get it off your chest. Get a chest. What was it with his chest?

Gordy stepped in, looking more ashen-faced than he did when the police car stopped at the park. "Hey, you two. C'mon, now. We're all friends here. What do you say we go get something to eat?"

Cooper didn't answer. *We're all friends here*. That was the problem, wasn't it? Maybe *that* was just another lie. Hiro let them down by ditching school. Going to the hospital. Making her own plans. Griping about the Code every time they got together. Some friend.

"C'mon, Coop," Hiro said, her voice daring him. Egging him on. "You were ready to say something a minute ago. I want to know what it was."

Gordy put a hand on Hiro's shoulder. "Hey, I think we'd better— "

Hiro slapped his hand away. "I want to know what Coop was going to say." She poked Cooper in the chest. "Let's hear it, Coop. If you can do it without lying that is."

"Is that all you think I do? Lie?" She didn't get it. Didn't see how he *had* to lie. "And what about you? What do you call what you told your Mom today about being sick? A little white lie? A half-truth? You say you're sick of the lies, but you're no better than me."

Hiro's mouth opened just a bit. Maybe she was surprised at what Cooper said. Maybe she realized for the first time that she really did lie to her mom. Cooper had no idea—and told himself he didn't care. But when the tears welled up in her eyes, he knew he'd made a direct hit. He saw *his* pain in her face. And hated himself for doing it.

Hiro backed her bike away from them. Without another word she straddled it and headed down the street.

Her reaction twisted Cooper two ways. On one end, happy he'd scored a solid point. On the other a panicky desperation to apologize and make it right.

"Brilliant." Gordy glared at him and shook his head. "Are you going to let her leave without patching this up?"

Why did *he* have to patch things up? He was trying to protect them all, wasn't he? They'd made it safely this far because he'd made sure they stuck to the Code. It was the only real option they had. And a good one. Silence is golden, right?

"Call her back," Gordy said.

Cooper watched her biking away. Her black braid beat a furious tempo against the middle of her back.

He fought the urge to call her back. He had a right to be steamed. To stall until *she* turned around and came back. Until she saw he was only trying to help.

"Coop." Gordy's voice hinted at disbelief. "She's not going to come back."

She stood on the pedals, picking up speed. Every second the separation between them grew farther. They were supposed to be *friends*. How did this happen?

"Hiro," he called. Probably not loud enough.

She didn't turn back.

"Hiro, hold on!" He shouted this time.

She must have heard him, but she didn't turn. It was like last night. The roles were reversed this time. Now he knew how she must have felt when he rode away. He jammed the baseball in his pocket and held the bat against the handlebar.

"Let's catch her," Cooper said, mounting his bike.

A police siren immediately behind them nearly made him drop the bat. It only bleeped on for a second, but enough to freeze him in place. He turned just as a police car pulled over to the curb behind them. The door opened, and a patrolman stepped out.

"Can I talk to you boys for a moment?" The officer shifted his gun belt as he walked toward them.

Cooper glanced back toward Hiro. She was nearly a block away now. She had obviously heard the siren and stopped, with one foot down. She stared for a moment, then pushed off and rolled away.

She abandoned him again.

"Excuse me," the police officer said. "Were you two playing ball in the park ten minutes ago?"

CHAPTER 32

Gordy thought about running. It was instinct—and stupid. Instead, he sat on the bike and watched the cop approach.

The policeman looked like he just walked out of an ad for a health club. Blonde buzz cut, baby face, and a chest that looked as powerful as the gun strapped at his waist. M. *Stryker* was engraved on a nametag pinned above his chest pocket.

Gordy imagined himself sitting on a stool with a bright light on his face with this guy interrogating him. In one minute he'd confess. To anything.

The officer stepped onto the curb and nodded toward Coop's baseball bat. "You were just in the park. Right?" He towered over them. Gordy figured his head would only get to the guy's shoulder. Coop might make it to his nametag.

"Yes, sir," Coop said.

The policeman sized them up. Like he was wondering how either of them could have gotten away from desperate robbers.

Gordy did a little figuring himself. This guy seemed bigger than the goons at Frank's.

"We were just knocking the ball around a little," Coop said.

"I was watching," Stryker said. "By the bridge?"

"Uh-huh."

Gordy's red sweatshirt was hard to miss. He was relieved Coop didn't deny it.

"You swatted a couple of nice hits there. Why'd you stop?"

Coop shrugged. "We were just messing around a little. Have to get back to do some homework."

That sounded good, but Gordy knew that was a lie. He kept his eyes on the cop's eyes. To look at the ground now would send a signal. A bad one. He couldn't mess this up.

The policeman nodded. "Where do you go to school?"

"Plum Grove."

That seemed to interest him. "Seventh grade?"

Here we go. He knows. He knows.

Coop sat a little taller on the seat. "Eighth."

Maybe he was asking some easy questions, calibrating his own "baloney detector." *Stick to the truth, Coop.*

"What were you doing down by the creek bed when I rolled up?"

"Looking for the ball."

"It seemed like a funny place to play ball, with the creek right there. Why not use one of the diamonds?" He looked at Gordy this time.

Gordy shrugged. "We weren't playing a game. Just knocking it around a little. There were only three of us."

Stryker looked back at Cooper. "What happened to your friend? It looked like she rode off in a hurry."

Friend? Hiro *was* Coop's friend, but something was definitely changing.

Coop looked down. "She's mad at me."

No half-truth there. "Totally steamed," Gordy said. He couldn't figure this guy out. Was he stalling until backup came? Maybe Detective Hammer himself? Or maybe he just had to ask enough questions until he decided whether or not to haul them in.

"Why is that?"

"I'm trying to figure that out," Coop said. "We were having a good time. Then she said something that got me frustrated. So I guess I said something not so kind back to her."

"Like reminding her how she lied to her mom," Gordy said.

The policeman cringed. "That will do it."

Cooper let his hands drop to his sides like the situation drained all the strength out of him. "She got all upset and rode off. I was just going to go after her and talk to her when you pulled up."

"Probably best to let her cool down a little."

Coop looked down the block. "I just don't get it. Everything was going great."

Gordy looked for Hiro too. He couldn't help it. Like he'd expected her to come back. Gordy wondered if she ever would.

Coop turned back to face the cop. "I just wish I could figure girls out."

Stryker laughed. "That, my man, is a question you'll struggle with all your life. Women are mysterious creatures."

"Crazy, if you ask me," Gordy said.

The cop laughed again. "But try to live without them. You can't."

Gordy wasn't so sure about that. But Coop nodded like he agreed. He really seemed busted up about things with Hiro. If it was an act, he was good at it—and he ought to consider trying out for the school play.

The cop stepped onto the curb. "Women are wired different. They're like computers. Complex. Unpredictable. Temperamental. Sometimes they drive you nuts."

"And sometimes they crash," Gordy said. "Like our friend Hiro."

Stryker gave Coop a pat on the shoulder. "Give her a little time before you talk to her. She'll be back around."

Coop didn't look convinced. And honestly? Gordy had to go with him on that one. Which made him feel kind of sick inside. It was always the three of them. They stuck together—and he'd do just about anything to keep it that way. To get it back. Stryker walked around the front of his police car. Suddenly he turned. "Do either of you have a cell phone?"

There it was. The cop made it sound like a casual request. He dropped the big question when their guard was down. Smooth.

Gordy stuffed his hands in his pockets and pulled them out empty.

"I've got mine," Coop said.

"I just needed to make a call," Stryker said. "I was hoping maybe I could just borrow one for a minute."

Right. Just long enough to look at the number and slap the cuffs on him. Gordy could kiss the rock they'd hidden the Walmart phone under.

Coop pulled out his *real* cell. "You can use mine."

Stryker took the phone, punched in a number, and put it to his ear. He wasn't on for more than a minute, and he handed it back with a smile, apparently satisfied neither of them were the mystery witness. For now.

Coop waited until the police car turned a corner and drove out of sight before he said anything. "Well, *that* got my heart pumping."

"Good. Maybe you can get mine going again." Gordy held his hands out in front of him. "Look at my hands. They're all jittery."

They mounted their bikes and began a slow pedal home.

Gordy should have been happy, but the way things ended up with Hiro put a big shadow over things. He hoped the cop was right about letting her cool off. That everything would be okay tomorrow. But somehow he didn't see how it could. Not unless Coop turned in the hard drive and broke the Code. Which wasn't going to happen.

"How upset would you say Hiro is?" Coop broke the silence.

Gordy shot him a quick glance. "On a scale of one to ten, I put her at least a seven." At *least*.

"Great."

Gordy replayed the way her face looked before she rode off. "Maybe eight."

"Or nine," Coop said.

Gordy shook his head. "Not nine. She'd have tried to deck you at nine."

The little joke didn't do anything to lighten Coop up.

"But still," Coop looked down the block, like he was hoping he'd see Hiro pedaling toward them. "Eight is pretty bad."

"Your crack about her lying to her mom really got her." Lying. That's what it all came down to. The lies were ripping the three of them apart. He saw Coop's side of it. Hey, if they could just hang together until the police picked up the goons, they could put all this behind them. But he understood Hiro's side of it, too. And Hiro was coming unglued. Like the lies were toxic, and it was killing her. Killing all of them.

Coop coasted for a moment. "Think she'll spill?"

"No way. Not Hiro." Gordy hoped it was true. "The three of us stick together. Right?" But even that didn't seem to be true. Not anymore.

Cooper didn't answer. Like he sensed something had changed. Gordy *had* to think of a way to patch things up.

They rode to Coop's drive in silence. Gordy hoped she'd be there. Waiting for them. Wanting to end the tension between. He scanned the front porch. The gate in the cedar fence to the backyard was closed. No bike. No Hiro.

Maybe Coop had the same hopes. He definitely looked disappointed. Gordy tried distracting him. "So what's next?"

Coop coasted to a stop and swung his leg over the bike. "I have another letter to write. And deliver. You want to meet after dinner?"

Gordy nodded. "I'm in."

Coop smiled, but his eyes weren't smiling a bit. "You're always in." He clapped him on the back. "Thanks."

Gordy knew what Coop meant. Gordy also knew that Cooper's smile would have looked a lot better if Hiro were with them right now.

"Lucky we hid that phone," Coop said. "You think he really believed us?"

"Totally. Don't you?"

"I guess so."

"*Guess* so?"

Coop kicked a stone off the drive. "It's just that if he didn't totally believe us he might try to check out our story."

Gordy shrugged. "He let us go without even frisking us. What's left to check?"

Coop didn't answer for a long moment. "What if he goes snooping by the creek and finds the phone?"

CHAPTER 33

I've got some good news, and some bad news," Dad said. He took a last bite of mashed potatoes and leaned back.

Cooper held his breath. He had a feeling part of the news had to do with the police interviews. Maybe they got past the hurdles.

"What's the bad news, Carson?" Mom's eyebrows went up with a pleading look that lined her forehead.

"Don't worry, Babe. It's not *that* bad."

Which set Cooper's stomach a bit more at ease, but it still felt like a knotted dish towel.

"I have three tickets to the Ringling Brothers and Barnum and Bailey Circus. The greatest show on earth."

"Yes!" Mattie jumped up from her seat and ran around the kitchen table. "We're going to the circus!"

"A satisfied client offered me the tickets. They didn't cost me a thing."

"When?" Mom picked up the calendar.

"This Thursday night."

"That's Halloween."

"Uh-huh."

"We're going to the circus in two days!" Mattie circled the table again with her arms out like wings.

"The problem is," Dad looked at Mom. "With only three tickets one of us will have to stay back." He pointed at himself and shrugged.

Cooper imagined being at the Allstate Arena with hours of acrobatics and amazing stunts. It would be a good place to get his mind off things.

"Will there be ponies?" Mattie stopped running and grabbed Dad's arm.

"Absolutely."

Mattie jumped up and down. "And clowns?"

"All over the place."

Clowns. Cooper could see it now. Three rings with guys in clown getup. "Hold on, Dad," Cooper said. "I'll stay back."

"What? And miss all the fun?"

"The way I see it," Cooper said, "you bringing home *The Getaway* was like bringing me tickets to the circus, the Super Bowl, and maybe even Disneyworld all wrapped up together."

Dad smiled. He beamed, in fact. Cooper scored some points with that one.

"Mattie can see some ponies and have some one-on-one time with you and Mom."

It was settled pretty quickly. Dad and Mom would take Mattie. Cooper would stay home. He wouldn't have to look at clowns for three hours.

After dinner he made an excuse to do homework on the computer in the family room, but he worked on the letter instead. Cooper had it pretty much written in his mind, so he was able to type it fast and print two copies without anyone coming near. One copy he folded and sealed in an envelope right away. The copy for *The Herald*.

After deleting the letter on the screen, he took a sheet of plain paper and pressed his hand flat on it, making sure every finger made full contact. He held it there for a full thirty seconds, wanting to be sure the oils from his hand left clear prints. Taking a pen, he traced his hand on the paper so the police would know exactly where to dust for fingerprints. He folded the second copy of his letter, along with the handprint sheet, and then slipped it into a different envelope. But he didn't seal it.

Cooper met Gordy in *The Getaway* at eight p.m. The battery-powered camping lantern Cooper kept in his bedroom sat on the middle of the cabin table, casting strange shadows behind Gordy.

"Think Hiro will show?" Cooper laid the two envelopes on the table.

"Not unless she has a brain transplant."

"How do you know?"

Gordy squirmed a bit. "I talked to her just before I came over."

"What?"

"Yeah, well, I knew you were pretty upset with how she left us and stuff, so I thought I'd talk to her and, you know, smooth things over."

"So what did you say?"

"Well, that you were pretty steamed at her for ditching us, but I thought you'd forgive her if she came back tonight."

"You told her *that*?" Cooper leaned back and raked his hands through his hair. "She's going to think I'm an idiot."

Gordy nodded. "That's pretty much what she said."

"Great. What about you *smoothing* things over?"

"But she *did* want to know what the policeman said."

Cooper thought about that a moment. That meant she still cared what happened to them. It wasn't much, but he'd take whatever he could get. "What did she think about how we handled his questions?"

"She didn't really say."

"Nothing?"

"Well, okay. She just said 'more lies.' And that was about it."

That's just about what Cooper would expect her to say. "You told her what time we were meeting?"

Gordy nodded. "She said not to count on her being here."

Cooper stared at the lantern and let the words sink in. So that was that. It was just him and Gordy now. Like old times.

"Coop?" Gordy peered out the cabin window into the darkness. "You think we should give it up?"

"NO!" Cooper shouted, making Gordy jump.

"We can do this." Cooper tried to slow himself down. "Just a little longer. Give the police a little more information so they find those guys. If we turn ourselves in now we're in just as much danger as we ever were."

Gordy shrugged and kept his eyes on the table. "It's just that Hiro says—"

"Hiro says? I *know* what Hiro says. She didn't like the Code from the beginning. Do you want to leave, too?"

"No," Gordy held up his hands. "I'm with you, Coop. It's just that Hiro had a couple of good points when she was talking to me, and—"

"She's delirious," Cooper said. "She thinks we can trust the cops. Well we *can't*. And I'm not about to walk into a trap. If you want out, let me know right now and I'll do this myself."

Gordy looked confused. "I said I'm with you. What more do you want?"

Cooper felt a twinge of guilt. He leaned back against the booth and sighed. "I'm sorry. I'm on edge, I guess." He checked his watch. "Wanna hear what I wrote?"

"Sure."

Cooper unfolded the letter to the police and started reading.

"*Rolling Meadows Police,*

This is my last letter. Here is more proof that I was at Frank 'n Stein's at the time of the burglary. That I am your witness. My backpack was on the back table. Inside was a book titled Adventures in American Literature. There was no name in the backpack, or on my sweatshirt.

I checked Frank's pockets for the keys while the burglars were upstairs in the office opening the safe. His left front pocket was empty except for a 4"x 6" photo of a Halloween party. His right front pocket had papers and change.

You should have found a big knife on the floor on the customer side of the front counter with my fingerprints on it. They will match the prints all over this letter. To make it easy, I tried to leave a good print on the next page.

The knife came from a rack near the back door. It isn't the same knife as the burglars used with Frank. There should be a small cut under his chin where they stuck him to make him give the combination to the safe.

This information should prove I was there and not just looking in a window. I am telling the truth. The guy with the clown mask almost caught me. He got my house key. He said he would find me and my family if I went to the police. He used the stool from the video game to break out the front window when I got away because I locked the front door behind me. I still have the keys.

I'll turn the phone on at 3:30 p.m. Wednesday. Don't waste your time trying to get me to come in or bring the hard drive. I've given you all the proof you need. Just find those three men. The one with the Elvis mask was about the same height and weight as Detective Hammer.

Talk to the guy who almost hit me with his car. The burglar chased me. He told the people he was a cop. Ask them for a description. I didn't see him.

The night of the burglary an SUV pulled out from behind Frank 'n Stein's. I saw it from Dunkin Donuts. It was dark, so I didn't get a good look at it. One headlight was out. And they're still in town. One of the robbers told me to leave the surveillance hard drive by the bell tower Sunday night. I left a note saying I wouldn't give it to anyone—not even the police. They were waiting, and they chased me. Same SUV. Headlight still out. I got away, but they got my bike and turned it into a pretzel. They mean business. Don't waste time looking for the witness who chooses to be silent. Find these men before they try to silence me for good.

Signed,

Silence is Golden"

Cooper looked up. "What do you think?"

"Maybe you should put something about Lunk."

"*Lunk?* Hiro said that? I honestly don't think he had anything to do with it. We have no proof." But that was only part of it. He looked down at his hands. "If they question him, he might just happen to suggest they check out a guy named Cooper MacKinnon."

Gordy nodded and held up his hands in a peacekeeping gesture. "You're right. And I think you've covered all the bases. Especially that part about talking to the witnesses by Dunkin' Donuts." He nodded. "Yeah, I think it's good."

Cooper folded it and slipped it back in the envelope. "Now all we have to do is deliver it."

"Where are we taking it anyway?"

Cooper looked at his cousin and held up a set of keys. "Frank 'n Stein's."

CHAPTER 34

"Why *there?*"

The two boys made their way out of *The Getaway* cabin and into the cool night air.

Cooper shrugged. "Who'd suspect it? If the cops are watching the library, they may also be watching the mailboxes and who knows where else. They'd never figure I'd go back to Frank 'n Stein's." Cooper stepped over the transom and hurried down the ladder.

"Are those *the* keys?" Gordy followed him down the ladder.

"Yep."

"Wait a second." Gordy jumped the last few steps to the ground. "We're *not* going inside, are we?"

Cooper stuffed the keys in his pocket. "It will prove I have them. They'll know I'm the one who was inside."

"No way. You're crazy," Gordy said.

Cooper made a goofy face. "So are you. It runs in the family."

"Gee, thanks."

Cooper could read Gordy's face even in the pale moonlight. He looked torn. Like he wanted to be supportive, but he was scared, too. And who wouldn't be spooked at the thought of going back inside Frank'n Stein's after closing? Just thinking about it creeped Cooper out. "It will be okay. We're doing the right thing."

"Do we even know what the right thing is anymore?" Gordy said it quietly. Almost like he was talking to himself.

Cooper acted like he didn't hear it. Was Hiro messing with Gordy's head?

"Hopefully this will make everybody happy."

"Impossible," Gordy said. "The cops won't be happy until they get you out of hiding, and the goons won't be smiling until they make you disappear for good."

"There's a happy thought." Cooper jogged toward his bike.

Gordy trotted alongside him. "It's strange, you know? The good guys want to make you talk, and the bad guys want to shut your mouth permanently. It's like both sides want to get their hands on you, but for opposite reasons. Unless, of course, the cops really are bad—then everyone wants to wring your neck."

"Real comforting," Cooper said. "Then I guess I want to disappoint everybody."

Gordy glanced at him. "You got a good start with Hiro on that one."

Coop let that sink in. Gordy definitely pegged that one right.

Gordy's face got serious. "You think we're making a mistake by not going to the cops? I mean, how can *all* the police be bad?"

Cooper could tell Gordy had been thinking about it pretty hard just by the way he asked. He could almost see the doubts gnawing at Gordy. Hiro really *was* getting through.

"I don't want to take a chance," Cooper said.

Gordy clapped Cooper on the back. "If this wasn't so stinkin' dangerous, it would be kind of a good adventure, you know?" Apparently Gordy wanted to change the topic, or at least the mood.

Cooper smiled and shook his head. "Let's get rid of this letter."

They rode side by side down the darkened streets in silence. The most direct route to Frank 'n Stein's was through the park, and at this time of the night they should have it all to themselves. Kimball Hill Park didn't have many trees, but those it did have were big and tended to be grouped together in clusters. The moon was bright enough to cast long black shadows beside them.

Cooper tried to peer into the shadows to see if anything or anyone lurked there. His imagination conjured up images of men crouching in the pools of darkness. They wore masks. Always masks. He stood on the pedals. If anything was out there, he wanted to have some good speed behind him. The rush of the crisp fall air forced his eyes to water. The wind moaned in his ears. It seemed to be alive, an unseen presence warning him to go back.

Gordy pulled ahead and took the lead over the footbridge and onto the bike path bordering the west side of the creek. Kirchoff Road lay dead ahead, and the bell tower loomed beside it.

When they neared the bell tower, Gordy skidded to a stop behind a towering maple. He laid his bike on the ground. Cooper did the same. The two boys crouched in the shadows and watched the traffic on Kirchoff Road.

Cars were sparse, and in the next five minutes they never saw a police car prowl by. Except for Mr. Stein's car, the parking lot at Frank 'n Stein's stood empty. Nothing looked out of place. Still, the police could be watching the place through a set of binoculars.

"If the police come, just get out of there. Don't wait for me. Tell my Dad everything. Tell him I'm sorry about all the lies."

Gordy nodded.

"And tell Hiro," Cooper paused. What would he want to tell her if he could? "Aw, forget it."

Gordy grabbed his arm and pointed. "Look."

The lights went out in Frank 'n Stein's kitchen. Mr. Stein plodded into view, shrugging on his jacket while he walked.

The bell tower chimed out the half hour like a giant grandfather clock. Cooper checked his watch. Half past nine. Mr. Stein stepped outside, locked the door, and trudged to his car.

"Poor guy looks beat," Gordy said.

Gordy was right. The co-owner was probably covering Frank's hours and his own. Trying to hold it all together without his partner and friend. He looked more stooped over than Cooper remembered, like he carried an extra weight on his shoulders. Maybe this next note would lead the police to the burglars, and things would lighten up for all of them.

"Think Frank will make it?" Gordy said it so quietly, Cooper barely heard. "I mean, there's always hope. Right?"

"Yeah," Cooper said. "There's always hope." Gordy didn't need to know what he really thought.

By the time Mr. Stein pulled out of the lot and drove down Kirchoff Road, Cooper's heart was beating like the bell tower. He hated to leave the cover of the shadows, but it was time to move.

"Let's just get this done. On the way back we'll grab the phone."

Gordy nodded.

Cooper walked the bike out of the shadows, straddled it, and bumped his way along the grass. The two of them followed the bike path through the tunnel under Kirchoff Road and out the other side.

Frank 'n Stein's stood on the rise across the creek. Except for the neon lights, all the other lights were off. Just like last week. Cooper shuddered and felt for the envelopes in his back pocket.

Cooper coasted for twenty yards then turned into the parking lot. He stopped next to the front door and hopped off his bike. Gordy stopped right behind him. He didn't get off his bike, but held Cooper's in place for a fast getaway if needed.

Pressing his face up against the glass, Cooper peered inside. To a casual person driving by, or even a cop, it would look like he'd tried to get there before they closed but missed it by a few minutes.

The dining room was as still as a graveyard, with all the creepiness of one too. Halloween decorations were out in force. A skeleton hung against a dark backdrop. Somehow it seemed totally wrong to put the decorations up after the robbery.

The donation jar for Frank's hospital expenses was on the

counter again and over half full with dollar bills and change. Cooper wondered if the lottery tickets Mr. Stein bought paid off. It looked like he'd be ready to buy more soon. The picture over the counter of the two partners had an addition now too. A handmade sign hung below the smiling image of Frank. *Please pray for my partner and friend!*

Cooper felt a twinge of guilt. He'd barely prayed for Frank at all. The only prayers he'd spoken lately had to do with getting himself out of a jam. Somehow the Code of Silence had kept him from talking to God, too.

Frankenstein himself stood where he always did, guarding the ordering counter. Some guard. He didn't do so well the other night. The eight-foot mascot seemed to be looking right at Cooper, smiling, like they shared a secret. He was part of their Code of Silence, and right now Cooper had a whole lot more confidence in the green-faced monster staying quiet than he did Hiro.

"Are you going to leave the letters or what?" Gordy whispered.

"In a second." Maybe he shouldn't take the time to open the door. With one more glance toward the road, he whipped the letters out of his pocket and tried sliding one end under the door. The words *Give to Rolling Meadows Police* stood out like the neon lights in the windows. The other was addressed to the Daily Herald. The envelopes jammed and bent. He tried another spot. No luck.

"Hurry."

Cooper fished the keys out of his pocket. His hand shook. *Get a chest, Cooper. Get a chest.* He took a deep breath, held it, and slid the key in the lock.

"Good thing Hiro *isn't* here," Gordy whispered. "Breaking and entering. You're really busting the law now."

Terrific. Cooper turned the key, and the latch clunked open. He pulled open the door, and a burglar alarm pierced the silence. Shrill and pulsing, the siren screamed loud enough to wake the dead—or get them killed.

CHAPTER 35

He dropped the envelopes inside and grabbed the keys, not bothering to lock the door.

"Move!" Cooper hopped on his bike.

They pedaled hard out of the parking lot. In a moment they scooted out of sight in the tunnel below Kirchoff Road. It would be a great place to hide, but it was way too close to Frank 'n Stein's.

"Keep going!" Cooper's voice echoed against the cement and steel of the tunnel. Even the alarm sounded louder under the road.

Gordy stood on the pedals and whipped out of the tunnel on the other side of Kirchoff.

With each turn of the crank Cooper's mind hurled accusations at him. *You've blown it this time. You're going to get caught.* Even the wind rushing against his face seemed bent on holding him back. He pulled alongside his cousin, making Gordy hunch over and drive harder, taking the lead again. In moments the two of them raced into the shadows of Kimball Hill Park.

His original plan called for a roundabout, casual ride from Frank 'n Stein's, one that wouldn't look suspicious. Maybe they were being watched right now. He needed to think. Map a safe route home. Making a beeline for the house may lead the cops right to him.

"Hold up, Gordy!"

His cousin shot him a questioning look. Only when Cooper hit the brakes near the giant maple tree did Gordy react. He skidded to a stop next to him.

"What's wrong?"

"Nothing." Cooper dumped his bike. "Just want to be sure we haven't been spotted." The spot gave a perfect view in all directions, including a clear shot of Frank 'n Stein's. He crouched down to rethink.

"Lousy alarm," Gordy said, breathing heavily.

Cooper could still hear it, even at this distance. It was like the diner had a life of its own. It was calling out to the police, telling them where he and Gordy hid.

"Well, Hiro really missed it," Gordy said.

And Cooper missed Hiro. In a way, the letters started out as a way to show Hiro they could help with the investigation without revealing their identity, without compromising their safety.

"Coop." Gordy nudged him and pointed just beyond Frank 'n Stein's.

Two police cars raced with their lights flashing, sirens off. They squealed onto the road and headed west for Frank 'n Stein's. Two more squad cars roared in from the opposite direction. All four cars converged on the diner. The policemen scurried out of their cars like ants from a damaged anthill.

"Somebody heard the alarm," Gordy said.

"Or maybe it's wired directly to the police station."

Cooper's plan didn't include his letter being discovered so soon. Not until the next morning when Mr. Stein opened up. He watched two officers approach the door. Another pair split up and ran along each side of the building toward the drive-thru menu sign in the back. Two more fanned out in the parking lot of the apartment building next door, walking between the cars and even dropping down to check underneath them.

"They came quickly," Gordy said.

Too quickly. And two of them from the direction of the library. They *were* scoping the place out. If he'd dropped the letter at the library, they'd both be sitting in the back of a squad car right now.

"We got out of there just in time," Cooper said.

Four more cars pulled up with blue and red lights flashing madly. The parking lot looked like some crazed light show gone bad. Two officers ran down the embankment where the creek passed the diner.

"Weird." Gordy crouched down on the bridge. "Here we are watching them while they're looking for us. It's like attending your own funeral."

"Which is exactly what we'll have if we don't get out of here," Cooper said. "We'll forget picking up the phone tonight. They'll widen the search zone quick."

After a quick scan in all directions, the boys crept out of the cover of darkness and mounted their bikes. In a moment they crossed the footbridge and sailed along the creek path toward Campbell Street at the other end of the park.

Fifty yards from Campbell Street a police car cruised into view. The boys pulled into the cover of some trees, dropped their bikes, and waited. The cruiser combed the sides of the road with its searchlight.

It looked like something out of an old science fiction movie. The beam reached far into the park, exposing every bench and rock in its path. It was an alien, searching for them. Sniffing them out.

Cooper and Gordy hid their bikes behind some brush and pressed themselves against the trunk of an ancient oak. The light inched their way. Cooper looked back toward Frank 'n Stein's. Several cars peeled out of the lot, joining the search. "Here they come."

"We gotta get out of here," Gordy said.

"Right." Cooper watched the cop car inching down Campbell. "As soon as he's out of sight, we're gone." The police had a net in place, and they intended to pull Cooper in. He couldn't let that happen.

"When is this going to end?" Gordy muttered.

Cooper knew the feeling. It all seemed so crazy. They were hiding from the police like any other criminal.

The searchlight crept across the brush. Cooper held his breath, praying the police wouldn't see the bikes in the shadow behind it. One reflection off the metal and they were nailed. Game over. The light splashed against the oak casting a pillar of darkness behind them. Neither of them moved. Cooper didn't breath. Light bleached the ground on either side of the tree and stopped. He expected it to keep going, but the beam stayed locked in place.

"What's he doing?" Gordy whispered. "Think he sees us?"

Both of them were in the dark. The cop couldn't possibly see them. But did he suspect something? Was he getting out of his car, walking this way to investigate? It made sense, and Cooper fought the urge to bolt.

Gordy leaned his forehead against the tree. "Please make him go, God."

He said something else, but Cooper couldn't make it out. He listened for a car door, or some sign the policeman was coming their way. He wished he could peek around the edge of the tree, but to him the searchlight was like a giant laser beam. If it touched him, even for an instant, he'd be toast.

The light started moving again. It crossed the tree, surging full strength on the other side, and kept burning its way across the park away from them.

Cooper let out a shaky breath. *Thank you, God. Thank you, God.*

They waited no more than thirty seconds before going for the bikes. Cooper didn't want to risk another police car using a searchlight on the park.

"We're not still going to take a roundabout route, are we?"

Cooper shook his head. "Too risky now." Before heading to Frank's they'd mapped out a return route with lots of turns to be sure they weren't followed. "We'll keep our eyes open, but let's go straight home." All he wanted was to get back and stay there. For about a month.

They watched the police car weave its way around parked cars lining Campbell. The searchlight probing for its quarry. It was past them now, and creeping farther away by the second.

"Let's make a run for it," Cooper said, swinging a leg over his bike. Gordy nodded and did the same.

Cooper took off, building up as much speed as he could. The two of them zipped across Campbell Drive, crossed through several yards, and into the maze of winding roads in the residential area.

In record time he made it to the house and rode through the gate to the backyard. Gordy followed and both of them leaned their bikes along the shed.

"I'll pick mine up tomorrow," he panted, heading back toward the gate.

Cooper wanted his own breathing to even out before he went in the house. He opened the shed, wheeled his bike inside, and tossed the keys to Frank 'n Stein's in the plastic barrel.

He hustled over to Gordy so he could lock the gate behind him. Cooper didn't need to remind him to make sure the coast was clear. He didn't think either of them would ever stop looking over their shoulders.

Gordy stopped and peered toward the street. "No more letters. Right?"

"Not a chance."

Gordy nodded once. "Good." He leaned out the gate, glanced both ways and then looked back at Cooper. "You think Frank 'n Stein's got a new hard drive for their security cameras?"

Cooper added up the days. "Maybe. Why?"

"You had your face up against the window, and um … "

Gordy didn't finish his thought. He didn't have to. If the cameras were up and running, they'd just captured a view of him pressing his face up to the window. As clear as the picture of the owners hanging on the wall.

CHAPTER 36

Cooper's stomach felt almost as bad as when he'd flipped off the bike at Dunkin Donuts. Like there was an entire gymnastics team inside his gut practicing their floor exercises. Fudge bounded over to greet him the moment he walked into the house.

"Hey, Fudge." Cooper reached for her.

She plowed right into him, nearly bowling him over as she did. Tail swinging, she nuzzled and poked him with her nose.

"Easy girl." He reached for the back of a kitchen chair to steady himself. Sweat trickled through his hairline. His stomach felt full of lava. He pulled the hoodie over his head, and a wave of dizziness swept over him.

Mattie skipped into the kitchen, then stopped and stared at him. "Cooper's home," she called. "And he looks sick."

His breath came in short pants. Too weak to run, he plodded for the bathroom and dropped on all fours in front of the toilet. Fudge walked beside him, ears plastered flat to the sides of her head.

He gagged once, and the volcano erupted.

"Cooper's hurling!" Mattie shrieked and ran out of sight.

He coughed, and his stomach squeezed out the last of it.

"Cooper, honey!"

Mom's voice. She knelt beside him and stroked his back.

Cooper's throat burned. He cleared it several times, then spit in the toilet and leaned his elbows on the seat.

"Feeling a little better?" Mom stroked his back.

Cooper nodded. His stomach still felt shaky, but better.

"When you're ready, I want you to march right up to bed. Looks like you've got the flu."

Cooper knew it wasn't the flu, but he didn't argue. He flushed the toilet and sat back on the floor. Fudge sat beside him with sad eyes. The close call. The police. The fear of the security camera picking him up at the window. Trying to stay alive was killing him.

An hour later he stared at the ceiling above his bed. His stomach better, except for the dread that stomped around inside. Kicking at him in an uncontrolled tantrum. Reminding him of everything that went wrong—and things that still could.

Two good things came out of his little rush to the toilet. First, everyone stayed clear of him. He was quarantined to his room. Only Fudge was allowed visiting rights. That meant nobody would be asking him questions, and he wouldn't be telling any lies. It was something.

But the best thing was that this would be his ticket out of school tomorrow. He wouldn't have to worry about Miss Ferrand getting suspicious, or Lunk cornering him with more questions. If nobody could get to him, this would practically guarantee the Code of Silence wouldn't be broken as long as he was home "sick." Hopefully long enough for the police to catch Elvis and the Clown. And Mr. Lucky, the one with the cowboy boots.

If he played it right, maybe he could milk this for a *couple* days. He calmed himself with that thought. He'd spend the time trying to figure out his next move. Maybe he'd call Hiro. Patch things up. Somehow.

Cooper scratched Fudge behind the ears. Her presence was comforting. He wasn't completely alone in this. Poor Gordy would be on his own tomorrow at school.

He should call Gordy. Tell him he wouldn't be there. But talking to Gordy over the phone about any of this seemed risky. What if someone overheard on Gordy's end? By now he'd be in bed. Calling at this hour would generate a bunch of unwelcome questions. Maybe he could call him in the morning before school.

He felt guilty he wouldn't be there for Gordy, especially because of how he'd felt when Hiro bailed. Would Gordy face questions from Miss Ferrand? From Lunk? And he couldn't count on Hiro to help. She'd probably love to see Gordy spill his guts. Gordy would be alone. Maybe the Code wasn't so secure after all.

CHAPTER 37

Hiro sat on the edge of her bed with all the lights off except the desk light with the green glass shade. She set her phone in its circle of light, and checked just to make sure she hadn't missed a text.

Did the police take Coop and Gordy in for questioning? She shouldn't have left them there. There were a lot of things she shouldn't have done. Like agree to the Code in the first place. And deliberately deceive her mom.

When Coop rode off angry the night before, she'd felt so incredibly lonely afterwards. He didn't come back. She'd dosed him with his own medicine tonight. And somehow she'd poisoned herself at the same time.

Hiro stood and walked silently to the closet, opened the door, and reached for her dad's Chicago Police jacket. Sliding it off the hanger, she buried her face in it, drawing in the smell of the leather.

She slipped it on and stood for a moment, feeling its weight. Its strength. The sleeves hung below her hands, and she pushed up the cuffs.

"I messed up, Dad," she whispered. "And I don't know what to do."

She sat on the floor next to her bed and hugged herself. "If you were here I wouldn't have done this. We'd have worked this out together."

She opened the jacket and studied the star hanging from her neck. Dad's star. The circular seal of the city of Chicago sat in its center. The words Chicago Police wrapped around it. SGT. KENJI YAKIMOTO was engraved in a banner that wrapped around the top of the star. Surrounding the seal on the bottom were a series of letters and numbers. EOW 2–22–2009. EOW. End of watch. The day he died in the line of duty.

"I still need you, Dad. Your watch wasn't over with me." She hugged herself again. "I'm in trouble here."

Her mind played back events over the last five days. All they'd wanted to do is keep the horror of what they'd seen a secret. Locked up tight so it couldn't escape. Now the secret had them. And no plan of escape seemed to come without a high risk. A price.

Break the Code, and I'll lose a friend. If there was anything left of their friendship to lose. But if she didn't break the Code, she might lose him to the robbers.

Could Dad see her now? Could he hear her? She wanted to think so. But she knew her Heavenly Father saw. He heard. And He cared.

"Help me know what to do," she whispered. "I want to stop the lies." She wiped her eyes with her dad's sleeves. Like he might have done if he were there. The feel of leather against her cheek made her heart ache even more. "Protect us, Father. Bring Coop back. And Frank."

She reached for her phone and checked for missed calls, even though she knew better. No call from Coop. She could be waiting for one all night. As she stared at her phone, an idea formed.

She should call Coop. She really wanted to. But he wasn't ready for what she had to say.She dialed Gordy instead. He picked up on the second ring.

"Hiro!" he said. "I'm glad you called. We delivered the second letter—but to Frank's this time because we were afraid the cops might have the library staked out and Coop used the key at Frank's but the alarm rang and we had to hightail out of there and we almost got caught because the cops were waiting by the library and swept the park with searchlights." Gordy paused for a breath.

"Gordy," she said and sat down on her bed. "Slow down. I want to hear *everything*."

Hiro rocked herself. He filled her in on the night's events.

She listened silently, her idea taking shape. "Gordy," she said when he stopped talking. "I've been thinking about what you told me earlier. About what Miss Ferrand said to the class today. I need you to give me her phone number."

CHAPTER 38

Hiro woke up early Wednesday morning, still wearing her dad's leather jacket. Her stomach cramped as she remembered the message she left last night. If Miss Ferrand checked her messages before she went to bed like she said she'd do, the tip about Lunk and his dad would already be in police hands. Lunk's dad may already be in custody. That thought eased her stomach a bit.

They should have done it days ago. Why couldn't Coop see that?

And now she needed to do something else that was long overdue. She dialed her brother. She took a couple of deep breaths while the phone rang.

"Officer Yakimoto."

"Kenny? I need to talk to you." Just get out there and say it. Get it done.

"How's my little sister?"

"What if I think I know someone who might be involved in the Frank 'n Stein's robbery?"

Ken didn't answer.

"Kenny?"

"I'm here."

Another pause.

"You know this for a fact, or are you playing junior detective again?"

She stood and paced. "Well, I have a pretty good hunch."

Ken laughed, and Hiro could feel the heat rising in her cheeks.

"Neal Lunquist works there. His dad is in town. Looks like an ex-con to me. And I think they were involved."

"Old news," Ken said. "RMPD got a tip last night and they checked it out."

"I hope 'checked it out' means they have him in custody. The night of the robbery I heard them arguing in the parking lot."

"The parking lot? As in the *crime scene* lot?"

She didn't like his tone. "Yes, I went there because-"

"Because you think you're a cop," he interrupted, "but you aren't."

Hiro reached up and touched the necklace. She would have her own star one day. Not a miniature one hanging from a necklace, but full size — the real deal.

"You made that call," her brother said. "Am I right?"

"Actually, I did." She wasn't ashamed of it one bit.

Ken was silent for a long moment. "I have a buddy with Rolling Meadows. We went through the Academy together. The way I heard it, the tip went straight to Hammer. He's one tough dude. Now drop it."

"What?"

"Hammer will run down that lead. If there's something there, he'll find it — but you stay out of it."

She let that sink in. Actually, what he said made sense.

"Hiroko. You still there?"

"Yeah. Just thinking about what you said."

"Good. And remember it." He paused. "But if you tipped off the RMPD already, why are you calling me?"

She'd struggled with that same question through the night.

"Hiroko, what is it you *aren't* telling me?"

There it was. A direct question. And deep down, what she was hoping to get. A question that would force her to tell the truth.

She took a deep breath and let it out slowly. "Hypothetically speaking, what if I know the student who witnessed the robbery?"

"Know? Or are we talking about hunches again."

She felt small. Weak. Her stomach cramped so hard she sat on the edge of the bed and hunkered over. "Know."

"You're telling me you know *Golden Boy*?"

"Golden Boy?'

"Yeah, that's what the guys at RMPD call the one who wrote the letters. They got a second one last night."

Hiro felt a twinge of guilt about the second letter. She didn't even know what it said. "Okay, *hypothetically*, let's say I know Golden Boy."

"Tell him to go to the RMPD. Straight to the man in charge of this investigation. Detective Hammer."

"But what if he thinks Hammer is part of the gang that did it."

"Ridiculous."

"That's what I told him," Hiro said.

Ken didn't answer for a moment. "Hypothetically, of course."

"Of course. Right." *That was sloppy.* Technically, she didn't want to be the one to break the Code. She just wanted to start things rolling. "What if *you* talked to him?"

"To Golden Boy?" Ken laughed. "Trying to ruin my career?"

"*Ruin* it? This would help it."

"Right," Ken said. "*Arlington Heights rookie cop finds key witness in Rolling Meadows robbery.* That makes a great headline, but it would be political suicide."

"You're a policeman, not a politician."

Ken laughed again. "Same thing."

This wasn't going the way she'd hoped.

"Listen," Ken sounded serious now. "Anything I learn from a witness is going to go according to protocol. Right up the chain of command here in Arlington Heights—and then to Rolling Meadows. If there's a dirty cop in the mix he's likely to hear about it."

"Dirty cop?" Hiro pressed the phone to her ear. "You don't honestly think any police are involved, do you?"

"No idea. But then that's the point. A good cop is careful and doesn't make assumptions."

His words hung there. That's exactly what she'd been doing. Assuming Coop was totally wrong. Paranoid.

"Listen, Hiroko," Kenny's voice dropped to a whisper. "This robbery wasn't just some amateur snatch and grab. These were professionals."

Kenny talked so quiet, Hiro had to tab the volume up a couple bars on her phone. "Are you saying *organized* crime?"

"I'm not saying anything. To *anybody*. There was a lot of money in that safe. A *lot*. And the wrong people found out."

People. He said *people*. This was bigger than she'd ever thought. And if organized crime was involved, there *could* be dirty cops—in high places.

"Golden Boy's letter last night made it sound like the men who tried to kill Frank Mustacci are looking for him. Now why would a couple of pros stick around looking for an eyewitness? Why not skip town?"

She'd wondered the same thing herself. "Why?"

"Hey, *you* want to be the cop. Think it through."

"They wouldn't stay in the area at all. It makes no sense. Unless ..." Her mind started spinning. What if they weren't the decision makers? What if they were taking orders from someone else? Someone who expected them to clean up their mess ... or else.

"Unless what?"

"They were hired muscle."

"Bulls-eye."

"Then we're talking mob connections or something," Hiro whispered. "And that would explain why the police want the witness so bad. And the surveillance drive."

"And they're going to get both. Today."

Hiro sucked in her breath. "What are you saying?"

"I'm not sure. Word I got was they were going to bait Golden Boy."

Hiro started pacing again, the phone in one hand, clutching the star in the other. "Bait him? What would that look like?"

"Don't know. They said he'll turn *himself* in."

Coop wouldn't do that, unless somehow they tricked him into turning himself in. Which would be a good thing, actually. *He'd* break the Code—not her. And the police would get the hard drive and maybe the evidence they needed to put some big time criminals away.

Unless, of course the police were involved. Then turning himself in would be ... *suicide.*

"Kenny, what would *you* do?"

"If I were Golden Boy? Lay low until I could figure out who I could trust."

Hiro stopped pacing. Exactly what Coop had been doing. Trying to do, anyway. "And what if you were *me*?"

"I'd warn my friend he might be walking into a trap," Ken said. "I'd tell him this was bigger than he can possibly imagine. I'd let him know that if organized crime *is* behind the robbery, powerful people will want him dead ... *hypothetically* speaking, of course."

CHAPTER 39

Wednesday morning Cooper overslept, totally missing his chance to call Gordy. Once he was awake, time crawled by. Other than the dread in his stomach, he felt fine. His strength returned. By noon he started pacing the room, wondering what Hiro was doing and if Gordy had blown their cover yet. He half expected a police car to pull up to the curb, and every ten minutes or so he checked the window.

The text message from Hiro came just about the time he'd be heading to lunch if he hadn't stayed home.

RMPD plans to trap you today.

That was it. No details. And the thing that really gnawed at him was this. *How did she know that?* Which is exactly what he wanted to ask her. But right now things were way too iffy between them. He didn't want to make it worse.

The good news, if this could be considered good news at all, was that at least she'd warned him. That was something.

Maybe Gordy told her about the second letter and she had one of those feelings. But he didn't need to be a detective to know the police would try to trap him. He was sure that was why Hammer had asked for more proof.

He debated whether or not to send a response to Hiro, but

how would it look if he didn't? He tapped out a quick thanks and sent it. It made sense to keep any bridge of communication open between them.

He hoped she'd send a response back, but when nothing came, he went back to thinking about his next move.

If he was going to avoid the trap, he'd better know what it was. Maybe they'd try to keep him on the phone long enough to locate him. By 3:30 Hammer would have cars everywhere in hopes to net him. The timing had to be the key to their little trap. He'd have to mess up their little timetable.

Mom left the house early for work and wouldn't be back until just before Mattie got off the school bus. Dad was shooting a photography job in Schaumburg and wouldn't be home until dinnertime. By the time he'd downed his lunch, Cooper knew what he had to do.

"C'mon, Fudge." Cooper grabbed the leash and clipped it to her collar. "We're taking a little walk."

Fudge trotted happily beside him. She didn't seem to care where they went. Maybe if she knew, she'd be as nervous as he was.

"Here's the plan, Fudge. The police expect me to turn on my phone at 3:30 again. And they'll be ready." Cooper figured they weren't about to let him slip away again. They'd have police cars all over. Maybe even plainclothes cops in public places looking for a junior high kid with a phone. But this time he wouldn't wait for the call. He'd call Detective Hammer himself—early. An hour and a half before Hammer would expect it … and hopefully that meant he wouldn't have the net set up yet.

Cooper kept a close watch for any suspicious-looking people in the park. It seemed he and Fudge were alone. The phone was exactly where he'd left it. He took a piece of paper out of his pocket with the Rolling Meadows police number on it. Taking a deep breath, he powered on the phone and dialed the number.

"Detective Hammer, please." Cooper used his high voice and the paper tube, just like before. Fudge looked up at him and cocked her head.

He counted off the seconds while on hold. The phone clicked at twenty-seven.

"Hammer."

"It's me. Silence is Golden." Cooper looked around.

"You're early. Skipped school today?"

Cooper cringed. How easy would it be for Hammer to check attendance records? He had to cover up his mistake. "I'm between classes—so I've only got a minute. You got the letter with more proof, just like you asked. What are you doing to find the real robbers?"

"Not as much as I could if I had the security tapes," Hammer said. "I want them."

"Can't. I explained that."

"You ever heard of obstruction of justice, kid? This is crazy."

Cooper checked his watch. "Not from where I stand."

"Really? And exactly where is that?"

Like he would really tell him. "O'Hare Airport. United terminal." It was the first place that popped in his head. "I'm leaving the country." He wished he could.

"Funny," Hammer said. "Now you listen good. I have a suspect in custody. But I can't hold him without something concrete. I need the hard drive."

Cooper's heart kicked it up a gear. "You've got one of them?"

"Absolutely. I think we've got Mr. Lucky. Got a solid tip from a student at Plum Grove. We picked him up a couple hours ago. Found the guy hiding out in a shed. Turns out the guy has a very interesting record, and he's related to an employee."

Cooper was too stunned to answer. *Lunk's dad is Mr. Lucky. They got him. Thank you, God!* "What about the other two?"

"We'll find them. He'll be ready to bargain when he sees we have the surveillance data. And when you bring it in, I'll have you identify him in a lineup."

He hadn't expected this. Wasn't prepared. Cooper looked around. No police cars in sight. Could it be true?

"You there?"

"I can't identify him. I never saw his face."

"Don't worry about that yet. You might be surprised at some things you'll remember."

"Yeah, uh, does this mean you believe me?"

Hammer chuckled. "Absolutely. Unless you don't show, that is."

Cooper wanted to shout. Call Hiro and Gordy. Celebrate. And apologize. Looks like Hiro had been right about Lunk. "Honest?"

"Trust me, kid."

Trust him? He couldn't trust anybody. How much time had passed?

"I can only hold him twenty-four hours unless you come in." Hammer's voice hardened. "He had a key in his pocket. Looked like a house key. Says he got it from somebody—but won't say who."

Cooper's stomach clenched. A house key? *His* house key. They really got him. "He must have gotten it from the guy with the clown mask."

"That's the way I see it. But he's got lockjaw now. I think the surveillance tape will loosen that up."

So they had Mr. Lucky. But that still didn't guarantee that Elvis and the clown weren't cops. What if Hammer was working with Lunk's dad, Mr. Lucky? What if they just wanted to smoke him out?

"Mr. *Golden*. You still there?"

"Yeah." And that was a problem too. He'd been on the phone too long. Again. He had to think.

"So give me your address so I can pick you and the hard drive up. I'll bring the key. If it fits your house you won't even have to identify Mr. Lucky on a lineup. Your key will pin him to the crime."

It sounded on the level. And easy. But if Hammer was part of it, he'd be leading him right to his house. "How long do I have?"

Hammer sighed. "This isn't a game. You said you wanted us to find the guy. Now you won't even ID him? You really want me to cut him loose?"

"No. NO." Cooper caught himself. Had he just answered in his normal voice? "How long?"

"Without more proof he'll walk tomorrow morning. Ten o'clock."

"I'll call." Cooper hit the END button and powered off his phone. How long had he been on? Two minutes? Three? He looked around the park and beyond to the street. No police cars. Yet.

"C'mon, Fudge. Let's get out of here."

CHAPTER 40

Gordy had something new in common with Hiro. Both of them were ready to skin Coop alive.

"No call, no nothing," Gordy said. He sat at the table chowing down a burger. "How about that for a friend?"

Hiro picked at her food, like she wasn't sure if she wanted to eat it or not. Neat little carrots in a plastic bag. Celery sticks all cut to the same length. And some kind of health-nut sandwich on whole wheat. No wonder she didn't tear into her lunch.

"He's changed," she said. "It's like his conscience is gone. Honestly? I don't think I'd sit at his table if he *were* here today."

Which was another thing that ticked Gordy off. Coop was messing everything up. How could a guy hope to keep the three of them together if he kept saying bonehead things like he did last night?

And if he didn't keep the three of them together, what then? Where would he even fit? He'd stick with Coop, probably, but they'd both be miserable. Hiro was part of them. She belonged.

"I called Miss Ferrand," Hiro said. "Left a message."

"I figured," Gordy said. "The way she hugged you before class. How much did you tell her?"

"Only my theory about Lunk and his dad."

Gordy drained a milk carton. "Good. Coop trusts him way too much, if you ask me."

Hiro pulled open the seal of the plastic bag holding the raw veggies, then zipped it closed again. "I feel good. Really good about this."

Gordy eyed her. "If you feel so good, how come you're not eating?"

Hiro looked down at her food and fumbled to open the sandwich bag. "Just thinking, I guess."

"You going to come with me to Coop's after school?"

"No." She shook her head. "Not a chance. But I was talking to Ken this morning ... and I have a message you need to bring him."

CHAPTER 41

Once he got back from phoning Hammer, Coop went to his room and stayed there. He needed time to think.

Fudge curled up on the rug beside his bed. Her body looked totally relaxed, but she didn't sleep. Every time Cooper looked at her, she was looking at him. Like she was giving him the space he needed, but keeping an eye on him at the same time.

He should be feeling relieved. The police had a suspect in custody. Exactly what he'd been hoping and praying for. Well, hoping. He hadn't been praying as much as he should. Why was that? Cooper knew the answer had something to do with the Code of Silence. It was hard to ask God for favors when you were lying through your teeth to everybody else.

But right now he had to focus on a new game plan. If they had Mr. Lucky, he had to do everything he could to keep him in custody. And that would mean breaking the Code. The thing was, if they caught the robbers, the Code wasn't really needed anymore. Right?

He still had a squirrelly feeling about Hammer. He wanted to trust him, but he wasn't sure he could. What if he was the guy in the Elvis mask? It would be a perfect cover. Who would suspect a police detective? Maybe Hammer masterminded a little side business of robberies to add to his pension. What if Hammer met Lunk's dad before? What if they were friends? "Business associates." Maybe he'd done other jobs for Hammer in the past. They helped themselves, and helped each other.

Or maybe Lunk said something to his dad—even innocently. Maybe Lunk mentioned something about his new job and the safe and how he kept a lot of money inside. Lunk's dad may have contacted Hammer, and they could have planned the job together.

The possibilities looped through his head. One thought rose to the surface. He was running out of time. If he didn't do something, they were going to find him anyway. The police would win the little legal battle to do the interviews. Or they'd do a little DNA sampling and haul him in. If he waited for them to put it together, they'd pick him up on their own terms. And if Hammer was really part of the robbery, that meant trouble.

No, he couldn't just wait to see how things turned out. Not anymore. He pulled a spiral notebook out of his backpack and started sorting things out on paper.

1. Lunk's dad is Mr. Lucky. Need to avoid Lunk.
2. Hammer may be Elvis. Can't go to police station alone.
3. If I don't break the Code by tomorrow at 10:00, Lunk's dad will walk.
4. If I don't break the Code, they may find me soon anyway.
5. Need someone to go with me—someone I can trust.

Cooper put down his pen and reread the list. They had a suspect now. A *suspect.* That changed everything. "I'll tell Dad and Mom tonight."

He looked at Fudge as he spoke. Her ears perked up, but she didn't even raise her head.

"I'll get the security hard drive, and we can all go to the police station together. Dad. Mom. Hiro and Gordy too. It will be safer to go as a group."

Working out a plan was sort of like trying on a new pair of shoes. You laced them up and walked around a bit, seeing how they felt. He did the same with the plan. Spilling the beans tonight was an idea that took a little getting used to. Cooper needed to see if it was a good fit.

He ran outside to the shed and dug through the plastic barrel. He pulled out Frank's set of keys to the diner. They jangled a bit, and his mind flashed back to Frank 'n Stein's kitchen. Cooper jammed them in his pocket and reached for the hard drive. Tucking it under one arm, he hurried back to his room with Fudge shadowing him the whole way.

He stashed the diner keys under his bed next to the phone from Walmart. But he dropped the security hard drive right on top of his pillow and stared at it. Part of him wanted to cover it up. The other part wanted to leave it in plain sight as a symbol of what he had to do.

His gut felt a little jazzed. Like he'd taken too many rides at a carnival on a full stomach. Only this was a carnival ride he couldn't seem to get off. Staring at the fish tank, he let his mind drift like the fish inside. He thought about the horrible secret he'd been protecting, and the lengths he'd gone to keep it from being uncovered.

Cooper didn't like what he'd done, but it had all been necessary. If he had to do it all over again, he'd do it the same way.

Or would he?

Of course, if he could change anything, he'd change *where* he was last Thursday night. If only he'd never gone to Frank 'n Stein's, he wouldn't be in this mess. But then who would have gotten paramedics to help Frank? Frank might have laid there all night . . . and been dead in the morning.

Images of Frank crept into his mind. Frank getting beaten and crumpling to the floor. Pushing those pictures out of his mind, he flopped onto his bed.

He thought of Gordy. Did anybody question him at school? Did he stick to the Code? Cooper looked at his clock, wondering why Gordy hadn't stopped by yet. School had been out for over thirty minutes. He wanted to talk to Gordy, but then again, that would only bring him closer to confessing everything to his parents. Now that the police had Lunk's dad, it would all be over soon. His stomach churned.

He heard a car door slam outside. *Cops*. He peeked out the window and saw Mom and Mattie come up the front walk.

Fudge tore down the stairs to greet them. Cooper shuffled along behind her. He didn't feel a bit sick, but didn't want to get Mom suspicious about his miraculous recovery either.

Mattie burst through the door just as he got to the bottom stair. She waved, smiled, and hurried toward the kitchen, humming some nameless tune. Totally carefree. Just like his life before the Code.

Mom closed the door and walked over to him. She gave him a hug and felt his forehead. "No fever. How do you feel?"

"Good enough to go to school tomorrow." Originally he'd planned to stretch this sick routine out for another day if he could. But now that the police had a suspect and Cooper was going to tell his parents about what really happened, it didn't really matter anymore.

"But I think I'll take it easy and stay in my room for awhile," Cooper said.

"Okay," Mom said. "I'll bring you some soup and crackers in a bit."

"Sure, thanks, Mom. That'd be great."

Cooper trudged back upstairs with Fudge right behind him. Cooper plopped on the bed, and Fudge sat on the floor and leaned in close. Cooper stroked her head. "And what's the story with Hiro, Fudge?" He pictured Hiro in his mind the last time he'd seen her. Something about her eyes when he accused her of lying to her mom. The pain. Like he'd physically hit her. "I hate the way she looked at me."

Hiro didn't understand, or maybe *wouldn't* understand was a better way to put it. Following the Code was a matter of life and death. At least for Cooper up until now. She seemed to get that at first, but somewhere along the way she got confused.

Or was it him?

Cooper swung his legs over the side of the bed and sat there. What about the things she said about him? Her face drifted into his mind. But it wasn't the smiling, loyal Hiro he saw. It was the face that showed the hurt and pain she felt. And the loss of respect for him.

If he broke the Code of Silence, maybe things would get back to normal with Hiro. Maybe. Their friendship had taken a real hit. He knew it. But was the damage permanent?

The doorbell tore Cooper from his thoughts. Fudge bounded out of the room and down the hall barking and howling as she went.

"It's Gordy," Mattie called.

Cooper hustled down the front hall and stepped outside. Gordy stood waiting on the front porch. He started in as soon as the door closed behind Cooper

"I can't believe you ditched me today. I mean, I was totally on my own."

Cooper motioned for him to lower his voice. "I was sick."

Gordy glared at him. "Now you're lying to me, too, huh?"

"Lying?"

"Oh, come on. This is Gordy you're talking to. You can't tell me you really had the flu."

"I threw up last night. If you don't believe that, ask Mattie. She was there."

Gordy put his hands on his hips. "That was last night. But I bet you felt *fine* this morning."

Cooper looked down at the decking of the front porch.

He leaned in close. "You *ditched* me. Me."

CHAPTER 42

Cooper looked up. He expected his cousin's face to look angry. Instead he saw hurt.

"Sorry, Gordy."

"Before Hiro, it was always the two of us. We stuck together no matter what. Right?"

"We still do."

Gordy waved him off. "Then Hiro was like one of us, until she couldn't stand it anymore."

"Couldn't stand *what*?"

"How you've changed."

"What?"

"But in my heart I defended you. I stuck up for you because we always stick together. We cover each other's backs. Until this morning. And now even I can't defend you anymore."

"C'mon, Gordy." Cooper put his hand on Gordy's shoulder. "Calm down."

Gordy brushed Cooper's hand away. "What if Miss Ferrand questioned me today?"

"Did she?"

"No. But she *could* have. And you didn't care."

Cooper could feel his cheeks getting warm. He fought to keep his own voice down even though he felt like shouting. "Of course I care. You *know* I care."

Gordy looked at him. His eyes narrowed. "You expect me to believe that?"

"It's the truth."

"Truth?" Gordy shook his head. "Do you even know what the truth is anymore?"

"Huh?"

"That's what I figured." Gordy turned and trudged to the porch steps and sat down.

Cooper stood watching, his mind replaying what had just happened. Gordy didn't trust him anymore. *Gordy*.

"Maybe Hiro is right," Gordy said.

"About what?"

"Forget it."

Cooper sat on the step next to him. "No, tell me. What did Hiro say?"

"Can't." Gordy pretended to lock his lips with an invisible key. "I promised I wouldn't."

Gordy never kept secrets from him before. Never.

"When did you talk to her?"

"Last night after I left here. At lunch today. After school too. What difference does it make?"

A whole lot of difference in Cooper's mind. Gordy was spending time with Hiro without him. Lots of time.

"Anyway, I need to deliver a message from her." He paused like he was trying to be sure he worded it just right. "She talked to her brother right before school today."

"She talked to Ken?" Cooper couldn't believe it. But that explained the text message and where she got the inside scoop about a trap being laid for him. "Did she tell him?"

Gordy shook his head. "Just talked about the case."

"Ken isn't stupid," Cooper said. "He'll figure it out. What was she *thinking*?"

"Relax. She didn't break the Code. You want to hear this or not?"

What he really wanted to hear was an explanation from Hiro. But he didn't want Gordy to clam up either. "Yeah, sure. What did her brother say?"

"Some of the Arlington Heights cops are buddy-buddy with some of the boys in blue from Rolling Meadows. The word is they want the person who wrote the letters *bad*."

No news there.

"The cops call you 'Golden Boy'. Did you know that?"

Cooper thought about the way he signed the letters. *Silence is Golden*. "It makes sense, I guess."

"And Ken said that Hammer was going to nail you when you called back or something. They weren't going to let you slip away this time."

Cooper smiled. "I figured they'd have police patrolling all over at 3:30. So I was one step ahead of them. I called them early before they had the net in place."

Gordy looked relieved. "You got the phone without me?"

"Yep. And I made the call. Hammer seemed really surprised too. He tried to keep me on the phone, but I never saw one patrol car. I caught him totally off guard." Cooper glanced back toward the front door. "And I've got some *really* good news for you."

Gordy looked at him, his eyebrows raising slightly.

Cooper paused for a moment. "They got him."

"Who?"

"Lunk's dad."

"You sure?"

"Somebody from Plum Grove called in and gave them a tip."

Gordy smiled. "It was Hiro. Called Miss Ferrand's number."

Cooper stared at him. "You know that for a fact?"

"I gave her Ferrand's number last night. And Ferrand hugged her before class."

A little alarm went off in Cooper's head. Hiro and Gordy weren't just together a lot. They were meeting and making plans without him. They were taking matters into their own hands and leaving him out of the loop. Hiro was gone, and she was taking Gordy with her.

"So they got him, huh?" Gordy looked like he was going to burst. "This is fantastic. Hiro called this one right."

Hiro was taking charge. And she could have blown the whole thing. "What did she tell Ferrand?"

"How she overheard the conversation between Lunk and his dad. How he's living in the shed. That they should check it out. Search the shed for masks or money."

She didn't really do anything wrong. It wasn't like she breached the Code. Not exactly. But she'd certainly torn another hunk away from their friendship. "And neither of you thought of talking to me about that first?"

"Look," Gordy said. "She kept telling you to tip the police off in the letter or the phone call. You wouldn't do it . . . so she did."

Cooper stared at the ground. *Let it go. Let it go. Don't take it out on Gordy or you'll drive him away. Admit it. You were wrong about Lunk—it's as simple as that. But the Code kept us alive, didn't it? That has to count for something. Hiro has to give me a little credit.*

"Coop? It's over, right? They got him. That's what we've wanted." The anger was gone from his voice now.

"Yeah," Cooper said. "Maybe it is." But it didn't *feel* over. Not nearly.

Gordy walked back up the stairs and sat on the railing. "So how come you're not doing cartwheels across the lawn or something?"

"They want me to bring in the hard drive and identify him on a lineup."

Gordy looked deep in thought. "Actually go there—as in turn yourself in?"

Turn yourself in. Cooper didn't like the way that sounded. Maybe he got so used to keeping a lid on this that even the thought of going to the police didn't seem like anything to celebrate. But it was time to break the Code for good. "If I don't, he'll walk."

Gordy's eyes widened. "But wait a second. What if—"

The front door opened and Cooper's mom walked out on the porch. "Hi Gordy. Looks like your cousin will be in school tomorrow."

Gordy eyed him. "For sure?"

Cooper nodded. "Yeah, I feel good."

Mom smiled and gave Gordy a hug, then walked back toward the door. "I'll put fresh sheets on your bed. You'll feel even better."

Cooper waited until she disappeared inside. "Okay. What is it?"

"I'm not sure. Ken didn't have any details, but it was pretty clear the police planned to try some other tactic this time. Something different."

"Whatever it was, it didn't work."

"I dunno," Gordy said. "Hiro wanted me to warn you that the police were setting some kind of trap. She said her brother used the word 'bait.' They were going to 'bait' you so you'd turn *yourself* in."

"*Bait* me?" Cooper's mind raced, filling in the blanks. He stood and paced the front porch. "Hammer said they had Mr. Lucky. That I needed to identify him, or bring in the security camera hard drive."

"Think it's true?"

"The part about Lunk's dad—absolutely. But can I trust Hammer? *That's* the question."

Gordy nodded. "Think he's using Lunk's dad to bait you?"

"Oh, yeah." Cooper plowed his hands through his hair. It made sense. Hiro's conversation with her brother added even more doubts about trusting Hammer. "And I was ready to take the bait. Hook, line, and sinker."

He wished Hiro was with them right now. He wished that wall between them wasn't growing. The call to Ferrand and the conversation with Ken proved it was. But she did send Gordy to warn him. That was a plus.

"What if he never even hauled Lunk's dad in?" Gordy said.

Cooper nodded. He could hear Hammer's voice in his head.

You really want me to set him loose? An icy chill crept up his back. Now the idea of marching in there with the hard drive didn't sound like such a good idea, even if his parents came with him. How hard would it be for Hammer to destroy the evidence?

"We need to rethink our next step. I was ready to go in. I mean, I dug out the hard drive and everything. It's sitting right out on my bed."

Gordy's eyes opened wide. "Didn't your mom just go up to change your sheets?"

CHAPTER 43

Stupid, stupid, stupid. Cooper bounded up the stairs two at a time. Fudge shouldered past him and pulled ahead, even though she couldn't possibly be sure where he was going. He burst into his room just as his mom dropped a wad of sheets on the floor. For a second he stared at the bundle wondering if she had somehow rolled the hard drive up inside.

"Looking for this?" Mom held up the computer component.

"Yeah, thanks, Mom." Cooper stepped forward and reached for it.

Mom pulled it back. "Not so fast. First I want to know what this is all about."

Stupid mistake. He'd have to wing it. "An auxiliary hard drive. You know, a backup."

"*Whose* hard drive?"

"A friend from school. They got a new computer with tons more memory. They didn't need the backup space anymore so he offered it to me." He gave what he hoped looked like a casual shrug. "I figured we could always use the extra memory so I took it."

She bounced it in her hand like she was testing the weight. More like testing the truth of his story. "And why hadn't you told us about it?"

He had to turn this around. Get her to stop asking questions by asking some of his own. "He gave it to me Tuesday. I got sick and forgot all about it. I put it on the bed so I'd remember to tell you. That's where it was, right?"

"Yes, but— "

"If I were trying to hide it, why would I leave it on the middle of my bed?"

She didn't answer.

Cooper was getting good at this little diversionary tactic. But he knew this could still go either way. He had her playing defense now, which is where he wanted her. If he let up the pressure, she'd jump back on offense. But push too hard, and she'd likely push back. "Gordy is going to help me hook it up this weekend. Sound okay to you?"

"Maybe. What's this boy's name?"

Busted. "Jeff." Where he came up with that name, he didn't know. It was the first name that popped into his head.

She eyed him. "Jeff?"

"Uh-huh. Jeff Williams. His family just moved here from Canada." Sometimes the more outrageous the lie, the more believable it was. Nobody would expect someone to lie that openly, so they figure it's the truth. Politicians did it all the time. He reached for the hard drive.

She pulled back again and wagged a finger at him. "Not so fast, Cooper MacKinnon. I think I'll hold onto this and see what Dad says tonight." She tucked it under one arm, picked up the bundle of sheets, and started out of the room.

Not good. Time for the trump card. "Don't you trust me?" He tried to paste a surprised, hurt look on his face.

Mom turned. "I've always trusted you, Cooper. But that doesn't mean that sometimes I shouldn't check to be sure I can *keep* trusting you." She smiled and left the room.

Cooper stood there for a second. Fudge looked at him with eyes that seemed to know everything. She looked disappointed in him. Or worried for him. She had good reason to be.

He followed his mom down the stairs to the laundry room. She put the hard drive on the counter and started feeding the sheets into the machine. It was crazy. Every cop in Rolling Meadows would love to get their hands on that little thing. So would the men that sent Frank into some kind of twilight zone between life and death. And here it was, just sitting out where anyone could see it.

"Did Gordy go home?"

How was he going to get the hard drive hidden again? What would he tell his dad?

"Cooper?"

He snapped his attention back to his mom. Too late. Her eyes flicked to the hard drive. *Stupid.* Cooper wanted to kick himself. She'd followed his gaze and caught him looking at it. That would only fuel her suspicions.

She cocked her head and looked at him. "Is Gordy still here?"

"I think so, but I'll check." He trudged to the front porch, relieved to dodge any questioning about the hard drive. Gordy must have read the situation just by looking at his face.

"She saw it?"

Cooper nodded. "Confiscated it too. Wants to talk to my dad about it."

"We're dead." Gordy jammed his hands in his pockets and turned away. "Now what?"

"I'll figure out something." Cooper hoped he sounded more confident than he felt. But if his dad plugged the auxiliary drive into the computer, and he would, he'd figure out Cooper was the mystery witness. Goodbye Code of Silence.

"Hiro wanted me to tell you one more thing."

Cooper groaned. "There's more?"

"Ken wondered if somehow organized crime was involved."

"Now there's a comforting thought." This whole thing was getting insane. Organized crime? He wanted to think through that possibility. What it would mean. But right now, at this moment he had to figure out if he should turn himself in or not.

He glanced over his shoulder at the house. The last thing he needed was for his mom to overhear. He stepped off the porch and headed for the driveway, motioning Gordy to follow. "The real question is this. Do the police really have Lunk's dad in custody or not?"

"And how are we going to find out?"

Cooper thought for a minute. "We could see if Hiro could ask her brother."

"What if *he* gets suspicious?"

Gordy was right. Asking questions like that would be risky. "Why do you think Hiro warned me?"

"She's your friend."

"You sure about that?"

"Definitely. She may be steamed at you, but deep down we stick together. Right?"

Cooper felt a twinge of guilt. He should have set his alarm so he could have warned Gordy before school this morning. In a way he really *had* ditched Gordy today. And things with Hiro were pretty shaky. Still, it was a good sign that Hiro warned him. Maybe their friendship hadn't taken quite the hit that he thought it did.

"Isn't that right, Coop? We stick together."

"Yeah, always. And I'm sorry about ditching you today. Really sorry."

Gordy nodded. "It kind of hurt, you know?" He gave Cooper a sideways glance. "But I'm okay now."

Neither of them said a word for a minute or two.

"Okay. Let's figure this out. If they really have Lunk's dad, also known as Mr. Lucky, somehow I need to go in or he'll be back on the streets," Cooper said. "But if they don't have Mr. Lucky, and I show up at the police station ..."

"You're toast," Gordy said.

"Or worse," Cooper said. "I turn myself right in to Detective Hammer, and he just happens to have an Elvis mask in his trunk ..."

"In which case," Gordy made a fake gun with his hand and put it to his head, "he'll be giving *you* a ride in the trunk too."

"Thanks, Gordy." Cooper wrestled with his thoughts. Turning himself in seemed more and more risky. If he could be sure they really had Lunk's dad in jail it was a pretty safe bet that Hammer was clean. Then he'd tell his parents everything. Maybe they'd call a lawyer. Or give an exclusive interview to the Daily Herald. The more people he told the better.

And if Hammer was involved in the robbery somehow, with enough people knowing, Hammer couldn't touch them. What would be the point? It would be too late to stop Cooper's eyewitness testimony, and the surveillance hard drive would be turned in as evidence. In a sense, Cooper would handcuff the cop.

But if Lunk's dad wasn't in jail, Hammer was dirty. What else could it mean? He'd probably have to talk to his parents anyway, but at least he'd know who the enemy really was. An idea started forming.

"We need to know if Lunk's dad is in jail."

Gordy grinned. "Sure. We just go to Lunk's house and ask if his dad can come out and play. Sounds easy."

Cooper shook his head. "We check Lunk's shed. See if he's inside."

"Great idea," Gordy said. "We just bang on the shed door. He'll come out and pound both of us."

"Not if we don't get close to the shed."

Gordy looked confused. "How you going to do that?"

Cooper checked over his shoulder. "With the potato gun."

CHAPTER 44

Gordy's eyes brightened. "We could shoot from far enough away where he'd never see us."

"And if he did, we'd have such a lead on him that he'd never catch us," Cooper said.

"After dinner?"

Cooper nodded. It wasn't much of a plan, but it was something. The best part was that Gordy seemed to have forgotten all about being mad at him. If only it would be that simple with Hiro.

"I'll bring the potatoes," Gordy said. "Think you can meet at seven?"

"I'll have the Spud-zooka ready."

Gordy met him at exactly seven wearing a dark hoodie. The side pockets sagged under the weight of a pair of the biggest Idaho potatoes Cooper had ever seen.

"Where did your mom get *those*?"

Gordy handed one to Cooper. "The farm must be near some nuclear energy plant or something. Maybe they're radioactive."

Cooper tested the weight and handed it back. "Let's go." He grabbed the homemade potato gun, hairspray, and ramrod. "Good news about the hard drive," he said. "I'll tell you on the way."

They stuck with the shadows, weaving their way from tree to tree. He waited until they were several houses away. "My dad called. The photo shoot he's on is running long. He told us to eat without him. He won't be home until late."

"Which means," Gordy said, "you're off the hook for tonight."

Cooper checked both ways and hustled across the street. "Tomorrow too."

"How do you figure?"

"My parents and Mattie are going to the circus tomorrow night. So I don't think it will come up until Friday."

"Which will give you another day to figure out how to explain things."

Cooper didn't answer. He knew he didn't stand a chance if his dad got the least bit suspicious. His only hope was that the police find the robbers before that happened. Which brought him back to tonight. He intended to find out if the police *had* hauled Lunk's dad in, or if the police cooked up the story as bait.

Brittle leaves huddled along the edges of the street as high as the curbs. Cooper and Gordy shuffled through them, every step crunching as they went. Cooper held the Spud-zooka low at his side. To someone passing in a car it might look like he was carrying a five foot length of PVC pipe, with one end a little bigger than the other. To someone who had ever used a potato gun, they'd recognize it right off. In the darkness of the night, Cooper figured nobody would even notice.

"I called Hiro," Gordy said. "Asked if she wanted to come with us."

"I bet that went over big."

"Yeah. She pretty much said we were crazy. If it was up to her, the Spud-zooka should have been permanently retired after the last time."

Cooper smiled, picturing her giving a lecture on the topic. "I wish ..." He couldn't finish the thought. How would he say he wished things weren't messed up between them?

Gordy eyed him. "Wish what?"

"Nothing," Cooper said. "We're getting close."

The single story house Lunk's mom rented was almost perfectly square. One of blocks and blocks of tiny two-bedroom homes that put Rolling Meadows on the map over fifty years ago. A narrow asphalt drive ran along one side of the house.

Cooper and Gordy circled around the back of a home several doors down. They hunkered down for several minutes to allow their eyes to adjust to the darkness of the backyard. A shallow strip of trees bordered the back end of the lot and continued well past Lunk's. It would have been better in the summer when the trees still had their leaves, but the trees would still give them some cover.

Sticking to the tree line, they worked their way through the next couple of yards and stopped a lot and a half away. The metal shed was easily visible in the moonlight.

"Looks like somebody is home." Gordy pointed toward the light streaming out from under the sliding door.

"We'll find out soon enough." Cooper jammed a potato into the open end of the PVC pipe. The sharpened edges of the pipe peeled off the excess potato, leaving a solid two-inch spud-slug in the pipe.

Gordy unscrewed the cap to the four-inch wide PVC section attached to the other end. "Ready?"

Cooper gave him a nod.

Gordy sprayed a four-second count of hairspray into the combustion chamber and screwed the cap in place. Cooper used the ramrod to push the potato down the barrel to the chamber loaded with hairspray fumes, compressing the mixture in the process.

Dropping to one knee, he shouldered the potato gun and aimed it toward the shed.

"Here we go," Gordy whispered. He reached over and flicked the igniter mounted on the bottom of the combustion chamber.

WOOOOMPH!

The bazooka gave a little kick and launched the potato.

"Too high," Gordy said. "Cleared the roof of the shed by a good three feet."

A dog started barking somewhere beyond the shed. Cooper watched the door of the shed, hoping it would open. Nothing.

"Let's reload."

Within thirty seconds Cooper was aiming at the shed again, but a little lower this time. "Okay."

WOOOOMPH!

The potato rocketed out the barrel. BANG! It disintegrated against the side of the corrugated steel shed with the sound of a brick crashing into a metal garbage can. The dog barked furiously.

"Direct hit." Gordy slapped him on the back and crouched down beside him.

The shed door flew open. A man stood silhouetted against the opening. Shoulders hunched, fists raised, ready for a fight.

"Bingo," Cooper whispered. Hammer said he'd be holding him until 10:00 a.m.

The back door of the house opened and Lunk ran out. The two talked for a moment. Cooper couldn't hear anything they said, but Lunk's dad acted pretty upset. He circled around the shed, apparently looking for whatever made the sound. Stopping near the point of impact, he picked something off the ground and smelled it.

"Mashed potatoes," Cooper whispered.

The man threw it to the ground and brushed off his hands. He looked at the side of the shed and the shrapnel pattern on the ground. He held his arm out straight, as if trying to determine where the shot came from. Lunk's dad pointed directly at them.

Lunk stopped and looked too, but apparently their vision hadn't totally adjusted to the darkness.

Cooper's heart thumped out a warning.

"Run or stay?" Gordy whispered.

"Wait." Cooper watched to see if they made any move toward them.

Lunk jammed his hands in his pockets and shuffled back into the house.

"Think he's going in for a flashlight?"

Cooper didn't answer him. He kept his eyes on Lunk's dad.

The man stepped back inside the shed and an instant later the light went out.

Cooper strained to see. The shed door was still open, but without the light it was impossible to see the man in the shadows.

"Let's run for it," Gordy hissed.

Could the man see them? Cooper wished for more leaves on the trees. *Stay still.* Sometimes that was the best cover a guy could get. If they took off now, Lunk's dad would spot them and probably give chase. But even if he did, they'd have a yard and a half lead on him.

When in doubt, don't. Don't *what*, though. Don't stay or don't leave? Probably don't go out and shoot the gun in the first place.

Cooper saw something move. Lunk's dad crept out of the shadows and took a step their way. This guy wasn't letting it go.

"Okay, nice and easy, back the way we came." Cooper barely whispered.

A twig snapped somewhere behind them, maybe a house or two away. Cooper grabbed Gordy's arm and scanned the tree line. The faint sound of leaves rustling helped him zero in on the spot. Someone was there. He could see him hunched over trying to use a tree as cover. *Lunk!* He hadn't just casually gone into the house. He'd gone out the front door and circled around. They were trapped!

CHAPTER 45

Did Lunk see them? Cooper tightened his grip on the Spud-zooka and ramrod.

Gordy must have seen Lunk too. They couldn't go forward toward the shed, and Lunk blocked the way they came. That meant cutting through the neighbor's yard right between the two.

Cooper pointed the direction. Gordy nodded.

Springing to his feet, Cooper bolted from the woods with Gordy right beside him. Lunk's dad came crashing toward them from the right. Lunk hotfooted in from the other side.

Cooper vaulted over a sandbox and dodged a bicycle just barely visible in the moonlight.

"STOP!"

Lunk's dad. It had to be. But it fueled Cooper's sprint between the houses and toward the street. Gordy raced right alongside him, legs pumping at a speed only raw fear produces.

"STOP NOW!"

The man's voice wasn't as close, but sounded just as angry. They were stretching the distance between them. Across the street and between another set of houses. Cooper didn't let up. Outrunning Lunk's dad was one thing, but Lunk could be a different story. Not that Lunk was quick—he was determined, though. And if he got his hands on one of them, he'd slow them down in a hurry.

Fence. The cedar planks had to be six feet high.

Cooper paced his strides to give a leap at the right moment. Grabbing the top of the wood, he swung a leg up and jumped to the other side. He landed on his feet, narrowly missing a patio chair.

Gordy wasn't as lucky. One foot got tangled up on lawn furniture and he came down hard, slamming against a grill.

Keeping one eye on the fence, Cooper grabbed him and pulled him to his feet.

"Hurry!"

Gordy hobbled next to him, favoring one leg. "Slow down, Coop," he said. "My ankle."

Slow down? Grabbing him by the arm, Cooper yanked him ahead. "You're going to get us caught." *Run, Cooper. Leave Gordy behind or you'll both be dead. He can hide. He'll be okay.* The thought flashed in his head. It made sense—but he couldn't. Wouldn't. He pulled harder.

Wincing with every step, Gordy built up to a rocky gallop.

Cooper led them through the backyard and alongside the house. As they rounded the corner he glanced back to see someone struggling to get over the fence. Streetlights illuminated the front yard. They'd be sitting ducks out here.

He grabbed Gordy's sweatshirt and pulled him toward an overgrown set of bushes lining the front of the house. The lights from inside spilled out the front windows, leaving the shrubs in heavy shadows. A lap dog hopped onto the back of the couch and yapped out a warning.

"Shhhhhh." Gordy held his hands up as if to show the dog he meant no harm.

"Hide!"

Cooper dove to the ground and army-crawled his way to the back of the bushes, pushing the spud-zooka ahead of him. He could smell the dirt and leaves as Gordy wriggled beside him. When they reached the brick of the house they stopped.

Seconds later heavy footsteps rustled through the leaves on the side of the house. Lunk passed them and stopped no more than twenty feet in front of the bushes.

The dog kept yapping from inside the house. What if the owner came out to see what was wrong?

Lunk glanced toward the house and barked back at the dog. The dog went crazy. Breathing heavily, Lunk bent over, rested his hands on his knees, and scanned the street in both directions.

Cooper willed Lunk to leave. *Just go. Give it up.* He hated the helpless feeling of hiding, but at the same time realized if they hadn't gone for cover, Lunk would probably be wailing on one of them right now.

The sound of more footsteps came from around the side of the house.

"Where'd they go?" Lunk's dad jogged up beside his son.

"Lost 'em."

The man swore. "I'd like to have gotten my hands on them."

Cooper could imagine that. Lunk and his dad tag-team wrestling him and Gordy. Cooper prayed. Told God how stupid he was and promised he'd be smarter in the future, even with the potato gun. A desperate prayer for sure. But he prayed anyway. He heard Gordy's heavy breathing beside him. Was *he* praying too? Cooper hoped so.

One thing was for sure. Hammer *had* been trying to bait him. Lunk's dad obviously wasn't being held. This bit of information changed everything.

"Split up," the man said, pointing to his left. "I'll go the other way. Whistle if you see something."

Lunk jogged off in one direction, his dad in the other.

"How's your ankle?" Cooper whispered.

"Throbbing." He hiked up his knee and massaged his ankle. "I hit a nerve or a funny bone or something. I don't think I twisted it bad."

"We'll stay put until we're sure it's clear."

"Think he recognized us?"

Cooper thought for a moment. "It's too dark." He hoped he was right.

"Thanks for waiting for me," Gordy said. "For a minute there I thought you were going to ditch me again."

Again. That stung. Cooper already lost Hiro. He couldn't lose another best friend. But a few minutes ago he'd almost done it. He'd actually considered leaving him behind. Ditching him. "We stick together. Right?"

He saw the faint glow of Gordy's teeth form a smile.

"Yeah, we stick together."

Cooper shifted his position to keep watch on Lunk and his dad. *We stick together.* And it felt good. He was the one who always tried to look out for Gordy and Hiro. When did he start looking out for himself? What was *wrong* with him?

The dog still barked, but it didn't sound like his heart was in it.

"It was a good shot," Gordy said.

"What?"

"The Spud-zooka. Nice hit."

Cooper imagined how it must have startled old man Lunquist. He laughed quietly. "Does that mean you're glad we did it?"

"Definitely. As long as we don't get pounded into mashed potatoes ourselves."

Cooper kept a close watch on the street. "Hiro would have wet her pants if she were here."

"You got that right." Gordy repositioned himself. "And good thing you didn't just turn yourself in."

He had Hiro to thank for that. He didn't want to think about what might have happened if he walked into the Police Department with the surveillance stuff. And if organized crime *was* in the mix, Hammer wouldn't have to touch him. He'd just let the wrong people know his identity.

Something moving caught his attention. "They're coming back."

The boys lay completely still. Lunk and his dad met back at nearly the same spot. The lap dog had another fit.

"Long gone," the man said. "Probably a couple of your friends from school."

"I don't have any friends."

Lunk's dad didn't say anything for a long moment. "Well, whoever they are, I'll be ready for them if they come back tonight."

Fat chance. Cooper wasn't going to come back tonight or any other night. Get home. That was the big goal now. To his room. His bed. Hide out there for a couple of days. Or weeks.

"You need to leave."

Lunk's voice. Cooper held his breath.

"You still worried about the little visit from the cops?" A deep voice. Strong. Like a DJ.

"Mom is."

"They asked some questions and left. They've got nothing on me."

So they did stop by. But they didn't haul him in. What was going on here? How could Hammer not arrest him—unless he was covering for him somehow?

"Mom's got a good job. Since you've come back so have her migraines."

The man spit. "Women."

"You've got money now. You got what you came for."

The senior Lunquist swore. "I need a couple more days. I've got a loose end to tie up. Could use your help."

Gordy squeezed his arm. Like he was thinking the same thing Cooper was. Cooper was the loose end. He had to do something before Lunk's dad got to him. And if the cops didn't arrest him before he left town, they might never catch him.

"I'm going back," Lunk said.

"Any idea who'd throw a potato at the shed?" Mr. Lunquist shuffled through the leaves alongside him.

Lunk rounded the corner of the house. "I intend to find out."

CHAPTER 46

Cooper had been right from the beginning. Police *were* part of this. And not just any cop, but the detective in charge of the investigation himself. How else could you explain why they let Lunk's dad off? *And* Hiro was right, too. Lunk's dad was part of it. He was Mr. Lucky. He and Hammer were both in this. And likely some organized crime connection was the common denominator that tied them together.

Cooper didn't move after Lunk and his dad disappeared around the corner of the house. The yapping inside the house died down.

What if Lunk hid in some shadows nearby. Watching. Waiting. Cooper kept still another few minutes, then inched out and crawled to the side of the house. The backyard looked clear. He motioned for Gordy, and minutes later the two hustled down the street. Gordy had an arm around Cooper's shoulders like they were in a three-legged race.

By the time they got to Gordy's house, his cousin hardly limped at all.

"Tomorrow is Halloween." Gordy stood at his door before going in.

Halloween. For an instant Cooper saw the group picture Frank had always been so proud of. He wished Frank could show it to him one more time. And he would give anything to be in a new photo with Frank like that again—even if he hadn't had a growth spurt yet. But there would be no group photo this year—or most likely ever again. He pushed the thought back and his mind drifted to the unholy holiday approaching.

"I can't imagine it being any scarier than tonight."

Gordy grinned, but it faded just as fast as it appeared. "You'll be there, right? At school?"

"Yeah, but I may be wearing a disguise."

Gordy grinned again, but this time it stuck. "Costumes are a great idea. Maybe I'll come as a hostage or something."

"A hostage?"

"Yeah, I'll put some duct tape over my mouth and nobody will get anything out of me."

If only it was that easy. "Tomorrow." Cooper waved, and crept across the street to his place. He stashed the Spud-zooka in the shed and hurried into the house.

With surprising ease he lied to his mom about where he'd been. He convinced her he wanted to go to bed early so he'd be strong enough for school the next day. Now there'd be no chance of his dad confronting him about the hard drive either.

Fudge followed Cooper to his room and curled up on her rug when he shut the door. He sat at his desk and stared at nothing in particular. Clearly he'd avoided another disaster. He'd avoided Hammer's little trap. But he'd created another problem in the process. How hard would it be for Lunk to suspect they'd been the ones behind the fiasco tonight?

He swiveled in his chair to talk to Fudge, but she was already asleep. Her ears and feet twitched in random spasms. What did dogs dream about anyway?

She gave out several quiet yips like she was having a nightmare.

He sat next to her and stroked her head. Startled, she tensed and tried to get to her feet.

"It's okay, girl," Cooper soothed. "It's me."

Her tail thumped against the hardwood floor.

Cooper lightly touched the tips of the fur just inside her ear. Her ear danced involuntarily. He did it again until Fudge stood, gave a full body shake and sat down to scratch her ear with her back paw.

He laughed and tussled her ears. "Okay, Fudge, lay down. I won't mess with you anymore."

Ears flat to the sides of her head, she lay back down but kept her eyes open and on him.

"Don't you trust me?" He scratched behind her ears and his mind jumped to Hiro. That's what happened with her. She stopped trusting him or lost her respect for him. Maybe both.

Which was really crazy when he thought about it. "Everything I did helped protect her and Gordy. Even Mom and Dad. And Mattie. If I talked, all of them could have gotten hurt. Or killed."

Fudge gave him a doubtful look.

"You don't believe me?" Cooper eyed her back. Sometimes it seemed she understood everything he said to her. "Then why did I do it?"

Fudge nuzzled his hand and licked it. Like she was trying to comfort him. Like she understood the truth and knew it would be hard for him to accept. Which was a ridiculous thought. Dogs aren't mind readers. How could she know anything about his motives?

A thought popped into his head. A question, really. *Was the Code of Silence really about protecting your family and friends, or was it all about protecting yourself?*

His mind replayed the events of the last week. It had all seemed so simple at first. So logical. Silence is golden. Right? Keep your mouth shut and nobody gets hurt.

Except people *did* get hurt. Hiro, for one. He'd tested their friendship to the breaking point and then some. He'd done it to Gordy, too.

The Code seemed like the right thing to do at the time. But since when did living a lie become the right thing to do? The Code wasn't solely built on a vow to stay quiet. It was about living a lie, and doing everything they could to keep anyone from discovering the truth. And that meant more lies. And lots of deception.

Cooper didn't like the thought of that. He looked around his room. Looked for something to get his mind off this. But all he could think about were the lies.

He told more lies in the last week than he could count. To Mom and Dad. To teachers, police. Anybody and everybody. He hadn't just broken trust. He'd trampled it. Shattered it into as many pieces as the lies he'd told.

Most of all he'd been lying to himself. How could he have ever figured this would all work out fine ... or go away? Lies don't work that way. They have a way of circling back and showing up just when you don't want them to.

He started pacing the room. He didn't want to think about this anymore. It was almost over. They'd stuck to the Code and they were still safe almost a week later. Nobody was breaking into their house at night to shut him up permanently. He was alive, and sometimes that's what mattered most.

He slumped down on the bed and looked at Fudge. She looked at him with sad eyes. Like Hiro had been talking to her.

"Don't give me those eyes, Fudge."

She didn't blink. And deep in her eyes he sensed the truth. He may be alive, but with all these lies, how could he live with himself?

But he had to. A little longer and things would work out. He was sure of it.

"God, please," Cooper whispered. "Get me out of this."

Did God hear the prayers of liars?

He had to shake that kind of thinking. He couldn't let fear get the best of him. He had to do something. It was obvious now that the robbers would never be picked up. Hammer would see to that. And Cooper's notes to the police only made the search for him more desperate.

Time was running out. Of that he was certain. If Lunk figured out he'd been the one with the potato gun, it wouldn't be hard to piece the rest together. Lunk would gladly tell his dad so Mr. Lucky could handle the loose ends and get out of town. His heart kept bringing him back to the same course of action. Something that twisted his gut just to think of it.

"Have I gone too far, girl?" Lying comes with a high price. He was seeing that now.

"It's never too late to tell the truth, is it?"

Fudge didn't look convinced.

And deep down ... neither was he.

CHAPTER 47

Cold and overcast. A typical Halloween in the Midwest. Cooper headed for the bus stop feeling like he hadn't slept all night.

"What happened to you?" Gordy jogged over, barely limping at all. "Let me guess. This is your Halloween costume ... and you're a zombie."

"Didn't sleep so well."

"I'm not surprised." Gordy held up one finger. "Hammer's looking for you." Gordy held up a second finger. "Some very nasty goons—who probably work for some underworld kingpin, see you as a loose end." Third finger. "You've got the situation with Hiro." Fourth finger. "Lunk." Fifth, "Miss Ferrand acted like she wanted to talk to you."

"Gee, thanks, Gordy. That makes me feel a whole lot better."

Not that he hadn't been thinking of those things all night. Add to that a growing sense of guilt. That's the only thing Cooper could call it. A feeling that all his lies, all that wrong couldn't possibly be right. He'd begged God to bring in the robbers so this whole thing would just go away. Then maybe Hiro would forget all about it too, and things would get back to normal.

He looked down the block. "I wonder where Hiro is..." Even if she showed up now there wouldn't be enough time to talk things out with her.

"I think she's getting a ride from her mom."

Which was a polite way of saying he *knew* she was getting a ride from her mom.

"Wants to avoid me that bad, huh?" Cooper stared down the block. He'd done this to himself. He should have talked it out with her sooner. Giving her space only seemed to be widening the gap between them.

"I wouldn't put it like *that*."

The bus turned onto Fremont. "How would you put it?"

Gordy didn't answer for a moment. "Here comes the bus."

The morning dragged. At 10:00 Cooper's mind flashed to Hammer. By now the detective knew the little plan to bait him didn't work.

When Cooper and Gordy walked into Miss Ferrand's class, Hiro wouldn't look at him. Not good. On the other hand, Miss Ferrand couldn't *stop* looking at him. He sensed her analyzing him. Maybe she was trying to decide whether she should hold him after class for a little one-on-one chat.

When the bell rang, Miss Ferrand watched him leaving class, but never stopped him to talk. Weird. And Hiro didn't talk to him either. Awkward.

The only one who wanted to talk was Lunk. He sat right across from Cooper and Gordy at the lunch table. Two burgers sat on his tray. Two bags of chips. Three cartons of milk. Just like Gordy.

"So, MacKinnon." Lunk squeezed ketchup packets onto each burger and leaned forward. "You going to tell me what's going on, or do you want me to guess?"

"What?" Cooper tried to screw a confused look on his face.

"Tuesday you were real serious about ditching Ferrand. You write *I didn't do it* all over the bathroom stall. Don't try to deny it. I know it was you."

Cooper stared at him and didn't say a word. He tried to put on a stone face, not showing any emotion at all. Out of the corner of his eye he saw Gordy give him a confused look.

Lunk took a bite of his burger, worked it into one cheek, and kept going. "Wednesday you play sick and don't even come to school. So don't act like you don't know what I'm talking about. You going to tell me what's going on?"

"Nothing's wrong. I'm fine."

Lunk snickered. "Right. So I'll guess." He took a huge bite from his burger and started chewing like he was enjoying putting Cooper on edge. "It's about last Thursday night."

Cooper took a bite from his sandwich and pointed at his mouth with a shrug. He made a big act of chewing. His mind raced for an answer. A lie that would come across as believable. With an exaggerated swallow, he cleared his throat.

"What are you talking about?"

A smile swept across Lunk's face. "I thought Christians weren't supposed to lie. You know exactly what I'm talking about."

Cooper didn't answer. He couldn't think of anything to say.

"You're the one the police are looking for."

And the one your dad is looking for.

Lunk's smile disappeared. "You were there." He leaned in close. "Frank 'n Stein's."

"Me?" Cooper turned to Gordy like he'd just heard something funny. Gordy looked like a kid caught shoplifting.

"You wrote the letter in the paper. I believe you didn't hurt Frank," Lunk said.

You know I'm telling the truth about that because your dad hurt him.

Lunk pointed at Cooper's chest. "But you didn't exactly help him either."

Cooper felt his cheeks getting warm. He took a sip of his milk.

Lunk leaned his forearms on the table. "I think you need my help."

Right. Cooper reached across the table and lifted the bun off a burger. "What's in those burgers you're eating?"

Lunk stood and grabbed his tray. "Wrong time and place for this discussion. I'll catch you later."

By the look on his face, Cooper figured he would, too.

Lunk swung a leg over the bench and sauntered away. Cooper sat stunned.

"Now what?" Gordy whispered.

"Not sure," Cooper said. "We can't talk here."

Gordy nodded. "*The Getaway* after school?"

"After my parents leave for the circus. At 7:00."

"Should I tell Hiro?"

"Why bother? She won't come anyway. She did a nice job of disappearing for lunch."

Gordy shook his head. "I'll talk to her on the bus."

Cooper didn't see Lunk at school the rest of the day, but a growing uneasiness made him look over his shoulder almost as often as he looked ahead. He saw Hiro, but she avoided him like he avoided Lunk. Her mom even picked her up at the end of the day.

"I told you Hiro won't come when we meet tonight." Cooper pointed at Mrs. Yakimoto's car. "She won't even ride on the same bus as me."

"Her mom is taking her to see Frank." Gordy hefted his backpack over one shoulder. "She told me about it just after lunch."

That figures. Cooper had a clear view of Hiro's window and watched to see if she'd turn. If she'd even look their way.

Hiro sat there looking straight ahead while her mom pulled out of the lot.

She can't even look at me. "Forget it. It doesn't matter."

Gordy started up the steps of the bus. "Don't act like you don't care. This is Gordy you're talking to."

Cooper followed him into the bus and plopped onto a seat next to him. His mind stayed on Hiro. She'd changed somehow. Really changed.

Cooper wished they were riding their bikes. Just to feel the wind in his face. The freedom.

"I'll talk to Hiro," Gordy said after they got off at their stop. "*The Getaway* at 7:00. Right?"

"Right."

Gordy jogged toward his house.

Cooper needed time to think. What would he say to Lunk? If Lunk told his dad his suspicions, it was all over anyway. He pictured Lunk's dad wearing a latex mask. Imagined him coming to Cooper's house for a little midnight visit.

The sight of his dad's truck in the drive helped him shake the thoughts from his head. They'd be leaving for the circus soon. It might have been a good way to forget things, but then there was the issue of the clowns. No thanks.

"Cooper." Dad stepped out the front door. "Hop in the truck."

"Where are we going?"

"Frank 'n Stein's."

CHAPTER 48

Cooper froze.

His dad walked around to the driver's door and pulled it open. "I feel bad I didn't have a ticket for you tonight. The least I can do is take you out for a shake."

Cooper took a deep breath and blew it out. "Aw, don't worry about it, Dad. I'm fine. Really."

"Hop in. It'll give us a chance to catch up."

Just about the last thing Cooper would like to do. It almost ranked up there with talking to Lunk or Miss Ferrand. He climbed into the cab and buckled up, stealing a quick glance at his dad. If he suspected something, his face didn't show it. Cooper's mouth went dry. Maybe this was about the hard drive.

Dad filled the short drive with talk about a couple of photo shoots he'd lined up. Cooper tried to think of something to say if his dad asked what was going on in his life.

When Frank 'n Stein's came into view, Cooper noticed the boarded-up window had been replaced. To other people it would look like the place was getting back to normal. Cooper wondered what normal really was.

The moment they swung open Frank 'n Stein's front door, the aromas of Italian beef sandwiches and Chicago-style hotdogs greeted him like old friends. The place still smelled like heaven, but his memories conjured up a scene definitely south of there.

Mr. Stein stood at the counter. His face lit up in recognition when he saw Cooper.

"There he is!" He smiled. "One of our best customers."

People always say something like that when they can't remember your name. Mr. Stein tried. He really did. But nobody could remember names like Frank did. Frank's picture greeted him from the top of the donation jar. And it looked like they needed a bigger one. The jar was packed.

It didn't feel like a typical Halloween, even after the way Mr. Stein had decked the place out with Halloween decorations. A Jack-o-lantern sat on the ordering counter, complete with a candle. The walls of the empty dining area had been covered with a stone block mural to look like a dungeon. A life-sized human skeleton hung from chains on one wall. It looked way too real for Cooper's liking. The jaws of the skull hung aghast, like it recognized Cooper and knew his secret. Cooper imagined it was himself. In a way it was. He'd been a prisoner of this place ever since the robbery.

Black and orange crepe paper twisted together along the borders of the dining area—a hopeless tangle that couldn't be separated without some major tearing. Webs stretched from the neon signs to the windowsills. Fist-sized plastic spiders clung to them.

The more he saw, the more keyed-up he felt. Taco Bell would have been a much better choice. He kicked himself for not suggesting it to Dad. But if he had, that might have looked suspicious. Taco Bell was okay for a change, but everybody knew Frank 'n Stein's was his number one.

"The place looks great, huh?" Dad pointed at the Frank 'n Stein monster mascot grinning at them from the corner. It seemed to be in its element now. The grin somehow bigger. Creepier. Like it looked right into his jeans pocket and thought the missing house key was an inside joke between the two of them.

Mr. Stein slid a large order of fries and two shakes across the counter. Dad led the way to a table. *The* table. The one he normally sat at with Gordy and Hiro. The one he sat at last Thursday night before everything changed.

Cooper slid into the booth and did his best to push it out of his mind.

"So tell me what's going on with my boy." Dad took the lid off his monster shake and poked a straw deep in the creamy vanilla.

What could he say? Something safe. Trouble was, no safe topics existed in his life right now. Talk about school? Sure. Miss Ferrand is ready to have him psychoanalyzed. He'd just made a graffiti wall out of one of the bathroom stalls. He took a handful of fries. "I can't think of anything to talk about right now."

Nothing he *wanted* to talk about anyway. At least it was partially true.

"How's Gordy doing?"

Cooper took a deep draw from his chocolate shake. "He'll be jealous you didn't invite him."

His dad laughed. "I believe it. He can really pack it in."

Cooper wished Gordy was here. He'd probably do some goofy thing to get the conversation going in a good direction.

"How about Hiro?"

Bingo. He'd just pressed his finger on a bruise. Like a mental version of the Battleship game, his dad just scored a hit. His eyebrows moved together slightly as if he noticed Cooper's hesitation. If he didn't say something quick a lot more questions would follow—and Cooper would be sunk.

"Well, I haven't seen too much of her this week." He poked his straw up and down through the plastic lid, making a squeaking sound. "She was sick one day. I was sick another. Today we missed each other all day. Her mom picked her up from school, so we didn't get to talk on the bus." All of it true, but intended to misdirect him. So that really made it all a lie, didn't it?

"That's too bad."

Cooper's tactic worked, but he didn't exactly feel happy about it. It only intensified a sense of isolation. Like he was all alone and in a place he shouldn't be.

"I really like that girl. And she's a good friend." His dad leaned back and smiled, staring up at the ceiling like he was playing back a scene from his memory. "Yeah, good friends are a gift from God."

One he'd underappreciated. "She's really something," Cooper said.

"A real sweetheart." Dad nodded as he spoke the words. Like he'd just realized the truth of what he said. "But she's tough, too. Doesn't take guff from anyone."

Don't I know it. Loneliness knifed through him. Next to Gordy, she was his best friend. *Was.* He'd messed that up good.

He'd messed everything up. He'd twisted the truth and lies together like the crepe paper crisscrossing the room. And he didn't think he could untangle it by himself.

For a moment Cooper felt an urge to spill the whole thing. Just tell Dad and let him help sort this mess out.

Tell him. A lump swelled in his throat. Why not? *Tell him now.* Deep down, he knew he needed help. For the first time in a week he cracked open a door he'd never planned to open. The one that he'd hidden the truth behind. Dad would know what to do. He'd understand and forgive him. He'd been fooling himself to think it was *his* job to protect the family—or that he could. Dad was the one who needed to do it. But how could he if he didn't even know the family was in danger?

The thought gave him a rush of something. Adrenaline? His breathing came in quick, shallow breaths. Not adrenaline. Hope. *TELL HIM.* He gripped the edge of the table as if to steady himself. Okay. He'd do it.

Remember the Code. The words struck him just as hard as if they'd been delivered with a fist. What was he thinking? How would he even start? His dad would be so disappointed in him. Plus, talking here didn't seem right.

The side door swung open from the kitchen and Mr. Stein

walked into the dining area. "Well." He walked toward their table and wiped his hands on a white apron stretched around his waist. "Thanks for coming in." He swung a chair around from one of the other tables and sat down. "Kind of a quiet day."

"Carson MacKinnon." Cooper's dad extended his hand. "And you know my son, Cooper, I imagine."

"Cooper." Stein smacked his forehead with his palm. "The face I know. The names?" he shrugged. "Frank is the great one with names."

"How is he?" Cooper's dad settled back in the seat.

Cooper squirmed.

"Better. Stronger every day."

Yeah, and Mr. Stein was overly optimistic.

Carson MacKinnon raised his eyebrows and glanced at Cooper. "What a relief, huh? Still in a coma?"

Mr. Stein squeezed his eyes shut and nodded.

Cooper's dad hesitated. Like he was giving a moment of silence in honor of the co-owner of Frank 'n Stein's. "Police have any more leads?"

"Aw," Stein slapped at the air. "They're chasing ghosts. Kids, actually. Got themselves tied up in a legal skirmish at the school so they can interrogate the kids. It's nuts. I think they've spent more time looking for the mystery witness than looking for the robbers themselves. Sometimes I wonder if they think the mystery witness was actually *involved* in some way. Like a gang initiation or something."

Cooper put the straw in his mouth and sucked hard on it. He needed to look busy so they wouldn't guess how shaky he felt inside.

"You don't think kids were involved?"

"Absolutely not. Not in a bad way, anyway. And the police haven't actually *said* kids were, but the way everything came down ... it just made me wonder."

Cooper's dad had that look he got sometimes when he was trying to word a question just right. "So what's your take on it—if you don't mind me asking?"

Stein leaned forward. "I believe it happened just like the letter in the paper. Some kid witnessed a robbery by professionals. The kid wasn't part of some gang. If he was he wouldn't write the letter. And no kid could take Frank down like that." He looked at the floor. "No kid *would*." He looked at Cooper. "Everybody loved him. Right?"

Cooper nodded, but no words came.

"The police can't get that through their heads. They're so hellbent on finding that kid—oh, excuse my language," Mr. Stein put a hand to his mouth. "Truth is, some boy out there is scared to death while some real bad guys are probably halfway across the country, spending Frank's money."

"If the witness is innocent, why doesn't he just turn himself in and prove he didn't do it?"

"Like the letter said, he thinks at least one of the robbers is a cop. He doesn't dare go to the police." Stein shrugged. "How can he? He doesn't know who to trust."

Dad swirled his shake with his straw. "I guess I see what you mean."

"The kid needs some protection. Some help. The police are trying to chase him down like he's a fugitive or something." He balanced his chair on the back two legs. "If there is a dirty cop, this kid can't go to the police by himself. I wouldn't either if I were him. It could be a trap." He looked at Cooper again. "Does that make sense?"

"Totally." Finally someone who really understood.

"Well, I wish the police would understand. They're going about this all wrong. This kid needs a friend. Not threats. All they're doing is scaring the kid into hiding." He waved an arm toward the window. "I'd like to put a banner in my windows. "'Come on in, kid. I believe you. Talk to me and I'll march right into the police station with you and the hard drive and show them myself.'" He shrugged. "Well, enjoy the shakes. I'd better get back to work." He smiled. "Time for me to shake a leg, and all that."

Cooper smiled back. What he really wanted to do is shake his hand.

CHAPTER 49

After some major begging by Mattie, Cooper's parents left early for the circus so they could watch the elephants being fed. Personally, Cooper thought the workers running cleanup behind the elephants would be the real show. Swinging the big coal shovels around to keep from being knee-deep in a real mess. Like he was now. More like neck deep.

Now that his dad was gone, all Cooper wanted to do was talk to him. Spill it all. He'd missed the perfect opportunity to do it at Frank 'n Stein's. Now it would have to wait, and the guilt he felt seemed heavier than ever.

They left Cooper with a giant bowl of bite-size Snicker bars to hand out to trick-or-treaters. Like he was really going to open the door for strangers wearing latex masks.

For a moment he pictured himself opening the front door and Detective Hammer standing there wearing an Elvis mask with some other cop in a clown mask behind him. Lunk's dad, Mr. Lucky himself, would be there too—and maybe "Guido" and "Lonnie" or some of the other boys from the underworld.

"Trick-or-Treat," they'd shout. "Thanks for opening the door, but you didn't need to bother. We have a key."

Would the robbers treat him to a trip to the hospital ... or the county morgue?

Cooper wasn't about to take a chance. Lunk had already connected enough dots to know Cooper was the witness his dad was looking for. Halloween night would be a perfect time to lead the robbers to his door.

He grabbed a piece of paper and a marker from his backpack. He wrote *Happy Halloween—take a piece of candy* in big letters and taped the paper to the edge of the bowl. Opening the front door a crack, he looked both ways and set the candy bowl on the porch deck. Fudge lunged at it, but Cooper grabbed her collar and pulled her back inside.

"Not for you, girl."

Cooper threaded his way through the house turning off lights, locking doors, and checking windows. If anybody stopped by for a visit, he wanted it to look like nobody was home. Fudge kept right on his heels with her tail wagging like this was some new kind of game.

By 6:30 he pulled on a black hooded sweatshirt and slipped out the kitchen door into the backyard. He wanted to get out of the house, and he needed some time to think. He hustled straight to *The Getaway* with Fudge trotting alongside. Climbing the ladder he swung a leg over the rail and crouched on the deck.

"You stay down there, Fudge. You're on guard duty tonight, okay?"

She didn't seem to like it any better than he did. She let out a single yip in protest.

"Quiet, girl. I don't want everybody to know I'm in here."

He opened the cabin, slipped inside and closed it up again. He needed some light, but wasn't about to power up the lantern. The cabin windows would glow and tip off somebody he was inside.

He lifted up the bench and pulled his dad's old duffle bag out from the storage compartment underneath. Rummaging through it quickly, he found the flashlight, pointed it at the floor, and clicked it on. A bright circle illuminated the decking under his feet. *Dad did get it fixed.* He tucked the duffle away, but left the flashlight on the table. He wondered if even the flashlight might be seen too easily from outside. He eyed a book of matches and a stubby candle on a brass stand.

Sitting on one bench, he struck a match and lit the candle. It wouldn't create enough light to be noticed outside, but it helped to chase out the shadows inside. He turned off the flashlight and waited.

Looking out the window, he checked to make sure the gate to the front yard was closed. If it wasn't, Fudge would be in that candy bowl in seconds.

He cupped his hands around the candle to take the chill out and peeked out the window every couple minutes. *The Getaway* made a perfect hideout, and with Fudge prowling around in the backyard, he felt safer here than in the house. But was anyplace really safe?

Not anymore. Not since he'd seen the robbery. Cooper turned that thought around in his mind. No, that wasn't really true. Was it just the robbery that had him hiding out in the boat on Halloween? Was it the robbery that had him looking over his shoulder at school?

No. It was the lies. The Code of Silence. The thing that was supposed to keep him safe worked like poison on him. Eating away at him. Destroying his friendship with Hiro. The robbery didn't do all that. It was the decision he made *after* the robbery. The decision to hide the truth in order to live. And every time he lied, he'd been dying a little bit more.

A thump along the side of the boat startled him. He puffed out the candle and stayed perfectly still. Holding his breath, he listened. Why hadn't Fudge barked?

"Coop," Gordy hissed from outside the cabin door. "You in there? It's me."

Gordy; that's why Fudge didn't bark. Cooper let out a shaky breath. He unlocked the hatch and stepped back. Gordy swung open the door. And he wasn't alone.

"Trick or treat," Gordy said. He gave a little wave and a goofy grin spread across his face.

Cooper looked past Gordy to the girl half hidden behind him.

"Hiro?" Cooper practically whispered her name.

He backed up and sat down on the bench while the two shuffled inside. Cooper relit the candle and searched Hiro's face to try to read what state of mind she was in. Maybe she'd thought about things and wanted to set things right too. Whatever was on her mind, she didn't let it show on her face.

Gordy sat on the bench opposite him. Hiro stood.

"I filled her in on the stuff with Lunk." Gordy shrugged. "She wanted to come."

Cooper attempted a smile. He hoped it didn't look as stiff and awkward as it felt. "Glad you're here."

"I won't be staying," she said. "I just have something to say, and then I'll leave the two of you to do whatever it is you plan to do."

"Okay," Cooper said, uneasiness growing. "Sure you don't want to sit?" He motioned toward the bench next to Gordy.

"Positive." She looked at Gordy, then back at Cooper. "I went to see Frank again today. My mom took me after school."

Cooper nodded. For a moment he wished he could have gone with her. Talked to Frank—even though he couldn't answer back.

"And Frank is coming out of it—the coma."

"What?" Cooper stood. Finally, a little light at the end of the tunnel. "That's great!" He looked at Gordy, but his cousin didn't look one bit excited.

"Yeah, I'm really relieved about that," Hiro said. She didn't look very relieved though.

"So he's going to be alright—I mean he'll make a full recovery. Right?" Cooper looked at Gordy and back to her again. Both of them looked glum.

"What am I missing here? You both act like he's going to die or something."

"Coop," Hiro's voice dropped to a whisper, "he *is* going to die."

CHAPTER 50

Cooper took a step back. "What?"

She folded her arms across her chest and hugged herself. "He figured out who was behind the robbery, remember?"

How could he forget? Frank had puzzled the thing together just before they put him in the coma.

"They realized he knew. That's why they meant to kill him. *Kill* him." She let the words sink in. "They obviously thought they did. And when he ended up in a coma, the scumbags were still okay. I mean it's not like he could possibly identify anybody. Right?"

Cooper nodded and pieces fell in place. "But if he climbs out of the coma, he's a lot bigger threat to the robbers than we ever were."

"Exactly," Hiro said. "If my brother is right, and organized crime is involved, they won't tolerate any loose ends."

Cooper slumped down on the bench. "They'll kill him."

"Dead men tell no tales. Right?" Gordy raised his eyebrows and drew one finger across his throat like a knife.

Hiro shot Gordy a sideways glance. "They tried once. They just messed up on their first attempt." She pulled the braid from over her shoulder and picked at it. "But they won't make that mistake again. Unless we do something, an innocent man will die."

In his heart he knew that was true. Why is it whenever he

thought he was seeing the light at the end of the tunnel it turned out to be an oncoming train? "But what about the police? Don't they have a guard at his hospital—"

"Police?" Hiro cut him off. "Thanks to us they don't know he *needs* protecting. Because they think it was a random robbery. They don't know the danger he'll be in. And if Detective Hammer *is* part of this, he'll have total access to Frank. Nobody will stop him."

Cooper pictured Elvis creeping into Frank's hospital room as he slept.

"Unless we tell." She stood with her hands on her hips watching him.

Cooper propped his elbows on the table and buried his face in his hands. He should have told his dad. He should have never set up the lousy Code in the first place. Yeah, Frank needed protection—and that meant going to the police. Hiro was right. But what about trusting the police? It would be risky to just walk into the police department and announce they'd seen the whole thing. Two cops were involved. That meant Hammer had a partner somewhere—a partner who would do anything to protect their dirty little secret.

"Well?"

Hiro had an "all business" look about her. Like she'd deliberately steeled herself so she wouldn't back down.

"Let me think."

"Think? What's there to *think* about? An innocent man is going to die because of you!"

"Me? I never hurt Frank—and I never would!" Cooper's leg started jumping under the table. *Not now.* He pressed his hand down on his knee. Hard.

"You're leaving him unprotected—and that's just as bad," she said.

"What if we talk to the *wrong* cop," Cooper said. "We could all be taking a risk."

Hiro took a step closer. "Yeah, and one we have to take. We were *wrong*, Cooper. All of us. We should have told our parents and gone with them to the police. The dumb Code and all the lies just made it worse on all of us."

The words sliced through him. He could feel his cheeks grow warm. He wanted to throw something. Anything. Just go out on the deck and chuck something as far as he could. Maybe even Hiro.

Get a grip, Cooper. Don't blow this. God, please help me. Help me process this right. I don't want to make this mess even worse.

"This isn't going to go away," Hiro said. "The longer we wait, the worse this is going to get."

Listen to her. Hiro was right. About a lot of things. The Code *had* made things worse on all of them—and it was all his idea. So many things happened that he hadn't seen coming. Like Frank's life being in danger. *Again.* "He's actually out of the coma now?"

Hiro shook her head. "In and out. He recognized me. Talked to me."

"What did he say?"

Her eyes pooled immediately. "Said he was glad to see me. To know I was okay." She swiped back tears. "Asked if you and Gordy were alright, and when I told him you were, he said 'Thank God.'"

Cooper felt like someone had just wrung him out. "Did he tell you who was behind the robbery?"

"Didn't get a chance. When he started talking, nurses ran in and Frank slipped back into the coma. The head nurse explained this happens as they're coming out. They may go back and forth a bit, but she seemed very excited. He'll probably be awake sometime tomorrow."

Gordy cleared his throat. "Which means we have to move fast if we're going to keep him safe."

Hiro folded her arms across her chest again. "We need to break the Code. We need to go to the police."

The instant she said it something inside him grabbed at it. This was truth. Cooper nodded. "You're right."

He could see her shoulders relax.

"You mean it?" Her voice sounded softer—like the old Hiro.

"Definitely." More than anything, now. "I just want to figure out the best way to do it."

Her shoulders tensed again. Her chin went up and her eyes narrowed. She stared at him like she was reading his thoughts. "Don't play games with me, Cooper MacKinnon. I'm not going to let you stall this. We go tomorrow morning together, or Gordy and I will do it ourselves."

She didn't trust him. Didn't trust *him*. He saw it in her eyes. Cooper glanced at Gordy. His face looked apologetic. Obviously they had this whole thing decided before they ever climbed onto *The Getaway*. Break the Code with us tomorrow morning or we'll do it without you.

He'd done it to himself. Why hadn't he seen it before? All the lies, the deception, the half-truths were their own type of poison. It had a toxic effect on their friendship. Hiro already distanced herself from him. Now even Gordy seemed to be pulling away.

If I had a chance to do this all over again, I'd do it so different. The truth of that thought swept over him. *God forgive me. Please forgive me.*

"Did you hear me, Cooper?" Hiro's voice sounded hard again. "I'm not letting you stall me."

Cooper looked down at the candle. "I'm not stalling." The flame flickered and danced. Squirming like his own gut. He felt like he'd fallen into a sewer. Only the sewage was his own dishonesty. He reeked with it. "I'm so done with the lies," he whispered. "I'm sick of it."

Gordy and Hiro stayed quiet. Maybe they didn't know what to say or had the good sense to let him think. But their silence allowed the truth to fully surface in his mind. And he didn't like what he saw. The Code *was* his idea. All his. He pushed it. Enforced it. And with every day they followed the Code, he got them deeper into a mess. And now Frank's life was in danger. Because of him.

"It wasn't supposed to be like this," Cooper said. "It was all about our protection." The flame settled into a glowing taper. "Mostly my own, I guess." But if saving his hide meant losing the things he valued most—like best friends, and self-respect—then he'd made a very big mistake. Huge.

"I thought this would be like, you know, *silence is golden*. I mean, even the word *golden* sounds so *right*. But it wasn't golden at all. It was fool's gold. It was dark and wrong. Evil. I never thought it would turn out like this. Never."

The candle flickered and bounced. It looked harmless enough, but fire was fire, and thanks to him all of them were going to have to walk through it.

"Somehow I lost my compass. I got us into this mess. It's my fault. I'm so sorry." He glanced up at Hiro. "I won't let you down."

Her eyes glistened in the candlelight. A single tear escaped and raced down her cheek. She didn't seem to notice. Instead she gave a slight nod and smiled. Just a half smile. But it was something.

Gordy stood and slapped him on the back. "I knew you'd come around. I told Hiro you would. Talked her into giving you one more chance."

Hiro didn't say anything. Maybe she was still playing it safe.

Cooper studied her face. "Got a plan?"

"Tomorrow morning," Hiro said. "Each of us talks to our parents. Tell them what happened. Then we all meet here at nine o'clock. We take the hard drive and go to the police. Together. Agreed?"

"Agreed," Gordy said.

Something bothered Cooper. Not the plan so much as the timing of it.

"Coop?" Hiro's voice had the slightest shake in it.

It felt like déjà vu or something—the three of them making a pact. Only last time he'd been the one pressing for a commitment.

Her eyes weren't hard and cold—the way she'd looked when she came in. He saw desperation. Pleading. Like she wasn't just fighting for Frank. She was fighting for their friendship. She was trying to save *him*. Hiro was determined to do the right thing and that meant leaving their friendship behind if she had to. Somehow he knew that. She was moving on to a new place but she was throwing him a lifeline.

But there was a flaw in her plan. He was sure of it. "What if tomorrow is too late?"

Hiro stared at him. Her lips parted slightly like she wanted to say something. Or maybe it was realization hitting her.

"If the hospital notified the police that Frank is coming out of the coma, and Hammer *is* a dirty cop . . ." Cooper left the thought hanging for them to process.

Gordy's eyes widened. "They'll try to get him tonight."

"Oh, no." Hiro shook her head, fresh tears forming. "What if you're right?"

What if Frank was *already* dead? Cooper couldn't go there. "All I'm saying is that if we're going to do this, we have to do it tonight."

Gordy slumped down in his seat. "My parents are at a Halloween party. They won't be back until late."

Hiro nodded. "My mom is with them."

"We could go to the police ourselves," Cooper said.

"Without even talking to our parents first?" Gordy looked at him. "And if Hammer is in on it . . ." He looked at Cooper, then at Hiro. "I mean—that's a lot more risky."

Of course Gordy was right. Cooper knew that. And the sense that this was all his fault flooded back over Cooper again. How could he have ever thought any good could come from being dishonest?

"If we go together," Hiro said, "it would be a *little* safer."

Gordy eyed Cooper. "You don't think they'd try something with all three of us, do you?"

How could he answer that? If the men were desperate enough to keep their sorry tails out of jail they'd do anything. And there may be a lot more they were hiding. Things that would come out if they were being investigated. Things they would want to keep hidden—at all costs. And if this involved organized crime in any way, they'd have the muscle and the means to do it.

"Coop?"

Cooper shook his head. "Maybe not." But his mind kept saying something different. They needed their parents. The risk was too great even if all three of them went. How could he let his friends put their lives at risk for a mistake he'd made? If something happened to one of them because of him—he might as well be dead. He could never live with that.

In that instant he knew what he had to do. Goosebumps rose on his arms. He might not be able to protect himself anymore, but he could still protect *them*. His mouth went dry. If going to the police turned out to be a trap, he wasn't about to let his friends walk into it. *God help me. God, please help me*. A plan began to take shape in his mind. He just needed time.

"Okay." Cooper checked his watch, calculating how much time he'd need to work out his strategy. "It's almost 8:00. We can hold off a little bit. Not much. Let's meet back here at say, 11:00. Maybe our parents will be home by then."

Gordy shrugged. "Maybe we should just wait here until they come home."

"No—not here," Cooper said. He said it way too fast. Almost blurted it out. He took a deep breath. Tried to look calm—however that's supposed to look. "I just need some time," Cooper said. "Alone."

Hiro studied his face. He didn't dare look away for fear she'd know he was hiding something. He definitely felt she was trying to read his mind. And with that women's intuition stuff, sometimes it seemed she could.

"So let's make sure we're all agreeing to the same things." Hiro didn't take her eyes off him while she spoke. "We meet at 11:00 pm. Tonight. We'll talk to our parents—then we'll go to the police. Together. Are we all agreed?"

"Agreed." Gordy didn't hesitate.

Cooper didn't want to lie. Not anymore. Not to his very best friends in the world. But he had to. One more time. Not for *his* protection. This time it was all about *their* safety.

"Coop?" Hiro's voice was soft. Tinged with something else. Hope? Maybe. But it sounded a lot more like fear to Cooper. She knew him better than anybody. Did she guess what he planned to do?

He took a deep breath and whispered a silent prayer in his heart. *Forgive me, God. Just one more stinking lie, and if you get me out of this, I'll never lie again.* He looked at Gordy, then back at Hiro. "I'm in."

CHAPTER 51

Hiro ducked out of *The Getaway's* cabin and took in a deep breath of the cool evening air. *Thank you, God.* This was a huge answer to prayer. Massive. Coop hadn't lost his conscience — he'd silenced it. But it seemed to be speaking to him now.

Yet she still didn't feel as relieved as she thought she would. Maybe it was the thought of talking to her mom or going to the police. But that is exactly what she'd wanted to do for days now. Was it Frank? She idly rubbed her dad's star hanging at her throat and tested the thought. Tried it on. No … Frank was going to be okay. She knew it.

It had to be Coop. She felt a definite heaviness the instant she thought of him. Gordy, on the other hand, looked like he could float off the deck. Like he could vault over the boat's rail and land on his feet in the yard below.

The way Hiro saw it, Gordy had been through a lot in the last few days. He never said it, but she knew. He'd put himself in the middle — working both sides to try to bring the three of them together again.

The three of them. Again the heaviness. Would it be the same? How could she ever trust Coop again? Even now, she felt he was holding back. Hiding something.

Coop joined them on deck just as Gordy climbed over the side.

"Hiro, can I ask you something?" Coop took a step closer and smiled. The smile looked stiff. Plastic. Like he wanted to look casual but wasn't feeling that way at all.

Hiro paused.

"What's it like ... when you get that *feeling*?"

A chill swept over her. How could she describe it? "It's a sense of doom." Like walking down a dark street and knowing someone or some*thing* is following. She felt her dad's shield. "Sometimes it is so strong it feels like the room is getting smaller or darker. Like you know something terrible is going to happen and there is absolutely nothing you can do to stop it."

He nodded. "Is that how it felt just before you heard about your dad?"

She felt the tears well up. She didn't want to cry now. "Yeah."

"And the other night, at Frank's ... before the robbery?"

"Exactly." But she didn't want to go back there. Not now. She didn't feel strong enough.

"*That* is spooky," Gordy said.

She swung one leg over the rail and started down toward him.

"Hiro." Coop called her name just barely loud enough for her to hear.

She stopped and looked at his face.

"Got any feelings like that now?"

She shook her head, and the heaviness in her heart seemed more pronounced. "Maybe just a sense that we're running out of time."

CHAPTER 52

The minute Gordy and Hiro left the yard, Cooper climbed out of *The Getaway* and ran to the back door of his house. Fudge bounded alongside him, ready to be part of whatever came next. If only she could.

But this time he had to work alone. No Gordy. No Hiro. If things went south, well, at least he wouldn't be dragging anyone else with him. He slipped inside a kitchen that had no color at all, only shades of gray near the windows and black in the shadows. He didn't turn on the light, but whipped out his cell phone and dialed his dad.

"C'mon, Dad, pick up. Hear the phone."

"Hello."

"Dad? I—"

"This is Carson MacKinnon. Please leave a message after the beep."

Nuts. Cooper redialed, but with no more luck than the first time. He hung up and tried to think. Fudge nuzzled his hand. For days he'd been totally focused on keeping everything secret. Now the Code felt like a time bomb in his hands. He had to get rid of it before anyone else got hurt. Before somebody bought Frank a transfer from a hospital bed to a coffin.

He checked his watch. For his plan to work, he needed his dad to pick up that phone. Now. With his back against the wall, he slid down and sat on the floor. He dialed again, praying that somehow his dad would hear the ring over the noise of the circus. When he got the answering machine this time, he knew he had to leave a message.

"Dad? It's me. I need to talk to you. I need you here. I didn't want to do this over the phone, but I don't know what else to do." He looked around in the dark kitchen. "I've been lying to you and Mom all week. I am so sorry. I—", Cooper paused.

Was he sure he had to do this? He took a deep breath. No turning back now.

"I was at Frank 'n Stein's last Thursday. I saw everything. There were three men. The two I saw wore masks. They had cop pants on, so I was afraid to go to the police. Gordy and Hiro were there, too. We just barely escaped. One of the robbers got my house key. Said he'd find our home and kill us all if I told."

Fudge stared at him, ears flat to her sides. Like she remembered the night. Remembered smelling Frank's blood on his pants.

"So I made Gordy and Hiro form a pact of silence with me. I was hoping the robbers would be caught and we'd stay safe. It was wrong and stupid." Warm tears ran down his cheeks.

He sat on the floor in the darkness with his back against the kitchen wall. "I'm the 'mystery witness' the police are looking for. They don't know about Hiro and Gordy. This thing has gotten so out of control." He hiked his knees up to his chest.

"I think Lunk's dad is one of the men. And I think Detective Hammer is involved too. There's one more cop involved, so it could be anybody." Why had he ever lied in the first place?

"Anyway, Hiro told me Frank is coming out of the coma. And he knows who was behind the robbery, so if I don't move fast, somebody might finish the job. Gordy and Hiro are meeting here tonight at 11:00, but I'm not waiting that long. I just didn't want them to be in any more danger than I've already gotten them in.

I'm the one who got them into this mess—and I'm going to get them out of it. I was hoping you and I could do it together."

The words poured out. Gushed out. And as they did, the magnitude of his lies became more and more clear. Why hadn't he done this before? Why didn't he see it?

He'd been digging himself into a pit. A grave. And he'd been dragging Gordy and Hiro in with him. Now he had to dig out before it swallowed them whole.

He looked at the clock on the phone.

"I need you to come with me to the police before something happens to Frank. I'll wait here ten minutes before I go to plan B. If I don't hear from you I'll call you one more time to tell you what I'm going to do."

He pushed the disconnect button and sat there, heart racing. He'd spilled. Broken the Code. But he felt better. Cooper shook his head and checked the clock. Nineteen minutes to be out of the house. Barely enough time.

Cooper hustled up to his room and grabbed a notebook. Reaching under his bed, he found the phone he'd used to call the police and slid it in his back hip pocket. He felt for the diner keys and pocketed them along with his own cell. He grabbed his flashlight from beside his bed, turned it on, and set it on the desk. The light swiped across the lined paper and left a bright circle on the wall. He pulled out a pen and started writing.

Dear Gordy and Hiro,

I'm so sorry for the lies. So very, very, sorry. It was all wrong—and all my fault. I see that now. None of us would be in the mess we're in if it wasn't for me and the stupid Code. Which is why I'm going to break the Code now without you. I got us into this, and I'm going to get us out of it. I have a plan, but it's risky. If something happened to one of you I could never forgive myself. If I haven't gotten here and destroyed this note before you're reading this, something must have gone wrong.

CHAPTER 53

He scribbled as fast as he could, briefly outlining his plan—just in case. Ending it was the hard part. Would this be it? Would he ever see them again?

You're the best friends a guy could ever have. If I get out of this somehow, I'll never lie to you again, or ask you to lie for me. I was stupid. I can't undo things, but I can make sure Frank stays safe. And I have to try to fix things so you two aren't in danger either. –Coop

He checked the time, turned off the flashlight and gave his eyes a moment to adjust to the darkness. Six minutes. He'd squared things with his parents, and now with his friends. But he was still missing someone. A *big* someone.

"I'm sorry, God." He whispered, but knew God heard him just as clearly as if he'd shouted. "Help me fix this mess—and please, don't let Frank die."

Coming clean with God should have made him feel better. And it probably would if he could stop thinking about what he had to do next.

"Let's go, girl." He moved through the house without turning on one light. Fudge trotted beside him the whole time. He flicked his flashlight on once in the laundry room. The hard drive sat right where Mom left it. Stuffing the hard drive in his pocket, he noticed his hand shaking. *C'mon, Coop. Get a chest.*

"Alright, Fudge," he whispered. "Let's get this note to *The Getaway* before I go."

Cooper opened the back door, and after being sure it looked safe, jogged across the yard. Fudge's chain jangled as she loped beside him. Climbing into the boat, he unlocked the cabin door and ducked inside. He left the note centered on the table. Flicking his flashlight on, he laid it on top of the note so they wouldn't miss it. The batteries would easily last long enough to do the job. He did the same with his dad's flashlight, just to be sure. Backing out of the cabin, he left the wooden door unlocked.

Back down on the ground, he ran to the shed and pulled out his bike.

"Almost done, girl." He slipped back into the house and held the door for her to follow. "The rest I do on my own." She looked at him and cocked her head to one side as if questioning his judgment. Cooper questioned it himself. He kneeled down and gave her a quick hug.

He was right on schedule—but hopelessly late at the same time. Days late. He should have done this sooner. He pulled his phone out and dialed his dad, praying he'd pick up.

When the recorded message started, Cooper felt weak. The beep sounded, and he outlined the final details of Plan B. He finished with a simple, "Please forgive me. I'll never lie to you again. I love you and Mom. Mattie too." He disconnected—and felt strangely distant from his family. He was all alone in this—God help him. And he was going to need it.

Suddenly Fudge stiffened, ears alert.

"What is it girl?"

Fudge let out a howl and bounded down the hall.

"Fudge," Cooper hissed. "Come back."

She didn't even *look* back. Cooper followed at a distance. She was in the family room now, barking at the window.

Kids trick or treating?

Cooper moved silently through the hall, staying completely within the shadows. A silhouette darkened one pane. Somebody was there. Cooper could make out hands cupped around a man's face, trying to see inside. And he wasn't looking for candy.

They found me. Please help me, God. Please help me.

Apparently Fudge's barking shook up the intruder, because a moment later the head was gone. But where?

Fudge ran to another window and barked. By her tone Cooper knew she didn't see anything. She was still trying to scare the guy off. Cooper prayed it worked. It certainly was doing a number on him.

Suddenly she bolted to the front door again, barking like crazy. Somebody was there. *It's one of them.* They have the key.

Arms out in front of him to feel the walls, Cooper hurried to the kitchen, thankful he'd left all the lights off. He had to get out of here. Now.

Fudge barked like mad in the other room. Maybe she would provide just the diversion he needed to get away.

He crawled to the back door and wished he could stay. Just hide here in the darkness until his dad got home. But that wouldn't help Frank now. And the man out front wasn't about to wait either.

After straining to see any movement in the backyard, Cooper reached for the handle and opened the door. Fudge never saw him sneak out the back. And he hoped whoever was creeping around outside didn't see him either.

CHAPTER 54

Silently, Cooper crept to the back gate with his bike. He peered through the cedar slats toward the front yard. A bright Halloween moon gave him a clear view, but that also meant he'd be easy to spot. The guy could be in any of the shadows along the house and Cooper would never see him.

He lifted the latch and opened the door just a crack. A gust of wind swirled a gang of leaves out from the darkness. Cooper raised his hands, ready to fight. Nothing came at him. He stared into the shadows.

This was nuts. Either he had to get back in the house and lock the door, or get on his bike and ride. He had no protection here. Whoever was out front would likely circle to the backyard. Cooper would be trapped. He could hear Fudge barking inside. Even she wouldn't be able to help now.

Okay. Okay. Let's do this. Cooper heaved open the heavy wooden gate. The hinges moaned as he swung a leg over his bike and stood on the pedals. Every muscle strained as he pumped to get up speed. Cutting across the lawn, he kept wide of the shadows along the house and raced straight for the street.

Out of the corner of his eye he saw something move. He glanced over his shoulder. Someone ran right for him.

"Stop!"

Legs churning, he picked up speed.

"Stop!"

Lunk's voice. But Cooper wasn't about to stop now. And certainly not for him. Where was Lunk's dad? He pedaled harder.

The wind howled in his ears, drowning out everything but the sounds of his own prayers looping through his head. *Please, God. Please, God. Please, God.*

He banked the corner off Fremont and onto School Drive, staying in the middle of the street. He didn't dare look back. As much as Lunk claimed to care about Frank, his loyalty to his dad was greater.

If Lunk's dad was with him, they'd give chase by car. Cooper cut right onto Campbell Drive, jumped the curb and flew through Kimball Hill Park. They'd expect he'd be heading to the police and try to head him off—but that's where they'd figure wrong. Instead of taking the footbridge, Cooper flew out of the park and through the parking lot toward Kirchoff Road. The same route he'd taken home just a week before. There was no time to take the tunnel.

The hard drive pressed against his leg with every turn of the pedals, and the rhythm kept him cranking like a machine. Pain stabbed his side but he still didn't let up his pace.

He saw the OPEN sign switch off at Frank 'n Stein's. Perfect. Checking for cars, he whipped across Kirchoff. Frank's set of keys were in his pocket. He'd use them if he had to.

Cooper saw Mr. Stein shuffle into the kitchen. "Mr. Stein!" Skidding to a stop, he dumped his bike by the front door.

"Mr. Stein!" Cooper stood panting on cement legs and banged on the glass door.

Stein turned and smiled. He pointed to his watch and shrugged.

"Let me in. Please." He glanced over his shoulder. "I'm being chased."

The smile slid off Mr. Stein's face and he rushed to the front door, fumbling with keys as he went.

Cooper heard the bolt slide and he yanked the door open.

"Cooper?"

"Lock it!" Cooper pulled the door closed behind him.

Stein locked the door and scanned the lot as he did. "Who's chasing you?"

Cooper held up one hand, trying to catch his breath. "I'll explain. But I need to hide."

"Behind the counter." He pointed. "Hurry."

Scooting through the opening, Cooper ducked behind the counter. He was back. Hiding behind the very same counter but on the other side this time. The side Frank had been on.

Mr. Stein squeezed through the counter and stood, back to the kitchen, but still looking out the front windows. "So what happened? You break a window or something?" He grinned.

Cooper shook his head. "Somebody was at my house—trying to get in, I think." He could see the confusion on Mr. Stein's face.

"So you came *here*?"

"My parents are out. And I had to talk to you, and then someone was sneaking around the house."

Mr. Stein still looked confused. Cooper took a deep breath. Time to break the Code, for the second time.

"It's, ah, about the robbery."

Stein's jaw opened slightly and his eyes bored into Cooper.

"I saw everything. And they're on to me."

"You?" Stein took a step back. "Exactly *what* did you see?"

"I didn't hurt Frank. Honest. There were three men."

Mr. Stein eyed him. Like he was trying to decide if Cooper was telling the truth.

"Look, they came to my home. They're going to kill me. And Frank, too, unless we can stop them."

"Frank?"

"He knew who was behind it. I could tell by something he said. And now he's coming out of his coma."

"What?"

Cooper nodded. "Look, we have to do something before they find me, or hurt Frank."

Mr. Stein reached under the counter by the register and pulled out a handgun. He jammed it in the back of his pants' waistband.

Cooper stared. "Is that real?"

"Sure is. And loaded." Mr. Stein wiped his palm on his apron like the gun left some invisible film on his hand. "I borrowed this after the robbery. Nobody is ever going to rob us again. Don't worry. I'm not going to let anybody get at you or hurt Frank."

Cooper felt himself relax. He was safe now. He'd done the right thing.

Someone banged against the front windows, making both of them jump.

"Mr. Stein," Lunk's voice called from outside. "I know MacKinnon's in there. Don't trust him. He's playing some kind of game. He was here the night of the robbery. I'm sure of it."

Mr. Stein hesitated.

"He's hiding something, Mr. Stein. Let me in or I'm going to the police."

The co-owner moved toward the opening.

"Don't do it," Cooper pleaded. Lunk would never go to the police. He'd be turning in his own dad. "He's lying." It seemed strange, him accusing someone else of being a liar. "I-I think he may be involved in the robbery."

"Neil Lunquist?"

Hiding was pointless now. Cooper stood. Lunk was at the door, his face pressed up to the glass between cupped hands. What was Lunk up to? This had to be a trick to get Stein to open the door. Maybe his dad was hiding around the corner.

"Open up. Please." Lunk shrunk away from the door and raised his hands as if to show he came in peace.

Cooper shook his head. "I don't like this."

Mr. Stein patted his belt. "I can handle him. But I need to get down to the bottom of this." He scooted through the opening in the counter.

If Mr. Stein knew about Lunk's dad, he wouldn't go near that door. Cooper had to say something. Stop him.

Mr. Stein slid the key into the lock and turned the latch.

"Wait, you don't understand," Cooper practically shouted.

Stein cracked open the door but held it there. He gave Cooper an over-the-shoulder "this better be good" look.

"I think his dad was one of the robbers—and that Lunk told him about the safe."

Lunk yanked the door open and glared at him. "I never did anything to hurt Frank Mustacci." He shook a finger at Cooper. "And neither did my dad." He pushed past Mr. Stein and charged Cooper.

CHAPTER 55

Cooper took a step back. Lunk vaulted over the counter and grabbed fistfuls of Cooper's sweatshirt. Staggering backwards, he tried to regain his balance. Something caught his legs and he slammed to the floor.

Lunk followed him down, his weight knocking the wind out of Cooper when they landed. Pinning him to the floor with one hand, Lunk cocked back his fist.

Cooper closed his eyes and jerked his head to one side. Searing pain exploded below his right eye. He couldn't see, could hardly breathe.

Lunk's fist hammered him again.

Cooper felt like his eye would burst. He raised his head, squirmed to get free.

Lunk landed a punch squarely on Cooper's nose, snapping his head back to the tile floor. Then Lunk was gone.

Through bleary eyes Cooper saw Mr. Stein drag Lunk to his feet.

"Let me go!" Lunk struggled to get loose.

Mr. Stein held him steady. "Back off, Neil, or I'll give you a taste of your own medicine."

Cooper felt warm blood running from his nose to his chin.

Tasted it on his lips. His face burned and tingled like he'd been dragged across the parking lot. He propped himself on one elbow and lightly touched his eye.

Lunk's shoulders slumped, and he stopped fighting.

"Now," Mr. Stein relaxed his grip. "I'm going to lock the door so we don't have any *more* visitors. Don't move. Understand?"

Lunk nodded, but glared at Cooper.

Mr. Stein was back in seconds. He hefted the stool from the arcade game over the counter and walked through the opening himself. He set the stool in front of Cooper and motioned Lunk toward one in front of the drive-thru window several feet away. "Sit."

Cooper got up and sat on the stool. Lunk retreated to the drive-thru window several feet away and did the same.

Mr. Stein handed Cooper a small stack of napkins and studied his face.

"You're going to have one nasty shiner. Let's get some ice."

Cooper blotted his nose and mouth and stared at the bright red blood on the napkins. The image of Frank's bloody apron flashed in his mind.

Ice cubes rattled through the soft drink dispenser and Mr. Stein caught them in a white dishtowel. He twisted the towel and handed the pack to Cooper.

"Alright, Cooper." Mr. Stein crossed his arms across his chest and leaned against the counter. "Explain what's going on."

Cooper eased the pack onto his throbbing eye. He took a deep breath, and broke the *Code of Silence* for good. Shattered it. Every detail—except the facts that Hiro and Gordy were with him.

When he'd finished, Mr. Stein shook his head and whistled. "So you think it was cops?"

"They wore cop pants." He put the ice pack down and traced the swelling with his finger.

"And you believe Neil gave his dad, also known as 'Mr. Lucky,' information about the safe. Is that right?"

Lunk jumped off his stool. "That's a lie!"

Mr. Stein took a step forward like he expected Lunk to start round two.

"Honest, Mr. Stein, I didn't know anything about the safe—and if I did, I wouldn't have told anybody, especially my dad."

Cooper watched Lunk with his good eye. The other was closing up fast. "Frank figured out someone on the inside was involved."

"Baloney." Lunk sat back down, an angry scowl creasing his face. "I wouldn't do anything to hurt him."

He sounded convincing. And Mr. Stein seemed to be buying it. "What about your dad?"

Lunk glared at Cooper. "My dad is a total loser. I admit that. But he never hurt Frank either."

Mr. Stein looked like he didn't know what to believe. "Cooper, do you have any proof that Neil's dad was involved?"

"Hiro saw Lunk and his dad arguing right here the night of the burglary. Lunk wanted him to stay out of sight."

Lunk thumped the counter with his fist. "What does that prove?"

"And I heard you and your dad talking after we launched the potato at your shed."

"That was you?" Lunk clenched his fists, but stayed on the stool.

"You told him you wanted him to leave," Cooper blurted out. "You said he had the money. That he got what he came for. That he needed to leave town."

Lunk's chin shook. "You don't know what you're talking about." He looked angry enough to do more face painting with his fists. "The cops came to our house and asked my dad some questions. Then they left. If they had a shred of evidence, don't you think the police would have hauled him in?"

"Not if the detective was covering for him." Maybe Lunk didn't have any idea what really happened. He sure seemed to believe what he said. And he backed it up with his fists.

Lunk's head dropped forward. "My dad drifts in whenever he really needs cash. My mom gave him a couple hundred bucks.

That's it. He'll blow most of that on booze." He looked up through shards of dark hair. "He hurts my mom. Scares her. Makes her worry too much." He sniffed and wiped his nose on his sleeve. "She needs me to protect her. I just wanted him to leave."

Cooper's throat swelled and burned like the area around his eye. Whatever Lunk's dad had done, Lunk didn't have anything to do with it. Cooper had misjudged Lunk. For a long time.

Mr. Stein took a deep breath and blew it out loudly. "So Cooper, what made you come to me?"

"I knew you'd believe me after the things you said this afternoon. And if you didn't, the security camera footage would back me up."

"And I could go with you to the police. Is that right?"

"That was my plan. I wanted to wait for my dad and tell him first, but he took my family to the circus. When I heard Frank was coming out of the coma I knew I'd have to do it on my own. We have to hurry to protect him."

"Do you have the hard drive?"

Cooper fished it out of his pocket. The connecter cables were still sticking out of it. He handed it to Mr. Stein and immediately felt relief. Freedom.

Mr. Stein bounced it in his palm a couple of times like he was testing its weight. "This is all we need. This changes everything."

Lunk stood. "Are you going to play it?"

Mr. Stein motioned for him to sit back down. "First I'm calling my lawyer. We'll let him decide what to do next."

Mr. Stein punched a number into his cell and disappeared around the corner of the dining area to talk. An uneasy silence separated Cooper and Lunk.

Cooper wished his dad was here. He checked his watch. 9:30. Maybe this would all be over before 11:00. He'd get back to *The Getaway* and get rid of the note to Gordy and Hiro. As soon as they got there he'd tell them it was done. That Frank was safe, and they had nothing more to fear.

Mr. Stein rounded the corner, snapped his cell shut, and leaned against the counter again. "He's on his way."

"Does he believe me?" Cooper shot a glance at Lunk.

"He has no reason not to." Mr. Stein paced again. "And what's more important, *I* believe you." He stopped and looked at Cooper. "You did the right thing tonight. A brave thing. Don't worry. This will all be over soon."

This will all be over soon. How many times had Cooper tried to comfort himself with those very words over the last week? One lie followed another like links in a chain. *This will all be over soon.* And with every lie the chain got longer, heavier. Imprisoning him.

Cooper's phone rang. He snagged it from his pocket and checked the screen. Hiro. Probably wanting to talk him into meeting earlier. Too late for that now. Best to just not pick up. Stall her off. He stuffed it back in his pocket and let it ring.

"Will your lawyer make sure Frank gets protection?"

Lunk's voice shook Cooper free from his thoughts.

Mr. Stein nodded. "Count on it."

Cooper felt a measure of relief. Frank was going to be okay—something he never thought he'd be able to say after seeing him the night of the robbery.

He wondered if blood still stained the carpet running along the counter. He scanned the carpet looking for the telltale marks. Frank's head had been just about exactly where Mr. Stein stood. If he would just take a step to one side or the other with those fancy looking cowboy boots he'd be able to tell for sure.

Cowboy boots. Cooper froze. He'd seen them before. With the gator skin toe piece. Standing in almost exactly the same spot as he'd seen them the first time.

God, no. No, please. Cooper felt dizzy. Lightheaded. His stomach swirled like the stitching on Stein's boots. Lunk had been telling the truth. His dad wasn't the third man in the robbery. It was Mr. *Stein.* And now he had the hard drive. He had a gun. And he had *them.*

CHAPTER 56

Gordy checked the driveway from his bedroom window again. He couldn't remember a time he was more anxious to see his parents' car pull up.

He wished he'd stayed with Coop. But then, it was pretty clear Coop wanted to be alone. Which hurt just a little. Maybe Coop felt the same way when he heard that he'd been making plans with Hiro. He recognized the look on his cousin's face.

Since when did they start keeping secrets from each other? He thought about that for a minute. It was when they started keeping secrets from everybody else. When they agreed to leading a secret life with the Code of Silence. Never again.

But Coop was back now. They were together again. Tonight they'd break the lousy Code for good. Things were going to be okay with the three of them. And Frank would be safe. But still, his stomach felt knotted again.

Maybe it was the thought of going to the police. Sure, that still scared him. But the thought of trying to keep what they'd seen a secret any longer scared him more.

He looked down the street at Coop's house. The lights were still off. He checked his watch. Over an hour to go. He stood and paced. This waiting was driving him crazy. He stared through the window again — and saw a vehicle cruising the block. Slow. With one headlight out.

NO. He dropped to the floor and peeked through the corner of the window. It was an SUV. It passed Cooper's house, then sped up and suddenly turned off Fremont and disappeared around the corner. *They were looking for Coop!*

Gordy's phone vibrated in his pocket. He saw Hiro's name flash onto the screen just as he picked it up. Her mom must be home.

"Hiro?"

"Have you talked to Coop?"

She sounded out of breath. And scared.

"No . . . you?"

"Just tried. He's not picking up."

Gordy's stomach twisted. "Maybe he's-"

"I'm getting a bad feeling about this. Real bad. And dark."

Gordy pressed the phone closer to his ear and bolted from his room, taking the stairs to the first floor two at a time. "Meet me at Coop's — now."

"Already on my way."

He stopped at the front door, checking the street in both directions before racing across the front yard. "Be careful. I just saw an SUV cruise by the house . . . with only *one* headlight."

"Dear God, no," Hiro cried.

"The feeling." Gordy's mouth went dry. "Is it getting worse, or darker?"

Hiro let out what sounded like a sob. "By the second!"

CHAPTER 57

Cooper's mind whirled back to the robbery. Suddenly it all made sense. The moment the guy in the Elvis mask mentioned the safe, Frank realized it was an inside job. Knew it was *his partner.* Someone aware of his personal safe and that he kept a lot of money inside. No wonder Mr. Lucky stayed in the car during that part of the robbery. He couldn't take the chance that his partner might recognize him.

Stein started pacing back and forth along the kitchen side of the counter. "So your parents are out at the circus?"

"Yeah, but I left him a message on his cell." He said it too fast. Did it sound panicky? *Slow down, Cooper.* "I told him I was coming here to talk to you."

Stein clenched his jaw. Like this was bad news.

Cooper looked past him toward the front door. He had to get out of here. Now. And he had to bring the hard drive with him. If Stein looked at it he'd see Gordy and Hiro were there too.

Cooper still had the keys in his pocket. But how could he get past Stein? Maybe if Lunk helped, but he didn't have a clue as to who Stein really was or the danger they were in.

What if I'm wrong? What if Mr. Stein just happened to have the same type of boots as the robber? Cooper wanted to believe that but he knew it was a stretch. Still, Cooper had to be sure.

He dug in his pocket and pulled out his cell. Cooper tried to sound casual, but his voice didn't even sound normal to himself. "I think I should try my dad again."

"Let's hold on that call," Stein said.

The hair prickled on his arms. *Stein has no intention of letting me make a call.*

"My lawyer will be here any minute. Let's just sit tight."

Lawyer? Did he really call a lawyer? Maybe. He certainly was going to need one now. Cooper checked the parking lot. But what if Stein called *them*? What if he called Elvis or Mr. Clown? He had to get out of this place. *Get out or die.*

Cooper stood. "I think I'll park my bike better while we're waiting."

"Sit down." Stein plastered on a smile. "We wait for the lawyer."

Every bit of doubt dissolved. Stein was the man.

Stein walked to the front window. He peered down Kirchoff Road and checked his watch.

He could run for the back door, but what if it was locked? Stein would pick him off like a target in a shooting gallery. The gun was the problem. Cooper stared at the handle of the revolver sticking out from Stein's belt. Could he get it? Bolt off the stool and grab it? He had to try *something* before whoever Stein called showed up. *God help me. God help me.*

He motioned to Lunk so stay quiet with a finger to his lips. Lunk definitely looked confused. Cooper stood silently and slipped through the pass-thru in the ordering counter. Stein's back was still to him — only five feet away.

"Mr. Stein!" Lunk shouted.

Cooper lunged for the gun — felt the grip in his hand.

Stein whirled around and swung a backhand at Cooper's face. The blow blinded him for an instant, but he managed to tug the gun free.

Lunk plowed into him and took him down in a rough tackle. Cooper slammed down hard, the gun skittering out of his grip. He clawed for the gun, but Stein's boot came down on his hand hard.

Stein scooped up the revolver and pointed it at Cooper. "Easy, boy." Sweat trickled down his forehead. "Move back into the kitchen. *Both* of you."

Lunk rolled off. "What?"

"Move." Stein motioned toward the stools with the gun.

Lunk looked totally confused. "I was *helping* you."

"Noted," Stein said. "Now get on the other side of the counter. Quickly."

Lunk shuffled around the counter and sat. Cooper followed.

Stein waved his gun at Cooper. "Put your cell on the counter."

Cooper obeyed, but left the phone from Walmart where it was.

"Mr. Lunquist, do you have a phone too?"

Lunk shook his head.

"Turn out your pockets."

Lunk stood slowly, pulled out his pockets. Empty. "What's going on?" Lunk looked at Stein, then at Cooper.

"He's the inside man," Cooper said. "Aren't you, Mr. Stein?"

"What?" Lunk whispered.

If Lunk was afraid, his face didn't show it. Only disbelief.

"I was wrong about your dad, Lunk. Mr. Stein is 'Mr. Lucky.'"

"Now I know you're crazy, MacKinnon." Lunk stood.

Stein leveled the revolver directly at Lunk. "Sit down, Mr. Lunquist."

Lunk's jaw opened slightly and he sat back down.

"Sorry, guys." Stein looked like he really meant it. Like this whole thing had gotten a lot bigger than he ever figured it would. Just like Cooper's lies. "How did you know?"

"Cowboy boots."

Stein shook his head and gave a half smile. "What are the odds of that?" He opened the register and pulled the bills from the tray.

Twenty's, ten's, five's, one's. He stacked the currency, folded them in half, and jammed them in his pocket.

He was robbing his own store. Again.

"Thanks to you," he looked directly at Cooper, "it looks like I'm going to need a little traveling money."

"The guy you called isn't a lawyer, is he?" Lunk looked like the energy had just been drained out of him.

"No," Stein glanced at Cooper, "and not a cop either. Hammer was on your side. Lucky for me, you didn't figure that out sooner." He reached into Frank's hospital fund jar and pulled out the bills.

Not a cop. He'd been wrong the whole time. About so many things. Hiro had misjudged Lunk but she pegged the cop part right. At least Hiro and Gordy weren't tangled up in this. But if Stein looked at the hard drive, they were doomed.

"Why?" The question came out before Cooper could stop it.

Stein slid the hard drive in a paper sack. "I've had a streak of bad luck lately. I borrowed from some people who don't like late payments. Big money. They don't mess around when it comes to money—not with that many zeroes behind it."

Hiro's brother was right. The robbery was connected to organized crime. Whoever he'd called wasn't coming to help. They were going to clean up Stein's mess.

"Gambling?" Lunk's voice was so quiet Cooper could hardly hear it.

Stein nodded. "When the debts piled up, I knew Frank's safe was the answer. He never trusted banks, you know."

"He shouldn't have trusted you either," Cooper said.

"Nobody was supposed to get hurt. If Frank had kept his mouth shut everything would have been okay." Stein shrugged. "Guess a little of my bad luck rubbed off on him."

"What will happen to Frank?" Lunk's voice shook.

Mr. Stein slid the sack next to the register and sighed. "I really don't know. Nothing, I hope. But it's out of my hands now."

Out of his hands? What did that mean?

Lunk clenched his jaw. And his fists.

"Lunk," Cooper said. "I'm sorry I suspected your dad in this. I messed up."

Lunk waved him off and shook his head. "I had it wrong too." Lunk studied Cooper's face. He seemed to be doing a bit of damage assessment. "Sorry about your face."

Stein's phone rang. He shifted the gun to the other hand and fished his cell from his pocket. He listened for a moment. "The back door is open." He looked out the front window. "But there's a bike out front, too. Make that two bikes. Listen, can't we—." He paused for a moment, shoulders slumping. "I'll unlock the front door."

Stein clearly wasn't calling the shots here.

He snapped the phone shut and pocketed it while moving through the opening in the counter backwards. "You boys sit tight." Backing all the way to the front door, he kept his eyes on the boys and after digging in his pocket, pulled out a small ring of keys.

Run. Was it his voice or someone else's? Cooper couldn't tell. But this was his chance. Cooper glanced at Lunk. Eyes bright, Lunk seemed to be thinking the same thing.

"Back door." Cooper whispered so only Lunk could hear him.

Lunk answered with his eyes.

Cooper heard the lock in the front door slide open.

He bolted from his chair and ran through the kitchen, Lunk right behind him.

"Stop!" Stein roared. "I'll shoot!"

"Keep going," Lunk shouted.

Suddenly the back door burst open. A man stepped inside wearing an Elvis mask and holding a gun.

CHAPTER 58

Hiro saw Gordy pounding on Cooper's front door when she rode up. She dumped her bike on the grass and ran up to the front porch. Fudge barked like crazy from the other side of the door.

"Coop? It's me. Gordy. You in there?" He looked at her and shrugged.

Hiro read Cooper's note to potential trick-or-treaters and instantly knew where to find him.

"*The Getaway*." She bolted off the front porch and ran for the gate in the cedar fence with Gordy right behind her. The gate hung wide open ... and the dark feelings closed in a little more.

"Coop!" She called for him even as she climbed over the transom of the Getaway. "It's us." She knocked on the wooden hatch. "Coop?"

Gordy reached around her and opened it.

Hiro squeezed past him and stood inside. The flashlights illuminated a note on the table. Snatching a light, she began to read.

Gordy looked over her shoulder. "What does it say?"

Her eyes flew over the words. "No, no, no, Coop. *NO!*"

"What!?" Gordy reached for the note.

Hiro pulled it away and kept reading. "He's doing this without us. And he's in trouble. I know it."

She could feel it. Stronger than what she'd felt a week ago at Frank's. More like the suffocating darkness she'd felt just before the police officers showed up at their door with the news about her dad. "God, no. Not Coop. Please, Father, not him, too." The words blurred on the page, and she crumpled the note and threw it to the cabin floor.

Gordy picked it up and tried to read it by the moonlight streaming in from the porthole. "Where did he go—does it say?"

She nodded, already dialing 9–1–1. "Frank 'n Stein's."

Gordy looked ghostly pale in the light of the flashlight. "I'll get my bike."

CHAPTER 59

Both boys stood with their hands above their heads in the back of Frank 'n Stein's kitchen.

"Told you I'd find you." Elvis fished a key out of his pocket and held it up. Cooper's key. "Guess we won't be needing this anymore." He tossed it at Cooper's feet. "But then again you won't either."

Elvis kept a wide stance with the gun trained on the boys. He clapped Stein on the back. "Well, Mr. Lucky. Maybe your luck is changing."

Gun still in hand, Stein gave a little nod.

"Either of them have cell phones?"

Stein nodded. "Already got 'em."

A third man hustled through the front door and made his way through the kitchen. He held a gun in his hand, with a second one stuck in his belt.

"Both bikes are in the creek. We're all set." He didn't wear a mask, but his hoarse voice worked like a vocal ID. Mr. Clown.

Elvis stepped forward. "Into the cooler." He nodded toward the walk-in freezer.

Freezer. Brown's Chicken. *No. Not there. God, help us.*

"Please . . ." Cooper pleaded with Mr. Stein.

Stein looked away like there was nothing he could do. Elvis was clearly King.

Elvis took a step closer. "Get inside and sit tight. We need to explain to Mr. Lucky how he's going to tie up some loose ends."

"We'll keep our mouths shut." Lunk looked at Cooper. "Right?"

Cooper nodded.

"Like you planned when you came here tonight?" Elvis snickered. "Move." He raised the gun.

We're the loose ends. Cooper pulled the heavy latch and swung open the insulated metal door. A blast of frigid air met his swollen face. A single light bulb illuminated the small room. Dozens of boxes filled the metal racks lining both sides of the freezer. He stepped inside with Lunk right behind him. *Please, God. Please, God.* He hiked his shoulders up, cringing at the thought of a bullet ripping through him at any moment.

The door slammed behind them like a vault. Or maybe a crypt.

"I thought they were going to shoot us," Lunk said over the noise of the high-powered fan whirring inside. "Think they'll leave us here to freeze?"

Cooper shook his head. In his gut he knew Elvis wasn't going to leave anything to chance. Not this time. "They'll make sure we're dead before they leave. He's going to make Mr. Stein do it." He feared the door might swing open at any moment. He and Lunk would face a firing squad.

Lunk nodded, eyes wide—like he knew. These guys weren't about to leave any witnesses around to identify them. He looked around the freezer and pointed at the ceiling. "What about crawling out the vent?"

The duct was big enough, and they could stack boxes to make a stairway up, but the vent cover was a problem. About twenty screws held it in place. "We'd need a screwdriver. Got a pocketknife?"

Lunk shook his head. He climbed up the rack and pulled on the vent cover. It didn't budge. Jumping back to the floor he stood there, wrapping his arms around himself against the cold.

Even if they had the tools, Cooper doubted they'd have time. He dropped to his knees. "God, forgive me, I've been wrong about everything. Save us. Show me what to do. Keep Hiro and Gordy safe. And Frank."

"You praying?" Lunk squatted down beside him.

"Yeah."

"Good."

Cooper stood, scanning the freezer, but kept an eye on the door. An emergency handle and latch assembly provided a sure escape for someone accidentally stuck inside, but they had the opposite problem. How to keep the robbers outside from getting in? He looked at the handle and back at the metal racks. An idea flashed through his mind.

"Thank you, God." Instantly he unbuckled his belt and whipped it through the loops on his pants. "We need to be sure they can't open the door."

Cooper threaded his leather belt through the door handle, wrapped it several times around the one of the metal uprights for the shelves, and buckled it.

Lunk pulled on the belt to test it. "That'll slow them down." He took off his belt and did the same, testing it with a hard pull. It held fast. His breath chugged out in little white puffs of steam. "This metal door." He looked at Cooper. "Think a bullet could get through?"

The door was thick, but probably filled with insulation, not solid metal. Cooper looked around. Boxes and boxes of frozen hotdogs, beef, and buns were neatly stacked on the racks. He lugged a box of hotdogs off the shelf.

"Let's stack 'em in front of the door. Make a shield."

Lunk and Cooper stacked boxes like madmen.

When the wall of cartons reached waist high Cooper stopped and dug in his back pocket. *The phone.* He pulled it out and held it for Lunk to see.

"You have *two* phones?"

"I'll call for help." He turned on the power button and waited for the phone to come to life. *C'mon, c'mon.*

"You call." Lunk reached for another box and hefted it onto their growing shield. "I'll stack."

Cooper pushed the SEND button, redialing the last number he'd called. He held it to his ear with a shaking hand. *Please, God. Please, God.*

On the third ring someone picked up.

"Hammer."

"It's me—! I need help!"

"Golden boy?"

"Yeah—Cooper MacKinnon—, I messed up."

"Where are you?" His voice was tough. All business.

"Locked in the freezer at Frank 'n Stein's. They're going to kill us."

"Hold on, buddy. I'm on my way."

Lunk slid a box in place. The wall stood nearly to his chest.

Cooper pocketed the phone, grabbed a box, and started another row along the bottom to make the wall double thick.

Someone tried to pull the door open, then pounded on it.

Both boys stopped.

"Open the door. Now!" The voice was muffled, but not enough to miss the rage in it.

Someone yanked on the door again. The belts held.

"Last chance, boys. We just want to talk."

Cooper eyed the belts. "God please don't let them get in here."

"Get down," Lunk hissed. He dropped flat on the ground.

Cooper pressed himself against the icy floor next to him.

And the men opened fire.

CHAPTER 60

Gunshots thundered from outside the insulated room. Bullets ripped through the door and slammed into the boxes. Others thudded high into the wall on the opposite side of the freezer. It sounded more like Fourth of July than Halloween.

Cooper felt the makeshift wall of boxes shudder every time a bullet lodged in it. He hugged the ground, wishing he could burrow through it to safety. He heard himself screaming.

Lunk tucked himself in a ball next to him, screaming as loud as the gunfire itself.

The gunfire stopped. And so did Cooper.

Lunk's screams morphed into sobs and moans.

Cooper kept his head low but spoke directly into Lunk's ear. "Follow my lead." Lunk looked at him with wild eyes. He blinked once, then nodded.

Blam! Blam! Blam! Bullets slammed into the wall of boxes.

Cooper kept his eyes locked on Lunk's. "Scream."

Cooper shrieked and hollered while Lunk did the same.

Gunshots came faster now like two guns were blazing.

Cooper drew one finger across his throat and put his hand over Lunk's mouth.

Lunk seemed to understand. He clenched his teeth like he was determined not to let out a sound.

"No!" Cooper howled, rolling onto his back. "You killed him. I won't talk. Please, stop!"

Three more shots.

Cooper stopped abruptly. Lunk watched him wide-eyed.

Two more bullets hammered the back wall. Cooper kept his mouth shut.

Pieces of insulation, scraps of cardboard and smoke filled the air. Cooper's body tensed, bracing for another round, but nothing came. Were they reloading? Did they leave?

Somebody pulled on the door again. The belts did their job.

Cooper put one finger to his lips. Lunk nodded.

"One more clip."

It sounded like Elvis, but Cooper couldn't be sure.

The room exploded in gunfire. The second shot took out the light bulb, covering them with darkness and shards of glass. The blackness brought its own terror, and a strange sense of protection at the same time. Bullets slammed into the boxes or the back wall.

Eight shots. Maybe nine. Cooper lost count, but his ears rang with the echos of them. Then silence. The kind of silence when you just know something is about to jump out at you.

Icy fingers reached up from the floor and gripped his gut. *So this is what it feels like to be in the county morgue.*

Light from the holes in the door cast eerie beams against the back wall. Frosty, smoke-like swirls twisted and turned in the beams like they were squirming in the agony of death.

Are they gone? The question looped in his brain. *Or are they waiting outside the door—listening just like me.*

Cooper started shivering. He felt Lunk's hand on his shoulder, pressing hard. Trying to let him know he was alive or trying to keep him still—he couldn't tell. *Don't worry, Lunk, I'm not going anywhere.* Try leaving now and they'd probably get shot. Wait for help, and they may freeze to death. Maybe he'd been shot and was dead already.

He thought he heard more gunfire. Distant though. Definitely not inside. And maybe they weren't even gunshots at all.

Cooper didn't close his eyes, but he prayed. Thanked God they'd made it this far. Prayed the men were gone. Promised God for the umpteenth time that he'd never lie again.

"Th-think they're g-gone?" Lunk whispered.

"I h-hope s-so." Cooper's teeth chattered.

"You p-prayin'?"

"Yeah."

"Don't stop."

The beams shining through the bullet holes broke for a moment. Somebody passed by the door.

Lunk gripped his shoulder tighter. He'd obviously seen it too.

Somebody pulled on the door again. Like the sickos wanted to see the bodies.

Suddenly his phone rang. Both boys jumped like someone had given them a jolt from a pair of defibrillator paddles—but they kept their mouths shut.

It had to be Hammer. He was the only one who had the number. *Where was he?* If Cooper answered the phone, Elvis and Mr. Clown would know he was still alive and they'd try to finish the job. Clenching his jaw tight, Cooper laid absolutely still and let the phone ring.

CHAPTER 61

Gordy rode hard and didn't let up. Even with the wind roaring in his ears he heard faint pops in the distance. Like fireworks. *Or gunfire*. His stomach twisted and he swallowed back an urge to heave.

By the time he entered Kimball Hill Park, the Halloween night sky glowed with flashing red lights from the direction of Frank 'n Stein's. It looked like the world was on fire. His world was.

He glanced over his shoulder to make sure Hiro was still behind him. He'd put real distance between them, but she was flying, too. No way could he slow down to let her catch up, though.

Gordy's legs burned, and a cramp tortured his side. But he didn't let up. He was getting what he deserved. He shouldn't have left Cooper. Should've followed his gut and stuck with him. If anything happened to him he'd never forgive himself. Never.

He sailed over the arched footbridge and nearly got air as he reached the top, then cut a hard left to pick up the bike path heading toward Kirchoff Road. Standing on the pedals to get maximum speed, he got a better view of Frank's. Police cars were angled all over the lot. Not neatly parked in parking slots, but like they pulled in, slammed on the brakes, and left the car wherever it stopped.

Coop got in over his head this time. He went swimming in the deep end of the pool. *And I wasn't there to help.*

An ambulance roared down Kirchoff road and squealed into the lot, siren blaring. A fire truck rumbled behind it. Gordy sliced down the path under the road along Salt Creek. Something shiny stuck above the surface, reflecting red lights from the police cars. Handlebars.

Coop's bike. Dumped in the creek. The water stood deathly still like the bike had been there for some time.

God, please don't let Coop be in there! Don't let it be too late. He scanned the surface for a floating body or a telltale sign of a struggle on the bank. Nothing. He gave the creek one more look, just to be sure. The water looked black.

Forcing himself to look away, he wheeled up to Frank 'n Stein's and skidded to a halt. He dropped his bike on the grass and pushed his way through the gathering crowd. Only when he pressed against the yellow crime scene tape did he stop.

Most of the lot was taped off in a zigzag pattern from post to car or tree. Police patrolled the perimeter, making sure nobody tried to press closer. A half-dozen officers stood around one of the squad cars off to the side. Spectators gathered on balconies of the nearby apartments.

Gordy drove a fist in his cramped side and motioned to the closest officer. "My cousin is in there."

The man held up both hands warning him to stay back. "We're still securing the area." He parked himself in a position where he'd instantly see if Gordy ducked under the tape and tried to make a run for it.

"Securing the area?" Gordy choked out the words. "What does *that* mean?"

"Nothing good."

Hiro's voice. He'd forgotten about her for a minute, but somehow she found him. Sweat trickled down from her forehead. Tears flowed from the corners of her eyes.

"Why are so many cops here in the lot, then?" Gordy felt helpless. "Why don't they go in and help?"

"A small team went in a few minutes ago." A stranger next to Gordy pointed toward Frank's. "The others probably have to wait until it's safe to go in."

Safe? Coop, what did you get yourself into? He looked at Hiro. Normally any kind of police activity would have her mesmerized. But now she looked small. Weak. Biting her lower lip and rubbing the police star necklace.

The policeman's radio squawked out a message. Gordy couldn't catch what was said.

Hiro obviously got it. "It's secure. They need paramedics." She squeezed her eyes shut. "Not Coop, God." Tears streamed down her cheeks." Please, Father, not Coop, too."

Two paramedics hustled toward the building carrying some sort of medical bags. Two others rushed behind guiding a wheeled gurney.

Gordy wanted to follow them. Help somehow. Do *something.* He lifted the tape, but the cop eyed him until he lowered it again. He had no idea how Hiro's intuition thing worked. All he knew was that he had a really strong sense of dread that Coop's plan had gone terribly wrong ... and he hoped he wasn't right.

But he wasn't the one with the spooky ability. That was Hiro's department.

"What are you thinking," he asked.

She didn't answer, but shook her head and buried her face in her hands.

Gordy's stomach sunk. She didn't need to say a word. Her face said it all.

CHAPTER 62

Cooper heard someone swear. "Get me something to pry open this door."

He tried to think. If they got the door open, it was all over. Staying low, he reached into his pocket and dug out the phone, now silent.

Where is Hammer?

Someone tugged at the door again. "Together now. Heave!"

A sliver of light came through.

No! God, please, save us! Cooper flipped open the phone.

"Slip that pipe in there."

The sound of metal on metal—*they have their pry bar in place.*

"We're g-going to d-die!" Lunk's voice came in a choked whisper.

Cooper missed the button. Cleared it out. Tried again. Pushed SEND.

"On three, two, one—HEAVE!"

The wedge of light widened, then with a loud snapping noise, the room flooded with light.

Lunk clutched onto him. Cooper dropped the phone and held him right back. Too late for phone calls now.

He heard a phone ring—in the doorway.

"You rang?" Hammer's voice. "Cooper—you okay?"

Cooper looked at Lunk and smiled. "We're o-okay. Frozen, but okay."

He stood and squinted into the light. Detective Hammer never looked so good. And other policemen in deep blue uniforms. Here to protect and serve. And save.

"Let's get you out of there." Hammer pulled a box off the makeshift barrier wall, handed it to a cop behind him and pulled off another to make a narrow pass-through.

Lunk squeezed through first, with Cooper following on shaky legs. The insulated door looked like a screen door now. The bullet holes riddled the door from top to bottom. The robbers obviously weren't taking any chances.

Hammer inspected the wall of frozen hotdogs. "Did you two build that wall of wieners?"

Lunk threw an arm around Cooper's shoulders. "That was my buddy's idea. Tying the door shut too."

"Brilliant." Hammer squinted and cocked his head to one side. "Saved your lives."

"And I'll never forget it," Lunk said.

"Detective Hammer," Cooper said. "Frank Mustacci needs protection. He guessed who was behind the robbery. That's why they tried to kill him."

"I got a call from a couple of your friends right after you called me. Two of my boys are already with Frank."

Relief swept through him, but he instantly tensed. "Hiro and Gordy—they're the ones who called—they need protection too."

"Not anymore." Hammer pointed out the front window. "The two dirtbags who shot up this place are sitting in one of the squad cars out front. Nasty characters, both of them."

"You sure you got the right guys?"

"Oh, yeah." Hammer smiled. "One of them had a latex Elvis mask in his pocket."

Lunk strained to look past them. "What about Mr. Stein?"

"We'll get him. He won't get far."

"He had this beautiful place." Lunk looked around the kitchen.

Hammer put a hand on Lunk's shoulder. "Seems Joseph Stein liked the casinos better."

Lunk still seemed to be in a state of disbelief. "So he robbed his own store."

Hammer shrugged. "For him, it was the perfect solution. He just didn't figure on witnesses." He clapped Cooper on the back.

Several officers moved aside so a team of paramedics carrying medical cases could get through. Cooper recognized one of them instantly. The guy from the Rolling Meadows fire station who always waved when Cooper rode by.

"Hi," the man smiled. "I'm Dave Rill. I need to check you out here."

"And as soon as he's done, I've got more questions for you two." Hammer said.

"I'll tell you everything you want to know," Cooper said.

Hammer gave him that sideways look and nodded.

"And you won't need that baloney detector either."

Officer Hammer took off his mirrored sunglasses and smiled. "Looks like you finally got yourself a chest."

CHAPTER 63

The parking lot looked like some kind of emergency vehicle light show. At least eight police cars, two fire trucks, and two paramedic trucks — all with lights flashing. Cooper stepped out the front doors of Frank 'n Stein's alongside of Lunk and Officer Hammer.

"Coop!" Hiro called from the other side of the yellow POLICE LINE DO NOT CROSS tape barrier. Gordy stood next to her waving.

Cooper pointed. "They're the ones who called you."

"They were with you the night of the robbery?"

"Yeah."

Hammer motioned for Hiro and Gordy to join them.

Gordy ducked under the tape and raced over. Hiro hesitated for just a moment to wipe her cheeks, then ran to catch up.

She slammed into Cooper and hugged him tight. "I saw all the police cars and the paramedics." Hiro looked up at him. "I thought you were dead."

"God answered my prayers."

She squeezed him tighter. "Mine too."

"We came back to the boat early," Gordy said. "Hiro had that spooky feeling. Found your note." He stared at Cooper's face.

"Looks like you've moved from arcade games to the real thing. Can you see out of that eye?"

"Clearer than I have in a week."

Hiro clenched her fist and shook it at him. "If your face wasn't already so messed up I'd let you have it."

Hammer laughed. "Oh I can see this is going to be a fun night."

Lunk stared at his shoes and suddenly looked awkward. Out of place.

Cooper pointed at him with his thumb. "And God sent Lunk along like a guardian angel."

Lunk raised his eyes and stared at Cooper through strands of dark hair. "An angel?"

"It took two belts to keep that door closed. And both of us working on that wall."

The faintest smile crossed Lunk's lips.

"Well, next time, NEXT TIME, we all stick together," Hiro said, poking Cooper in the chest. "That's what we always do. Right?" She hooked one arm through Gordy's arm, and the other through Cooper's. "And that goes for you, too, Lunk. Seems to me we *all* need to stick together."

"Yes Ma'am." Lunk held up his hands in mock surrender. "Whatever you say, Hiro."

She nodded her head toward Cooper and Gordy. "With friends like these I could use a guardian angel too."

Lunk grinned and jammed his hands in his camouflaged pants.

Gordy reached up and swept an arm around Lunk's shoulder.

"Alright gang," Hammer said. "I hate to interrupt this little reunion, but it's time we all *stick together* and get down to the station. We'll get your parents to join us. Then comes the really hard part. I'm going to need statements from all of you—and nothing but the truth."

Cooper started toward Hammer's police car. "The truth? That'll be easy." He smiled at Gordy, Lunk, and Hiro. "It's the lies that are really hard."

CHAPTER 64

EPILOGUE

One Week Later

The night before Frank 'n Stein's *Grand Reopening Celebration Week* began, Frank threw a private party. Cooper stood at the back of the dining area, taking it all in. The diner didn't seem to have a "creep factor" anymore — and not just because all the Halloween decorations were down. Likely it was because the room was filled with so many of the people Cooper cared for most in the world.

His mom sat at a table with three other ladies. Hiro's mom. Gordy's mom. And the big surprise was Lunk's mom. Cooper had seen her before, but never looking as happy as she did right now. They chatted away, laughing and talking over each other.

Mattie sat at a table by herself, humming and drawing pictures of ponies on a sketch pad.

Cooper's dad stood near the ordering counter with Gordy's dad and Detective Hammer. They all looked toward the kitchen while Hammer pointed and motioned with his hands. Probably going over some of the events of Halloween night. A night Cooper would never forget — and in some ways, didn't want to.

Like the moment his mom and dad burst into the police station. Dad hadn't gotten the phone message until after the circus.

He said that after hearing Cooper's confession, he busted every speed limit getting to him.

Cooper never wanted to forget the way his dad rushed to his side and held him. Or the way his mom wept, thanking God over and over for answering her prayer. Cooper never wanted to forget how good it felt to confess everything to them in person, and to know his parents forgave him completely.

But most of all he didn't want to forget a promise he made to himself that night—never to lie to his parents again.

"Coop, get over here," Gordy called from their usual table. Hiro sat next to him.

Just as Cooper slid into the booth, Frank Mustacci stepped out of the kitchen carrying a large tray of monster shakes. He looked like himself again. Strong. His cheeks had good color, and the bruising around his eye was nearly gone. He wore a new white apron for the event. No blood stains. Lunk followed with a tray in each hand, loaded with orders of fries.

Frank stopped at Cooper's table. "Okay, my dear friends. Time to celebrate."

"Oh yeah!" Gordy stood and reached for a shake.

Lunk helped Frank distribute the food around the room.

Frank circled back to where he started. "And now," he said, raising his voice so everyone could hear, "I want to thank each of you for joining me tonight at this little party."

Lunk set down the empty trays and glanced at Cooper. He stood in the aisle, looking a little stiff. Like he wasn't quite sure how to fit in—but he wanted to. Cooper slid over and motioned for Lunk to join him.

"This has been quite a couple of weeks," Frank said. "Actually, it seems like less than that—but maybe that's because I spent half of it in a coma."

Everybody laughed.

"I thank God every day that I'm alive, and for my very special friends at this table." He took a step closer and put his hand on the back of the booth. He looked directly at Cooper. There was life in his eyes. "And as a small token of my appreciation, I'm giving all four of you free monster shakes and fries for the next year."

Gordy jumped to his feet and pumped his fist in the air. "Yeah!"

Cooper smiled. Maybe this would trigger a growth spurt of his own.

"I'm going to take good care of this bunch," Frank said. "I know Hiro wants to be a cop, and Cooper a fireman, but at some point I'm going to need a new partner. Maybe one of the other boys will fill that spot someday."

"Gordy will eat all the profits," Hiro said.

The group laughed again.

Lunk sat up a little taller and looked toward his mom. She smiled back at him. Cooper tried to imagine Lunk as partner. Wouldn't that be something?

Frank kept talking, but Cooper's mind drifted. Mr. Stein still hadn't been found, but it was only a matter of time. Life could get back to normal now. Whatever that was. With Lunk, Gordy, and Hiro around, there was likely going to be another adventure. Hopefully Hiro wouldn't get to play cop again too soon.

He glanced over at her and found she was fingering her necklace, looking at him. She raised her eyebrows and gave a little nod. Was she reading his mind or something?

The corners of her mouth curved into the slightest smile.

Cooper smiled back. Hiro knew him so well it was spooky.

Frank finished his speech, and the room broke into applause.

Lunk stood and shook Mr. Mustacci's hand like he'd just received a promotion. And in a way, he had.

Cooper dug in his pocket, pulled out a quarter, and slapped it on the table in front of Gordy.

Gordy picked it up. "What's this for?"

Hiro sighed. "He's going to teach you those trick moves on that *classic* arcade game."

Gordy laughed and was on his feet in an instant. "You're on."

"Wanna join us, Hiro?" Cooper said, standing. "Just think about it. The forces of good and evil locked in mortal combat. It'll be an adventure."

Hiro smiled and shook her head. "I've done enough of that lately. And I've got a feeling we'll be doing it again for real—sooner than you think."

Cooper laughed, grabbed his monster shake, and followed Gordy toward the game. Somewhere, deep inside, he believed Hiro was right. A slight thrill rushed through him, a crazy mix of fear and excitement. He rubbed down the goosebumps forming on his arms and made another promise to himself. Whatever happened, next time he'd do the right thing.

A WORD FROM THE AUTHOR

Code of *Truth*

White lies, half-truths, fibs, whoppers, and bamboozling, there are all kinds of cutesy names we use for lying. But there's nothing cute about lies. Cooper started with a *Code of Silence*, but in the end he was determined to live by a *Code of Truth*. Smart move.

As we saw with Cooper, lies start off ugly and only get worse, leading to more and more lies. So why do we lie, anyway? Generally there are four main reasons.

1. To avoid something uncomfortable or unpleasant. Often this has a lot to do with being put on the spot—and instead of finding a tactful way to be truthful, we tell someone what we think they want to hear. It is about making things more convenient or comfortable for us. Let's say your friend has a small part in a play—and they totally bomb. But of course you aren't about to tell *them* that. You'd feel like a jerk. Afterwards, they ask what you thought of their performance. "*You were great,*" you say. "*Next time you should audition for the lead.*"

2. To avoid punishment or consequences. We messed up. Did something that will get us in trouble. We decide to cover it up. But then someone questions us about it, so we put on an innocent face. "*I didn't do that. It wasn't me.*" This reason is all about avoiding discipline—even if we deserve it.

3. To get something we wouldn't get with the truth. In these situations, we lie to gain an advantage or a privilege. This is deception purely for our own selfish motives. If we could rank lying by degrees of nastiness, this is often the most devious type.

"*I just got invited to go out with some friends.*"

Your mom gives you that look. "*Not until your homework is done.*"

"*I don't have any homework. I finished everything before I left school.*"

Of course that isn't true—but you figure you'll find a way to get it done before class tomorrow. This type of lying is about getting something we'd never get if we told the truth.

4. To protect ourselves or someone else. This is exactly why Cooper started the Code of Silence. It was all about protecting himself. His family. His friends. When it involves protecting someone else, lying can appear noble at first, but it doesn't always end up that way. And with a little thought and effort, there are other ways we can find to stay safe or keep someone else safe without relying on lies to do it.

If we understand the types of reasons and situations that tempt us to lie, it can help us avoid dishonesty.

Let me mention just a few things about lying and honesty because if we get this right …

By the end of *Code of Silence*, Cooper made a promise to himself not to ever lie to his parents or anyone again. That can be a tough promise to keep, but a good one to try. If we really commit to being honest, in the long run, everyone would be so much better off.

If Coop were talking to you right now he'd urge you not to twist or hide the truth—or ask your friends to. He'd encourage you to tell the truth—all the time. I think that's pretty good advice. And Coop ought to know. He learned it the hard way.

The hard way. That's the thing about lies. It seems like lying is the easy road, but it really is the hard one. Imagine you are in a situation where you must make the decision to tell the truth or tell a lie. If you knew 100% that you'd get caught in the lie, you wouldn't bother telling it, right? It's good to remember that God has the ultimate "baloney detector". We can never fool him.

As for me, I'm lining up with Coop, Hiro, and Gordy. I'm striving to be honest. Always. To live by a *Code of Truth*. How about you? Will you join us? Honesty always pays off in the long run. And that's the truth.

—*Tim*

For Further Reflection

1. Cooper's plan not to tell anybody about the robbery they witnessed *sounded* okay at first, but how was it really like lying?
2. Cooper thought the only way to stay truly safe was to stay quiet. Was that really the only way to stay safe? What could he or *should* he have done different?
3. Cooper pressured Hiro and Gordy to be dishonest, too. Hiro felt really uncomfortable with agreeing to the Code. What could she have done instead?
4. Even when Cooper didn't come right out and lie to his parents, he deceived them by allowing them to believe something he knew wasn't true. How is deceiving someone just another form of lying?
5. When friends or someone else pressures you to lie, or to deceive someone else, how can you handle that in a way where you won't be dishonest?
6. Cooper was afraid of what would happen to him if the truth came out. How does fear tempt us to lie—and what can we do when we're afraid to tell the truth?
7. Detective Hammer claimed he could tell when someone was lying with his built-in "baloney detector". Cooper figured Hammer would see right through Gordy, for sure. Even if we could fool our parents, or teachers, or whoever, ultimately who *never* gets fooled? What difference should that make as far as how honest we choose to be?
8. As Cooper continues with the Code, the lies begin to unravel his friendship with Hiro, and even with Gordy. How does dishonesty destroy even the closest relationships?
9. Cooper's lies bought him some temporary safety, but he found the price tag of honesty was a lot higher than he figured. How did it affect him when he saw he'd lost the respect and trust of Hiro and Gordy? How would it affect you if you lost respect or trust in the eyes of parents, friends, or others?
10. If Coop, Hiro, and Gordy didn't tell the truth, Frank Mustacci might have been killed. How do innocent people get hurt when others lie? Can you think of some examples?

We want to hear from you. Please send your comments about this book to us in care of zreview@zondervan.com. Thank you.